SAM AND JAMES
THE MISSING TEEN

THE SEQUEL TO A POLICE ACTION

AA FREDA

iUniverse

SAM AND JAMES:
THE MISSING TEEN

Copyright © 2019 AA Freda.

All rights reserved. No part of this book may be used or reproduced by any means, graphic, electronic, or mechanical, including photocopying, recording, taping or by any information storage retrieval system without the written permission of the author except in the case of brief quotations embodied in critical articles and reviews.

This is a work of fiction. All of the characters, names, incidents, organizations, and dialogue in this novel are either the products of the author's imagination or are used fictitiously.

iUniverse books may be ordered through booksellers or by contacting:

iUniverse
1663 Liberty Drive
Bloomington, IN 47403
www.iuniverse.com
1-800-Authors (1-800-288-4677)

Because of the dynamic nature of the Internet, any web addresses or links contained in this book may have changed since publication and may no longer be valid. The views expressed in this work are solely those of the author and do not necessarily reflect the views of the publisher, and the publisher hereby disclaims any responsibility for them.

Any people depicted in stock imagery provided by Getty Images are models, and such images are being used for illustrative purposes only. Certain stock imagery © Getty Images.

ISBN: 978-1-5320-6027-4 (sc)
ISBN: 978-1-5320-6029-8 (hc)
ISBN: 978-1-5320-6028-1 (e)

Library of Congress Control Number: 2018913954

Print information available on the last page.

iUniverse rev. date: 01/14/2019

1
THE ABDUCTION

The van is parked at the end of a dead-end street. No cars have come by since it arrived an hour ago. He glances at the clock on the dashboard—only fifteen minutes to go. He lifts his head and stares across the vast, empty lawn behind the building. The high schooler will come through the gray metal back doors of the school at four thirty. She will be with her schoolmate. His target and her friend will come across the lawn and walk by on the other side of the street from his van. He's been watching this young lady almost every day since he accidentally laid eyes on her a month before. The girl's daily schedule varies—except on Thursdays. On Thursdays, she always comes out at exactly four thirty, and always at this exact spot.

She's a real beauty—tall, blonde, and rosy cheeked—and, despite being so young, she has a nice figure. The teenager is still a virgin—he's pretty sure. During the entire month that he has been stalking her, he has never seen her spending time with any boys. Owning her is going to be a real pleasure for him; he's been dreaming about her every night. His day is not complete until he catches a glimpse of his princess.

The two metal doors in the back of the building swing open. The girls come rushing out, arm in arm and laughing. He glances down at the clock—four thirty. A smile spreads across his face: *Perfect,* he thinks. The object of his affection, accompanied by her friend, is sticking to her Thursday routine like clockwork. It is the only day of the week when she is not picked up by her mother and the only day she walks home—always with the same friend.

The girls leave footprints in the light dusting of freshly fallen snow as they cut across the lawn. He stares at his princess intently. Seeing his beauty so close increases his excitement; there is a hardening in his groin.

"Turn around and follow them," he barks at the driver as soon as the girls pass. "Make sure you don't get too close. Give them plenty of room and stay at least a block behind; we don't want them to notice us."

They trail the girls for five blocks, and the teenagers turn right—the same route they have taken every time he's followed them. Three more blocks and they turn left. A few seconds later, the van takes the same turn. A quick look around the neighborhood assures the abductor that there is no one around. It is dusk, and there are no streetlights; this time of year, dusk comes early.

In four more blocks, his prey says goodbye to her friend. The schoolmate dashes into her house. In another block, he watches *his* teenager going into *her* house—a large, two-story Spanish style stucco home with a red-tiled roof. There are gates in the front. They watch her lift the latch on the gate and let herself in. The house is huge; the property takes up almost half the block. His passion disappears as the girl makes her way up the long, winding walkway.

The van pulls up and stops in front of the gate. He takes another quick look around the street and sees that it is empty. They wait in front of the house for a few minutes.

"What are we waiting for?" the driver asks him.

"Pull up the street and turn around," he orders without replying. The old van goes up the block and makes a U-turn.

"Stop right here. Turn off the lights and the engine," he commands.

"Now what?" his accomplice asks.

"We're waiting for her mother. She usually goes to the beauty parlor to get her hair and nails done on Thursdays. If my calculation is correct, the girl's mom should come home at around five thirty. I'm just making sure of her schedule one last time."

They sit and wait, looking vigilantly at the house. He watches as an occasional car drives by on the street. No one has come out of a home or walked by on the sidewalk. At 5:27 p.m., a silver Mercedes sedan pulls into the driveway. They watch as a dark-haired woman makes her way up the long drive. The garage door opens, and the Mercedes disappears into the garage. They continue to stare at the garage as the door comes down automatically behind the vehicle.

"Right on time," he says, a wry smile spreading across his face. "This is going to be so easy. There's nobody around. We'll have plenty of time to pull it off."

"Who *was* that lady?" his partner asks.

"The girl's mother—Elizabeth Campos. There's a kid brother in the house, too. Twelve years old. The only other person we have to worry about is the maid, but she's got Thursdays off. The schedule couldn't be better."

"What about the father?"

"I've done my work on this family. He doesn't get home until after seven. I followed him one day, he works in Santa Fe. The guy we *really* have to worry about is the kid's grandfather, Henry Greenwald. He's got money, and he's got friends in high places. Hell, this family owns most of the big railways in the Southwest.

"In fact, Greenwald *could* be a problem for us," he says, almost to himself. "He can push the police around—maybe judges, too. I bet he'd offer a reward. Yeah. I bet Greenwald will have everybody looking for her."

He leans back in his seat, stares straight ahead for a moment, and grins. "It won't do him any good. We'll be long gone before Greenwald even has a chance to get started."

"What's her name? The girl?"

"That lovely young lady has a beautiful, classical name—Penelope," he says, and another broad smile appears on his face. "Most of her friends call her Penny, but the Penny stuff will stop as soon as *we* have her. No common name for my princess. We'll call her by her full name. She will be as pure and faithful to me as Queen Penelope was to Odysseus."

He's still grinning as he dreams of what will be.

"When are you going to do it?" the driver asks.

"Next week," he answers. "It *has* to be next week," he says adamantly, coming back to the moment. "We need to be out of my cousin's house by next Friday. He called me last week and said he'll be back on Saturday. He wants his house back, so we need to move on."

"What's the plan?"

"We'll park the van right here in front of the Campos house next Thursday around four thirty. Penelope should get here no more than ten minutes later. When she shows up, I'll jump out of the van holding a piece of paper with an address on it. I'll act confused, tell her I'm lost, show her the address, and ask if she can help me. When she comes over to look at the note, I'll snatch her and throw her into the van, then jump in behind her. You'll drive off and head for home. We'll have at least an hour's head start—probably a lot longer, as her mother's first instinct will be to start calling her friends to ask if they've seen her daughter. I'm guessing the police won't be called until at least seven.

"It doesn't really matter *what* time the police are called—it'll take the cops some time to investigate before they send out the bulletin. For all we know, the alert may not even go out until the next day. We'll leave that night, before the police have time to get their act together. This week, we'll stock up on all the provisions that we'll need to lay low for a while. I'm thinking that a month's supply should be about right. I've got a place in Arizona, just outside of Yuma, all set up. We'll stay there for a bit until I can figure my next move."

"Are you going to ask for ransom?"

Annoyed, he looks over at the driver. "*Ransom?*" he shouts angrily. "No—no ransom, even though she'd fetch a nice sum. The Greenwalds would pay a king's fortune to get her back. No, I don't want money for that goddess. She is going to be my *wife*. I want to get to know every part of her body. She is going to be *mine*. I will be the first man that young maiden will ever experience—and the last. She'll never forget me." The man pauses, staring out the window. His dark eyes and his pointed shaped beard make his profile look menacing.

"Yes, indeed," he muses, "it's going to be so nice deflowering that beautiful young virgin."

"How do you know she's a virgin?"

"She's a virgin all right," he replies with certainty in his voice. "I'm absolutely positive. This whole time that I've been watching her, I've never seen her with a boy. I dream about her every single night; it's going to be wonderful. She has an angelic beauty. Just imagining what it will be like to take her flower sets my blood on fire. I can't stop thinking about her."

He sits up in his seat and turns to his partner. "Come on—start the car. Let's get out of here. No need to take any chances of being noticed."

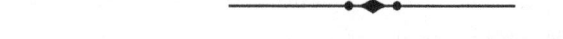

At a little after four the following Thursday afternoon, the same van pulls up at the school. It stops behind the only car parked in the street.

"What are you doing at the *school?*" he yells at his partner.

"Aren't we going to wait for her?"

"Not *here!* In front of her *house,* you idiot!" He nearly comes out of his seat. "We can't snatch her *here*—someone might see us. Weren't you paying attention to anything I said to you? We're going to grab her in front of her *house,* where the streets are empty and there's no one around. Get out of here before someone notices us!"

The van pulls out from behind the car and begins making a U-turn.

"Watch out for that guy!" he shouts at his driver.

The van comes to a screeching halt.

"Why don't you watch where you're going?" the man in the street yells at the people in the van. "You almost hit me!"

The passenger rolls down the window and sticks out his head, "Sorry!"

As they pull out, he looks over at his partner and shouts, "Pay attention, you idiot! You almost screwed everything up."

They drive to Penelope's house and park the van in front. He looks at the clock on the dash: 4:20 p.m. *It won't be long now,* he thinks. It's a clear, cool January afternoon in Albuquerque, New Mexico. The street is completely deserted. He keeps staring at the side-view mirror, watching for the girls. He turns to his partner.

"It shouldn't be long now," he says. His excitement is growing as he anticipates her.

"Let's go over the plan one more time—I don't want any more screwups. I'll grab her and shove her into the van through the sliding door on the side. Then I'll jump in behind her. As soon as I'm in, you drive off." He pauses. "No more messing up," he warns his partner. "You know the route. Don't speed and be sure to obey all the traffic signals. We don't want to get stopped by the cops."

"What if the girl starts screaming?"

"Don't worry—I'll shut her up. I've got duct tape to put over her mouth. I've also got rope to tie her up so she can't move. Just concentrate on your job and don't worry about mine. You almost hit that guy earlier. A mistake like that could have botched the entire plan." He looks at the mirror once more. "There they are!" he shouts. "Start the engine."

He looks into the mirror and sees Penelope saying goodbye to her friend. She walks near the van. He jumps out in front of her.

"Excuse me, young lady. I seem to be lost. Do you know where this address is?" He holds out the note. She comes over to have a look. He slides open the door and heaves her inside. Immediately, he jumps in and slides the door closed. Penelope tries to get up, but he shoves her back down placing his body on top of hers so that she can't move. His hand is behind her head, pushing her face to the floor.

"What are you waiting for? Drive!" he yells at his partner.

The girl tries to push him off her and lets out a scream. He pulls her up by the hair and slaps her across the back of the head.

"Shut up! I don't want to hear another sound out of you." She begins to cry as he shoves her back down and turns her onto her stomach. He grabs her hands and begins to tie them behind her back.

"Please let me go!" she sobs.

"I said shut up!" he shouts, slapping her on the back of her head and reaching over for the roll of duct tape. He tears off a piece with his teeth. He lifts her by her hair and rubs the tape over her mouth.

"There—that should keep you quiet." His breathing gets heavier as he looks around for the other piece of rope. It's dark in the van, and he can't seem to locate the cord. Finally, he sees the cord in the corner, he leans over and grabs the rope. He uses the rope to tie her ankles together. He looks down at the young lady and turns her to him. Tears are flowing down her face.

"Don't be afraid, little darling," he says, stroking her hair. "I'm not going to hurt you. You just do as I say, and everything will be just fine."

He checks the rope ties one more time. Satisfied that she is secure, he crawls his way to the front and jumps into the passenger-side seat.

"Do you still remember the way?" he asks the driver.

"Yeah—I know where I'm going."

"Good," he says. "Just make sure you obey all the traffic laws; we don't want to get stopped," he says, repeating his earlier instructions. He looks back at Penelope, who is sobbing but not moving. "Perfect," he comments, sitting back and taking a deep breath. "Absolutely perfect." He grins fiendishly.

They get to their house and pull into the driveway. The driver shuts off the engine.

"Get out and take a look up and down the street to make sure there's no one around. When the coast is clear, we'll take her out of the van and get her into the house."

His partner jumps out. A moment later, the partner opens the door and leans in. "All clear!"

"Good," he says and jumps out. "Come over here and give me a hand getting her out."

He jumps into the van. "I'm going to remove the tape and untie your feet. You make a sound or try something, I'll smash your head in." He says to Penelope.

He's helping the girl out of the van when a car appears unexpectedly and heads down the street toward them. The driver of the car turns to look at him. The driver appears to take no notice but simply continues on and pulls into his driveway a few houses down the street.

"Crap!" he shouts. "Come on! Hurry up and get her inside! I thought you said the coast was clear!" Once inside the house, he turns to his accomplice, "I've got a good mind to give you a beating. Lucky for you, I don't have time! We can't wait any longer. That guy may have seen something and could be calling the police right now! Hurry up and help me load the van."

Elizabeth Campos's Mercedes pulls into the garage at five thirty as it does every Thursday evening. Once inside, she heads for the kitchen, turns on the lights, and places her bag on the counter. She opens the fridge, takes out a bottle of water, twists off the cap, and takes a sip. She heads upstairs and passes her son, Mark's, room. The door is open. He is playing with his toys on the rug. Her daughter's door is closed. She opens the door and looks into the empty room. She closes the door and goes back to Mark's room.

"Mark, where's Penny?" she asks.

"I don't know, Mom. She hasn't come home from school yet."

She walks into the bedroom and calls Mary, Penny's friend who walks home from school with her. Mary's mom, Jennifer, answers the phone.

"Jennifer, is Penny at your place?" she asks.

"No, she's not here," Jennifer replies.

"Is Mary there?"

"Yes, Mary is here. Why? What's the matter? Is something wrong?"

"Can you ask her if she came home with Penny today, please?"

Jennifer puts the phone down and runs to ask her daughter. She comes back almost immediately. "Mary says she walked home with Penny, like always. What's the matter? Is Penny not home?"

"No, she's not, and I'm worried."

"I'll be right over," Jennifer tells Elizabeth.

Elizabeth decides to call her husband. His secretary answers. "I'm sorry, Mrs. Campos—your husband went to a meeting and will not be returning to the office. He said he would head straight home after the meeting."

She hangs up and hears the doorbell. She runs to the door. It's Mary's mom. "Any news?"

"No, nothing. I'm very concerned; I was just about to call the police."

Elizabeth gets on the phone and calls the police. Instead of coming right over, they ask her more questions than she can bear. *Did you recently have an argument with your daughter? Does your daughter have a boyfriend? Have you checked with all your daughter's friends?* The questions just keep coming. Finally, the distraught mother, totally frustrated, plays her ace.

"My father is Henry Greenwald. If you don't get someone here immediately, I will have him call the chief of police, the mayor, and the governor!"

Fifteen minutes later, two policemen are at her door. They begin the interview. After about twenty minutes, one of the cops asks, "Does your daughter have a boyfriend? You know, sometimes they sneak off without telling the parents."

"No! She doesn't have a boyfriend—and she doesn't sneak!"

"Mrs. Campos, sometimes kids don't tell their parents everything," the policeman insists. "You'd be surprised the things some teenagers keep from their parents. Are you *sure* she doesn't have a boyfriend?"

"Well, if she didn't tell me, then I wouldn't know, *would* I?" she fires back, becoming agitated. "My daughter walked home with her friend Mary, just like she always does every Thursday. Her friend lives right down the street. The walk between there and here is no more than two minutes—there's no way she could have gone somewhere else. Shouldn't you be out there looking for her?"

The other cop cuts in. "You're quite right, Mrs. Campos—we need to start looking for her," he says. "We just need to make sure we have all the correct information. How old did you say your daughter was?"

"She just turned fourteen; she's a freshman at the high school."

"What's her height and weight?"

"She's five seven and weighs one hundred and ten pounds or so."

The cop is writing in his notepad. "You say she's a blonde. Does she have any other distinguishing features?"

Elizabeth thinks for a second. "No, I can't think of anything right now. Oh, wait, she has blue eyes."

"Do you have a current picture of your daughter?"

"Yes," she replies. "I'll go get it for you." She goes into the bedroom and comes back out with a framed picture of her daughter Penny.

"Can I have this photograph?" the cop asks her.

"Yes, of course. Let me take it out of the frame for you."

A few minutes later, two plainclothes detectives, Hector Rodriguez and Frank Fallon, arrive. The scene at the house becomes surreal. Police are everywhere. The detectives pull aside the officer who took the notes.

"What do you have?" Detective Rodriguez asks the cop.

"A fourteen-year-old girl comes home from school with her friend who lives down the street. Between there and here, she disappears. No reason for her disappearance. These are my notes," he says, handing Rodriguez his pad. The cop leans over and whispers in Rodriguez's ear, "These people are well-connected. Henry Greenwald is the missing girl's grandfather."

"Thanks," says Rodriguez, who takes the pad and tears out the page of notes. He gives the pad back and walks into the living room, where Elizabeth and Jennifer are sitting on the sofa.

He takes a seat on a wing chair across from the women. "Mrs. Campos, I'm Detective Rodriguez, and this is my partner, Detective Fallon. Would you mind if we ask you a few questions and go over a few details with you?"

Elizabeth shakes her head no.

"Any possibility your daughter may have gone somewhere else after leaving her friend?"

"None whatsoever," Elizabeth answers unequivocally. "She *always* comes straight home—that's why I'm so worried."

"I wouldn't worry too much, Mrs. Campos," Rodriguez comments. "These incidents usually turn out to be harmless. You'd be surprised how often the cause of a child's disappearance is something totally innocent."

Elizabeth leans forward and fixes Rodriguez with her gaze. "Are you going to take this seriously, or do I need to call my father, Henry Greenwald?"

"No need to call, Mrs. Campos. Believe me, we're taking this matter very seriously. Normally, we wait twenty-four hours before we begin a search…"

"Twenty-four hours!" Elizabeth shouts and jumps up. "I'm calling my father. *Right now!*"

Rodriguez leaps up and takes her arm. "Please, Mrs. Campos, have a seat and let me finish. There's no need to call anyone. We don't plan on waiting twenty-four hours. I can see that in this instance we need to go beyond normal procedures."

Elizabeth sits back down. So does Rodriguez. "As I was saying," Rodriguez continues, "normally we wait twenty-four hours in these types of cases. However, regarding your daughter's disappearance, we'll get to work immediately."

He looks straight at the distraught mother and clears his throat. "Mrs.

Campos, I don't mean to alarm you, but we need to consider that your daughter may have been taken for ransom. If it's all right with you, I would like to bring in some technical people. They'll put recording and tracking devices on your phone in case the kidnappers call and make a ransom demand."

"Do whatever is necessary."

"Good. I'll get a crew in here right away. They'll be here around the clock. Do you have any problem with the squad being here?"

"No," Elizabeth replies. Her eyes fill with tears. "As I said, do whatever you have to do. Just bring my Penelope home."

Mr. Campos does not arrive home until eight. A spectacle awaits him when he gets there. Nearly a dozen police cars are in front of his house. Half a dozen uniforms are in his foyer when he walks in.

"What the hell is going on?" he asks to no one in particular. "Did something happen to my family?"

The detectives take him aside and begin telling him what has happened. The police get the phone book of all the family's friends and acquaintances and begin calling each one. The police question everyone—Mary, Penny's friend; Mark, Penny's brother; and the neighbors up and down the block. The detectives spend hours interviewing Penny's parents and looking for any clues.

The cops go door to door, canvassing the entire neighborhood. In the end, they come up empty-handed. They are no closer to solving the disappearance than when they started. An all-points bulletin throughout New Mexico is issued around ten o'clock that night. At about the same time, Penny and the kidnappers are approaching Lupton, Arizona, just past the New Mexico border.

The police leave the Campos house just after one in the morning, but they come back a few hours later, at around dawn. This time, a technical team arrives to set up the telephone recording equipment. There have been no calls from the kidnappers with any demands. The authorities distribute hundreds of copies of Penny's picture and round up a dozen volunteers to begin posting the photos throughout the community. Penny's face makes the local news that morning on television. A few hours later, her case goes national.

Detectives go to the school to interview Penelope's teachers and classmates. The maid, Magdalena, comes in after her day off, and a detective immediately begins interviewing her. Elizabeth who is completely traumatized, stays in her room and takes tranquilizers to calm herself.

Around noon, after stopping over and comforting his daughter, Henry Greenwald, Penelope's grandfather, shows up at the police station. Mayor Abernathy and Police Chief Franks arrive a few minutes later. The three men meet in Captain Richard Belmont's office. Greenwald has an aura of self-importance that immediately marks him as the one of the four who is in command.

"What are you doing to find my granddaughter?" Greenwald asks the captain.

"We have every available officer at the precinct working on the case, sir," Belmont answers.

"Has the FBI been called in?" Greenwald asks. There is cold anger in his voice.

"Not yet, sir. We don't *know* yet if this is a kidnapping." Captain Belmont replies. "The FBI doesn't usually get involved in a missing person investigation."

Greenwald turns to Mayor Abernathy. "Is this the way that police matters are handled in your city? Your captain here seems to be taking my granddaughter's disappearance very lightly. What could this be other than a kidnapping? Of *course* she's been taken. Are your other detectives as ill-equipped as Belmont here to participate in this investigation?"

"Now hold on a sec, Henry," the mayor responds. "Belmont is one of our best men…and he has had experience with missing children cases. Why not give him some time? I have every confidence he'll find your granddaughter."

"Time? We don't *have* time!" Greenwald yells out. "While you all are acting like the Keystone Cops, my granddaughter is out there somewhere facing God only knows what kind of terrible danger." Greenwald points an intimidating finger at Abernathy and adds, "Call the damn FBI! If you're not going to call, just say so and *I* will call. I want you to get every available man in the entire Albuquerque police force on the case—not just the ones at this pint-size station. Call the governor and get the state troopers working on the case immediately.

"You get me?" he adds, tapping the mayor on the chest with his finger. "My granddaughter comes back alive, or you're all finished!" With his threats having been issued and his demands having been made, Greenwald storms out of the office.

Mayor Abernathy turns to his chief and his captain. "Solve this case," he says to them in his sternest voice, and then he, too, storms out of the office.

Chief Franks turns to Captain Belmont. In the first calm voice of the meeting, he asks. "You got anything? Please tell me that you've got something…"

"We *may* have a lead, Chief."

"A real lead? Or are you just saying you have something to get me off your back?"

"No, this information could be promising. One of the detectives interviewed the maid and she says something is not right between the father and the daughter. She suspects that the father may be sexually molesting his daughter. The father doesn't have an alibi for the time the daughter went missing. I'm sending some men later today to interview him."

"What the hell do you mean *later today*? What are you waiting for? Get the maid and the father down to the station and grill them. Dig out all the skeletons. I'll call the FBI and the state troopers to make sure that you have plenty of manpower. If the father *didn't* do it, we're going to need help, because then we will have to go farther afield. You grill that father! You better *hope* we can solve this problem that simply."

Chief Franks pauses for a second and wipes his brow. "This is the type of affair that can break us, Belmont. If you don't solve this case, you'll be back pounding the beat and I'll be there alongside you. Put the pressure on everyone. Work around the clock if it's necessary. Cancel all leaves and vacation requests."

Penny's father is brought down to the station and is interrogated for nearly six hours. Late that night, the detectives release Campos and drive him home. The next morning, Belmont calls the detectives into his office.

"So, what happened?" he asks the detectives. "I hear you released Campos. Why'd you let him go?"

"We had nothing, Captain," Detective Fallon tells him. "The maid had no specific proof that he molested his daughter—just a feeling. The only reason Campos is still a suspect is that he doesn't have a good alibi. Campos says that he went to a meeting in Espanola that was over around two thirty. He claims that he stopped at a bar in Santa Fe and had a few beers. He got to talking to some people and lost track of time. When Campos got on the road, he realized he was tipsy, so he pulled over. He fell asleep in the car and woke up around seven, when he started for home.

"We've got a man heading right now to Santa Fe and Espanola to check out Campos's alibi. There's another crew tailing Campos everywhere he goes. Until we come up with something more, that's all we can do. We don't want to push him too hard and have him lawyer up. Let him believe he's in the clear. When we get all our facts together, we'll yank him right back."

"All right, you stay on him. Something about his story stinks. We need to find out what."

"Yes, Captain. We're not letting up, believe me."

The captain rubs his hands through his hair. "What a way to start a new year. A kidnapping of the granddaughter of the most influential man in New Mexico. We don't solve this case we won't see 1970, I can promise you." He turns to his men. "You got anybody else?"

"There's a groundskeeper at the school." Fallon looks at his notes. "A Hernando Martinez, who says he saw a suspicious-looking guy hanging around the schoolyard a couple of different times. This Martinez fellow says he's pretty sure he saw that same man on Thursday. We're bringing Martinez in to see a sketch artist this morning." Fallon and Rodriguez stand up. "That's all we got, Captain. If you don't mind, we'd like to get back to work," Fallon adds.

"You do that, boys. I'm going to need you to help me out here. I've got everybody riding my ass. The governor even called me earlier and tore me a new one. This case is a ball-breaker, believe me."

"We'll do our best, Captain," Fallon says as he and Martinez walk out of the office.

The next morning, the detectives are back in the captain's office, and they are excited.

"What do you have?" Captain Belmont asks. "Anything good?'

"The girl's father's alibi doesn't check out," Rodriguez informs him. "The man's meeting in Espanola was over right after lunch, around one—not two thirty as he told us. Nobody at the bar Campos said he went to after the meeting remembers seeing him."

"Son of a bitch! What are you waiting for? Go pick him up!" Belmont shouts.

"I don't know, Captain," Fallon speaks up. "This guy Campos doesn't look stupid. He must have known we would check his alibi. Something doesn't seem right."

"Since when are criminals smart?" the captain challenges him. "Bring Campos to the station. If he can't satisfy you about his whereabouts on Thursday evening, book him. Either Campos comes clean or he's going to jail. Why isn't Campos coming clean? What father wouldn't do everything possible to find his daughter?"

They pick up Bernard Campos and bring him in again. The detectives work together at first to get the interview started, and then take turns grilling him, pushing harder and harder. Campos continues to be evasive. Finally, Detective Rodriguez has had enough.

"Get up," he says to Campos. "Put your hands behind your back."

"Why? What are you doing?" Campos tries to push Rodriguez off him.

"I'm booking you," Rodriguez yells at him. "I've had enough of your bullshit. Your daughter is missing, and you couldn't care less. You've been feeding me a sack of crap. Maybe a couple of days in the slammer will make you see the light." Rodriguez grabs Campos's wrist with one hand and jerks his handcuffs from a back pocket with the other.

"Wait! I'll talk. I'll come clean." Rodriguez sits back down. Campos tells him a new story of where he was that afternoon his daughter disappeared.

"Stay here," the detective says to Campos when he's finished. "I'll be right back. You better hope this latest tale that you're spinning checks out. I'm getting sick and tired of all your bullshit."

Rodriguez walks out of the interview room. His partner, Fallon, is asleep on one of the benches.

"Come on." Rodriguez shakes him to wake him up. "Let's go see the captain."

"What, you got something?" Fallon jumps up and runs after him.

They knock at the captain's door and hear him holler, "Come in." When he sees the men, he demands, "What do you have? Good news, I hope?"

"The scumbag now says he has a mistress in Santa Fe," Rodriguez says. "He didn't want his wife to know about her. That's why he lied to us."

"Do you believe him?"

"If he had told us about the lover right off the bat, I might have believed him," Rodriguez responds. "But since he lied to us before, I'm not so sure. Frankly, that guy is a piece of crap. He sickens me; he's more worried about his affair being discovered than he is about his daughter being found. He has yet to ask anything about the investigation—and that has got me thinking."

"You two get up to Santa Fe right away," Captain Belmont orders. "Don't send anybody else—I want you to handle this personally. Come down hard on the mistress. If you think she's lying, break her. Tell her she'll have the cell right next to her boyfriend. Let Mr. Campos know that he's going to be our guest for a little longer. Put somebody on him while he's here and make sure he doesn't get anywhere near a phone to tip off his girlfriend."

Later that night, the detectives are back in the captain's office to give him an update.

"So, what's the story?" Captain Belmont asks them. "What did you guys find out?"

"His alibi checks out," Detective Fallon reports. "Campos was with his girlfriend in the afternoon. A neighbor remembers seeing him go into the woman's house. They had dinner at a local restaurant. We interviewed a waiter who remembers the couple. Says he'll never forget them. They had a table in the back and she had her head in his lap between courses."

"Crap," the captain says. "All this fucking time wasted just because that douchebag wouldn't tell us the truth. Don't release that dirtbag yet—let him sit in the station and sweat for another couple of hours. That's what he deserves for giving us the runaround. So, where are we now on the case? You got anything new?"

"Well, we have the sketch given to us by the groundskeeper at the school—you know, the sketch of the man he saw lurking by the school the day the girl was taken. It's a decent composite. Gave us a good description of the car, too. That could be promising. Other than that, we got nothing."

2
The Trip Home

Two months after the kidnapping James stares out at the vast, empty farmlands. The 66 light blue Mustang is speeding along at seventy-five. Little does he suspect on this drive that the kidnapping of that young girl will have such a major impact on his young life. This time of year, the Kansas fields are lying fallow. The land is barren—a stark, dark, empty place made even gloomier by the cloudy skies. The emptiness of the landscape reminds him of where he was in his life just two weeks before. Only an occasional other car is on the highway. The window is cracked open, letting in some of that cold March Kansas air. These are the same fields that he flew over two months ago when he returned from Vietnam.

He turns and stares at the beautiful young blonde woman sleeping in the seat next to his. Her head is resting against the passenger-side front door of the Mustang. A smile appears on his face. *What a doll!* he thinks. *This must be a dream.* How could such an unpleasant, gloomy human being such as himself manage to attract such a joyful, beautiful woman? The only possible answer is that he must be dreaming. James turns back to the long, empty road in front of him.

Sam begins to stir from her sleep. She rubs her eyes, stretches, and turns to look at James. She glances at the clock on the dashboard; it's four thirty. She stretches her arms once more and yawns.

"How long have I been sleeping?" she asks.

He looks over at her and smiles. "Five or six hours."

"What?" Guilt sets in. She begins to question him furiously. "Why didn't you wake me? Aren't you tired? Isn't it my turn to drive? You must be exhausted! You've been driving since six this morning."

He gives her another smile. "I did try to wake you when I stopped for gas, but you were out cold."

"I'm sorry," she says. She yawns once more and rubs the back of her neck. "I guess all that running around this past week in New York City with you must

Sam and James: The Missing Teen

have really knocked me out. The fatigue finally caught up with me. I don't know how you do it, James. Don't you ever sleep?" She stretches again. "Do you want to pull over and let me drive? I can take a turn now—I feel rested."

"I'm okay for now. Maybe when I stop for gas. We're on a quarter of a tank, so we'll need gas soon. I can stop sooner if you're hungry. You slept right through lunch."

"I'm good. I can wait until we stop for gas," she replies, looking out the window at the seemingly endless Kansas landscape.

The week in New York City with him was great. Best of all, she had convinced him to return to Colorado with her. *More* than convinced—not only had she persuaded him to come back, but he had also proposed and given her a ring. His out-of-the-blue proposal went way beyond her wildest expectations of how her journey to the city would end.

After all, he had come home from his tour of duty in Vietnam, and instead of stopping to see her in Colorado, as he had promised, he'd gone straight home to New York. He had broken up with her and ended their relationship. And he had done it without coming to see her.

Instead, he'd written her that awful breakup letter—the letter that contained all the lame reasons why he could not be with her any longer: how he wasn't good enough for *her*, and how she was too good for *him*. He'd actually advised her to find someone else and get on with her life. Things would be so much better, he had insisted, if he were no longer in the picture. The letter offered one crappy reason after another why they should not be together.

But James made a big mistake: after finishing with all his bull crap, he had admitted that he loved her, because he signed the letter *"Love."* And she knew then that she would never let him go.

She packed her bags, went all the way to his home in New York, and demanded that he look her straight in the eye and tell her his true feelings. She gave him a choice: either retract the statement that he loved her or keep her in his life. No running away or hiding behind letters or telephones. It was time for him to man up, look her straight in the face, and tell her the truth.

Now she is returning to Colorado Springs with an engagement ring on her finger. What a wonderful turn of events! The result is far better than she ever could have hoped. She looks over at him once more and smiles.

"Any regrets, James?" she asks. "Are you sorry at all that I came to New York and got you?"

James turns to her and replies, "No regrets." He pauses for a moment and adds, "I'm sorry that I didn't come right home to you when I got out of Vietnam as I promised I would."

She leans over and gives him a kiss on the cheek. "You're forgiven…as long as you really don't have any second thoughts. I wouldn't want you to come back to me just because you feel sorry for me. You *are* coming back to me because you love me, right?"

"Sam, may I tell you something?" He pauses and swallows. "When my plane was landing at the airport in New York on my return from Vietnam, I felt really happy. I'd survived that awful war. But despite my joy, something was missing, and there was an emptiness deep within me. I just didn't feel like I was returning *home*. Yeah, there was serious relief that I had made it through the war, but there was also a wide hole of gloom underneath that relief.

"A few hours ago, I spotted the first road sign for Colorado. When I saw that sign, a thought hit me. The sentence *I'm returning home* popped into my head. *Finally, I'm coming home. This is where I should be.* The emptiness was completely gone. That's how I felt when I saw that road sign for Colorado."

Sam leans over to his side and kisses him on his cheek. Tears well up in her eyes as she says, "That is the sweetest thing."

James turns his eyes to her for a brief moment. "Sam, I'm so sorry I didn't come straight home to you as I promised I would. I'm so sorry that I hurt you and put you through that pain. That's the last time I will ever hurt you—I swear."

She gives him another kiss on the cheek and slides her hand between his legs. James looks down at her hand and turns to her. "What are you doing? There's no place to pull over."

"You don't have to pull over. I can handle everything while you're driving." She moves closer to him, unfastens his pants, and yanks down the zipper.

"Ow!" he screams in pain.

"What's the matter?" she shouts, and recoils.

"Holy crap, you caught my dick in the zipper! God, it hurts!" he yells. Tears of pain begin rolling down his face.

"Oh, James, I'm so sorry," she says, sliding over to help.

"Stay away!" he hollers and looks for a spot on the road to pull over.

James stops the car and stares down at his crotch, where a vital part of him is caught in the zipper. His member is no longer hard, which makes matters worse. "Geez, that hurts!" he says, grimacing in pain.

"Let me help you get it untangled," she says, as she moves toward him once more.

"Stay away," he warns her. His face is an angry beet red. "This is not like getting your jacket caught in a zipper. That's my skin caught in there. It's gripping my most prized possession."

James begins pulling the skin gently away from the zipper. "Fuck, that hurts!" He cringes, stops for a moment, and takes a deep breath. One final yank and he manages to get it free.

"Look at the welt." He shows her his penis; it has a large red mark on it.

Sam looks. "At least it's not bleeding," she says and then bursts out laughing.

"You think this is funny?" He scowls.

"No," she says, trying not to giggle.

"I hope it doesn't leave a permanent scar," he says as he begins to drive off.

"I hope it *does*. A scar would give it some character," she says and bursts out laughing again.

As they get back up to speed on the highway, he turns to her. "Well?"

"Well what?" She raises her brow and looks at him.

"Aren't you going to finish what you started?" he says, gesturing toward his dick, which is still exposed. "Why do you think he's still out—to get air?"

"I thought you were in pain..."

"I *am* in pain, but that doesn't mean I'm not horny. Just keep your hands off the zipper."

"You could be on your deathbed, dying in agony, and you would still want a blow job, wouldn't you?" she remarks. She moves over, bends down, and puts the head of his penis in her mouth.

"You're damn right," he says, rubbing the back of her head and smiling. "Just be very gentle. Remember, that's a wounded warrior down there."

"Move the seat back a little." She is mumbling because his penis is in her mouth. "I'm hitting my head on the steering wheel."

She is very gentle when she first starts, simply licking the head, too afraid to go much lower and cause further damage. Feeling his hand caressing the back of her head, she puts his penis deeper into her mouth. Since he's not complaining of any pain, she begins moving her head up and down more vigorously. When she's done, she raises her head and looks at him. "So, are you happy? Did I make up for hurting your precious boy?"

"No, you'll have to lick his wounds a few more times before he'll forgive you," James answers, giving her a cunning grin.

"Well, that's just too bad for him, because that's all he's getting," she fires back. "Pull over at the next gas station, please. I need to rinse out my mouth and brush my teeth."

Sam comes out of the ladies' room and walks toward James, who is pumping gas into the Mustang.

"Are you hungry?" he asks when they get back on the road.

"Not really."

"We should stop and eat something," he says. "You haven't eaten all day. You didn't eat breakfast, and you slept through lunch. We've got a good three hours before we get to Colorado Springs. I'm sure there's no food in the house."

"Kathy may have bought some food."

"What? Why would Kathy have bought food?"

She looks at him and her face flushes. "Oh my gosh—I forgot to tell you. Kathy is staying with us. She had to run to Texas for a few months to take care of her sick mom, and she lost her apartment. When she came back, she didn't have a place to stay, so I let her stay with me. I hope you won't mind…"

"No, of course not. I like Kathy; she can stay as long as she likes. We have the extra bedroom, so it won't be a problem. I still feel we should stop and get something to eat."

"Okay. I'm just really eager to get home—that's all. If you want to stop, we can do that. I *am* a little hungry."

Sitting in a booth at a roadside diner, they order two deluxe cheeseburger platters.

"This place looks pretty good," he says to her. "The bathrooms are really clean." This is his strictest criterion for a good restaurant. Then he asks her, "What're your plans for tomorrow?"

"I have to work. I've got the early shift and absolutely have to be there by nine thirty."

"Can't you take the day off? You're probably going to be really tired tomorrow."

"I'm sorry, James. I can't." She shrugs. "I'd love to take another day off, but I'm going to be managing my own department in a couple of weeks, so I can't take any more time. The store was good enough to give me the week off to go to New York City. What about you? What are you going to do tomorrow?"

"Tomorrow morning, I'm going to unpack our bags and do laundry. I'm sure we'll be too tired to do the wash tonight. In the afternoon, I'm going to go to Colorado College and talk to the admissions people. I might as well get that ball rolling. The sooner I know my status, the better."

The waitress comes over and brings them their order.

"Do you think you'll have any trouble getting admitted?" she asks him after taking a bite of her cheeseburger.

James takes a sip of his drink and sits back in his chair. "It's hard to say. There *could* be some problems. I didn't have the best grades in my first two years of college in New York—not even a C average. I don't believe the new college will be breaking out the champagne or bringing out a welcoming band when I show up."

Sam puts a fry in her mouth. "What are you going to do if they don't accept you?"

"Oh, they'll accept me; I *am* getting in," James says confidently. He takes a large bite of his cheeseburger. "Getting rejected is out of the question. It's just a matter of how hard a fight the admissions people want to put up before they give in. They have no idea as to the kind of person they'll be dealing with."

"I don't know, James. Maybe you should have a backup plan."

James is defiant. "No, Sam. Backup plans are for losers. A backup plan is an admission that you won't win. The first step to *losing* is the backup plan. This is a fight that I *have* to win. I'm getting in—and that's final."

James is right about the drive: almost exactly three hours later, they are heading down the street to their home—the bottom of a split-level house. The landlady, Mrs. Smythe, lives upstairs.

"Would you mind bringing the bags in?" Sam asks him when they pull up to the house. "I want to run in and tell Kathy the good news."

Not waiting for his response, she hops out of the car and dashes for the front door. She unlocks the door and runs in. "Kathy? Kathy, are you here?" she hollers as soon as she gets inside the house. Kathy comes out of her bedroom.

"Oh my God, you're home!" Kathy shouts. She runs up and hugs Sam. Then, just as quickly, she pulls away and asks, "Where's James? Don't tell me that he said no and stayed home?"

"No, he's outside. He's unpacking the car." She starts to smile.

Kathy hugs her again, squeezing harder this time. "Oh, I'm so happy for you!"

"Look." Sam shows Kathy the diamond engagement ring on the finger of her left hand.

Kathy lets out a scream and begins jumping up and down. She reaches over and hugs Sam again. "You're engaged! Let me see that ring again!"

Sam is smiling broadly as she proudly puts her hand out. Her friend takes a closer look.

"It's beautiful," Kathy says.

"Oh, Kathy, everything went perfectly. I'm so happy. I knew he loved me."

"His love won't last long if you make him lug all the bags by himself," James hollers as he carries in the four bags inside the open front door and drops them.

Kathy walks over and gives him a hug and a kiss. "Welcome back, stranger. It's so nice to see you again."

James squeezes Kathy tightly and gives her a kiss. "It's nice to see you too, Kathy." He pushes her back slightly and takes a look at her. "How's my tall, blonde Texan?"

"I'm well, James. Welcome back from the war. How about you? How are you feeling?"

"Really great, now that I'm back where I belong," he replies with a broad smile. "I hear you're going to stay with us for a bit?"

"Yes, if it's okay with you. Do you mind? I'll try not to overstay my welcome."

"Don't be ridiculous," he says and gives her another hug. "You stay as long as you want. Although all the men in Colorado will be jealous: I now have the two prettiest women in the state living with me." He looks into Kathy's face and changes the subject, still holding her. "I was so sorry to hear about your mom. How is she doing?"

"She's doing better," Kathy responds, breaking free of his embrace. "The doctors say the cancer is in remission. All we can do now is hope and pray that the cancer doesn't come back."

"Is that James that I saw from the window?" a voice calls from the doorway.

James turns around and sees his landlady. "Mrs. Smythe!" he shouts, and hurries over to give her a hug and a kiss. "It's so nice to see you!"

The lady gives him a slap on his shoulder and shoves him away from her. With her finger in his face, Mrs. Smythe says, "Don't play nice with me, young man. It's about time you came back to this beautiful girl. I'm very disappointed in you, James. You really hurt this wonderful gal—you broke her heart."

"I know, Mrs. Smythe, and I'm really very sorry." James looks at the ground. "Please believe me—it will never happen again. I'll never hurt her ever again, I promise you."

"Good," she says sternly. Then she points her finger in his face once again. "Because if there is a next time, I'm coming to look for you myself—and believe me, you won't be happy."

"I understand, Mrs. Smythe." James flushes. "Believe me, that won't be necessary. I'm never leaving her again, I promise. Thank you for watching over Sam while I was away."

"No need to thank me, James. She is a pleasure," Mrs. Smythe says as she turns to walk out the door. Her final words are, "Welcome home, James. I'm glad you got home safe and sound. Good night, everyone. Samantha, call me if you need anything."

"Good night, Mrs. Smythe, and thanks for everything," Sam replies. Sam looks at James. "I'm never going to let you break the promise you made to that woman."

"Don't worry, Sam. I have no intention of breaking my promise. Listen, I need to take a shower. Are my nightclothes in the same drawer I left them in?"

"Exactly where you left them," Sam responds. She walks over to lock the front door.

When James has left to get his things, Kathy turns to Sam and whispers, "Come on—let's sit on the sofa. You can tell me all about your trip."

After they are seated, Kathy says, "So, go on! What happened? How did you get him to change his mind and come home with you?"

"I was really nervous when I got to his house," Sam says, beginning her story. "I wasn't really sure that he still wanted me, Kathy. I knew that he loved me, but when I got there, I began doubting myself. We discussed everything over lunch, but James was still confused and wouldn't give me an answer. He asked how long

I was planning to stay in New York City, and I told him a week. Then he promised me he would give me a decision by the end of the week."

The young women stop talking as James comes out of the bedroom and heads for the bathroom. He looks over at the girls and is immediately suspicious. "You guys are talking about *me*, aren't you?"

They don't reply. "Well, at least be a *little* kind," he says, and heads into the bathroom.

"So, go on," Kathy urges Sam. "Finish the story."

"When James told me he needed more time to think about our situation, I got really concerned. That's when I decided that I was going to be on my best behavior, Kathy. No fighting, no shouting, no demands—just do everything he says, I told myself. I met his family and friends, and we went out every night. Everywhere that he wanted to go, we went. Everything that he wanted to do, I did. By the end of the week, I was sure that I had succeeded—and I was right. You see? He's home, and I'm so happy about it!"

"But what about the engagement ring?" Kathy wants to know. "You couldn't have possibly been expecting to get engaged. You *had* to have been surprised…"

"*Surprised?*" Sam sits up and looks at the bathroom door. "I was in complete shock. All I wanted was for him to come back to me. When he proposed, I almost fainted." Sam pauses for a moment. "Kathy, I'm so happy, and I'm so glad that you, my best friend, are here to share this joy with me. Will you be my maid of honor?"

Tears roll down Kathy's face as she gives Sam a hug. "Oh, Sam, of course! I would be honored."

James walks out of the bathroom. Sam and Kathy stop talking once again. He looks over to where they are sitting on the sofa. "This silence when I come into the room is making me very nervous. Sam, do you know where we put the Vaseline?"

"Why do you need Vaseline?" Sam asks.

James stares at her. "Really, Sam, do you have to ask? You don't *know*? I want to put some Vaseline on the wound that you caused, so it doesn't scab."

"What wound?" Kathy asks.

Sam shakes her head at Kathy and whispers, "Not now." She turns back to James. "It's on the top shelf of the medicine cabinet."

After James goes back into the bathroom, Kathy asks once again, "What wound? What happened?"

"I was pulling down his zipper and caught his penis in it," Sam admits.

Kathy bursts out laughing. "What? Ouch! Oh my God, that had to hurt! Is he all right?" She is now laughing uncontrollably.

"He's fine," Sam says, making a dismissive motion with her hands. "He's just being a big baby."

Kathy is holding her hand over her mouth, trying to stifle her laughter, when

James comes out of the bathroom. He looks over at Sam. "You told her, didn't you? You just couldn't keep your big mouth shut."

Kathy can't control herself any longer. She bursts out laughing. "I hope you're not permanently handicapped," she yells.

"Very funny, Kathy. Why don't you come to the bedroom with me and find out for yourself?"

Kathy doesn't respond. She is still laughing.

"Aren't you coming to bed?" James asks Sam. "Aren't you tired?"

"You go ahead. I'm going to stay up and chat with Kathy a little longer."

"All right. Good night. Try not to stay up too late. You've got work tomorrow."

"I won't be much longer. Good night, dear."

As he's walking to the bedroom, Kathy calls out, "Make sure you don't abuse that little man of yours. He's injured!"

"Your concern is touching, Kathy. Maybe you should come and kiss him to make it better," he yells back from the bedroom.

3
THE REJECTION

The white van pulls into the dusty Sinclair station. The bearded man gets out of the vehicle.

"What'll be?" The attendant asks him.

"Five dollars worth of gas," the man replies.

"You've been here a few times but we've never been properly introduced. My name is Ralph." Ralph the attendant sticks out his hand.

The man pauses and stares at the hand that's been offered. "Isaiah," the man shakes Ralph's hand.

"So how do you like living in Yuma?" Ralph asks him. "Are you used to the area yet?"

"I'm only here temporarily. I'll be leaving in a few weeks. Right around Easter."

"I'll be sorry to see you go."

"I'm going inside to the grocery," Isaiah tells him. "I'll be right back."

"Sure, take your time. My wife is in there. She can help you."

Sam looks at the clock on her nightstand when she wakes up the next morning. It's seven o'clock—forty-five minutes before the alarm is set to go off. Hearing noise in the kitchen, she is sure that it's James.

She and Kathy had stayed up talking until three. Normally, she would have turned over and snoozed for the remaining forty-five minutes. This time, however, she decides to get up. She wants to talk to James about something that happened last night that has been weighing on her. She slides into her slippers and walks into the kitchen. James is pouring himself a cup of coffee at the counter.

"You're up early," he says when he sees her coming into the kitchen. "Do you want a cup of coffee?"

"Yes, please."

He hands her his cup and goes back to the coffee pot to pour another. He opens the fridge and takes out the milk, and then opens a cabinet and takes out the sugar bowl. Sam places her cup on the table, reaches into a drawer, and takes out two spoons.

"What time did you guys finally go to bed last night?" he asks.

"Around three," she replies, sipping her coffee.

"Three! You must be really tired. Are you sure you don't want to call in sick? You're not going to be very useful, anyway."

"Truly, I'm not that tired," she tells him as she sits at the table. "I slept most of the day yesterday during our trip. You did all the driving. Besides, I have no choice—I need to get to work."

"Do you want some breakfast?" he asks her.

"Not right now. Maybe after my coffee. I'd like to talk to you about something first."

"What's up? What did you want to talk to me about?"

She fiddles with her napkin and glances away from him. "This may sound petty, but you know last night when you flirted with Kathy…"

"What the hell are you talking about, Sam? I didn't flirt with Kathy," he says, cutting her off quickly. His voice is rising.

"Shh!" she says to him, turning around and looking at Kathy's door. "Not so loud! You might wake her…"

"Wake her! I've got a good mind to go and knock her right out of bed," he insists. "Did Kathy *say* I flirted with her?"

"No, she didn't *say* it," Sam says, becoming defensive. "It's something that I witnessed myself. Kathy doesn't have anything to do with this."

"Sam, what's going on? What's gotten into you?" He asks, calming down. "You're acting so strange. What did I say or do that led you to believe that I was flirting with Kathy?"

Sam moves uncomfortably in her seat and takes another sip of her coffee. "I'm talking about when you told her to come kiss him, to make it better."

"That's it?" James sits back in his chair. "A harmless remark like that? That's what has you so upset? Sam, you've got to know that I was joking. You know me, I can't resist a good comeback. Always trying to be funny. I can't believe you would get jealous over something so stupid!"

She sits quietly, says nothing, and just stares at her coffee cup.

James looks over at her. "I'm sorry, Sam, for making light of this. I can see that it's bothering you. Come on, get it all out. Tell me everything that's going on—I don't believe it's just one stupid comment I made last night. I've said much dumber things. What's really bothering you?"

"Do you remember when you were in Vietnam and Kathy brought those boys over here?"

"I do, Sam." He looks thoughtful. "But you took care of that problem. As I recall, you kicked the guy in the groin when he tried to get fresh with you, and also gave him a bloody nose. What does that episode have to do with last night?"

Sam shifts in her chair. "I had a long talk with Kathy after that night. She told me she brought that boy over to my place on purpose, trying to break us up. Kathy had a crush on you, James, and she was jealous of me. She brought that boy over just to cause trouble between us."

"Oh crap. Sam! I didn't know." He pauses for a moment as Sam's words sink in. "I always knew Kathy liked me, but I never thought it was anything more than friendship." He looks into Sam's face and asks, "If you feel so strongly, why did you offer to let Kathy stay in our home with us? Why set yourself up?"

"I trust you, James. I don't believe you would ever cheat on me. Kathy is my lifelong friend. She took me in when I first came to Colorado. After the night with that boy, she and I had a long talk. We cleared the air and straightened everything out. Now she needs a place to stay, and I'm returning the favor that she did for me. I just don't want you to say or do something that she might take the wrong way." She looks up at him with a sorrowful face.

"Not even jokingly, James. Please. Can you understand how I feel?" she continues. "Don't give her any encouragement. Will you do this for me, James?"

He gets off his chair, walks over to where she is sitting, and gives her a kiss. "Of course I will. I'll be more careful of what I say. Come on," he says, taking her by the hand.

"Where are we going?"

"To the bedroom. I just realized that it's been almost a year since I last made love to you in our bedroom. You've got a little time before you need to get ready for work. I want to make love to my one and only love."

When they are done, Sam heads to the bathroom to shower and get ready for work. James heads to the kitchen. Kathy is there with her back to the counter, sipping a cup of coffee.

"You're up?" James says to her when he sees her. "As late as you went to bed last night, I thought you'd sleep until noon."

"How can *anybody* get any sleep around here when you two are having sex? You guys are louder than two alley cats in heat. I'm surprised your landlady hasn't come down here. Unless she's deaf, she had to have heard your performance. The whole neighborhood probably heard you."

"I'm sorry; I'll try to be quieter the next time."

"It's not you. It's Sam," Kathy explains. "I've never heard so many moans, groans, and sounds coming from one person. I never realized that, Sunday-school-teaching, Bible-toting friend of mine is such a sex maniac."

James begins laughing. "She's not a sex maniac. To Sam, sex is an expression of love. She throws herself into the act of making love, just as she does into everything else we do together…out of feelings of love. Fully abandoning any inhibitions and giving in to all her desires is her way of expressing love."

"Well, whatever her reasons, she sure seems to be having a grand ole time," Kathy comments. She heads for her bedroom. "I'm going to have to buy earplugs while I'm staying here."

It's nearly seven in the evening when Sam gets home from work. She comes in the front door, puts her pocketbook on the chair, and heads for the kitchen.

"Hello," she says to Kathy, who is sliding a pan into the oven.

"You're late." Kathy looks up and smiles.

"Yes, the store manager called me in. He wanted to bring me up to date on what I missed the week I was out. What are you cooking?

"I'm baking some meat loaf for dinner. I thought I'd make some mashed potatoes and a salad to go with it, if that's okay with you?"

"Sounds perfect. Where's James?"

"I don't know." Kathy stands up and closes the door to the oven. "The last time I saw him was around two o'clock, when he was heading out to see the admissions officer at Colorado College."

"He's not back yet? I hope that's a *good* sign. I think that if he'd been rejected, he would be home by now."

They hear someone putting a key in the door. James comes walking in carrying a poster.

"Did they accept you?" Sam asks nervously when he comes in.

"No, they rejected me," he tells her nonchalantly. "They tried to beat around the bush and not give me a decision, but I insisted and forced their hand."

"I'm so sorry!" Sam exclaims. She walks over and tries to give him a hug.

"*I'm* not," he says, holding her gently away from his body. "I suspected they were going to reject me. Now the *real* action begins," he adds defiantly. "This battle has only begun. They have no idea who they're dealing with. I mean, I fought in 'Nam. Is the tent and camping gear we used when we went on our trip last year still in the shed in the back?"

"Yes, I guess so," Sam tells him. "Why? What are you going to do?"

"I'm going to camp out on the front lawn of the college admissions office until they accept me. I'm going to make a poster that says, *Vietnam Vet Needs an Education; Just Give Me a Chance.*"

James turns and looks at Sam and Kathy. His face is taut. "I deserve a second chance. I'm not asking for a handout, just a leg up. They sent me to war—or to '*a police action,*' as they called it. They owe me this much."

Sam asks, "How long are you planning to camp out?"

"As long as it takes. It's up to them," James says boldly.

The two women look at each other and burst out laughing.

"Are you crazy?" Kathy asks. "They'll just ignore you. You could be there for months."

"No, Kathy, I don't think they'll ignore me. The administration will have to do *something*; they can't leave me camped out right in front of the admissions office. Every prospective student and every parent will see me when they visit the campus. The college can't afford the bad publicity."

"What if they just call the police and have you arrested?" Sam asks.

"That would be *perfect*," James says with a crafty smile. "Look at all the press I'd get. They'll have me arrested and then I'll have the school exactly where I want them. The whole country will hear of my plight. A *Vietnam vet* being denied a chance for an education and getting arrested instead should get a lot of play in the news. Getting busted would be my one-way ticket to getting into school. Think of all the hippies who are going to college and refusing to serve in the army. Can't you just picture the outrage? I went to war, but they won't let me go to college. Think of the irony—what a great news story it'd make.

"No more time for talk now. I've got to get busy and get myself pinched," he says and leaves the kitchen.

Sam runs after him and grabs his arm. She smiles warmly, "Why don't you have dinner first? Kathy baked a meat loaf. You must be hungry; you haven't eaten all day. The camp-in can wait a little longer. There's probably nobody at the office right now, anyway. You'll be protesting to the dark, empty night."

"You're absolutely right, Sam." James turns around. "Might as well shower and take my time packing. Once I start my protest, I could be there for a while."

He heads for the bedroom, telling them as he goes that he will leave first thing in the morning, at the crack of dawn. "I want to be there when the admissions people have to pass me on the way to work in the morning. Let 'em have a good look at the man they're dealing with."

When he's gone, Kathy says to Sam, "You do know that boyfriend of yours is crazy, don't you? Absolutely certifiable."

Sam smiles at Kathy. "I know! Isn't he just wonderful? I just love him."

The next morning, around ten, Kathy walks into the kitchen, where Sam is preparing some sandwiches.

"What are you doing?" she asks.

"I'm making lunch for James. I'm bringing him the sandwiches before I go to work."

"He's really doing the camp-in?" Kathy shakes her head. "I can't believe it. I thought he'd change his mind after he slept on the idea."

"Then you don't know James," Sam informs Kathy. She opens the fridge, takes out two Cokes, and sticks them in a bag along with the sandwiches. "I better get going. He's probably starving. He left so early this morning, he didn't have time for breakfast."

When Sam gets to the campus, it's easy to find James. There are some thirty guys, many wearing army fatigue jackets, milling around a small tent in the middle of the big lawn. Some are sitting on beach chairs. James is standing, speaking to two of the men wearing fatigue jackets.

"Check out the skirt!" one of the men says to James when he notices Sam walking across the lawn.

James turns to look. "Put your eyes back in your head, Nieves. That's my girlfriend." He walks over to Sam and gives her a hug and a kiss.

"I thought you might be hungry," she says to him. She hands him the bag with the sandwiches and the Cokes.

He looks inside the bag and asks, "Why don't you have lunch with me? There's plenty of food in here for both of us."

"Okay. Who *are* all these guys?" Sam asks as she looks around the lawn.

"They're fellow Vietnam vets. I had to go inside the building this morning to use the bathroom. The campus security guards snuck out here and tried to snatch my stuff. Nieves and a few of the vets noticed and drove the guards off. Now they're all on watch, so it won't happen again."

"What is that smell?"

He takes a sniff and looks around. "Oh, a few of the guys are probably smoking pot."

"Are you doing dope, James?"

"Me, no, I can't afford to get pinched. This campus is probably loaded with undercover fuzz. I get busted for smoking pot and they'll never let me into the school."

Just then, Nieves comes walking over he's smoking a joint. "Damn, Coppi, if I had a beauty like her back home, I wouldn't be out *here*."

"Sam, this is Bobby Nieves. Bobby, this is my fiancée, Samantha."

"It's a pleasure meeting you, Samantha." Nieves puts the smoke in front of her. "Want a toke?"

"No thanks. I don't smoke. Did you serve in the same area of Vietnam with James?"

"No, I was in the Twenty-Fifth Infantry, much farther south, where the *real* action was in the war. James and his buddies just slept while the NVA slipped by them. We had to do all the mopping up of the men they let through."

"Very funny, Nieves," He turns to Sam. "Don't listen to him, Sam. He probably snuck off to Saigon every weekend. The only NVA he ever saw was on television when he got home."

"Listen up," Nieves tells James. "I've got three classes in a row, so I can't be out here this afternoon. Everything seems to be copacetic but just in case, we worked out a deal that someone will be here all day and night. If you want to take a break, just let them know. We called all the news stations and papers—maybe someone will pick up the story. Anyway, I'll see you later." He turns to Sam and says, "You don't happen to have a sister who is as pretty as you, do you?"

"No, but I have a good friend, Kathy, who isn't seeing anyone. I think she is prettier than I am."

"Prettier than you?" Nieves turns to James. "When this is over, we're double-dating."

After eating lunch with James, Sam heads off to work, leaving James to continue his protest with his army buddies. She takes her dinner break at six. Walking through the electronics department of the store, she sees two of her coworkers looking at a television.

"What are you guys watching that's so interesting?" Sam asks the women.

"They're interviewing this young Vietnam vet who is camped out on the college campus asking for the chance to be admitted," one of the ladies tells her.

"He's gorgeous," the other woman remarks. "Maybe I'll take a ride out to the school after work and find out if he's available."

Sam looks at the screen and turns to the woman. "He's *not* available. That's my fiancé," she says and walks away.

The next day, Sam has the late shift. She once again packs sandwiches for James.

"How long do you think he'll hold out?" Kathy asks her.

"I have no idea. He was there all night. James says what he's doing is really important. I've never seen him so determined."

"He was all over the news last night."

"Everybody was talking about him at work, too," Sam tells her. They hear someone unlocking the front door and see James hauling in all his camping gear.

"What happened? Did you give up?" Sam asks him.

"No. *They* gave *in*," a smiling James tells her as he puts down the gear. "They admitted me to the school. I won!"

"That's wonderful!" Sam shouts. She gives him a hug and a kiss. "Tell me exactly what happened."

"Come on, let's sit and I'll tell you guys all about it." He leads the two women into the living room.

"The dean's assistant came out early this morning and said they wanted to speak with me," James begins his account. "At first, I thought it was a trick to get me away from my tent. None of my buddies were around to guard my gear. I decided to follow her anyway, and she took me to his office. When I got there, the dean said that they were admitting me beginning in September. He said that I'll be on probation and need to keep a C average or above or else they'll kick me out—and no amount of protesting will get me back in. I had to sign a document agreeing to those terms."

Sam slides over on the sofa and gives him a kiss. "I'm so proud of you."

"I'm not going to start at the school in September, though. I'm going to wait until the spring semester."

"How come?" Kathy asks.

"It's about the money. After meeting with the admissions officer and with financial aid, we all felt that the tuition might be a burden. Even with the money I'd get from the G.I. Bill, I would still have to take out some loans. I'm going to take courses this summer and this fall at El Paso Community College. The school just opened up. Tuition is a lot less there. If I can get my GPA up to 2.0, the college will give me credit not only for the courses that I take at El Paso, but also for the credits I earned when I attended college before I got drafted. That will save me a year and a half at the school and will also save me money. I won't need any loans."

James turns to Sam. "By the way, you'll be happy to hear I also found work. You won't be supporting me."

"You did? Where?" Sam asks.

"An attorney came by during my protest and we got to talking. When he learned that I needed a job, he asked me if I wanted to be a process server."

Sam looks confused. "A process server? What's that?"

"You serve papers and summonses on people that the lawyers want to take to court. He'll pay me ten dollars for each summons that I serve. Should be a snap, I figure. Just walk up to the unsuspecting stiff and hit him with the papers. Really easy money. What can it take? Twenty minutes a day at most. The lawyer knows other lawyers who may want to use me. He's got four summonses that he wants me to process this week alone. The job should be perfect; I can do the work around my school schedule."

James leans over, pulls Sam to him, and gives her a kiss. "I can't believe how easily everything is falling into place. It's all because of you, Sam. You set me on a path and showed me that anything is possible." He gives her another kiss. "Thank you for coming to New York and rescuing me."

Sam's eyes begin to fill with tears. She pushes him down on the couch and gets on top of him. She gives him a kiss and says, "You are most welcome."

"Not again! I'm going to my room," Kathy calls out. She gets up and heads down the hall. "I hope you guys will be a little quieter this time. I don't think the neighborhood has quite gotten over your last performance."

4
AN ARREST

Detective Frank Fallon, heavy-set and gray haired, puts his sunglasses and his cowboy hat on the table and looks over at his partner, Hector Rodriguez, the first Mexican American to have made detective in the Albuquerque Police Department. They are the lead detectives on the Penelope Campos case. They are meeting at their favorite diner in Albuquerque, as they do every Thursday morning, to go over the weekly progress of their cases. It's a routine the two officers have followed ever since they became a team nearly four years earlier.

This week, the detectives have only one case: the disappearance of Penelope Campos. This Thursday morning get-together is both more important and more anxiety producing than usual. Right after their discussion, they are going to meet with Captain Richard Belmont, who will want a full update on the status of the investigation. The waitress comes over and pours fresh coffee into their cups.

"Good morning, Detective Fallon, Detective Rodriguez," the middle-aged waitress says to the men, nodding to each in turn. She wants to ask them about the case of the missing girl, but knows better.

"What'll it be, boys—the usual?" she asks, smiling.

They both nod in the affirmative.

"So, what do we have on the case?" Fallon asks Rodriguez as he lights up a cigarette.

"We've got diddly-squat," Rodriguez replies, running his hands through his thick, dark-brown hair.

"Man, we really stepped in fucking shit this time, didn't we? What are we going to tell the captain? We can't go in there with nothing," Fallon says. He moves his Stetson to the other side of the table. "All the politicians are running for cover. This Greenwald guy is getting ready to pull the trigger. If we don't solve this case soon, somebody is going down and us along with him."

"Maybe if we hadn't spent the last two weeks answering phones, we'd have gotten a little further along," Rodriguez answers. He smiles, showing bright, shiny teeth. "Greenwald's offer of a fifty-thousand-dollar reward was a huge fucking mistake. Every nutcase in the country is calling the station with worthless tips, and every officer in the station is on a wild-goose chase."

Rodriguez pauses. "Not that I can really blame the old man," he comments as he looks up. "It's been three months since his granddaughter's disappearance." Rodriguez takes a sip of his coffee. "Do you think she's still alive?"

Fallon waits before answering. The waitress arrives with their food and puts it on the table.

"Her chances don't look good," he says when the waitress is gone. He shakes his head; a frown appears on his leathery face.

"That young girl's face haunts me," Rodriguez says, buttering his toast. "I have three daughters; I can't imagine what it would be like if one of them went missing."

Not much is said for the remainder of the breakfast. Not much *could* be said. The detectives have nothing—not a single clue.

"I guess we better go face the music," Fallon says after finishing his third cup of coffee.

The station house is busy. The state troopers have brought in a team to work on the kidnapping with the local police. Almost every detective is on the phone.

Rodriguez looks at Fallon. "Look at how many guys are sitting here at the station answering phones. All these guys should be out pounding the pavement. Instead, they're sitting here answering calls from every crank in New Mexico—all because of that reward offered by Greenwald."

Fallon knocks at Captain Belmont's door and calls out, "Fallon and Rodriguez, sir."

"Come in," they hear from the other side.

The detectives open the door and see the captain, as well as a man in a suit sitting beside him. *Crap,* Fallon says to himself when he recognizes the Albuquerque chief of police.

Belmont gets right to the point. "Okay, Mutt and Jeff, what have you got?" The captain had adopted these nicknames for his lead detectives four years earlier, when he first saw the short, stocky Rodriguez and super-tall Fallon standing at attention together.

"We're still trying to locate the guy who was seen lurking at the school," Rodriguez answers.

"That's the same thing you said last week!" Captain Belmont throws up his hands, picks up a pad and slams it back down on the desk. "What the hell is taking so long?

"We'd have a lot more time to look for this man if we didn't have to chase down every so-called lead from all the calls coming in from these crackpots, Captain. Greenwald's announcement of a reward was a huge mistake," Fallon says in an obvious attempt to defend himself and his partner. All three of them know the excuse is getting old.

"Well, maybe if Mr. Greenwald sensed that the case was moving forward, he might not have felt the need to offer a reward," Chief of Police Franks says calmly. Fallon knows he is being scolded. The measured voice of his chief worries him.

"Yes, sir," he answers obediently.

The chief looks at his captain and frowns. "You know, I'm really disappointed in this investigation, Belmont," he declares as he starts to stand. "You're no further along than you were when you first began." Chief Franks straightens his jacket and, still speaking in his flat, composed voice, adds, "I'm going to leave and return to your office *next* Thursday at this same time. If we are still hitting the same impasse, you will take these detectives off the case. You will demote them back to uniform and send them back out to pound the beat. That, my dear fellow, will be your last official act as captain of this station house, because you'll be pounding the beat along with them. Do I make myself clear?"

"Yes, sir. Loud and clear," Captain Belmont responds.

"I'm sick and tired of being blamed by the mayor of this town and the governor of this state," Chief Franks mutters as he starts to leave the office. He opens the door, but before walking out, he turns to the three men and adds in an ominously quiet voice, "This case is a career ender."

The captain loosens his tie and looks at his two men. "Get the hell out of my office and get back to work!" As they turn to head for the door, the captain yells, "And solve this case!"

The two detectives go back to their desks.

"Now what?" Rodriguez asks Fallon.

"Let's start again from the beginning," Fallon suggests as he lights up a cigarette. "Let's pull out all the files and go over everything once again with a fine-toothed comb. We'll go back out and interview the witnesses all over again. We must have missed something—"

Suddenly, they see a detective come running by. They watch as he bursts into the captain's office.

"We got him!" he shouts.

Fallon puts out his smoke. The two detectives jump up and run into the captain's office, too.

"He tried to snatch another one, Captain," the breathless detective tells them. "Right at the same school. The girl broke free and took off. A patrolman who was on the scene gave chase and arrested the perp. It's the same guy from the sketch. They're driving him here as we speak."

"Where's the girl he tried to grab?" Captain Belmont asks him.

The detective pauses and looks confused. "I don't know," he responds. "I guess she ran home."

"All right." The captain sighs as he gives directions to Fallon and Rodriguez that he knew should not have been necessary. "Go to her house, pick her up, and bring her here. She'll need to give us a statement and identify the creep. Make sure you bring one of her parents with her."

Captain Belmont looks over at Fallon and Rodriguez. "Call someone from children's services to help with the girl. Get a search warrant and send a couple of men to the perp's house immediately." Both detectives nod. Belmont continues. "Make sure they search *everything*. Tell them to be *very* careful—not like bulls in a china shop. We need evidence to help find Penelope. Get somebody good out there; let's not screw this up. When the perp gets here, you two take him into the interview room and grill him *good*. Don't come out until you have a written confession—you hear?"

"We hear you, Captain," Rodriguez answers.

"You break that perp today or you will be back in uniform tomorrow. Got that?" the captain warns.

"Yes, sir," Rodriguez fires back. "We won't let you down," he adds. They leave to go sit at their desks to wait for the suspect, but they don't even get that far. As they're leaving Captain Belmont's office, two uniforms come walking in with the handcuffed suspect.

"Put him in the interview room," Rodriguez calls out the moment he sees them.

"So, how do you want to approach this?" Rodriguez asks Fallon.

"Let's start out nice and easy. Offer him a beverage. Get him to start talking. Let him explain what he was doing at the school. Don't challenge anything he says. Let him open up and trap himself with his own words. We'll ratchet up the questioning slowly. When the time is right, we'll drop the hammer and bring in the heat."

"Okay. Let's get started." The impatient Rodriguez jumps up from his chair.

"Not yet," Fallon says, trying to slow Rodriguez down. "Let him sit there for a few minutes by himself and get his bullshit story straight. The more he thinks he can fool us, the better off we are."

Twenty minutes later, Rodriguez looks at Fallon. "What do you think?"

Fallon nods his head. "Yeah, it's showtime."

They walk into the interview room.

"Good morning. I'm Detective Rodriguez, and this is my partner, Detective Fallon," he says to the pudgy, pimply-faced young man. "Your name is Mr. Peter Fontana—is that correct?"

"Yes," Fontana responds, squirming nervously in his chair.

"Mr. Fontana, do you mind if I call you Pete?"

"No, Pete is good." Fontana says with a nervous smile.

"That's good, Pete. Can I get you something to drink—water, coffee, or a Coke?" Rodriguez smiles, showing off his large, white teeth.

"A Coke, if you don't mind."

"Sure thing." Rodriguez turns to his partner. "Fallon, would you mind getting Pete a Coke?"

"Not at all," Fallon replies in a tone every bit as gentle as Rodriguez's.

Rodriguez turns to the suspect when Fallon leaves the room. "Make yourself comfortable, Pete. We just need to clear up a few things. This shouldn't take long." Rodriguez smiles once more and sits back in his chair. "So, tell me, Pete—what were you doing at the school this morning?"

About an hour has passed when the detectives hear a knock at the door. They go outside and find Captain Belmont standing there. "How's it going?"

"Fontana here says the whole thing was just a big misunderstanding," Fallon tells him. "Says the girl was heading into the street without looking and he reached out to save her from the oncoming traffic. For some reason—he doesn't know why—the girl screams, kicks him in the shins, and runs off."

"You believe his BS?"

"No, of course not, Captain." Fallon shakes his head. "We're just letting him talk right now. We'll start to apply the pressure soon."

"The young girl and her mother are here," the captain says. "We're getting a statement from the girl right now. Let's put him in a lineup so she can ID him."

"Why bother, Cap'n?" Rodriguez chimes in. "He's not denying that he grabbed her."

"Because I want the identification to be *by the book* and on the record. I don't want him coming back later saying we misunderstood what he said. Let's button everything up. Put him in the lineup and start squeezing him. Let's get to the Campos girl as soon as possible."

"Will do, Cap'n," Fallon responds.

After the lineup and the girl's positive identification of the suspect, the two detectives stand outside the door of the interrogation room and discuss their next move. "I'll go in and keep the dialogue going," Rodriguez tells Fallon. "I think he trusts me. You come in after about a half hour and ratchet it up."

"All right—go ahead," says Fallon. "I'll go have a cup of coffee and grab a smoke."

Fallon is having his coffee when another detective comes up and drops a box on his desk.

"What's this, Fusco?" he asks the detective.

"Take a look inside." Fusco responds. "We got these at the scumbag's house."

Fallon reaches in and takes out a stack of photographs. He looks through the stack. "Son of a bitch," he mutters. "How many are in here?"

"There must be hundreds. They're still going through his home."

"You got anything else?"

Detective Fusco smiles and reaches into the inside pocket of his jacket, pulling out three more photographs. "I saved the best for last," he says, handing Fallon the pictures.

Fallon looks at the photos and then tucks them in his shirt pocket. "Good job, Fusco," he says to the detective. He gets up, grabs the box of pictures, and heads for the interrogation room. He pushes open the door, slams the box down on the table, walks to the other side of the table where Fontana is sitting, and kicks the chair out from under the suspect, sending him flying onto the ground. Fallon reaches down, pulls Fontana up by his collar, and flings him against the wall. Rodriguez tries to step in, but he's too late to keep Fallon from grabbing the perp by the neck and starting to choke him.

"So, you like little girls, do you—you sick motherfucker?" Fallon yells, squeezing the guy's neck harder. Rodriguez manages to break Fallon's grip and release Fontana from the choke hold. Rodriguez looks at Fallon, who pulls the three photographs from his shirt pocket and shows them to his partner. They are pictures of Penelope Campos.

The door to the room opens. Captain Belmont sticks his head in. "Can I see you guys out here for a sec?"

"What's up, Cap'n?" Fallon asks him once they are outside the room. "I was just getting started."

"I see you started turning up the heat," Belmont answers. "Good. The groundskeeper from the school, Martinez, is here. Let's put the perp in a lineup and get a second ID."

After the lineup and a positive identification by Martinez, the detectives and perp are all back in the interrogation room.

"I think I'd like a lawyer now," the suspect tells them as he sits back down. "I'm tired and I want to go home."

"Okay. If a lawyer is what you want, you can have one," Fallon says to him. "But if a lawyer comes, you are *not* going home. You'll be booked and arrested. It's your call."

Rodriguez leans over the table. "Listen, Pete, we don't really care about the girl you tried to grab today. To tell you the truth, I believe you. I think that what happened with her was a big misunderstanding. We'd like to speak to you about another girl. This one." Rodriguez slides the pictures of Penelope Campos in front of Fontana. "She disappeared three months ago. You know anything about that?"

"No. I don't know the girl."

Fallon grabs him by the collar and shouts, "Then what were her pictures doing in your house?"

"Frank, please. Let him go," Rodriguez cuts in. "I'm sure there's a good explanation. Take a break and go get another a cup of coffee. Let me talk with Pete alone for a few moments. I bet we can straighten everything out."

When Fallon leaves, Rodriguez tells Fontana, "You'll have to excuse my partner. We're all very tense trying to find out what happened to this young girl. Something tells me that you can help us out, Pete. I've been doing this work for a long time, and I've got a feeling that you can help.

"I know sometimes things are not what they seem," Rodriguez continues. "It could be that we're all just misunderstanding you. Maybe you took this girl, Penelope Campos, for a ride to show her the countryside…you know, Rio Grande Canyon, or somewhere like that. Maybe you did something accidentally that frightened Penelope and she ran away. Perhaps while she was running, she tripped and hit her head on a rock. You got scared and panicked when you realized she was dead. I think the district attorney would understand that it was just an accident. Something as simple and innocent as that would explain everything—and then you could be on your way back home in no time."

"If I admit to that, I can go home?" the suspect says to him.

"Maybe—if your story checks out. We would have to talk to the DA first, but I'm sure he would be very sympathetic. After all, it was just an accident, right?"

"Okay, I'll do it."

"Good," Rodriguez says, rising from his chair. "I'll go out and get a pad and a pen and be right back. You get your story straight."

Rodriguez goes out to his desk and gets a pad and a pen. Fallon is standing outside. Rodriguez gives Fallon a smile. "We got him. Bring a pad and pen; he's ready to confess."

After the suspect signs the confession, Rodriguez goes in to Captain Belmont's office to give him the news. "We got it, sir; he's confessed. It's all right here in black and white."

"Thank God!" the captain responds with relief. "I'm calling Chief Franks right now to tell him. We still have time to gather the press for a news conference and make the evening news. Call the Campos family and tell them what's happened."

In an adobe house somewhere in the Sonoran Desert of Arizona, at around the same time that Rodriguez and Fallon are taking Fontana's confession, Penelope is sitting in a kitchen chair with the back of her head over a sink. Her eyes are closed. One of the kidnappers is putting dye onto her long hair. Shackles bind her ankles together. She is perfectly quiet, and her face is without expression.

"How's it coming?" the man asks as he walks into the house.

"We're done," his partner informs him. "Come on, sweetie, get up. Show your husband that amazing hair of yours."

"Beautiful! Absolutely beautiful," he says when she stands up and shows him. "You look like a brand-new woman." He unlocks the shackles and frees her. "Come on, let's go to the bedroom. I want you right now."

"Please, no more today," Penelope begs him. "My private area still hurts from this morning."

"Maybe you should give her a break," his partner tells him. "You've been doing her two and three times a day. She's only a young thing."

"Maybe you should mind your own damn business," he says to his partner. Then, turning to the girl, he says, "I told you—the pain will eventually go away. The more you do it, the easier it will get." He grabs her by the arm and begins dragging her toward the bedroom.

She resists his pull. "No! I don't want to!" she cries.

"Don't make me use the belt," he growls. Then he slaps her and drags her into the bedroom. When he closes the door, she lies down on the bed, pulls up her dress, and shuts her eyes while she waits for him to penetrate her. The pain begins as soon as he forces himself into her.

When he's done, he lies panting on top of her, looking down at her face. She has her head tilted to the side and her eyes are squeezed tightly shut. Tears have gathered on her face. He gets up, looks down at her: "Get up and get ready. We're leaving today."

"Do you want something to eat?" his partner asks him when he gets back into the kitchen.

"No. We better get packed and get going. We need to be out today."

"Where are we going?"

"I have an uncle who owns a place just outside of Ralls, Texas. It's empty right now. I called him today, and he said I could stay there. I've been there before—it's out in the middle of nowhere. No one's going to come around poking their nose into our business. I can find some work as a jobber in Texas, so we should be able to get by."

"Do you think it's safe to drive through New Mexico?" his partner asks him. "Aren't they still looking for her?"

"No, we're good. I read in the paper that they arrested some stupid stiff. They won't be looking for her anymore. She is now my permanent wife."

In the bedroom, Penelope has heard the entire conversation. Fresh tears are flowing down her face. He walks back into the room and shows Penelope the shackles.

"You won't have to wear these any longer. But you have to stay close to us—don't ever leave our side. Just remember, I *will* kill you and your entire family if you try to escape. You got that?"

She nods. He reaches into a bag and takes out a long robe and throws it on the bed. "Here, put this on. You'll be wearing it from now on." He walks out of the room.

She lifts up the cassock from the bed and slides it over her head. She notices a nail on the floor in the corner of the room and goes over and picks it up. Looking at the door to make sure it's closed, she bends down and scratches something on the wall behind the bed.

In the kitchen, the kidnapper reaches into the bag, pulls out a similar robe, and hands it to his partner. "Here—you'll be wearing one, too. We're all going to wear this garb from now on."

"Won't we look conspicuous in these clothes?" his partner asks. "We'll be drawing attention to ourselves. I don't like this getup."

"People will look, but they won't stare. In fact, they'll be bothered by our appearance and will become apprehensive. They'll look at the clothes, and not our faces. I'm more worried about *her*; people will be curious about her appearance, but they won't give her much more than a passing glance. We'll put a scarf over her head to hide her hair and draw attention away from her blue eyes."

"What if she makes a run for it now that she's no longer manacled?" the partner asks. "What's to keep her from running off the first chance she gets?"

"She's not going to run. She loves her family greatly, and she's worried that I might do something to them. She hasn't made any attempt to run away this entire time, although she's had the chance. It's because of her family, I'm sure. Come on, let's pack up the van. I want to get to Ralls as soon as possible. We have a long drive ahead of us. If we start now, we should be there by Easter."

5
IT'S NOT AS EASY AS IT LOOKS

James is up and has just finished making the coffee. "You're up early," he says to Sam when she comes into the kitchen and sits at the table. He pours her a cup of coffee and places it in front of her.

"What are you doing today?" she asks him.

"I'm going to the lawyer's office to pick up all the summonses that I need to serve. When I'm done, I'll pick up the forty bucks that I've earned. I can't believe how easy this job is. Do you want some breakfast?"

"No, I want to talk to you for a few minutes. "Can you stop what you're doing?" she asks. "Please sit for a minute."

He grabs his cup and sits across from her.

"Okay. What's up?"

"We *are* engaged to be married, right?"

"Sam, I'm pretty sure the ring on your hand proves that fact."

"So, when are we going to set a wedding date, James? We haven't set a date, and there doesn't seem to be any reason to wait. Why don't we get married?"

"There isn't any *particular* reason." He moves uncomfortably in his chair. "It's just that everything has happened so fast. We just got engaged. I thought we should wait until the pace slows. You know—until we establish a routine with my school and your job. We have a lot of stuff up in the air. When the dust settles, we can set a date."

"What's the difference?" She looks up from her coffee cup. "We're already living together as if we're married. We share our money. Why should we wait? Why don't we just get hitched and make it official?"

He takes a gulp of his coffee and takes a long look at her. His knowing look makes her uncomfortable. Finally she says, "What? What's the matter? Why are you looking at me like that?"

"So. This is a discussion about getting married, Sam? Nothing else?" He continues to stare at her. There is even a bit of suspicion in his eyes. Sam drops her eyes, takes a sip of her coffee, and avoids making eye contact with him.

"Yes. Of course there is nothing else. What else *would* there be?" she asks him.

"Sam, it's a good thing you're not a poker player, because you'd go broke. That face of yours is a dead giveaway. What you're really thinking about is written all over your face."

She finally looks up. "*What's* written all over my face?" she asks, her voice going up a notch as she begins to get testy.

"I'm thinking *children* are written all over your face. Are you asking about babies?"

"What about children?" she asks back, but her voice has gotten quieter. She knows he has discovered the truth.

"*Don't* try to tell me that you don't want children," he challenges her. "You want to get married, yes—but mostly you want to raise a family. Am I right, Sam?"

"Not *mostly!* Mostly I want to marry you—but, yes, I definitely want a family, and I don't want to wait forever. You want a family, too, don't you?"

"Yes, Sam, I do, but not for a while. I want to finish school, and I want to figure out what my goals are. I know you want a child. I know that you want to make up for the baby you could not keep last year. Believe me, I get it. You think that by having a child and raising it right, you might get the redemption that you're looking for. I want a family, too. Unfortunately, this is not the best time for us to start one. We don't have the means to give a child a decent home. Bringing a child into the world right now will put a lot of strain on us—strain that we can avoid simply by not rushing into anything."

James looks over and sees that tears are in her eyes—tears that are about to come spilling down her cheeks. He rises up from his seat, goes over, and squats down in front of her. He strokes her soft face.

"Please, Sam—don't cry. I didn't mean to make you sad. But we're young. We have time to have lots of children. I'm not asking you to wait forever. I just can't handle starting a family right at this moment. Do you understand?"

She wipes the tears from her face with her napkin. "Yes, I understand. No children at this time."

James goes back to his seat. "You need to promise me, Sam—no children unless we discuss it first," James tells her firmly. "Don't do anything crazy. We can't afford you getting knocked up."

"I promise I won't do anything unless I discuss it with you first," she answers meekly.

"Good. Now that we have settled that, why don't we go to city hall and get married on your next day off? I think that's Monday, right?"

"I'm not getting married at city hall," she says with determination in her voice. "We're getting married in June at my family's home in Lorenzo. I've always dreamed about getting married right in my backyard. My dad will perform the ceremony, and my mom will walk me down the aisle. Kathy and I are going to start shopping for my wedding dress next week. All my friends and relatives from all over Texas are going to be there."

"Why do I get the feeling that I've just been had?"

"You're the poker player—you tell me," she says, giving him a huge smile.

"What about *my* family? Aren't *they* invited? There's no place for them to stay in Lorenzo. I don't even know if they can *get* to Texas—especially to your hometown. It's way out in the sticks!"

"Stop making such a fuss! There *is* a motel. It's right in Lorenzo! And there's another one in Ralls, not too far from my house. And there are motels *and* hotels in Lubbock, which is no more than ten minutes away. There's plenty of room for your family. Oh, James! Our wedding is going to be so wonderful!"

That night when Sam comes home, Kathy is in the kitchen, preparing dinner.

"What are you cooking?" Sam asks.

"Pork chops, string beans, and a salad."

"What's in the oven?"

"I made some biscuits," she says, opening the oven to show them to Sam. "I'm leaving them in the oven so they stay warm. I hope James gets here before too long so we can eat them before they dry out. I bought some honey butter to have on them."

"With the amount of food you cook every night, I'm going to need to get back to the Y real soon to get back to working out. I put on two pounds just last week. Where *is* James?"

"I don't know. I haven't seen him all day."

"Oh, by the way, Kathy, I got you a job interview on Friday—it's in the ladies' wear department. One of their people just upped and quit and they need someone quickly. They're desperate, so it shouldn't be too hard to get the job. Just in time, too. After you get the job, we can all go on a diet and buy new clothes from you. All this good food does have consequences. Well, except for James. He doesn't seem to put on any weight, no matter how much he eats."

"It'll be nice going back to work," Kathy admits. "I was beginning to climb the walls in this place. Today I cleaned the entire house. After I get back to work, I need to get busy finding a nice guy like James."

"You know, Kathy, when James was camping out at the college in protest, he introduced me to this guy, Bobby. I told Bobby about you, and he sounded interested. If you want me to, I can have James introduce him. He's a veteran like James and going to school."

"What does he look like?"

"He's the same height as James, but stockier. He's got light-brown hair and a mustache. I'm not quite sure what color are his eyes, but I think they're brown."

"Sure, why not? It's not as though there's a line of men waiting at the door. Is he as good-looking as James?"

Sam smiles. "No one is as good-looking as my James, but he's not bad. Do you still have a crush on James?"

"Well, dearie, if you ever throw him out, you won't get him back—I promise you," Kathy answers with a broad smile.

"Don't get your hopes up! James isn't going anywhere. The only way he's getting out of this relationship is in a body bag. I'll tell him to call Bobby and fix you up the second James gets home! I don't want you getting any wild ideas about *my* boy."

They hear a key at the lock of the front door. After a few moments, James comes walking in.

"Yum, something smells good," he says, giving Sam a kiss. "I'm starving; I didn't have time for lunch."

"Where have you been all day?" Sam asks him. "I thought you said delivering a summons is easy."

"Well, I guess I was wrong. I didn't realize—though I should have—that no one actually *wants* to be served with court papers. If I'm not physically able to confront the person, they don't have to answer the summons *or* appear in court. People keep sneaking out the back door or pretending they aren't home. I chased this one guy for two hours in my car.

"Another guy kept me waiting in the lobby for two hours. Finally, the janitor told me that the guy had already walked out, dressed as a woman. Can you believe the lengths these people will go to just to avoid going to court? It won't do them any good, though. I'll get them. I'll just have to get a little more creative." He looks at Kathy and asks, "Do I have time to take a shower before dinner?"

"No, we need to sit down and eat before the food dries out." She begins setting the table.

"Anything else going on?" Sam asks James as she sits down to eat.

"Oh, yeah. I almost forgot to tell you: I'm becoming a private investigator."

"You're becoming *what*?" Sam and Kathy yell out in unison.

"When did this happen?" Sam asks. "Isn't that a dangerous job?"

"No, not this one. It has to do with what they call white-collar stuff—mostly it means just sifting through files and papers. One of the law firms said I can make a lot of money doing research for the attorneys."

"If it's just sifting through papers, why do you need to become a private investigator?" Sam asks as she picks up her knife and fork.

"Well, in the event that I'm called to testify, I need to be *licensed*, so that I can be considered an expert. The law firm that I talked to said that having a license is a really big deal. Anyway, from what they tell me, becoming an investigator isn't too hard."

Sam puts down her knife and fork and looks at James.

"What's the matter?" he asks her.

"You know, James, with all this law and private detective stuff going on, I'm worried that you'll forget about college. Don't you think that with so many distractions, you might screw up your education? I'm worried that you'll flunk out again, and that this time it will be for good. They won't give you another chance, James, no matter how long you camp out on their lawn."

James reaches across the table and places his hand on hers. "Sam, I won't let anything interfere with my schooling. My classes don't even start until summer. Believe me, I'm going to graduate. I've made a vow to myself. No screwing around; I swear. I've got something to prove. And it's not just about my education; it's about my success."

He pulls his hand back so he can grab another biscuit and continues. "Sam, it's going to happen—I promise you. I may not graduate at the top of the class, but I *am* going to get my degree."

"Okay, I'm convinced. I was just getting worried, that's all," Sam says. "By the way, speaking of school, what do you think about fixing Kathy up with that guy I met the day I brought lunch to you on campus?"

"Bobby?" James looks at Kathy. "Yeah, sure, I'll call him tonight. When do you want to go out with him?"

"Saturday is good, if he's available," Kathy replies.

"Sure. I'll call him right after dinner."

The next morning, Sam walks into the kitchen hoping to find James there, but the room is empty, and there is a note for her on the table. It reads:

Sam,

Got up early to get a start on my process serving. Tell Kathy that I spoke to Bobby and he is thrilled about the idea of going out with her. He'll pick her up at the house at eight on Saturday. He plans on taking her to the movies.

See you tonight.

Love,

James

Reading the way he ended the note makes her smile. *Love.* How hard she had to fight to get him to say that word. Now the word rolls out as if it's effortless for him to say.

"What are you smiling about?" Kathy asks as she walks in.

Sam looks up at her. "Oh, nothing important. I was just remembering something pleasant." She hands Kathy the note from James. "You're all set with Bobby."

"Oh, thank Heaven," Kathy says, looking up at the ceiling.

"By the way, don't make any plans for the Easter weekend. We're going to Lorenzo. My mother is throwing an engagement party for me. I haven't told James yet, so please don't tell him until I speak to him. I'm pretty certain he'll try to wiggle out of going. He'll give me a lot of crap about how he's so busy and can't go anywhere. So, don't say anything yet. I've got to figure a way to talk him into it. With James, these things are a process. You can't go at him directly."

"All right, mum's the word. That reminds me; I need to call *your* mom today."

"Why do you need to call my mother?"

Kathy is quiet for a moment, thinking about how to recover from her slip of the tongue. She is planning a wedding shower for Sam to be held when they are in Lorenzo, but it is supposed to be a surprise.

"Oh, you know. I *am* the maid of honor, after all! I just want to ask your mom if she needs me to do anything for the party…"

On Good Friday morning before Easter, Sam is deep in thought as she climbs out of bed. She still has not told James about the trip to Lorenzo. She just hasn't been able to think of a way to broach the subject. Now time has run out and she has no choice but to approach him directly. He's sure to put up an argument—she knows that, but there is no other way. Her parents are giving her an engagement party, and James needs to be there. He cannot miss something as important as an engagement party. She's prepared to fight; she will not give in to him in this instance. She can hear him making coffee in the kitchen.

"Good morning, sweetie," she says, going up to give him a kiss. She sits back at the table.

He pours her a cup of coffee and places it in front of her.

"What're your plans for today?" she asks.

"I'm going to a law office to collect the money they owe me. Two hundred and forty dollars. That's a lot of money. Forty for the summonses and two hundred for an investigation I did for them."

"You were right about the investigative work; it's working out great. The money is just pouring in. You are a complete genius when it comes to making money."

James looks at her sideways. She recognizes the look.

"What?" she asks.

"You know, Sam, if you want something *really* bad, you should offer to make it worth my while. This sweet-talking of yours isn't working. Offer me a blow job, and now you're talking."

"All right, it's a deal," she responds quickly with a big smile on her face.

"Wait just a minute. You answered a little too fast. What did I just agree to?"

Her smile gets wider. "I'll tell you, but it's too late for you to back down; we have a deal. There's no reneging on the deal we just made. No amount of protesting will change that." She leans forward in her chair and whispers, "A deal is a deal in my book, mister."

"All right, Sam, just get it out. We made a deal. I'll keep my end of the bargain—I promise. What did I agree to?"

"We're going to Lorenzo; my family is giving us an engagement party on Easter Sunday. I think Kathy is also planning a wedding shower for me on Monday." She sits back in her chair. There is a smug look on her face because she knows she's pulled off a coup by suckering him into going. And all she has to do is give him a blow job.

James smiles slyly back at her. "I already knew about the engagement party. Your mother called the other day and spilled the beans. I was just waiting to see when you'd get around to telling me. I told her I'd be there. No way would I miss our engagement party, Sam. I'm just as excited as you are about getting married. Come on—let's go into the bedroom. I want to collect on the deal we just made." He rises from the table.

"Oh no you don't! You sit right back down, mister. I'm not doing it! You pulled a fast one." She tries to push James away. "You were already going. You tricked me. There was no reason to make a deal in the first place, since you'd already agreed to go."

James pulls her up from her chair. "No reneging, remember? That's what you said. 'A deal is a deal in my book, mister.' I'm really going to enjoy this, Sam. And this time I want you to swallow it all. That's what you get for trying to be such a sneak."

That afternoon, James walks into the office of an attorney named Michael Barrett to hand in his voucher for the work he's done.

"Do you think I can get a check today? I could really use the money," he tells the bookkeeper. "I'm taking a trip out of town.

"Sure," she replies, "just give me a couple of minutes."

"James," a voice calls, "can you come into my office for a sec?"

"What's up?" he asks the lead attorney of the firm.

"Have a seat, James," Barrett says to him, pointing to a chair. "Let's chat a while. Let me get to know you better. You're from New York City, right? We're you born there?"

"No, I was born in Italy." James leans forward in his chair. "What's this all about, Barrett? You already know I'm from New York? Even if you didn't know, my accent would've given it away."

"I'm just trying to get to know you better, that's all. You don't act or speak like an Italian boy from New York."

"Oh, yeah! Is that right! How does an Italian boy from New York act and speak like in your eyes?" James tries to calm down. His blood is boiling. He's heard Barrett's type of comments before. He knows exactly the stereotype that Barrett is referring to.

"Why are you getting so angry?" Barrett says. "I didn't mean anything by it."

"That's a lot of bullshit, Barrett." James's voice gets louder. "You and I know exactly what you meant." James fixes himself in his chair and lets out a breath. He collects his thoughts after calming down. "Michael, I'm very proud of my Italian heritage and my upbringing. I will never run from that. There's nothing that I find more offensive than the stereotype Americans have of Italians. Every waking moment of my life is dedicated to proving that stereotype wrong. So if you have nothing further, I'll take my leave before I say something I may later regret." James stands up.

"Please, don't leave James," Michael pleads. "Sit a little longer." He points to the chair. "Please!"

James sits back down.

"I'm sorry that I offended you, James. That was not my intention, believe me. That was the last thing that I wanted to do. I was trying to pay you a compliment. You are an articulate and an intelligent young man. That's what I was trying to say. I'm so impressed with you that I'd like you to take on a very important assignment for me.

"I have an important client, and I'm going to meet with him in Santa Fe for a big settlement negotiation on Tuesday. His name is Henry Greenwald. Among his many holdings, he owns a railroad. Mr. Greenwald purchased some railcars, and he believes he's been shortchanged by the manufacturer. There's an outstanding retainer of two million dollars that Greenwald is holding. He doesn't want to pay the money. He asked me to look through the contract and invoices and come up with something to offset the claim. I had a junior associate take a look, but he couldn't find anything.

"Greenwald isn't the type of man to whom you can say, 'You're wrong,' if you get what I mean. He's used to having his own way. When he tells you he believes he's been shortchanged, what he really means is that he's not willing to pay the bill. So, what he wants in this situation is to be shown a way to get out of paying. I'm really screwed, James. If I don't come up with something, I'm pretty certain that I'll lose this account. Last year, Greenwald and his companies represented almost half of all my billing at the firm."

"I'm sorry, Michael, but what's all this got to do with me?"

"I want you to look through the Greenwald files this weekend and see if you can come up with anything."

"In that case, I'm *truly* sorry, Michael. This weekend I have to go to Texas to an engagement party that my in-laws are throwing for me and my fiancée, Sam. I won't have time to do any work. Besides, you said that someone looked through the files already and couldn't come up with anything. What makes you think I can? I don't know anything about contracts."

"James, I saw you work on the last matter I gave you. When you see a problem, you assess it and you come up with a solution. I've never seen anybody dissect a problem the way you do. You stay on the subject and think about it until the solution becomes clear in your mind. If anyone can find something in that contract, it's you. The files are right there on the desk; you can take them with you to Texas. Work on them over the weekend. I'll meet you at Greenwald's office in Santa Fe on Tuesday, and I'll pay you five hundred for the work."

James turns around and looks at the files on the desk. "All those files? You've got to be kidding me. There's no way I can finish them in three days."

"I know it's a lot. Christ, the contract alone is over twelve hundred pages," Barrett says, sitting back in his chair. "I made a fortune on this deal. There're eighty-seven change orders and amendments, not to mention two hundred and twenty invoices. I'm desperate, James. I need help. I'll tell you what—I'll pay you a thousand. And if you find something that we can use, I'll give you a five-thousand-dollar bonus to boot. Agreed?"

James looks at the files on the desk once more. "Can you have someone help me put the files in my car?"

6

LORENZO

"How are you doing back there?" James asks Kathy as they all start out on Saturday evening for Lorenzo.

"Just barely surviving. I'm going to be stuck with all the bags in the back seat for seven hours."

"I'm sorry, Kathy, but the trunk is full of all the files I need. We can switch places every hour."

"I can't believe you're going to work over the Easter weekend," Sam says.

"It's a thousand dollars," he reminds her. "And if I find something that they can *use*, I'll get a five-thousand-dollar bonus. Do you have any idea what that means, Sam? We'll have enough for a down payment on a house of our own. How can I possibly refuse?"

"How can you possibly go through all those files?" Sam asks. "The whole trunk of this car is full of papers. You won't have the time. Where will you even be able to work? My parents don't have the room. You'll just be lugging a lot of papers back and forth for nothing. Also, I was hoping to take a side trip and visit Aggie Hall in Amarillo. Now we won't be able to go see her because you'll be too busy working."

"We'll visit Aggie in June when we come down for the wedding," James says.

"Who's Aggie Hall?" Kathy asks from the back seat.

"She's the widow of a soldier that James served with in Vietnam," Sam responds. "James sent her some money to help her out. She used some of it to buy a trailer, and she is *so* grateful. Every single time I call her, she tells me to thank James. The twins call him 'Uncle James.' They were really looking forward to seeing 'Uncle James' after I'd told them we'd be passing through."

"This girl, Aggie, used *part* of the money to buy a trailer? Just how much did you give her, James?" Kathy asks.

"Can we just drop the subject?" James pleads. "What difference does it make how much I gave her? She needed the money and I was able to help—end of story!"

"Why are you getting so defensive?" Sam asks. "Nobody is being critical.

Why don't you ever want to talk about Aggie? You never even want to speak to Aggie when she calls."

"All right, you want to know?" he asks, his voice rising. "I gave her ninety-five hundred. Okay, are you happy? I told you the amount. Now can you both just get off my back?"

"Ninety-five hundred? My God, that's a small fortune!" Sam says.

James looks over at her. His face is getting red, and his voice is raised. "No, it's not, Sam. It sounds like a lot, but it's not. Aggie has three kids; she'll need every penny. I'm glad that she was able to buy a trailer so that they have a place to live. I'm glad that Hall's children have a place of their own and don't have to rely on Aggie's family for support. My buddy Hall hated taking handouts from his in-laws." He looks over at Sam once more and says in a much calmer tone, "Sam, I had the money and was in a position to help, so I did. I'm very uncomfortable talking about this. Can we please drop the subject?"

"Okay, we'll drop it. But I'd still like to visit Aggie one day."

"Of course you would, and so would I…and we will, though not during this trip. Let's talk about something else." James looks in the rearview mirror at Kathy, all bunched up in the back seat.

"How was your date with Bobby last week?" he asks her.

"It was okay."

"Just *okay*?" he pries. "No bells ringing?"

"It wasn't love at first sight—the way it was for you and Sam, if that's what you mean. The date was fine; I'll see where it goes. I've agreed to go out with him again. Bobby seems like a nice guy, but I'm not rushing into anything."

"How about your job? How do you like your new job at Sam's department store?" James asks. "You haven't talked about it much. Sam is always going on about her work."

"It's a job," Kathy says unenthusiastically. "Sam loves dealing with people. I'm not so crazy about it. Anyway, now that I'm working, I'm going to start looking for my own place. I've freeloaded off you guys a little too long."

"Don't rush," Sam chimes in. "You're no bother at all. Look at all the cooking you've done! Stay a little longer and sock away some cash. You'll need the money to furnish your new place. At least stay until after the wedding; I could use you in the planning."

"All right, you've talked me into it…but by fall, I'll definitely be out. Even though, I must say, I do love the evening performances you guys put on for my entertainment."

◆

Each of the two women falls asleep not long after that conversation. They're supposed to be taking turns driving, but that doesn't happen. Eventually, the car needs gas. James starts looking for a station in Amarillo. Not only does the car need gas, but he really needs to use the bathroom as well. Sam wakes up as James pulls up at the pump.

"Where are we?" she asks.

"Amarillo."

"Why didn't you wake me up? You've been driving the entire time. You must be exhausted."

"I wasn't tired, and you and Kathy needed the rest. You both worked today."

"Where are we?" Kathy asks from the back as she, too, wakes up.

"Amarillo," Sam answers.

"My God, I must have been exhausted! I slept the entire trip," Kathy remarks.

"Me too," Sam tells her. "Poor James had to drive the whole time."

"Do you think they have a bathroom in this gas station?" Kathy asks as they're pulling up to the pump. "I really gotta go."

"Me, too," Sam says.

The girls jump out as soon as James comes to a stop at the pumps. He gets out, too.

The gas attendant comes over. "What'll be?"

"Fill it up, and check the oil; I might be low a quart. Where's the men's room?"

"Inside to your right."

A van pulls up to the other side of the pumps. A passenger gets out—a tall, lanky man with a goatee. A teenaged girl is with him. The two head toward the station. James looks at them as they walk away. He notes the long, white robes they're wearing. *Must be some kind of religious garb,* he thinks to himself. *Freaks.*

"I'll be right back," he tells the attendant. "I need to use the restroom. If it's low on oil, top it off."

The man who just got out of the van is standing in front of the ladies' room when James gets there. James walks past him, avoiding eye contact, and heads for the men's room. When he comes back out, he steps around the man and bumps accidentally into the teenager as she is coming out of the ladies' room.

She looks up at him. "I'm sorry," she says and immediately looks at the man with the goatee.

James looks at the dark-haired young lady. "My fault," he responds. *What a waste,* he thinks. *She is really cute. Too bad she's probably part of some stupid religious cult.* Sam and Kathy are buying snacks at the counter. He goes back to the car and pays the attendant.

"I checked the oil. You're good," the attendant tells him.

James watches the van pull out as Sam and Kathy are getting into the car.

"Do you want one of us to drive?" Sam asks.

"No, we're okay. We've only got a couple of hours to go. I'm not really tired," James tells her, pulling out of the gas station.

Sam holds out a bag of chips. "Want some?" James reaches in and grabs a handful.

"Thanks! Is everybody in Texas a religious fanatic?" he asks Sam, talking around the chips in his mouth.

"Not fanatics, necessarily, but religion is big in Texas. Why do you ask?"

"I just saw a guy and his daughter back there in the gas station. Both of them were wearing those long vestments you see on the late news sometimes. She was really cute; I can't believe she's being brought up by those crazy weirdos."

"What makes you believe she was his daughter?" Kathy says from the back. "It could have been his wife. A lot of these sickos marry girls as young as thirteen. They say their religion permits the marriage, but I think they're just sick bastards."

"Texas is one weird state," James concludes.

"Yes. And this weekend you'll find out more about just how religious it is, too, when Reverend Powers tries to convert you," Kathy says.

"Uh...Sam?" James looks over at Sam. "What the heck is she talking about? Is your dad going to try to convert me?"

"No," Sam responds, looking back at Kathy and shaking her head, a signal to drop the subject. "Daddy *might* talk to you briefly about your religious views—after all, he *is* a preacher, and you *are* marrying his daughter. He'll probably want to know what your views are, that's all."

"You know, Sam, your dad better not go there," James warns her. His face is getting flushed—not a good sign with James. "It's none of his damn business what my religious views are. You better have a talk with him before he gets to me."

"It won't do any good," Kathy cuts in. "Reverend Powers is a preacher, and you're a sinner. In his book, he's saving your soul; no one can stop him from his God-given mission. There's nothing Sam can do about the talk. James, you're screwed—you're just going to be stuck hearing his entire sermon—so get prepared."

"I don't see what the big deal is anyway, James," Sam says. "Why don't you convert? You don't practice Catholicism. All you need to convert is to get baptized."

"I'm very happy with my faith, thank you, and I've already been baptized. There's no need to go through that again."

"No good, James. You'll have to be baptized again if you convert," Kathy says with a laugh. "You have to be *reborn*."

"Listen, ladies—you may not know it, but I already have a strong religious belief. I don't need another. In *my* religious creed, a person has just one requirement—and it can be summed up in two words."

"What are those words?" Kathy asks.

"*Be* and *nice*." James shrugs. "If people would just be nice to one another, we wouldn't need anything else. All this hallelujah religious crap is just a lot of bunk."

Sam looks over at James and says, "Please don't talk like that or make a scene in front of my dad, James. His lecture is just half an hour long, at most. Just listen to him and don't argue, please. I'll make it worth your while when we get home, I promise. Just be nice to him and everything will be okay…"

"Damn it, Sam, I wish you had told me before we started out! I would never have agreed to come along."

"I know. That's *why* I didn't tell you," Sam says with a sly smile.

The road to Lorenzo is deathly dull. It's nothing but open fields. This is the second time James has driven this trip. The last time was when he visited before he left for 'Nam. The trip is just as boring as he remembers. He's sorry now that he didn't let one of the women drive. He struggles to stay awake. It's nearly two in the morning when they get to Kathy's house to drop her off. Sam jumps out to let her out. Kathy pushes forward the back of the car seat and hops out of the car. She reaches back to drag out her luggage.

"I'll see you at church later," she tells Sam. "And maybe I'll see you there, too, James," she teases and runs off laughing toward the house.

James watches Kathy go into the house but doesn't move.

"What's the matter?" Sam asks when she notices that James is not driving off.

"I want to talk about that lecture from your father that I'll be facing later today."

"James, please—there's nothing that I can do about the talk. Kathy is right; I can't stop my father. When he gets on his religious hobbyhorse, there's nothing that anyone can do. Just sit there and listen; you don't have to make any commitments. I'll make it up to you when we get home—I promise. You can have anything you want."

James stares at her meaningfully; she recognizes the look. "Yes, even my cute little ass. Are you happy now? Can we just go, please? It's late. My family must be worried about us."

On Sunday afternoon at Sam's family home in Lorenzo, James finds a few minutes to take a break from working and reviewing the files he brought along. He uses the time to sit in the sun on the porch with Sam and Kathy.

"Did you know that you guys speak with more of a Texan accent down here than you do in Colorado?" James observes.

"What do you mean?" Kathy asks. "Our accent is the same wherever we are—no different here than anyplace else."

"No, it's different down here," James insists. "For one thing, you're louder."

"We're not any louder!" Sam shouts.

"Yup—there's a good example right there. It's not *just* the loudness, either. It's hard for me to explain. In Colorado, I wouldn't necessarily know that you guys are *from* Texas from your accent, but down here, there's no mistaking that Texas drawl."

Reverend Powers comes walking out, and the discussion comes to an end. "What a beautiful spring day," the reverend says. "I believe I'll go for a walk." He turns to James. "James, would you like to accompany me?"

"No, thank you, sir," James replies. He turns to look at Sam. This walk is a chance for her father's sermon that she warned was coming. "I drove most of the night, and I'm enjoying just sitting here and talking to the girls, if you don't mind. I need to get back to work soon, in any event. I'm just taking a short break."

The reverend will not let it go. "James, if you don't mind, walk with me for a bit; it's important. There's something I'd like to discuss with you. I won't keep you long, I promise. It shouldn't interfere with your work too much."

James looks over at Sam, who has a wry smile on her face. "Please," she mouths to him.

"Yes, of course," James tells the reverend. He gets off his chair. James creases his nose derisively at Sam as he walks away with her father.

Once they get about a block from the house, the reverend turns to him. "James, you don't practice religion much, do you? It's Easter. The most sacred day of our religion—I noticed that you didn't go to church."

"No, sir, I guess you're correct; I don't practice religion much," he replies, kicking a pebble down the road.

"May I suggest that maybe it's the religion that you're practicing that has turned you away? A different religious view might be more inspiring to you."

James stops just before he's going to kick another pebble and looks at the reverend. "Sir, I need to stop you. I know where this talk is going. It won't work."

When the reverend turns to face him, James continues.

"Sir, there are two people more important to me than life itself. One is your daughter, Samantha, and the other is my mother. Both of these women have strong religious convictions. There is nothing that I would do to interfere with those beliefs. My mother knows that I'm not a practicing Catholic, but she prays daily that one day I will come to my senses and become one again. If she were ever to learn that I've dropped Catholicism altogether, it would shatter her completely. Nothing that you can say to me today that would make me break my mother's heart."

"What about your children, James? Aren't you worried about how they will be raised?" the reverend asks. "What kind of spiritual example will you set for them?"

"My role as a parent, if Sam and I have children, will be to teach them moral and ethical values. They will have another wonderful parent to teach them their religious principles. I'll leave that part of the schooling to your daughter."

"So, you won't object if your children are not brought up as Catholics?"

"No, of course not. I would have no objection at all. Since I'm not a practicing Catholic, or have any conviction, it would be phony of me to insist on any particular religion for my children. I will leave their religious upbringing entirely up to their mother—your daughter Samantha.

"And sir, if I may add, I will try to follow a more religious path. Your criticism of me in that regard is absolutely correct. As I told you during our talk last May, I have a lot of faults. Do you remember that talk we had when you first met me last year? You told your daughter that you saw no redeeming qualities in me. That she could do a lot better than finding a worthless guy like me. I took your disapproval of me that day to heart and your displeasure affected me deeply. Since that day, I have worked very hard at trying to be a better man so that I could be a proper husband to your daughter. You're quite right—religion is one aspect of my life that's been lacking. Thank you for taking the time today to point that out to me."

The reverend walks over and places his arm around James's shoulders. "James, about that talk back in May—I want to apologize to you for my harsh criticism. My initial assessment of you was totally wrong. You are a hardworking, considerate young man. Most importantly, you are very devoted to my daughter. I still don't approve of the life the two of you are leading—but with your marriage, that objection will come to an end."

"You know, Samantha," the reverend says to his daughter after he and James get back and he's alone with her in the house, "I was totally wrong about James. He is truly a fine and honorable person. I can't express to you how happy I am that you two are getting married."

She runs inside and approaches James. "What did you say to my dad? He absolutely loves you. Did you agree to convert?"

"No, I didn't agree to convert. I told your dad how pleased I was that we had our talk. I said to him that he is absolutely right—I haven't been following a true religious path, and that I will try much harder going forward. My converting is out of the question since it would break my mother's heart, but I wouldn't object if my children were raised in a different faith. Then I thanked him for being so patient with me. Are you happy now?"

Sam puts her arms around his neck and pulls him toward her. She gives him a kiss and whispers, "Thank you. And to show my gratitude, you can have that cute little ass of mine for the entire week when we get home."

"Well, if your dad had said you would offer me *that*, I would have agreed to convert," James says, kissing her back. "Now if you don't mind, please get out of the room, I've got to get back to work."

At around five in the evening, Kathy comes over to the house. "Where's James?" she asks Sam.

"He's in my brother's room, locked up with his papers. He hasn't come out since he came back from that walk with my dad."

"How did things go with your dad?"

"Very well; they got along great. It's going to cost me when we get back home, but it's worth it. Come on—let's see what he's doing. He needs to get ready; the party starts in an hour." She walks up to James's room and opens the door.

"My God, look at all the papers!" Kathy cries out when they get into the room.

"Don't step on anything," James warns them.

"How can you *avoid* stepping on the papers?" Sam asks. "They're all over the floor."

"So go back outside! Who asked you guys to come in, anyway?"

"We came to remind you that you've got to get ready for the party. The guests will be here in an hour," Sam says.

"Okay—I'll start getting ready, but you two need to get back outside this room. I don't want *anything* moved out of place."

"How can you tell if anything is out of place?" Kathy asks. "Everything is scattered everywhere. Where are you going to sleep? There're papers all over your bed."

"Who said I'm going to sleep? I'm going to be very busy tonight after the party."

"Did you find anything?" Sam asks him.

"Yes, I did," he declares, picking up a large binder that's on the bureau. He opens the binder to show her.

"You read that entire agreement?" Kathy asks, sounding impressed.

"Yes, I did read most of the contract. It seemed to take forever before I got it finished." He frowns. "Most of the binder was boring—engineering and other technical stuff that I skimmed over. But I had to read closely everything else—otherwise, I would have missed what I found."

"What did you find?" Sam asks him.

James puts the binder in front of her. "See, right here on page 387—this paragraph?"

The women lean over to look.

"That's it? That little paragraph is causing this huge mess?" Kathy asks him, sounding like she doesn't believe him.

"Yeah—crazy, right? The contract is over twelve hundred pages long, and that little six-line paragraph is one of the most important pieces of the agreement. It's not surprising that no one has picked up on it." Turning to Sam, he asks, "Do you have some loose-leaf paper?"

"My sister has some. How many sheets do you need?"

"I need a lot; you better give me a whole stack. Bring in some Scotch tape, too."

When Sam comes back, he takes the stack from her and places it on a chair—the only empty spot in the room. He pulls a sheet off the top of the pile and begins to write. Then he pulls off a piece of tape to stick the sheet on the door. *Keep Out,* the signs states.

"Okay. Let's get ready to party; it's time for some fun," he says. "Is anybody using the bathroom? I need to take a shower and shave."

7
NEGOTIATIONS

The engagement party is great. Everybody has a super time. Sam and James receive lots of wonderful presents. There *is* one small problem with the presents: how are they going to get them back to Colorado Springs? There is no room in the Ford Mustang.

Immediately after the party, James gets back to work. That is what Sam finds him doing the next morning when she goes into his room.

"Did you get any sleep at all?"

"Yeah, I got a couple of hours." He gets up off the floor and begins to stretch.

"Do you want some coffee?"

"Yes, please. Coffee would be great! Call me when it's done; I need to take a break."

Sam comes into his room a few minutes later. James is on the floor going through some files. "There's a call for you; it's a man named Michael Barrett."

"What time is it?"

"It's five after eight."

"He's up early," James remarks. He gets up and heads for the kitchen. "You're up early," he says to the lawyer on the phone.

"How is it going?" Barrett asks him. "Did you find anything? Please tell me you found something."

"Yeah, Barrett, I found something. You're going to be very happy; you're going to look like a hero. Greenwald is going to be very grateful."

"So, what is it? I didn't get any sleep all weekend worrying about this."

"It's complicated. I really don't want to talk about my findings over the phone. Besides, I'm not finished yet." James pauses for a second. "Michael, I want to renegotiate our deal," James tells the attorney.

Barrett screams, *"What?"* James holds the phone away from his ear so his eardrum won't burst from the yelling the attorney is doing on the other end. Finally, the tirade is over, and Barrett calms down.

"Are you through?" James asks. "Good—then listen. I know the deal I made up front with you; you don't have to repeat yourself over and over. That was before I realized how much work was involved. I've been working day and night on this problem. So, here's the new deal: I want one percent of any findings that I uncover."

James pulls the phone away from his ear once more to avoid the shouting that is coming through. Sam begins laughing. Sam's mother has just walked into the kitchen.

"Who's shouting at James on the phone?" she asks Sam.

"It's a business associate," Sam whispers. "They're negotiating a deal."

"Michael, please calm down and listen to me," James says to the attorney. "Your shouting into the phone is getting us nowhere. And I'm very busy; I need to get back to work. You're so busy yelling that you're not thinking this new proposal through rationally. Under the old deal, the maximum I could earn was six thousand dollars. So, that means I would have to come up with at least six hundred thousand in findings to break even under this new proposition." Another tirade comes from the phone.

"Michael, I would not be renegotiating with you on a percentage agreement if I hadn't discovered more than the six hundred thousand. My results are big, Michael; you're going to look like a superstar and Greenwald is going to save a whole lot of money. I just want a little piece of the pie—that's all. I'm not being unreasonable. When you get a look at what I found, you'll agree that one percent is nothing."

There is silence on the other end of the phone.

"Michael are you still there?" James asks.

"Greenwald is going to be pissed," Michael says. "You know that, right? He doesn't like anyone not keeping his word. Once he makes a deal, he expects all parties to honor the bargain. That's why he's so upset with these people who built the railroad cars. Greenwald believes they didn't keep their promise."

"I don't care if Greenwald gets pissed," James replies defiantly. "I made the deal with *you;* Greenwald can take it or leave it. Call me right away with his answer, because there's still a lot of work to do. If Greenwald doesn't like the new arrangement, let me know and I'll stop working. I'll pack all the papers back in my car. You guys can muddle through the meeting without me." James hangs up the phone.

"You turned down six thousand dollars?" Sam calls out to him when he's done. "Are you crazy? You worked all weekend for nothing!"

"Good morning, Mrs. Powers," James says, ignoring Sam. "It's going to be another beautiful day, don't you think?" He turns and looks at Sam. "May I have that cup of coffee you offered, please?"

"Don't ignore me, James! You turned down six thousand dollars!" She pulls at his arm. "We could have used that money to put a down payment on a house or to pay for your schooling. What were you thinking? Why would you do something so stupid?"

"Fine—I'll get my own cup." James begins walking toward the cabinet.

Sam grabs his arm again and pulls him away from the cupboard. "Stop it," she yells.

"Lower you voice, dear," her mother warns her. "There's no need to shout."

"Mom, I'm sorry. I don't mean to yell, but do you realize what he just did?" Sam releases her hold on James and pleads her case with her mom. "James did all this work this weekend for nothing. He was supposed to earn six thousand dollars, which we could have used to put toward a down payment on a house." She glares over her mother's shoulder at James. "Then, without discussing anything with his future wife, he goes and blows the money. That's why I'm so angry—and that's why I'm yelling!"

"Sam, I didn't blow anything; we're just negotiating," James explains to her. "People do this all the time in business."

"He's right, dear," Sam's mother says. "Leave it to the man of the house. They're in a position to know better. Women should stay out of these affairs."

"Mom, that may be the kind of relationship that you and Dad have, but James and I have a different understanding." Sam is furious. She turns and scowls at James. "At least, that's what I thought before today. We discuss money problems out in the open before a decision is made. You don't go do something stupid and foolhardy without discussing the matter with your partner."

The phone rings, interrupting her. James answers. "Hello." Pause. "Yeah, Michael?"

Sam and her mom wait silently. Finally, James says, "Okay, that's his answer? Are you absolutely sure?"

"Fine," James says and hangs up the phone. He stands by the phone, not saying a word.

"Well, what did he *say*?" Sam finally asks.

"They took the deal!"

Both women begin applauding.

"Thank you, God!" Sam shouts, looking up at the ceiling.

"What's with all the racket?" Reverend Powers asks as he comes into the kitchen.

"James just negotiated a wonderful business deal," his wife tells him. She looks over at Sam. "You see, dear? I was right. You have to leave this business stuff to the men."

"How much are we going to make?" Sam asks him.

"We?" James looks at her and gives her a crafty smile. "Well, I still have a lot of work to do, but I believe *we* are going to make at least thirty thousand dollars. Now would you please pour me my coffee?"

Sam comes over, places her arms around his neck, and gives him a kiss. "I'm sorry I screamed at you. I just got so nervous. Please forgive me?"

"You're forgiven. May I have my coffee, now?"

"Certainly." She pours him a cup and hands it to him.

Reverend Powers pats James on the back. "Well done, young man."

It is nearly four thirty in the afternoon when James hears a knock on his door. He has worked the entire day, stopping only to have a quick sandwich. The hard work is paying off; he has made a lot of headway and is almost finished. James walks over, unlocks the door, and opens it. Sam and Kathy come walking into the room.

"Why did you lock the door?" Sam asks him.

"I didn't want to be disturbed."

"Wow, you've made a lot of progress!" Kathy observes. "Most of the papers are gone; I can actually see the floor again."

"Yeah, I'm almost done. I'm wrapping up and beginning to organize my files."

"I've got to go to the bathroom," Sam announces.

After she leaves, Kathy turns to James. "Don't forget we're giving Sam a bridal shower tonight at my house. You need to have her there at six—not before. Don't give it away; it's a surprise."

"Okay. You can count on me."

"I'm going to drop Kathy off at her house," Sam says to him when she comes back.

"Why don't I take a ride with you guys? I could use some fresh air."

"What do you want to do now? Do you need to go back to work?" Sam asks James after they drop Kathy off.

"No, I think I need a break. Why don't you drive and show me the sights? I just realized that I've been here twice and really haven't seen much of Lorenzo. Why not start by showing me your high school?"

"There it is," she says to him when they get to the high school, pointing to a small building. "Not really much to see, is it? What would you like to see next? There isn't actually much to Lorenzo."

"Let's just park here and talk. How was your day? You were gone so long."

"My day was great! I saw all my old friends. It was so nice to catch up with my friends again. They seemed so happy to see me. I even got to see an old boyfriend of mine."

"I'm not sure I like this part of the story."

Sam laughs at James's comment and then turns around to look at him. Her tone turns serious. "Thank you, James."

"Why are you thanking me?"

"I'm thanking you for coming into my life. You have no idea how happy you have made me. You probably aren't aware that today is our anniversary. It was a year ago today that I met you at that bar. You rescued me. I was drowning and you saved me." Tears begin to fill Sam's eyes. James leans over and pulls her toward him. He gives her a gentle kiss.

"We saved each other, baby. We were both lost and confused. It was our love for each other that pulled us out of the quandary that had us trapped. There's no need to thank me, Sam, because I owe you a debt of gratitude—every bit as much as you believe you owe me. I can't believe how happy I am today."

They sit looking out of the car as the sun begins to set on the horizon. She rests her head on his shoulder. He looks down and sees that the clock on the dashboard reads five to six.

"Oh, crap, you need to drive me to Kathy's!" James says.

"Why?"

"I just remembered that I've got a question your mom wanted me to ask her," he fumbles to explain.

"What do you have to ask her?"

"Your mom said it was personal; I can't tell you."

"Well, if you won't tell me, I'm not driving you there," she announces, sitting back in her seat and giving him her special, sly look.

"Come on, Sam," James begs. "Stop fooling around! Start the car and drive me to Kathy's."

Sam looks at him. Her smile gets larger. "I can't believe the skillful, conniving James can't come up with a believable story to use to get me to my surprise bridal shower."

"You know?"

"Yes, I know. Remember? I suspected Kathy was planning a bridal shower some time ago. Then the girls gave it away this afternoon."

"Well, can you please at least act surprised when you get there, so that the women don't think I was the one who gave it away?"

At five o'clock on Tuesday morning, James is up and busy packing his car. It can take at least six hours to get to Santa Fe, and the Greenwald meeting is at one that afternoon. The bridal shower went well. Sam is happy. Sam got more gifts from women who had not attended the engagement party. They decide to leave them in the attic of Sam's parents' house. Even if they can find a way to get them to Colorado Springs, there is no place to put them in their small apartment. They decide to wait until they have their own house and then bring them up. James heads back into the house and is surprised to find that Sam is already up, dressed, and ready to go.

"I didn't expect you up," he whispers.

"James, I know how important this meeting is to us," she whispers back. "Let's leave a nice note for my parents."

They drive to Kathy's house. She is sitting on the front porch. She runs over with her luggage and hops in the back seat.

"Wow!" James exclaims. "Everybody is up and ready to go! I'm impressed!"

"I got my marching orders from your fiancée last night," Kathy says as they drive off. "Be ready or else."

"Kathy, it almost sounds like you're afraid of Sam."

"You've been dating her for a year and you still don't know who you're dealing with, do you?" Kathy asks. It sounds like a warning.

"Oh, come on, Kathy," James says, looking at her in the rearview mirror. "Sam is such a sweet little thing. She's absolutely harmless."

He turns and looks at Sam. "How come you're not a part of this conversation? Don't you have anything to say?"

"I'm just listening," Sam tells him, looking indifferent.

"Let me ask you something, Kathy. If you and Sam got into a fight, who would win?" James asks.

"Sam," Kathy answers quickly and unequivocally.

"Really? I would've never have guessed."

"James, Sam could beat the crap out of any girl in our high school," Kathy insists. "Some of the guys, too. Nobody would mess with her."

"Really?" he asks, looking at Sam. "I'm going to have to be more careful around you from now on."

"You've got nothing to worry about," Sam tells him. "Just follow your religious creed, 'be nice,' and you and I will get along splendidly."

James pauses for a moment. "You know, that almost sounded like a threat."

"Just a piece of friendly advice," Sam says with a laugh. "How did you like the engagement party?" she asks.

"The party was great. I never knew you were so popular. I'm guessing that more than a thousand people were in your backyard. Or maybe just a couple of hundred. At any rate, it *felt* as though the entire state of Texas turned out. And they all brought a dish of food to pass. Your parents did a great job. They set up plenty of tables. How did you have the time to invite so many people, Kathy?"

Kathy leans forward and stage-whispers in his ear, "I didn't. The word just got out, and everybody showed up. There's no way I could have stopped them from coming."

"You were splendid, Sam," James tells her. "You remembered everyone's name and made all the guests feel important. You were so gracious! I just walked around in a daze, completely overwhelmed. Both of you were great; everybody had a wonderful time."

"Don't Italians have big parties?" Sam wants to know.

"We do, we do…but nothing like this party," James says. "Those people aren't all coming to the wedding, are they?"

Kathy begins laughing. "They won't stick around for the reception afterward," she answers, "but they'll be at the ceremony. You better show up, too, James; the whole state of Texas will be gunning for you if you don't."

"Don't worry, Kathy," Sam cuts in. "We won't need the whole state of Texas if he doesn't show. I'll kill him myself."

"Suddenly, I'm feeling very uncomfortable," James says.

They get to the offices of Greenwald's company in Santa Fe around twelve thirty. "I've got to run upstairs and get a cart for the files," he says to the women and hurries off into the building.

When all the files are packed into the cart, Sam asks him, "What time do you want us back?"

"I'm guessing about three," he says. "I can't imagine the meeting taking more than two hours."

When he gets up to the office, the receptionist whisks him right into the conference room. The meeting started early. The receptionist opens the door and lets James into the smoke-filled room. The attorney Michael Barrett is there, as are about half a dozen men from the opposing side. It is Mr. Greenwald who gets up to greet him.

"You must be James," Greenwald says, extending his hand and giving him a smile. James looks at the slender, gray-haired gentleman and likes him immediately. There is something about Greenwald's fatherly face that appeals to him.

"This is my chief engineer, Sam Stokes, and my chief financial officer, Rodney Pinkerton," Greenwald says. "I believe you already know Michael." Greenwald continues introducing his staff to James and follows by introducing James to the opposing side.

"James, you can take a seat next to me," Greenwald concludes. James takes a seat, between Greenwald and Stokes. Greenwald continues. "Go ahead, gentlemen. Sorry for the interruption. Please continue. You were saying…"

"Well, as we were concluding, Mr. Greenwald," one of the men from the opposing side continues, "you can see that we have completed our part of the contract. All the one hundred railroad cars have been delivered, on time and satisfactorily; therefore, the agreement has been fulfilled. As such, we would like the two million dollars in performance retainer that you are holding to be released at this time."

"I see," Greenwald comments, looking around the room to his men. "Anyone have anything to add?"

When no one answers, he looks over at James. "James, you looked at the files. What say you? Can we release the retainer at this time? Was the contract satisfactorily completed, as these gentlemen are maintaining?"

"No, sir, Mr. Greenwald, you shouldn't pay one cent more," James says firmly. "In fact, my calculation indicates that in addition to the money that you're holding, these guys owe *you* $1,150,000."

One of the opponents jumps up from his seat and points at James. "What's this lunatic talking about, Greenwald? We did our job and delivered all the cars. Now that it's time to pay the balance that's due, you're pulling this stunt? Is this some sort of scam? You're not going to get away with this swindle. We'll take you to court!"

"Gentlemen, please, sit down," a now-smiling Greenwald tells the men. "There's no need to shout and call names. This is a friendly meeting. Let's give James a chance to clarify his position."

When the men sit back down and the room is quiet, Greenwald turns to James. "James, can you please explain the basis for your calculation?"

"Yes, sir, I will." James bends down and pulls out the contract agreement from one of the folders. He opens the contract to the page that he had marked before the meeting.

"Right here, on page 387, there is a paragraph called 'liquidated damages.'" James looks over at the opposing side. "Would you like to see the section for yourselves?"

"No, we're familiar with the clause," the opposition responds. "What does that article have to do with anything?"

"The paragraph states that the weight of the cars is of importance for fuel-consumption saving." James looks at the opposing side again. "Are you sure that you don't want to take a look at the contract?"

"No, we'll take your word for it," growls the man who had protested earlier.

"The clause also states," James continues, "that if the delivered railroad cars are above this contractual weight, there shall be penalties assessed to the manufacturer." James looks over at the men. "That would be you guys. The penalties are to reimburse the buyer, Mr. Greenwald's company, for the cost of the extra fuel the cars will need to consume throughout the life of their service because of the added weight. According to the agreement, that calculation is as follows: for every pound that the cars are over that contractual weight, there is to be a penalty of fifty dollars."

James turns to Greenwald. "I calculated the cars overweight this weekend, sir. When you multiply the fifty dollars in penalty by the pounds that the railroad cars exceeded their allowed contractual weight––you are owed $3,150,000. When you take off the $2,000,000 in retainer that you're holding, Mr. Greenwald, these men owe you a balance of an additional $1,150,000." As James concludes his explanation, the hint of a self-satisfied grin makes a brief appearance on his face. He sits back in his seat.

"Now hold on a second, James," Greenwald's chief engineer, Stokes, calls out. "Our side made a lot of changes that added to the weight." Stokes turns to Greenwald. "Those were design changes that were requested and approved by *our* company, Mr. Greenwald. These people are not responsible for any extra weight incurred by our changes. They just complied with what we requested."

"That's right," a member of the opposing side chimes in. "Greenwald, you can't hold us accountable for the additional weight of the cars when it was your firm that asked for the changes."

Greenwald turns to James. "Well, James, what do you have to say? Is this an error on your part? Were these changes all approved?"

"No, Mr. Greenwald. I took into account all the change orders that were approved by your company." James picks up another sheet of paper and begins reading. "There were eighty-seven approved change orders in total for the project. However, there were an additional 222 changes to the design of the cars that were never approved by your company, Mr. Greenwald. Those changes are what led to the extra weight. Those unauthorized modifications are the only revisions that I used in calculating my final numbers."

Stokes blows a puff of smoke at James' face. "Well, we probably never got around to *documenting* the modifications," Stokes, the engineer, admits. "In our haste to complete this project on time, we never got around to putting the change orders in writing. I'm sure all these alterations were asked for and approved by us. Mr. Greenwald, it's quite simple—we just need to go back to recording the changes."

James looks at the engineer for a moment and turns to Greenwald. "Sir, I can't tell you what to do, but I can give you a suggestion."

"What's that, James?"

"You need to fire your engineer. He is either incompetent, lazy, or on the take—possibly all three. No one could've just *missed* documenting more than two hundred amendments. What does *documenting* the changes have to do with the timing of the deliveries?"

Stokes stands up and yells at James, "Why you…"

"Shut up, Stokes!" Greenwald shouts. "And while you're at it, pack your things and get the hell out of the office, too. You're fired!"

Stokes looks at Greenwald. "Mr. Greenwald, please…"

"I said get out, Stokes!" Greenwald says, cutting him off. "You've got ten minutes to pack your personal belongings and get off the premises. If you aren't gone by then, I'll call security and have them escort you out."

Greenwald looks at the men across the table. "Well, gentlemen, I'm sorry to disappoint you, but I guess you'll be leaving today without any money."

"We're taking you to court, Greenwald! You're not getting away with this," the spokesman from the opposite side threatens. "Your own engineer is on our side."

"Yes, I'm quite sure he is on your side. Unfortunately for you, he doesn't work here anymore. I'll send you an invoice for the money you owe me. Based on your attitude here today, I'm quite sure you won't pay the bill. So, I guess we *will* see you in court. Good day, gentlemen."

After they leave, Greenwald gestures at James and lets a smile take over his face. "This is quite an investigator you have here, Michael. I'm very impressed."

"Yes, I knew we could count on James," the attorney, Michael, answers. "That's why I used him for the job."

Greenwald looks over at his financial man. "Rodney, can you please give James and me some privacy? I'd like to speak to him alone for a few minutes."

Before Rodney leaves, Greenwald adds, "I believe we owe Mr. Coppi some money—one percent of $3,150,000. Isn't that right, Mr. Coppi?"

"Yes, sir. That's our agreement," James replies.

"Rodney, can you take a minute and write out the check? I'd like Mr. Coppi to have the check before he leaves today. I'm quite sure he could use the money; Michael tells me he's getting married soon." He turns to Barrett. "Michael, you can stay. I'd like you to be in on my discussion with James."

After Rodney leaves, Greenwald turns to Michael. "I'd like you to draw up a personal services contract between my firm and Mr. Coppi. Mr. Coppi will be on retainer to me for investigative work. The firm will pay Mr. Coppi one thousand per week, plus his expenses. Is that clear?"

"Yes, very clear, Mr. Greenwald," Michael replies. He turns to James. "Congratulations, James. This is quite a deal Mr. Greenwald is offering you."

"Are we in agreement?" Greenwald asks James.

"I'm sorry, sir, I don't understand? What does this agreement mean?" asks James, who has been caught by surprise at the turn of events and is completely confused. "Does such a contract mean that I will work for you exclusively from now on?"

"No, James, you can take on other clients. But when I call, you will come running," Greenwald explains. "Do you hear me?"

"Yes, sir—loud and clear."

"Good. Now that we have gotten that out of the way, James, your first assignment is to come with me to the Albuquerque district attorney's office on Thursday. There's a matter you may be working on for me. In any event, I'd like you to be there for the meeting; I'll need your investigative acumen. Speak to my secretary; she'll give you all the details." Greenwald extends his hand to James. "Thanks for all your help. I like a man who can work under pressure."

James shakes his hand. "Thank you, sir." James smiles and gets up.

"You can leave the files here," Greenwald tells James. "I'll see you on Thursday. I'm sure you won't forget to pick up your check on the way out."

As James is about to leave the room, Greenwald calls out to him, "James—just one last item."

James turns around. "Yes, Mr. Greenwald?"

"This will be the first and the last time you will ever renege on or try to renegotiate a deal with me," Greenwald warns him. "When you make a deal with me, you stick to the original terms. You got that?"

James smiles. "Yes, Mr. Greenwald. Understood."

Sam and Kathy are waiting in the car when James comes out of the building. Kathy jumps out of the front seat and gets in the back. James takes her spot in the passenger seat. He takes out the check and shows it to Sam.

"Thirty-one thousand five hundred!" he yells, with a broad grin on his face.

"Oh my God, we're rich!" Sam exclaims. She leans over to give him a kiss.

"Not so fast, Sam." James stops her. "We have to pay taxes on this money."

"What do you mean?" Sam asks. She is immediately concerned.

"I mean this is taxable income. We're going to have to declare the money at the end of the year. Greenwald's accountant told me he's going to send me a tax form in January. I'm guessing we'll get to keep only about twenty thousand, after taxes."

"That's still a lot of money," Sam says. She smiles as she starts the engine and puts the car in gear. "We'll still have enough to put a down payment on a house."

"Do you want to hear another piece of good news?"

"There's more?" she exclaims.

"Yes, there's more. Greenwald hired me to be his company's investigator. They're paying me one thousand a week, plus my expenses."

"One thousand dollars! Did I hear you right?"

"Yes, you heard correctly?"

"What does that mean? Why is he paying you that kind of money? Do you work for him? What does he expect?" Sam asks.

"No, I can still do other business with other people, but when Greenwald has a job for me, I have to drop what I'm doing and get on the case right away."

"What about your school?" Sam asks. "Are you giving that up? You fought so hard to get in. What if this Greenwald thing doesn't work out?"

"Yeah, I thought of that when I was coming out of the office. I think I'm going to open up an office, Sam. I can't work out of the apartment anymore. You saw the mess I made in your parents' home in Lorenzo. I can't run my business that way." James looks over at her.

"Sam, instead of using the money to buy a house, I'd like to use it to start up our own business. This investigative work could be very profitable for us. I already have Greenwald as a client. I'm sure there'll be more.

"I'm going to hire another investigator to work with me. When I'm in school, he can run the fieldwork. Sam, I made a vow to you and to myself that I'm going to graduate, and I'm going to keep that promise. To do so, I'm going to need another investigator to help me run things. I'll also need to hire an assistant for the office—you know, a person to do the paperwork, answer phones, and keep things organized."

"Can you afford an office and all those people?" Sam is leery. "That's going to cost a lot of money. Twenty thousand won't last long."

"Yeah, I'm sure I can. I did a quick calculation in my head while I was coming downstairs. The office expenses and the staff will cost me around thirty thousand a year. Greenwald's contract alone is going to bring in over fifty grand per year. That means I'll net over twenty thousand—and that's not counting all the other work that will come into the firm. You'll still have your job at the department store. Your salary will cover our living expenses until the business is up and going." James sits back in his seat and smiles.

"We already have the money to get started, Sam. We're going to do just fine. If I'm right and this business takes off the way I believe it will, we're going to have more money than we could ever have imagined. Just have some faith in me, Sam, and give me a little time. What do you say? Want to take a shot?"

James looks over at her for an answer.

"All right." She smiles. "Let's go for it."

He leans over and gives her a kiss. "That's my girl. You won't regret your decision, I promise you."

"Why don't you hire *me*?" Kathy asks.

James turns to Kathy. "You?"

"Yeah, me," she repeats. "Why don't you hire me to run your office? That's what I did at my other company—typing, bookkeeping, filing, and answering the phone. I did it all—I'd be perfect."

"You already have a job," he reminds her, "at the department store."

"I don't really like that job. I just took it because I needed the money.

I'm not like Sam; I don't like dealing with people. Please, James, give me the job. I'll work hard. I won't let our friendship get in the way. I'll be very professional."

"Yeah, why not?" He nods. "It's a deal—but don't quit the store just yet. Give me a few days to find an office."

8
THE PENELOPE CAMPOS INVESTIGATION

Sam looks at herself in the bedroom mirror the night they arrive home from Santa Fe. She is in her pajamas, dabbing perfume onto her neck. James comes out of the shower wrapped in just a towel and walks up behind her.

"That fragrance smells nice," he says, kissing her neck. His hands slide down her pajamas. He strokes her backside. She knows what is coming—that inconvenient promise she made to him in Texas. His hands come up and he grabs her breasts. There is no way she can get out of this chore. *Too bad,* she thinks, as she could have used some gentle loving tonight. He is still kissing her neck while his hands gently fondle her breasts.

"Any chance we can postpone my promise and do something else tonight?"

"Nope. Not a chance," he replies, guiding her over to the bed. She steps out of her pajamas. He leans her forward onto the side of the bed. She bends down onto her stomach. Her backside is up in the air. She can feel his hardened member against her derriere. She is face down on the bed as he moves closer. She feels a wetness on her skin as his member makes contact.

"You need to relax, baby, or I can't penetrate," he says to her.

"Easy for you to say." She pouts. "You're not the one getting that thing shoved up your butt."

James begins stroking and massaging her back. He bends over and nibbles on her earlobe. Under his gentle touch, she relaxes. She can feel his member entering her. Ever so slowly he begins his rhythmic sexual motion, his penis goes deeper into her behind with every thrust. She opens her eyes and lets out a moan, as he is now fully inside of her. The pressure of his penis inside her causes her to tighten. He leans over her and begins kissing her neck again. His hands reach up and gently fondle her breasts. She relaxes once again. He resumes his thrusts.

She lets out a sigh as she concentrates on the gentle stroking of his hands on her breasts. His hands drop down and he grips her by her hips. She braces for what is coming next. His pace quickens. His hands squeeze tighter on her hips, and he plunges himself fully into her ass.

"Oh, God," she groans. Her eyes close. "Please, James, be gentle."

His assault into her reaches a frantic pace as he gives in to his most basic nature. She feels him stop as he climaxes.

When he has finished, she pulls away from him, puts on her pajamas, and smiles over at him. "Are you happy?"

"Yes, very much, thank you," he replies as he puts on his pajamas. "That was hot."

Sam walks up to him and gives him a hug and a kiss. "I'm glad you enjoyed yourself. You're not really going to make me keep the foolish promise I made to you, are you?" she pleads. "You're not going to do this to me all week long?"

James smiles at her. "I should, just to teach you a lesson. That was a sneaky thing you pulled on me with your dad. But no, I'm not going to."

"Thank you," she says, giving him a kiss and beginning to walk to her side of the bed.

James grabs her arm. "Will you do me a favor? Can you put this act in your repertoire? Can we just do this from time to time? The last time we did this was a year ago. Can you throw me a bone and surprise me every once in a while?"

She gives him a parting kiss. "All right, we'll include this in our nighttime activity; we'll do it a little more often. It wasn't as bad as I thought it would be. Can I speak to you about something else?" she continues.

"What's up?" he asks, lying down on the bed.

She lies down next to him and begins stroking his chest. "Can we do a waltz for our wedding dance?"

"A waltz?" James sits up as if the question has caught him by surprise. "I don't know how to waltz."

"Neither do I," she says, sitting up with a pleading look on her face. "But we can take dance lessons together. There's a dance studio in town that teaches ballroom dancing. It shouldn't take long; we can go after work."

"So, in addition to all we've got going on, you want us to take dance lessons? Are you freaking crazy?" He begins to get up.

"Please, James, let's do it," she pleads, pulling him back down. "I always dreamed of dancing a waltz at my wedding. The lessons shouldn't take long—a couple of hours a week, maybe."

He takes a long look at her, sighs, shakes his head, and relents. "All right," he says. "But this is it. No more requests."

She moves over to give him a kiss and murmurs, "Thank you." She pulls him down on top of her. "What do you say? Are you up for a little more fun? That action before was good for you, but it left me wanting."

"Yes, I can go another round, but let me just wash up real quick. Don't lose that thought."

The next morning, James is in Michael Barrett's office. He looks at the pudgy, middle-aged man wearing a three-piece, pinstripe suit. Barrett's gray hair makes him look old. *He's probably not as old as he looks,* James thinks.

"What can I do for you, James?" Barrett's voice jolts James back to reality.

"Can you prepare me a little for the meeting on Thursday? What does Greenwald want from me at the district attorney's office?"

Barrett shrugs. "To be honest with you, James, I really don't know anything about the meeting," he says. "It's got nothing to do with Greenwald's business. We're meeting with the district attorney down in Albuquerque. It may have something to do with his granddaughter, who went missing three months ago. All I know is that they got the guy who *snatched* her, but they never found *her*. Why Greenwald wants us there, I haven't a clue. Your guess is as good as mine."

"Maybe I'll go down to the library and do a little research," James says.

"It couldn't hurt."

"Michael, would you happen to have contact information for Charlie McGill?"

"The private eye?" The change in subject catches Barrett by surprise. "Yeah, sure, ask my secretary. She'll give you all the information. Why are you looking for Charlie?"

"After the meeting with Greenwald, I decided that I may need some help," James tells him. "I'm going to open my own office. I want to hire Charlie."

"I think opening your own office is a great idea. I'm sure that Greenwald is going to keep you very busy. He's not paying you all that money for nothing."

"That's exactly what I was thinking. I'm new to this private-detective business. Charlie can be very helpful. I need someone with experience."

"Charlie's a good man. He's an ex-cop and a hard worker. He's a good choice. Did you find an office yet?"

"No. I was going to start looking next week."

"I've got two offices you can rent right here next to me," Barrett says. "I rented the extra space last year when I was considering expanding—but since then, I've had a change in plans. I can sublet the space to you really cheap—three hundred a month. Come take a look," he suggests to James, getting up from his desk.

They walk down the hall. Michael unlocks the door of a large office. In the room is a desk, a conference table, and filing cabinets. James looks around.

"Is the furniture included?" James asks.

"No, it's not included, but you can use it for a while. Then, later, if you want to keep it, you can make me an offer. Come on—I'll show you the other office."

They walk into another office. This one has a desk, a desk chair, and two guest chairs.

"Same deal on the furniture in this office," Michael says.

James doesn't speak. He walks to the window and looks out. *Time to negotiate,* he thinks. "Not much of a view; it overlooks the parking lot," he mentions to Barrett.

"That's true, but the rent is more than reasonable." Barrett is on to James and knows what's coming. "The building itself is first-rate. It has a nice lobby and an elevator, and the address is highly respectable. It's in one of the most desirable parts of Colorado Springs." Barrett pauses for a moment. "Well, what do you say? Do we have a deal?"

"Two hundred and throw in the *utilities* and it's a deal," James bargains.

"You are one tough negotiator," Michael says to him, shaking his head. "I'll tell you what. Two hundred and fifty and I'll throw in the utilities for twelve months. After that, you need to start paying."

"Two years' worth of utilities and we're good." James smiles and sticks out his hand.

Barrett laughs. "As I said, you are one tough cookie," the lawyer says. He shrugs and reaches out to shake James's hand. "I'll draw up the papers."

———◆———

That night after dinner, James is back in his new office with Sam and Kathy. "Kathy, you'll be out here in the reception area." He shows her. "Charlie and I will split the other office."

"Who's Charlie?" Sam asks him.

"Charlie McGill; he's the detective I want to hire to help me run the agency."

"What if he doesn't take the job?" Sam asks.

"It doesn't matter, Sam. If Charlie doesn't take the job, I'll have to hire somebody else. I told you earlier—I can't do this by myself. But I'm pretty sure Charlie will come on board. I called him today and he sounded interested. He's coming in on Friday to speak to me about the job." James turns to Kathy. "Kathy, you're the office expert. What else do we need to get this place up and running?"

Kathy looks around. "Telephones, of course. A desk for Charlie, a couple of chairs for the waiting area, a typewriter, a copying machine, filing cabinets, and some office supplies."

"Sounds like a lot of money," Sam remarks. She's still worried about the idea of an office.

"What do you say, Kathy? Is a thousand enough?" James proposes.

"A thousand? That's way too much." Kathy shakes her head. "I'm guessing more like five hundred—maybe not even that much. Most of the big stuff, like the typewriter and copying machine, we can lease."

James smiles at Sam. "You see, Sam? Not that much." He turns back to Kathy. "So, when can you get started?"

"How about tomorrow?" Kathy responds.

"Tomorrow? Don't you have to give notice to the store?"

"Believe me, they'll be happy to see me go." Kathy waves her hand dismissively. "I have no clue what I'm doing at that place. They'll be glad to get rid of me."

"All right, tomorrow it is. Hire a sign guy to paint the name of our new detective agency on the office door."

"What's the name?" Kathy asks.

"Sam and James Detective Agency." He beams, looking over at Sam.

Sam walks over, puts her arms around him, and smiles. "You're putting my name on the sign?"

James gives her a kiss. "Well, you *are* my partner, aren't you? It's your money, too, that's funding this operation. You'll be a silent partner." He looks at her and smirks. "That means keeping your big mouth shut!"

Sam slaps him on the arm.

James is riding with Michael Barrett to Albuquerque for the meeting with Greenwald and the district attorney, Simon Gold. When they get to the DA's office, Greenwald is waiting for them in the lobby. He has a woman and another man with him. The woman is the one whom James immediately notices. She is gorgeous.

Greenwald introduces him to the couple. "James, this is my daughter, Elizabeth, and my son-in-law, Bernie. It's their missing daughter that we'll be talking to the DA about this morning."

"Mr. and Mrs. Campos," James says to them after the introduction, "I can't tell you how sorry I am about your daughter's disappearance."

"Thank you, James," Mrs. Campos responds. "I hope you can be of some help. My father has nothing but praise for you."

As confused as he was before he got here, this last statement completely baffles James. Now, he is truly clueless. He turns to Greenwald for clarification. "Sir, before we go into the office, can you just take a moment to explain to me what I'm expected to contribute to this meeting?"

"Probably nothing, James," Greenwald comments, clearing up absolutely zilch for James. "You're here as an observer. Just listen to what the district attorney has to say. You have a knack for noticing details that are not obvious to the average person. Maybe you'll hear something that's being overlooked by the rest of us. I may call upon you for advice. Now, I believe we should head upstairs and meet with District Attorney Gold."

Upstairs, they are ushered into a conference room that James immediately thinks is not much of a meeting room. He sees an old, wooden, rectangular table with wooden chairs around it. A few minutes later, a large, burly man wearing a three-piece blue suit comes in, accompanied by a young, smallish woman. The young woman is struggling to carry three large files.

"Good morning. I'm District Attorney Simon Gold," the large man says as he walks in. "With me is Assistant District Attorney Myra Berkowitz." He gestures to the small woman, who continues to clutch the files. "Won't you all please have a seat?"

James is not absolutely sure that the old, rickety chair will be able support him. He takes a deep breath, sits down, and is relieved when the chair holds. There is a strange odor in the room. James takes a sniff and tries to recognize the smell.

"The reason we're here today is to give you an update on the case." Gold looks at Greenwald. "Henry, I'm very sorry to report that the case has hit a snag."

"A snag? What kind of snag?" Greenwald asks, his voice begins to rise in indignation.

"The defense has filed a motion to retract the confession made by the suspect," Gold informs him. "I don't believe the judge will throw the confession out, but you never know."

"Excuse me, Mr. Gold," James interrupts him. "May I see the confession?"

"Why is that important?" Gold fires back. He turns to Greenwald. "Henry, who is this young man?"

"This is James Coppi," Greenwald answers. "He is a private investigator that I use from time to time. Simon, I would really appreciate it if you would kindly cooperate and give Mr. Coppi whatever he asks for."

Gold turns to his assistant. "Myra, please give Mr. Coppi the accused's confession." Myra leafs through the file, pulls out a sheet, and hands it to James.

"As I was saying," Gold continues with an annoyed glance at James, "I don't believe the judge will throw out the confession—but if he does, I believe we still have a very strong case."

"Excuse me, Mr. Gold," James cuts in again. "Would you mind letting me see the police report?"

Gold huffs loudly to show his indignation. He looks at his assistant, who also appears annoyed. "Here," she says, handing James one of the thicker files. "The report is in there."

"Thank you, Miss Berkowitz." James has noticed that they're getting aggravated and tries to soften his approach. "Can I ask you what it is that I smell?"

"What?" Gold looks at him, utterly confused.

"The strange odor that's in this room; it's very noticeable," James continues. "What *is* it?" James looks around at the others. "Am I the only one who smells it?"

"We had a water pipe burst last year. It flooded the office," an agitated Gold explains. "The rugs got moldy. We're waiting for the city to budget enough money to replace the carpeting. Can we get on with the meeting now?"

The meeting goes on for about another hour. James does not interrupt again; he is busy leafing through the file. Indeed, he pays no further attention to the conversation at all. Gold is doing most of the talking. The meeting draws to a close. Greenwald looks at James, who is still reading one of the documents.

"James, would you like to add something?" Greenwald asks him. "You haven't said much."

"What?" James looks up from the paper he's reading. He looks at Greenwald and then turns to Gold. "You've got the wrong guy, Gold. Your man didn't do it!"

"What?" Gold yells, turning again to Greenwald.

"Henry, who is this character?" Gold's face is beet red. "This is just too much." He clenches his fists and sets them down heavily on the tabletop. "I'm not going to put up with him any longer."

"Now just a minute, Simon." Greenwald's response is equally loud. "Let's give James a chance to explain himself." Greenwald turns to James, lowering his voice. "James, what makes you say that they have the wrong man?"

"First of all, the confession, Mr. Greenwald." James rummages through the file and pulls out a sheet of paper and waves it in the air "It sounds like it's made up. There are words in the confession that I don't believe the suspect, Fontana, would have used. The words appear to have been dictated to him by someone else." James tries to hand Gold the confession. "Here, look for yourself."

Gold refuses to take the paper. "Young man, it's obvious to me that you know nothing about police techniques. It's very common for a detective to help a suspect with the phrasing and wording of a confession. Suspects sometimes get confused, and the detectives have to help them organize their thoughts. The criminal gets to read the confession before he signs it, and his signature attests to its accuracy. There's nothing underhanded about the procedure. If the perpetrator doesn't like the terminology, he can change the words."

James turns to Greenwald and continues to argue his point. "Sir, even if you agree with what he's saying, please look at the confession. It says, 'Fontana disposed of the girl at Rio Grande Canyon.' *Where* in the canyon? I can't believe that Fontana couldn't have given at least an *approximate* location—some sort of roadbed, or some kind of landmark. Why couldn't the detectives have gotten such details out of him?

"And if Fontana was *confessing*, why wouldn't he say what he did with the girl? Doesn't it stand to reason that the cops would have asked where he disposed of the body? If they did ask him, what was his answer? Wouldn't the police have wanted to know this last piece of the puzzle to lock up their case and make it airtight? The only possible answer is that the suspect didn't dispose of Penelope. That's why the body has never been found."

"What about all the other evidence?" Gold asks angrily. "The gardener who saw him at the school, the three pictures of Penelope found in his possession, and the similar attack the suspect made on that other girl at the same school."

The entire table looks at James and waits.

James begins. "I believe the gardener—I think his name is Martinez—*did* see the suspect at the school that day. Martinez gave an accurate description to the sketch artist, and he accurately identified Fontana in the lineup." James sits back in his chair and says coolly, "The testimony of Martinez has no significance. Penelope was not taken at the school. She was abducted in front of her home, right after she left her friend Mary. In fact, the gardener's testimony actually gives the suspect an alibi."

James turns to Greenwald. "You see, Mr. Greenwald, Penelope had already gotten out of school and had passed Fontana's car before Martinez ever approached the car. By the time the groundskeeper approached the car, Penelope was almost home. She was being abducted at the very same moment that Martinez was confronting Fontana."

James lifts a file from the floor containing the photographs. "As for the photos of Penelope, those were just three of 672 pictures discovered in the accused's home. None of the other young women who were photographed by the suspect were kidnapped. Lastly, as to the matter of the other young girl who managed to get away when Fontana tried to grab her at the school—I believe she was the subject of Fontana's first attempt at a snatching. He was so bad at the attempt that he screwed it all up. The girl was able to resist him and run off without any trouble. Fontana has no experience grabbing girls. That was his first and only attempt."

James moves forward in his seat. He looks at Greenwald and then at Penelope's parents. "If you want to find Penelope, you need to start from the beginning. This mystery is *not* solved. The police have the wrong man in jail. Penelope may still be out there."

"Henry, if you want to listen to this lunatic, be my guest," Gold says in anger. "The district attorney's office is not going to spend any more time or money investigating this case. We have the right man in jail—a man who has confessed to the kidnapping." Gold turns to the parents. "Mr. and Mrs. Campos, I can only imagine the grief you are experiencing," he says. "God knows that if it were my daughter, I would cling to any hope that she might be found. This man is a charlatan and can only cause you more pain. Please don't listen to him any further. This fool will only cause you more pain with his half-baked theories."

Gold gets up.

"Sit down, Simon," Greenwald shouts. His face is beet red.

Gold does not sit. Instead, he remains standing and tries again to protect the existing theory. "Henry…"

"I told you to sit down and shut up!" Greenwald insists, cutting Gold off and hollering so loudly that no doubt the entire building could hear him. Startled, Gold sits. "You don't want to reopen the investigation? Fine! Frankly, I don't want you *or* the police to do the investigation. Your attitude here today demonstrates to me that you couldn't solve the mystery, anyway. What I do want is *your* cooperation in James's investigation."

Greenwald draws himself up in his chair and places the palms of his hands on the table. "Gold, I don't know what happened to my granddaughter, but I aim to find out. I'm not going to rest until she's back home. Your office and the entire police department will give James your full support and allow him access to anything he needs in his upcoming probe."

Greenwald points a finger at Gold. "So help me, Simon, if I hear even the slightest peep from James that you are not cooperating, I will destroy you. You'll be through in Albuquerque, and any other place that you may end up. Do I make myself clear?"

"Very clear." Gold swallows. He clears his throat, turns to James, and says, "You will have our full cooperation in your investigation."

"Good," Greenwald concludes, waving dismissively to Gold and sitting back down. "Now if you don't mind, Simon, we would like to use your conference room in private for a few more minutes."

After Gold and his assistant have left, James turns to Greenwald. "Sir, I don't believe I *am* the right man for the job. District Attorney Gold is quite right; I have no experience in criminal matters. You need someone who is an expert in this field. This search is far too important to entrust to an inexperienced detective like me. Your granddaughter's life may be on the line."

"Well, James, unfortunately, I don't have anybody else," Greenwald replies, "so you'll just have to do the job. After all, you are on my payroll."

"Sir, please, I'll check around and find you someone more suitable," James continues. "You can take me off the payroll. I'll search around and find you—"

"That's enough, James!" Greenwald cuts him off brusquely. "You're the man I want. I trust you."

James sits back in his chair, completely floored by Greenwald's comments. All he can do is look away and shake his head in disbelief.

Mrs. Campos has been sitting quietly, but now she speaks up. "James, please help us," she says. Her eyes are filled with tears. "Every day I question myself: Why did I go to the beauty parlor that day? Why didn't I pick up Penelope as I usually do? The police don't seem to care. The case is closed in their eyes. Despite all their talk and so-called compassion, no one is lifting a finger to find my child. Please, James—won't you get involved? We're desperate."

"Find my granddaughter, James," Greenwald orders when he sees the emotion that has overcome James. "Is that clear? Put all these thoughts about how you aren't experienced enough out of your head. I have the utmost confidence in you, and I am a damn good judge of character. I'm *positive* that you can solve this mystery. So stop doubting yourself.

"As an added bonus, James, here's what I'm willing to offer. If you find my granddaughter and she is alive, I will give you a bonus of one hundred thousand dollars. You heard me right, James—one hundred grand. So get busy and find my Penelope." The gray-haired old man gets up and gives James a fatherly smile. "You'll do it, James. I'm absolutely certain you can solve this mystery."

9

SAM AND JAMES DETECTIVE AGENCY

John Dugan, a deputy sheriff for Ralls, Texas, is driving his patrol car on his rounds when he notices a van parked on the side of the road. He pulls up behind the vehicle. He notices the New Mexico plates and the van is up on a jack. A tire is lying on the ground, a man and a teenage girl are standing alongside the tire.

Weird bunch, he thinks to himself when he sees their religious garb. *There are a lot of freaks around these parts.* The man is wearing a long robe; the girl is, too. She has a straw hat on her head. The deputy opens the driver-side door of his car and reaches for *his* hat. He exits his police cruiser and puts his hat on his head, moving it from side to side to put it firmly in place.

"What seems to be the problem?" Deputy Dugan asks the man when he gets to him.

The guy smiles. "I got a flat and I don't have a spare. Can you give me a lift to a gas station nearby?"

"Yeah, I can do that. Grab the tire and put it in my trunk." The deputy takes a walk around the van and waves to the driver, who waves back. He walks up to the young girl. "What's your name, sweetie?"

The teenager looks over at the man. "She's very shy." The man answers for her.

"Is she all right?" The deputy asks. "She looks all flushed."

"Yeah, she's fine," he answers. "It's probably from being out in the sun."

The man turns to the young girl and says, "Sweetie, you get back in the van and wait with Chris until I get back."

Deputy Dugan walks to the back of his cruiser and opens the trunk. The guy puts the tire inside.

"Is the gas station far?" the stranger asks after he gets in the police cruiser.

"Not too far—maybe ten minutes," the deputy replies. "Where were you headed? The road that you're on is a dead end. It's pretty desolate out there."

"We just arrived from Arizona and will be staying in Ralls for a bit. My cousin has a house down that road and is letting us stay there."

"Is your cousin Russ Cooper?" Deputy Dugan asks. "His is the only house out there. He hasn't lived there in nearly three years."

"Yeah, that's my cousin."

"What ever happened to Russ? The last I heard, he had moved to someplace in New Mexico. Is he ever coming back?"

The man shrugs. "He did move to New Mexico, but I'm not sure where. I don't really know his plans. All I know is that he told me I can use the house as long as I want."

"There's the gas station," the deputy says, pulling into the place. "What's your name?"

"Isaiah," the man replies. "Isaiah Wheeler."

"Well, it's nice to meet you, Isaiah. Enjoy your stay in Ralls. I'm Deputy John Dugan. If you ever need anything, let me know."

The deputy gets out of the car and hollers at a man pumping gas. "Hey, Bubba, I've got a customer for you."

The deputy opens the trunk. Isaiah takes out the tire. "Bubba'll help you, Mr. Wheeler. He'll give you a lift back to your van when he's done. Have a nice day."

Detectives Fallon and Rodriguez are sitting in District Attorney Gold's office.

"All right, men, what did you find out about this kid, James Coppi?" Gold asks the detectives. "Is he going to be any trouble?"

"No trouble at all." Fallon smiles. "The kid has absolutely no experience in police work, period. He just got his private-detective license last month. This kid couldn't find his way out of a wet paper bag. You're getting all worked up for nothing, Gold."

"No, I'm not!" Gold leans forward. "Henry Greenwald likes this kid, and Greenwald can cause a lot of trouble for us. With his influence, we can all be out of a job."

"Well, you've got nothing to worry about," Rodriguez cuts in. "This guy Coppi doesn't have a clue as to how to conduct an investigation. Before he became a private dick, he was in the army. He hasn't done any police work at all."

"It just doesn't make sense." Gold taps his pen on the table and looks away from the detectives. "Why would a shrewd character like Greenwald have such faith in this kid? We've got to be missing something?" He looks back at the detectives. "How good is Fontana's confession? Are you sure we got the right guy?"

"We got the right guy!" Fallon assures him. "There's no doubt! Coppi will just waste a lot of time. He's not going to find anything."

Gold begins tapping his pen on the desk again and looks away from the men.

"Why get yourself all worked up? Why don't you offer the perp a deal?" Rodriguez says, breaking the quiet.

"A what?"

"A deal!" Rodriguez repeats. "The perp is facing life in prison. Offer him twenty-five to life. He'll take the deal, I'm sure. You'll get the matter off your desk. The case will be closed. And then this kid, Coppi, will have no place to turn."

"A deal, eh?" Gold stops tapping his pen. "That may not be such a bad idea. Once the suspect pleads guilty, the investigation is closed. Greenwald will be off my back."

"You're going to investigate a kidnapping?" a skeptical Sam asks James, sitting in the kitchen when he gets back from Albuquerque. "You're not a criminal investigator. I thought all you'd be doing is white-collar stuff."

"I know, Sam. I didn't want to take on the case, but Greenwald and the Campos insisted. I got backed into a corner."

"Call them back! You need to explain that they need to get somebody else. James, this is serious. A girl's life may depend on what you do. This is not like reading a contract or serving a summons."

"Sam, I tried to back out. Believe me, I know I'm not qualified. These people are desperate." He stares into Sam's face. "Sam, if you looked into the mother's eyes, you'd understand. This woman is beside herself. She blames herself for her daughter's disappearance. These parents have no place else to turn. I'm their last hope. Somehow, I've got to figure out a game plan." He gets up. "Sam, if this thing gets to be too much, I'll pull out." He pauses and swallows. "Sam, you might think I'm a cockeyed dreamer, but I think this girl is alive. I'm probably the only one who believes that she is still alive. And I'm going to find her."

James walks into his new office next morning. Kathy is already at work. Bobby Nieves is standing alongside her desk.

"What are *you* doing here?" he asks Bobby.

"I helped Kathy bring up some boxes," Bobby replies. He walks over and gives Kathy a kiss on the cheek. "I'll see you tomorrow night," he tells her.

"Anything else going on?" James asks her after Bobby leaves.

"Mr. Charlie McGill is waiting for you right over there."

James turns and sees Charlie sitting in one of the chairs. "Hey, Charlie, how are you?" He walks over to greet him. "Come into my office. Let's have a talk."

Charlie McGill is a burly man—some six feet tall, around two hundred and thirty pounds. Very little of that weight is fat. McGill always wears a gray Stetson hat and almost always has on a gray suit, a white shirt, and a red tie. The next half hour's talk is just casual stuff—nothing serious—as James tries to size up McGill.

"So, Charlie, why did they kick you off the police force?" James asks, ratcheting up the conversation after the small talk.

"What makes you think they kicked me off?" McGill squirms in his chair and flushes.

"Well, okay, Charlie." James sits back and smiles. "If they didn't kick you off, explain to me why you gave up your good job as a cop to be a poor, struggling private detective."

McGill stays silent and just looks back at James. James knows the answer already, because he has asked around. He's testing McGill. Will McGill come clean and tell him the truth?

"I was kicked off the force because of my drinking," McGill confesses.

"Then why should I give you a job?"

"Mr. Coppi, I can't tell you what to do. If I were in your shoes, I probably *wouldn't* hire me. Who needs a drunkard on his payroll?" McGill pauses for a moment, looking down at the floor. Then he raises his head and stares straight at James. "I lost everything because of my drinking. My wife, Emily, took my three kids and left. I hit rock bottom. I put my gun to my mouth and pulled the trigger. But the gun didn't go off, because I had sold the bullets the day before for a bottle of vodka—a fact I'd forgotten.

"That's when I went to AA and started to follow the program. I've been sober for nearly six months now. Two months ago, I went to see my wife. I can't believe that she actually took me back. After all the lousy crap I put that poor woman through, she has given me another chance. She's a wonderful lady, James. I don't want to let her down ever again. There are no more chances for me—this is it. I've got to make it this time, but I'm struggling to earn some money. Everybody knows my history."

McGill stops talking and rubs his hand through his thick, brown hair. "James, I'm a recovering alcoholic. You could be making a big mistake hiring me. But I will promise you this: I will break my ass for you, and I'll give this job everything I've got. It's not going to be easy, but I will try. Just give me a chance."

James looks at McGill. "The job pays a hundred and a quarter a week to start, and you start right now."

"Whew." McGill heaves a sigh of relief. "I really didn't think you were going to hire me. Thanks, James. I won't let you down. You won't regret this—I promise. So, now that I'm on board, do you want to tell me what case you're working on?"

"Penelope Campos."

"Who?" McGill doesn't immediately recognize the name. Then he thinks about it for a moment. "Is that the girl who was kidnapped in New Mexico?"

"That's the one. Henry Greenwald hired me to investigate."

"Greenwald, the millionaire?" McGill shakes his head. "Christ, James, I thought you were doing well, but not *that* well. If people like Greenwald are hiring you, you're playing in the big leagues. Why are you investigating *that* case? Don't they already have the guy? What's our job?"

"The guy who's in jail didn't do it. They have the wrong man. Our job is to find out what really happened to her. The police closed the case and won't reopen the investigation. It's not going to be easy, Charlie. She's been gone for nearly four months now." He looks over at McGill. "The only fact that I know for sure is that the girl wasn't kidnapped for money. The ransom demand would've come in by now.

"Monday, you and Kathy are both going down to Albuquerque with me to look over the case files. I'm guessing we'll be there all week."

"Good luck getting a look at those files," Charlie warns him. "The cops in Albuquerque won't cooperate, because they believe they got their man and the matter is closed. They're not going to show you anything. You have no idea how defensive cops can get."

"I'm way ahead of you, Charlie. Greenwald already read the DA the riot act, so they'll cooperate—believe me. Any trouble and we immediately call Greenwald. We won't make any friends, but we'll get what we want."

"What do you want me to do this week?" McGill asks him.

"Kathy has summonses that need to be served. I'm way behind on that work. If you have some time, stop by the library and look over some newspaper articles on the Campos case. Do you need money?"

"Can you advance me fifty against my first paycheck? I could really use some cash—we're two months behind on the rent."

James goes into his pocket, pulls out a fifty, and hands it to McGill. "You don't need to pay it back. Consider this your signing bonus." He looks at McGill suspiciously. "The money *is* for rent, right?"

"It's not for booze, if that's what you're thinking." McGill gets up and puts the fifty in his pocket. "I better get to work. You said Kathy has the summonses?"

"Yes. Just see her outside."

James looks at the clock and thinks, *Ten o'clock? Crap, that's all? What do I do for the rest of the day?* He gets up, stretches, and heads out of the office. Kathy and Charlie are speaking at her desk, but when James walks by, she interrupts Charlie.

"Excuse me, Charlie—one sec. Where are you going, James?"

"I don't know." James turns back. "For a walk, I guess. I've got nothing to do. Charlie is serving the summonses."

"Aren't you going to answer your calls?" Kathy prompts him.

"I've got calls?" He looks at her, entirely confused.

She hands him four messages. "Yes, you've got calls, boss. Get back in your office and call these people." She begins laughing. "You wanted this, remember?"

He comes out an hour later. Kathy is bent over a filing cabinet, arranging the files. "Any more calls?" he asks her. She shakes her head no.

"Good—then I'm going out. By the way, put McGill on the payroll for a hundred and a quarter. Don't make any plans next week. You're coming with McGill and me to Albuquerque; we're going to be there for a few days."

"Who's going to run the office while we're away?"

He shrugs, there's a blank look on his face. "I don't know. Who cares? If we're not here, there's nothing to run."

"What about the phones? Who will answer the phones?" Kathy asks.

"Kathy, why are you asking me all these questions? I don't *know* how to run an office. That's why I hired you."

"We'll have to hire an answering service," she says, thinking aloud.

"Answering service—perfect." He gives her a big smile. "You see? I knew you could figure it out. You're the best." He runs out the door before Kathy can fire any more questions at him.

He decides to surprise Sam and take her to lunch. He's been spending so much time on his new business that he's completely ignored Sam and her job. *Well, no more*, he thinks. *Time to get caught up.*

When he arrives at the department store, Sam is delighted and immediately goes to get her jacket.

"So, what do you do all day?" Sam asks him. The two of them are sitting at a booth in a diner. James has just finished telling her that he hired McGill. "Since you have everybody working for you, what do you do with *your* time?"

"I'm really busy. This morning I hired McGill, and after that I returned four phone calls."

She looks at him and furrows her brow. "You returned four phone calls? That's it? That was your busy morning? My poor baby," she says, smiling. "You must be exhausted. Maybe you should go home and take a nap after lunch."

"You know, Sam, if I had known I was going to be made fun of, I wouldn't have come to see you. I try to do something nice by taking you out to lunch, and that's the thanks I get? You make fun of me and my job." He throws down his menu on the table annoyed.

Sam laughs but manages to say, "I'm sorry. Go ahead—what do you want to talk about?"

"Tell me what's going on at your work. You're a manager and running your own department. How do you like your job?"

"I love what I'm doing," she tells him excitedly. "I love everything about the job. It gives me a chance to put my own personality into my department."

"How do you do it, Sam?" He leans forward in his seat. "How do you run things with so many people waiting for your instructions? I've got to be honest with you, Sam: I don't know what to do. I've never run anything before. Frankly, it scares the crap out of me. Thank God I hired Kathy. She at least knows how the office should work. I would be totally lost without her."

Sam smiles again at him. "Just give yourself a little time, James; you'll figure it out. Trust in yourself."

After he drops Sam back at her job, he realizes that things have changed for him and he needs to make adjustments. Granted, he's not used to running the show, but people are now relying on him for instructions and orders. Until now, he has just run his own life and, frankly, he has not done a very good job of it—at least by his own assessment. *The only good thing that's happened to me in my life since getting drafted is having met Sam. It's time for me to grow up and get busy. Life is no longer just about taking care of myself. People are relying on me. They are counting on me for my leadership.*

Crap, he thinks, *how the hell did I get myself into this mess?* Instead of going back to the office that afternoon, James decides to visit the office of every attorney in Colorado Springs and personally introduce himself and his agency to get the word out that the Sam and James Detective Agency is open and ready for business. By the end of the day, he's satisfied that he has put in an honest day's work.

10
COLORADO SPRINGS

Sam doesn't get out of bed until ten the following morning. Monday is generally her day off, but this week a coworker has asked to switch with her. Sam usually uses her day off to get caught up on housework. This morning, she hears someone in the kitchen.

That's odd, she thinks. Both James and Kathy should be at work. She goes into the kitchen. James is sitting at the table. He is reading the paper and having coffee.

"I thought you'd never get up," he says when he sees her. "I was about to come in and wake you."

"What are you doing at home? Why aren't you at the office?"

"Well, there's nothing doing there, so I decided to take the day off and spend it with you. We can go on a picnic. There's a park called the Garden of the Gods that I'd like to see. I already have the picnic basket packed and in the car, along with a blanket."

"I'm sorry, James." She goes to grab a cup of coffee. "I can't go. This week I worked on Monday, and today is my day off. I'm way behind on my housework. I've got three loads of laundry to take to the laundromat."

"I'm way ahead of you," he tells her after she sits down. "The laundry is already bagged and in the back seat of my car, waiting for us to take it to the laundromat. I'll come with you; we can get it done twice as fast."

"What about the apartment—the dusting and the cleaning?"

"We'll both do the housework when we come back. I'll help you. It's supposed to be a beautiful day. Let's put it to good use."

"All right. Let me take a quick shower and get dressed."

As they sit in the laundromat waiting for the wash cycle to complete, James reads some brochures.

"What are you reading?" Sam asks him.

"Just some brochures on Colorado Springs that I got from the welcome center. Did you know that Colorado Springs is, on the average, higher in elevation than Denver? Denver calls itself the Mile-High City, but Colorado Springs is the mile-high-plus-another-thousand-feet city."

"Why the sudden interest in Colorado Springs?" Sam asks, taking one of the brochures from him and looking it over.

"Because, Sam, if this is going to be our home, I want to know everything about the place," he replies. "When I was stationed here last year, I didn't pay the city any mind. I didn't think I'd ever come back. Now, I realize that this is going to be our *life*. This area is our future, so I want to know everything about the place. That's why we're going to the park today. We're going to make time every once in a while, to explore a new part of the city."

"Well, if you want to do some exploring, why don't we go look at some houses this afternoon after our picnic?" Sam suggests. "There's one in particular that I saw at an open house last Sunday. I'd love to show it to you."

James looks at her. "So that's what you've been doing with your afternoons after teaching Sunday school—sneaking around looking at houses."

"I'm not *sneaking* around," Sam says in self-defense. "You spend your Sundays at the Y working out and I keep myself busy looking at houses after Bible school. You've always known that I'd like us to get a place of our own. There's nothing secret about that."

"We won't have time this afternoon. Don't you remember all the housework that needs to be done?" James is in no mood to go look at houses. Besides, he already knows the house he wants—and he's pretty sure that he and Sam will not be on the same page about his choice. He needs time to develop a plan for how to convince Sam about his dream.

"We don't have to go *in* the house; we can just drive by," Sam persists. "You'll love the place." She smiles happily. "It's in a cul-de-sac. It's nothing fancy, but I think the place could be a nice starter home. What do you say? Can we go look?"

Backed into a corner, James leans over and gives her a kiss. "Sure, why not? As long as we don't have to go inside, it won't hurt to look."

When the laundry is done, they drive to the Garden of the Gods. James pulls into one of the parking lots along the edge.

"Are you sure you've got the right place?" Sam asks as she looks around. "There's nobody else here. Only three other cars."

"It's early afternoon; maybe people are still at work. It's just as well; we'll have the park all to ourselves."

"How will we know where we're going?"

"I've got a map," James replies. He gets out of the car and heads for the trunk. "I got it from the visitor's center. I'll be your tour guide," he adds as he opens the trunk and pulls out the picnic basket and blanket.

"This is nice," Sam remarks as she takes another look around.

"Absolutely beautiful," he agrees as he, too, pauses to have a look. "Aren't you glad I suggested this place?"

She comes over to give him a hug and a kiss. "Yes, this is a wonderful idea. Do you want me to carry anything?"

"No, I'm good."

No more than ten minutes into the walk, Sam stops suddenly. "What *are* those, up on the rocks?" she cries out. James looks up to where she's pointing.

"Oh my God, this is great!" he yells, excited. "Those are bighorn sheep; I didn't think we'd get to see them."

"Let's go back," she says, starting to walk away. "I didn't know there'd be wild animals at this place."

"Of course there are animals." He grabs hold of her. "We live in Colorado, where there *are* wild animals. That's what's *great* about where we live. Those sheep are harmless. Stop acting like a baby."

She moves up close to him and holds him by the arm. "You're going to have to stay close to me for the rest of the day. Look at the horns on those sheep. That one on the right looks angry. He looks like he's going to charge at me any second."

Some twenty minutes later, Sam is still holding on to James. "Look!" he says cheerfully. "Look up there. What does that rock formation look like to you?" He points up to some rocks.

She looks to where he's pointing. "I have no idea."

"That rock formation is called the Kissing Camels," James tells her eagerly. "Don't the rocks look like the humps of camels? Look up on top. Don't they look like camels kissing?"

"I guess—if you say so. Yes." She barely looks at the rocks.

"What's the matter? You really aren't into this? I *love* it!"

"I'm sorry, James, but seeing those sheep kind of freaked me out. I keep expecting some wild creature to jump out at any moment. There's no one around to help us if something happens. We can't even call for help."

"Calm down. Nothing is going to happen. Try to enjoy the experience."

"Look who's telling me to calm down: a boy from the Bronx. The only animals that you ever saw there were sewer rats."

He pushes her away and laughs. "Now, that was downright insulting. If you get attacked by an animal, you're on your own."

A little farther down the trail, she points to a rock formation. "What's that?"

James reaches into the basket and pulls out his map. "That configuration of rocks is called the Graces," he tells her.

"The Graces? I wonder why they're called that."

"I guess they look like spiritual ladies. Don't you think?"

"Yes—I can see that now that you point it out."

They finally come upon the area that he has said he most wants to see.

"Look at that boulder! It looks like it's going to fall over at any moment!" Sam comments.

"That's Balancing Rock," he tells her, all excited. "I wanted to see this rock formation most of all. Isn't it amazing? That massive boulder is slowly eroding away and will eventually fall. It's been eroding for thousands of years—maybe—a million. Come on, let's climb up closer to the rock. That's where we're going to put down our blanket and have lunch."

"Are you crazy?" she cries out. "It'll be just our luck that after a million years, today's the day that the massive boulder finally comes crumbling down, right on top of us while we're eating."

"That's the fun of it!" he exclaims and begins to climb up the rocks. "Come on," he calls to her. "Don't be a spoilsport!"

She shakes her head to clear away her fear and scrambles up the rocks. James lays the blanket down directly under the massive boulder and begins taking out the sandwiches.

"All I brought is peanut butter and jelly," he tells her.

"Yum! My favorite! I just hope those bighorn sheep aren't attracted to the smell."

"No, I don't think peanut butter is part of their diet. How about a Coke? It's probably warm."

After lunch, he lies down on his back and she lies alongside him. They gaze up at the massive rock. He pulls her to him and begins kissing her neck. She tilts her head back so that he can have more access. His hand slides up her sweater and cups her breast. He moves her onto her back, leans over her, and reaches down to unfasten her pants.

"What are you doing?" she yells, grabbing his hand.

"I'm trying to unbutton your pants."

"Why?"

"Why else?" he responds. "I want to make love to you."

"Right here, under this boulder?"

"Yes." James sits up and begins taking off his shirt. "Just think of it—we're going to make love under this massive rock that can fall down at any time. It's going to be so exciting."

"Never mind the rock," Sam says. "Look around. We're right out in the open. Anybody can come walking by."

"What are you talking about? We're completely alone." He points to the vast emptiness of the park. "Look, do you see anyone? We were walking for an hour and didn't see a single person."

"Whatever. I'm still not comfortable." She shakes her head and tries to get up. "It'll be just my luck that someone will come by just as we get naked."

"We'll wrap the blanket around us." He pulls her back down. "Even if someone does come by, no one will be able to see anything. Besides, I'll keep watch."

"But these darn rocks are so doggone hard," she continues to complain. "You'll break my back."

"No, I won't. I promise I won't put my entire weight on you. Come on—be a sport. It'll be fun," James pleads.

"The things I do for you!" Sam shakes her head. She sits up to pull off her sweater. "You *better* keep a lookout!" They finish undressing. He lies on top of her, pulling the cover over them.

"You better make it snappy," she barks at him.

"Stop spoiling it for me. You're taking all the fun out of the adventure."

"You better not get up too quickly or you'll crack your head on that rock directly above you," she warns him.

"Are you comfortable?" he asks her as he inserts himself into her.

"Yes, I'm fine. Stop kissing my neck and keep a lookout. You can't see anything if you're bent over kissing."

"You know, that was kind of fun," Sam admits when they have finished and are getting dressed. "The possibility that we might get caught actually made it more exciting. We should do this again. How was it for you?"

"It would have been a lot *more* fun if you hadn't kept asking me to look and see if anyone was coming."

She gives him a kiss and a smile. "Well, you were a great sentry. Come on, let's head back. I want to show you that house we talked about earlier."

"We'll have to look at your house some other time," James says, once again trying to avoid the search for the house. "We won't have time today. Remember, we still have all that housework waiting for us when we get home."

"It'll only take a minute—it's right on the way," she says excitedly. "Come on, let's hurry!" She begins walking faster. "We're just going to drive by. You'll love the place. It's absolutely beautiful."

"So, what do you think?" Sam asks James when they're parked in front of the house.

"Yeah, it's okay. It's nice." James shrugs, responding with indifference.

She gives him a long look and then turns to glare straight ahead.

That night after dinner, Sam is sitting on the sofa with Kathy, watching television, when James comes in, carrying two jackets.

"What's on the boob tube?" he asks.

"The news is saying that the Beatles might be breaking up," Kathy responds.

"Can't happen fast enough to suit me," he says.

"You don't like the Beatles?" Kathy asks. "Why not?"

"Because I'm not a teeny bopper and I don't like bands who cater to them."

He hands Sam a jacket. "Come on—let's go for our walk," he says to her. "It's a beautiful evening. The sunset over Pike's Peak is going to be spectacular."

"I'm not in the mood tonight," she tells him. "I'm tired from all the walking we did at the park today."

"Oh, come on. The sky is going to be beautiful. We don't have to go for a long trek. Let's just go to the park and sit on our bench. After the sunset, we can come straight home. Please, let's not just sit around here and watch tv."

Once they are at the park and sitting on their favorite bench, James asks Sam, "What colors do you suppose we'll see tonight?" James's arm is wrapped around her. She's resting her head on his shoulder. They have a view of Pike's Peak. There are still a few minutes to go before the sun sets behind the big mountain.

"I don't know," she answers coolly.

"I'm guessing it's going to be the oranges and reds. There's almost no cloud cover, so I don't believe it will be the blues and the purples. I can't understand why no one else has discovered this spot. It has to be the most beautiful place on Earth at sunset. You would think that thousands of people would flock to this very spot at sundown. You know, Sam, if God came down and told me that I had only five minutes left to live on this earth and I could pick any place to be for that time, this is where I would choose to spend those five minutes. I can't envision that even paradise is as beautiful as this spot. Don't you agree?"

"Yeah, it's okay. It's nice," Sam shrugs, responding indifferently.

James removes his arm from around her shoulder and sits up. "All right, Sam, get it out. You've been sulking ever since we came back from that house this afternoon."

Sam sits up and scowls at him. "I'm angry with you, James. You know how important a house is to me, and when I show you one, all you can say is, 'Yeah, it's okay. It's nice.' If you know how important a house is to me, why are you so dismissive? Why can't you show just the slightest bit of interest?"

"Because that's not the house, or the neighborhood, that *I* want, Sam. I don't want a starter house on a cul-de-sac," James says, making a circular motion with his hands to represent the cul-de-sac. "Geez, Sam, we can find that kind of house in any town in the United States. It's no more unique here in Colorado than it is in, say, in some suburb of Philadelphia.

"We live in the West, and we need to take advantage of everything the region has to offer. This area is changing, just like the rest of the country. We may never get a chance to live in this kind of open environment again."

"Well, what kind of house do *you* want?" Sam asks him. "I'm assuming you *do* want us to have a house of our own?"

"Of course I do," he replies after a pause. "Sam, I want a ranch."

She is totally quiet for a moment and then bursts out laughing. "A ranch? You know *nothing* about ranching. How is a nice Italian boy from the Bronx going to start herding cows?" She continues to laugh.

"Not cows," he says in self-defense. "I would never raise animals just so they could be slaughtered. I don't have the stomach or the heart to be part of killing an animal."

"All right, then." She looks at him dubiously. "What animals *are* you going to put on this ranch? I'm assuming you are going to have at least *some* animals?" she asks with a slightly mocking tone.

"Yes, I'm going to have animals," James answers. He gets up from the bench and looks back down at her. "You know, Sam, this is exactly why I haven't discussed my dream with you. I knew what your reaction would be. I knew you'd see my idea as just one big joke."

She reaches up and grabs his arm to pull him back down. "Come on, sit back down. I'm sorry. I'll be serious. Tell me about your plan."

James sits back down and looks straight ahead. The sun is setting at Pike's Peak, but he's not noticing the orange-yellow glow. "Sam, I didn't lose my college deferment. I gave it up voluntarily."

She turns him to face her. "*What?* Why did you do that? What happened?"

James swallows hard and begins. "I was struggling at school and thought I was going to lose my deferment. The dean called me into his office to discuss my standing. After a long meeting, he put me on probation and let me keep my deferment. Two days later, I walked into an army recruiting office on the Grand Concourse, gave up my deferment, and pushed up my draft date."

"Why did you do that?"

James stares straight ahead. "You know, Sam, I've given this a lot of thought the past four months, ever since I came back from 'Nam. The conclusion I come to is that I *wanted* to end up in Vietnam. Back then, I was really suffering—just wandering around aimlessly. I was doing drugs, popping pills, hustling at cards and pool. I had no direction." He turns to her and reveals to her his deepest-kept secret. "Sam, I may have been heading toward suicide."

"What?" she yells, sitting up straight. "Don't say that! It's not true! You weren't like that when I met you. You were smart, confident, and strong. You were the one that saved *me*."

"It was just an act, Sam. Down deep, I was really hurting. Even when I met you, I was still in a lot of pain. There was a time in Vietnam when I had massive headaches almost every day. I couldn't concentrate on anything. I don't have a clue how I survived that war."

She looks at him. "I remember that period. I was so worried about you."

James looks at her. "You *knew*? How did you know? I never wrote to you about what was going on inside of me. I never told anybody."

"You didn't have to say anything, James. The hurt you were feeling was clear in your letters. Your handwriting was all scribbled and illegible. It was obvious you were suffering. I can show you those letters—there in a box in my closet at the apartment. I was so worried about you."

James leans back on the bench. "That's why I didn't come straight home to you, Sam. I was still all fucked up. Still doing drugs, still without plans, and still wandering around aimlessly. How could I come home to you?"

"You weren't doing drugs when I came to New York. Believe me, I know, because I went through your clothes every night. I even searched your car." She notices him smiling slyly at her. "*Were* you doing drugs?"

"Tobi, at the front desk of the motel, was holding the stash for me."

"I'm such a fool. Of course you were on drugs. How else could you stay up all night long?" She turns to him. "Tell me the truth, James: are you still doing drugs now?"

"No, not anymore. No drugs since we left New York, Sam. I wouldn't even touch a pill because of you. There's nothing that I would do to disappoint you; that's how important you are to me." He sits up straight and faces her. "That's why I want this ranch, Sam. You want a home, and my response is to build you a castle. You want to raise a family, and my response is to have the best family possible. This ranch is going to have horses, Sam. I don't know what kind yet. The plan is still developing. Our children are going to be brought up in the wide-open spaces of the West. We're going to give our children the most wholesome life imaginable."

She reaches across and strokes his face. "You don't need to do all that. I'm happy just being with you. A modest home with a nice family is all I want. I'm not a princess in need of a castle. I'm just a simple girl from Lorenzo, Texas."

"Let me do this, Sam," James begs. "Let me do this for you. I put you through so much this past year; let me make it up to you."

"But you don't know anything about ranching."

"I didn't know anything about being a private detective and running my own business, either, but here I am doing both. Sam, I know I can make this happen. The realization came to me during the meeting with Greenwald. You should have seen me, Sam. I was running the meeting and they were listening. You don't impress a guy like Greenwald that easily—and believe me, he was impressed. After that meeting, I realized that, I wasn't a street punk from the Bronx any longer. I'm just as good as those men in the conference room."

"All right. How big of a ranch were you planning on buying?"

"Five hundred acres."

"Five hundred acres!" she yells out in disbelief and laughs. "Do you have any idea how big a piece of God's green earth five hundred acres really is?"

James bursts out laughing. "Frankly, no. It was the first number that came into my head."

"What about the cost? Where will we get the money? How long will we have to wait before we get our own home?"

"Just give me some time, Sam," he pleads his case. "I don't have all the answers right now." He pauses for a moment and considers. "How's this? Just give me until I graduate. If I don't have my ranch in three years, you can go buy any house, in any color, of any size, in any cul-de-sac of your choosing. How's that? That's it: three years. That's all I'm asking."

"So, let me see if I understand you correctly." Sam smiles, turns to look at him, and ticks off her fingers as she recaps his promises. "In the next three years, you're going to get married, graduate from college, successfully start up your business, and buy a ranch. Do I have it right, or is there something else? Did I miss anything?"

"No, that's it. You've got it right." After a pause, he looks at her. "You think I'm crazy, don't you? You're probably thinking right now that you're about to marry a lunatic."

She pulls him over to her and gives him a kiss. "Of course, you're insane. I've known it all along. What sane person would want to marry me?" She gives him another kiss. "But I wouldn't want you any other way. You're absolutely perfect."

She leans her head on his shoulder. They stare out at the dark night. "With all this talk, you missed out on your sunset," she says.

"I know, but I don't care. This is one of the best moments of my life. Opening up to you and telling you all my secrets felt so good. Thank you for being so understanding."

11
INVESTIGATING

On Friday morning, when James comes into the office, Charlie is talking with Kathy.

"I served eight of the twelve summonses you gave me yesterday," Charlie tells her. "Here's the list," he adds, handing her a slip of paper. "I'm going to go right back out today and take care of the remaining four."

"Stop by the office of the attorney Jonas Stark," Kathy tells him. "He called yesterday and says he has another summons that needs to be served. Do you know where his office is located, or do you want me to look up the address?"

"No, I'm good. I have the address." He turns around and sees James. "You got anything for me, boss?"

"No, we're good, Charlie," James replies. Then he notices Sam coming in.

"Well, look who's here! What a nice surprise. What are you doing here?" James goes over and gives her a kiss. "Did you come to make sure everybody at your agency is staying busy?"

"I'm doing some shopping and I stopped in to invite Charlie and his wife to dinner on Sunday. How about it, Charlie? Would the McGills like to join us for dinner on Sunday?"

"Sure thing," he replies. "What time?"

"Two o'clock."

"Great. I'll see you on Sunday," McGill tells Sam. Then he heads out the door.

Sam looks at Kathy. "How about you and Bobby? Can you guys make it, too?"

"I'll give Bobby a call and ask, but I don't think it will be a problem."

"Don't tell me—let me guess. I'll be barbecuing?" James asks in a fake whine. Then, in a more serious tone, he adds, "I'm really in no mood for cooking this Sunday. Sam, you knew, I leave the next day for Albuquerque. Why didn't you discuss this dinner with me first?"

"Stop your complaining," she scolds him. "You're not barbecuing. I'm cooking Mama Coppi's famous lasagna, followed by her equally tasty lamb casserole."

"You've got to be kidding. You don't know how to cook Italian!"

"Your mom gave me all her recipes," Sam tells him. "And she just sent me a jar of her tomato sauce. It arrived yesterday. Would you like to know how she makes her meatballs, James? She uses ground pork *and* veal. I have her recipes for the entire dinner. You don't have to do a thing so stop your complaining."

"When did you speak to my mother?"

"I call her every Sunday evening when you're at the Y. *Somebody* has to call your mother, since her precious Giacomo never calls."

"Who's Giacomo?" Kathy cuts in.

"That's your boss, Kathy. *Giacomo* means 'James' in Italian."

"Giacomo. I like that." Kathy smiles. Turning to James, she says, "It sounds European. Maybe I'll call you Giacomo from now on."

"Don't get smart," James warns Kathy. "You stick to calling me James! Then he turns back to Sam. "How do you communicate with my mother? She doesn't speak English, and I know you don't speak Italian."

"Oh, we manage. When it gets really tough, one of your sisters translates. Anyway, we speak just about every Sunday. I've got to go. I can't stand around and talk to you all morning; I need to finish the shopping before I go to work today." Sam gives James a kiss. "Maybe if you called your mother every once in a while, you'd know what's going on."

"You're amazing," he says to her as he opens the door to let her out.

"Did you know about this?" James asks Kathy after Sam leaves the office.

"Not the cooking part. I knew she spoke to your mom every Sunday, but I didn't know anything about the cooking."

"Those have got to be some of the shortest phone calls on record," James remarks, shaking his head. "What can my mother and Sam have to talk about? Neither one understands the other."

"No, they're on the phone at least a half hour," Kathy says. "They usually talk for quite a while."

"This is unbelievable." He shrugs, shaking his head once again. He looks over at Kathy. "Kathy, I'm going next door. I need to speak to Michael Barrett."

———◆———

"How come you're not wearing a suit and tie?" James asks Barrett when he walks into Michael's office. "You're in dungarees. Are you closing the place?"

"No. On Fridays, we always dress casually," Barrett says. "Unless clients are coming to the office, I let my staff wear whatever they want." He pauses. "What do you need, James?" Barrett asks. "Don't tell me you came in here to discuss how I dress."

"No. I need to ask a big favor. Can you arrange for a meeting between me and the accused in the Penelope Campos case? Can you reach out to the defense attorney and get me an interview with his client? I'll be in Albuquerque next week; I'd like to hear what the suspect has to say."

"I doubt that the defendant's attorney will let you anywhere near his client," Barrett says. "Anything the suspect tells you can be used against him at his trial."

"Tell the lawyer I'm on his side—I don't believe his boy did it and that I'm out to prove that the cops have the wrong guy. His man has nothing to lose. I'm quite sure no one else is trying to prove he's innocent. Anyway, please make the call and try to persuade the attorney to let Fontana meet with me. It's in his client's best interest."

It takes a little persuading, but Barrett gets it done. The defense lawyer agrees to a meeting between James and the suspect on Tuesday afternoon at one o'clock.

"It's all set," he tells Kathy when he gets back to his office. "You and Charlie are coming to Albuquerque with me first thing Monday. Make reservations at a hotel for two rooms for three nights. Charlie and I will share a room. Do you have anything else for me?"

"You need to return a call to Big W, a department store chain headquartered in Boulder. They want to speak to you about a security proposal. Henry Greenwald gave them your name."

Sam is busy preparing the food that Sunday morning for the dinner she is giving later in the day.

"Do you need any help?" James asks when he comes into the kitchen for coffee.

"I do! Would you mind peeling and cutting the potatoes for me, sweetie?"

"Ah, so now that you need my help, I'm a *sweetie*."

She gives him a big smile. "Yes, now you're a sweetie. There's a big bowl in the top cabinet. I need you to peel and slice all the potatoes and put them in the bowl. You'll also need to slice up some onions and mix them in with the potatoes, please. There's a bottle of olive oil in the cabinet under the sink. Stir three tablespoons of oil into the bowl with the vegetables."

"You're really on top of things, aren't you?" he says, reaching for the bowl.

"Yes, I've got everything under control. I just need a little help from you—and from Kathy, too, when she gets up. I don't know how your mother does it all by herself! This is a lot of work."

"I'm at your service, milady." James bows to her. "You can count on me."

"Good! After you're done with the potatoes, you can dust and vacuum the house."

That night, Sam and James are lying in bed. "How did I do?" Sam asks him. "It wasn't as good as your mom's, I'm sure, but the dinner came out pretty well."

"*Signora*, your dinner was *magnifico*. Better than I could have ever imagined. You're a natural. Did you notice Mrs. Smythe? She had three huge servings of your lasagna. I've never seen her put away so much food. The gravy came out great. Where did you find those sausages? Those sausages were as good as any I've ever tasted. I never knew that Colorado Springs had such a great butcher."

"A coworker at the department store told me about him. He's from Poland." She smiles as she gets caught up in his enthusiasm. "Wasn't the lamb in the casserole tender?"

"Yes, it melted in the mouth. You had sausages, meatballs, and pork ribs in the gravy. Only the *braciola* was missing."

"When we were in New York and ate at your mom's house, I know you loved the *braciola*. Your mother gave me the recipe for her *braciola*, but I was afraid to try making it this time. Maybe next time."

"Well, everything came out great, and everybody loved your food."

"The only one of the guests who didn't eat much was Bobby. He didn't seem to like my cooking," Sam muses.

James leans alongside her and gives her a kiss. "He was acting strangely all day. It wasn't about the food. Your entire meal was great. Something else was going on between Bobby and Kathy." James gets on top of her. "So, my wonderful chef, what would you like as your reward for the amazing feast you prepared today? Your wish is my command; I'm at your disposal."

She pulls him down and whispers in his ear.

"Of course." He smiles at her. "I'll get right on it. You just lie back and enjoy."

"Is the district attorney going to give us a hard time about providing the files?" Kathy asks James on the drive to Albuquerque early that Monday morning. She's driving his Mustang. Charlie is following behind in his Cutlass. They decided to take two cars, hoping that the extra mobility options will help them get twice as much done.

"I don't really know." James says, worried. "The district attorney said that all the files are ready for copying; I only hope he was telling the truth. I'm telling you, Kathy—I'm not going to allow any stonewalling. The minute I see that they're not cooperating, I'll call Greenwald. There's a girl out there who needs our help. I'm not going to put up with any games or delays."

"So you believe that the girl is still alive?"

"I refuse to form an opinion either way until I know more." He closes his eyes as he considers the question. He turns to Kathy. "Everybody tells me that she's probably dead, you know, since it's been over three months—but I'm not willing to accept that conclusion unless the facts are there. I'll let the evidence lead me wherever it may. If I don't keep an open mind to any and every possibility, I may overlook an important clue."

When they get to the district attorney's office, they are ushered into a conference room where there are eight boxes and eleven files stacked on top of a table.

"Holy crap!" Charlie says. "We'll spend a week copying this stuff and a year going through everything."

"No, we won't," James responds. "Charlie, there's probably nothing worthwhile in the files. If there were something here, they wouldn't have the wrong guy in jail, and the case would have been solved. Kathy will stay here and make copies of everything. You and I need to start the investigation from the beginning.

"Charlie, you'll need to go back to the girl's neighborhood, where she was kidnapped. Go door to door and interview everyone again. Don't leave out anyone; make sure you canvass the entire area. I'm going to interview the gardener at the school and Penelope's friend, Mary. We'll meet back here tonight and compare notes. Our only hope is that the police overlooked something. We'll zero in on the files once we find something new."

It takes James a few minutes after he gets to the school before he catches up with the gardener, Mr. Martinez. James has read the notes on the case, and he is familiar with the statement that the gardener provided to the police. Martinez's statement is pretty straightforward; the groundskeeper saw the suspect at the school the day that Penelope was abducted.

To James, Martinez's testimony is irrelevant and does not have anything to do with the kidnapping. The young girl wasn't kidnapped at the school; she was snatched in front of her house. The last person to see Penelope before she went missing was her schoolmate Mary, and she saw Penelope one block from the missing girl's house. Indeed, Martinez's statement actually gives the jailed man an alibi. If the suspect was at the school, there was no way that he could have also been at Penelope's house committing the crime.

James is just hoping that Martinez might remember something more. Anything—he will take anything at this point. He has looked at the picture of that beautiful young girl that he got from a newspaper clipping at least a dozen times. Her face preoccupies his every thought; he thinks about her constantly and refuses to believe that she is dead. If the police are correct and they have the right man in jail, then the girl is dead. On the other hand, if James's hunch is right and they have the *wrong* guy, she might still be alive. He asks himself if he is just indulging in wishful thinking. It's not like him to look at situations through rose-colored glasses. He's usually very practical.

"I'm sorry to bother you again, Mr. Martinez," James begins after Martinez starts protesting the idea that he has to go through his testimony once again. "I'm aware that you've already provided a complete and full statement to the police. You must realize, though, that the family is desperate—they're trying to locate their daughter. *You* have a family; I'm sure you can sympathize with how grief-stricken the family must be. Can you imagine losing one of your children and not knowing what happened to that child? So, please, if you don't mind, Mr. Martinez, take me through the entire event once more." James takes out his pad and pen and gives his agency card to the groundskeeper.

"There's not much more to say, from what I told the police when I spoke to them," Martinez replies, sitting on his tractor. "I was riding my lawn mower, doing my job, when I saw this guy parked in his car, right down the street. The man looked suspicious just sitting there, so I went up to him and asked him what he was doing. You know, it's a dead-end street. There's no reason for anybody to be there. Right after I faced him, he drove away. That's it—not much more."

"What time was that? Was that before the young girls passed by, or after?"

"The first time I approached him was before the girls passed by. The second time was after."

James stops writing and looks up at Martinez. "You confronted him twice?" he asks excitedly. "Are you sure of that, Mr. Martinez? In the police report, it doesn't mention that you confronted him twice."

Martinez thinks about it for a moment and nods. "Yes, it was twice—I'm sure. The first time I went over, a van almost ran me over. I remember yelling at the driver of the van."

"A van?" Once again, James feels excitement. "What kind of van?"

"I don't remember." Martinez shrugs. "It's a dead-end street, and cars are always coming down this street by mistake. They make a U-turn when they realize their mistake. Happens all the time."

"This happened before the girls came walking by—is this correct?"

Martinez takes his hat off and runs his hand through his dark hair. "Yeah, before they came by. The van was gone before the girls came out of school. Is that important?"

"Probably not, but we've got to look at everything. Are you sure you don't remember the color of the van? Think real hard, Mr. Martinez; it could be important. Maybe I can locate the van, and maybe the person or persons in the vehicle saw something that day."

"No, I'm sorry." Mr. Martinez shrugs again. "I really can't say. It was a light color—silver, gray, or maybe white. I'm sure it wasn't a dark color. I wish I could help, but that's all I can remember."

"What about the driver?" James questions him. "Can you identify the person driving the van? You said that you yelled at the driver. Did you get a good look at him?"

"No, I'm sorry. I don't really recall what either of the people looked like," Martinez responds, trying to remember.

"*People?*" James asks. "There was more than one person in the van?"

"Yes. There were two people in the van, but I can't remember what either of them looked like," Martinez repeats. "I wish I could be more helpful."

"Not at all, Mr. Martinez. You've been very helpful. Thanks for your time. If you remember anything else, please give me a call."

With nothing to do for the few hours before Mary, Penelope's classmate, gets out of school, James decides to check in on Charlie and see how he's doing. He spots Charlie coming out of a house right down the block from where Penelope was snatched.

"Anything?" James asks him.

"Absolutely nothing. Nobody saw or heard anything. It's a pretty quiet neighborhood. I don't think that anybody was out that afternoon. How about you? How did you make out with the gardener?"

"Martinez told me something new," he says. "I don't know if what he told me means anything important, but at least it's something. Martinez said he saw a light-colored van with two people inside around the time that Penelope was getting out of school. If we can locate that van, the occupants may have seen something that afternoon. They aren't mentioned in any police report, so I don't believe they were ever questioned. I'm going to drive over to the DA's office to look in on Kathy and see how she's doing with the copying. Keep going, Charlie. You never know. You might just get lucky and find that needle in the haystack."

"How's it going?" James asks Kathy when he gets back to the conference room. Stacks of papers are everywhere—on the table and on the chairs, too. The floor also has some stacks of papers. "What a mess!" he says. "How do you keep track of anything?"

"Don't you have anything to do?" she fires back.

"I see you're in a good mood."

"I'm sorry." Kathy begins laughing. "Making all these damn copies and keeping track of everything is no fun. The crappy copier they have in this place keeps jamming. Anyway, I've got all the copying done. Now I'm cross-referencing to make sure that I've got everything. Tomorrow, I'll develop a filing system so you'll have easy access to all the files you might need. How's that?"

"You're the best," he tells her. Then he gets the heck out of there. There is no way he can be helpful to her in the process.

He drives back to Penelope's neighborhood and parks his blue Mustang in front of her schoolmate Mary's house. Around three thirty, he notices the young teenager walking up the street. He decides to wait until Mary is in her house to question her. No need to scare this young woman by confronting her in the street. He gives it five minutes and then knocks on the door. Mary's mother comes to the door.

He introduces himself. The mother agrees to let him interview her daughter. It's not long before he realizes that Mary isn't going to be very helpful. Finally, he asks Mary if she noticed any cars parked on her street when she walked home with Penelope that day.

"No, I'm sorry. I didn't notice any cars," Mary replies, twirling her brown hair with her finger. "We just walked home as usual."

"Mary, do you know if Penelope had a boyfriend or a boy who was interested in her? In the picture I saw of Penelope, I could see that she is really cute. I can't believe that some boy didn't have a crush on her."

"No, Penelope didn't have a boyfriend, and I don't know of any boy who was interested in her."

That night, James, Kathy, and Charlie are having dinner at a diner close to their hotel.

"So, what's our plan going forward?" Charlie asks James.

"Charlie, you need to go back out tonight and finish canvassing the houses that you didn't get to today."

"Why bother? It'll just be more of the same."

"Please, Charlie, don't take that attitude. I know that you're frustrated and that there're a lot of dead ends. But we only need *one* break. We just have to keep plugging along and hope to get lucky. We got a small lead today from the gardener; we need more leads like that. Tonight, you go back out and finish the houses. Tomorrow, I want you to meet with the detectives who worked on the case. You're an ex-cop; they might open up to you. While you're talking to the detectives, I'm going to interview the prime suspect. Maybe I'll learn something."

James turns to Kathy. "What about you? What do you have?"

"I've separated the files into two sets. One set is from during the beginning of the investigation, and the other is from after the reward was posted. Greenwald announced a fifty thousand dollar reward to anyone who had any information on the missing girl. The reward set of files is three times the size of the investigation set. I don't believe there was much of a search done into the files after the reward was offered. The case was closed not too long after the reward was announced."

Later, he's in Kathy's room looking over the files.

"So, what's your opinion?" Kathy asks him. "Did I just waste an entire day making copies? There's probably nothing in any of the files."

"I'm sorry to say it, Kathy, but you're probably right. There's not likely to be much here," he responds dejectedly. "Tomorrow afternoon, after my meeting at

Sam and James: The Missing Teen

the jailhouse, I'll come back and go over the files with you. I want to see just the files that relate to the time after the reward was posted."

"Really?" She looks at him, baffled. "Why those? Aren't those the files with all the crackpot calls? They're mostly useless."

"Yes," he says. "They probably are, Kathy. I'm assuming the police investigated the first files and got nowhere. The crackpots weren't investigated because the case was closed soon thereafter. So if there's anything new and worthwhile, it'll be in the files with the crackpots."

Just before he leaves, he turns to Kathy. "You did an amazing job on these files, Kathy. Thank you."

Kathy gives him a smile. "You are most welcome."

◆

James is walking up and down the sidewalk in front of the county jail the next afternoon. He spots an older man wearing a three piece gray suit walking down the street toward him. The suit looks like it hasn't been pressed in months. He's toting a gray, worn attaché case. *Probably his lunch is inside the case?* James guesses. *That must be the legal aid lawyer Dingle.*

"Are you James?" The man asks when he gets to him.

"Yes," James extends out his hand to shake. "You must be attorney Dingle?"

"It's a pleasure to meet you," Dingle shakes his hand. "Come on, I'll show you the way in."

At the security gate, Dingle opens his attaché case to show the guard. James notices that indeed two sandwiches are inside. A brief walk down a long corridor, and they are in an interview room with Peter Fontana, the accused. James takes a hard look at the pudgy, pimply-faced young man. *He doesn't look like a kidnapper,* James thinks. *But then again, what does a kidnapper really look like?* Two black-and-blue marks are healing on Fontana's face.

"What happened to you?" James motions at the marks on the prisoner's face.

"Cell mates are not particularly fond of child molesters," Dingle answers for Fontana. "I got him a separate cell away from the rest of the jail population, but they still got to him. The prison guards were probably in on it."

"What do you want from me?" an annoyed Fontana asks, looking at James. "Why the fuck are you here?"

"I'm here to get your version of the story," James tells him. "I'm taking a fresh look at the case."

"Why? Are you going to believe me? I've been screaming my bloody head off for months now that I'm innocent. Those two mother fucking cops tricked me into signing that confession." A red-faced Fontana turns to Dingle. "Why is this guy wasting my time, Dingle? Look at him—he's just a kid…probably doesn't even know how to tie his own shoes yet. This is the fucking genius who's going to break the case? This is the guy that's going to outwit the filthy pigs who tricked me into confessing. Is this your idea of a joke?"

"As a matter of fact, Peter, James thinks you're innocent," Dingle tells him. "He comes well recommended from an attorney I know. James is actually on your side, Peter. It's in your best interest to tell him everything you know. It may be of some help with your defense. You've got nothing to lose by talking to him."

With Dingle's admonition, Fontana calms down and looks over at James. "What do you want to know? I'm not sure I know anything that can be of any help to you."

"All right, Mr. Fontana. Let's start from the beginning." James pulls out his notepad and starts the interview. "That Thursday afternoon, around four o'clock, you pulled into the block behind the school and parked your car. Then what happened?"

"I parked the car, and I was just sitting there, listening to some music. I was looking out at the yard, and I noticed this Mexican mowing the lawn. He kept looking over at me, checking on what I was doing. I could sense that he was going to come over and bust my chops. Sure enough, after a few minutes, the Mexican got off his tractor, came over, and put his dark, oily face into my window. 'What are you doing here?' he hollered at me.

"'Just sitting in my car listening to some music, minding my own business,' I shouted back. The Mexican got a little testy with me and told me that I needed to drive off. I told him to go screw himself, saying that he didn't own the street, and I wasn't leaving. He got pissed, but he left. He got back on his tractor and continued eyeing me."

"What about the van?" James looks up from his pad.

"What about the van?" Fontana asks, there's a confused expression on his face. "Who gives a rat's ass about the van that came by?"

Dingle jumps up from his seat, excited. "There was another vehicle there?" He looks at Fontana. "Why didn't you tell me?"

"It's a dead-end street," Fontana says to Dingle. "There's always cars coming up and making a U-turn when they realize they got no place to go. I didn't pay the van any real attention. The van drove up and was gone in a minute. There was nothing unusual about what they did."

"All right, Fontana. Take your time. This could be important." James gets very patient and deliberate. "Go back to that day. Did the van come straight up the block and make a U-turn?"

Fontana sits up in his seat and thinks for a moment. "No, it actually came up behind my car, stayed there for a moment, and then drove back out. It almost hit the Mexican when it pulled out. Too bad, too—if the van'd hit him, I wouldn't be in this mess today."

"How many people were in the van?" James asks.

"Two," Fontana tells him. "I think." He pauses for a second. "Yeah, two; I'm sure."

"Did you get a look at the people inside?"

"No, not really. The passenger had a beard. That's all I know. I didn't see the driver."

"What about the van?" James presses. "What make, model, or color was it?"

"I don't know anything about the make or model, but the color was white—I'm pretty certain." He thinks it over a little longer. "Yeah, definitely white."

"Are you sure about the man with the beard?" James continues to press him. "Think real hard, Fontana; this may be important. You said he had a beard. Are you sure?"

"Yeah. He definitely had a beard. That's all I remember of him—his beard. It was more of a goatee—not a full beard. You know a beard like you see on a beatnik or some of these Jesus freaks."

"All right, Fontana. Those are all the questions I have," James concludes. "Is there anything else about that day you might remember?"

Fontana shrugs his shoulders. "Nope. That's about it."

"So, does this new development about the van help?" Dingle asks James.

"It's hard to say. It would be nice if we could locate the van. Maybe the driver or passenger saw something—but then again, maybe they just made a mistake and went up a dead-end street, like Fontana said. In any event, it's a lead that's worth pursuing."

Back at the hotel, Charlie is waiting for James.

"So, how did it go?" Charlie asks him. "We got anything?"

"We got a small lead. It's worth checking out. It may be helpful." James tells him the details. Then he asks, "How about you? How'd you make out with the cops? You got anything?"

"I got nada," Charlie answers, "absolutely nothing. Just as I expected, the detectives became very defensive. They told me only enough to make it look like they were cooperating. So, now what? Where do we go from here?"

"Now the real fun begins, Charlie. We start digging through the files. Come on let's go to Kathy's room."

"Kathy, which stack contains the files from people who called after the reward was posted?" James asks Kathy when he's in her room.

"They're on the floor, on the right-hand side of my bed," she responds.

"You've got to be kidding me! We're not going through all those files, are we?" Charlie yells. "Those are just crazy calls; there's nothing in those records. It'll be a complete waste of our time."

"What do you care, Charlie?" James fires back. "You get paid for looking, not for finding. Everybody grab a file."

"What are we looking for?" Kathy asks.

"We're looking for any mention of a van—particularly one of a light color—and of a bearded man or a teenage girl."

"You do know that this could be a complete waste of time," Charlie repeats, continuing to try to persuade James to call off this part of the assignment. "Even if a van was there, that doesn't mean the people in the van saw anything."

"I know, Charlie, but right now it's all we have. It's the only clue that hasn't been followed up on. We need to follow this trail until it takes us no further. The van was there during the right time period. Let's find the vehicle and the people who were inside it and learn what they saw that day."

It's around seven when Charlie gets up to stretch his legs. "Are we going to go out and get something to eat? I'm getting hungry."

"Let's order room service. I'd like to finish these files tonight," James responds.

It's nearly eleven when Kathy yells out, excited, "I think I got something!"

James jumps up from his chair and hurries to look over her shoulder. "What do you have?"

"This guy called in and said that he saw a young girl that came out of a van and went into his neighbor's house across and down the street from where he lives."

"Two for two," James yells out, looking at Charlie, "a van and a young girl." He turns to Kathy. "Let me see that message."

James takes a look at the note and walks over to the phone.

"Isn't it a little late to be calling a witness?" Charlie asks him.

"He's more likely to be home at this hour," James tells Charlie. He makes the call. The guy is indeed at home and agrees to meet them first thing in the morning, before he goes to work.

The next morning, at seven, James is at the tipster's house with Charlie. "Do you know who lives in the house you saw the girl going into?" James asks the witness.

"No. I usually keep to myself," the witness tells him.

"How many people were with the girl?"

"There were two others," the man answers.

"What did the two people look like? Can you give me a description?"

"No, I'm sorry, I didn't get a good look." the man shrugs. "It was dark and they were gone in an instant."

"How about the girl, can you describe what she looked like?"

"No, sorry, as I said it was dark and it all happened so fast."

"Have you seen the van since you made that call?"

The witness shakes his head. "Not since that night."

"May I ask why you didn't call this in to the police right away? Why'd you wait?"

"To tell you the truth, I didn't make the connection," he answers. "When I heard about the reward, I took a shot. What do you think? Will I get a reward?"

"I don't know, the reward is not mine to give." James points to a house across and down the street. "That's the house, right there? Are you sure?"

"Yeah, that's the house. I'm sure."

"Okay, thanks. Here's my number." James hands him a card. "If you remember anything else, please give me a call."

The witness gets in his car and drives off to work.

James looks at Charlie. "There's only one way to find out."

James knocks at the door. A pudgy, gray-haired, middle-aged lady answers. He shows her his private detective ID. "Pardon me, ma'am. My name is James Coppi, and this is my partner, Charlie McGill. We're investigating the disappearance of a young girl, Penelope Campos. You may have heard the name; it was all over the news a few months back. Would you mind if my partner and I came in and asked you a few questions?"

Inside the house, the woman's husband is sitting on the sofa with the television blaring. "Max, these men are investigating the disappearance of that young girl we saw on the news," she hollers.

Max gets up and turns off the TV. "I thought they caught the man that did it."

"We still haven't located the girl," James says. "Until we do, the investigation stays open."

"What do you want with us?" the husband asks. "We don't know anything about her disappearance."

"I was wondering if you saw something back in January." James takes out his notepad.

"We weren't even here in January," his wife answers. "We'd been in Florida for several months with my sick sister."

"We let my cousin use the house while we were gone," Max speaks up. "He's a distant relative; we hardly ever see him. He always seems to show up when he needs something. Like this last time, when he asked to use our house while we were away."

"What's your cousin's name?"

"Wheeler. His name is Isaiah Wheeler."

"Does your cousin have children?" James looks up from his pad. "Maybe a teenage daughter?"

"No, no children. At least none that I'm aware of."

"Do you know where we can reach your cousin?" James asks him. "He might have seen something."

"I really don't know." Max scratches his behind. "I think he mentioned that he might head for Yuma, Arizona, but I'm not really sure. He's a drifter. He moves from place to place."

"What does your cousin look like?"

"Tall, skinny fella." Max demonstrates with his hands to show James the man's height. "Long, gray hair down to his shoulders. middle-aged, has a beard."

"Okay. Thanks for your help," James replies, and begins to leave. Charlie looks at James, confused. James turns around when he gets to the door.

"By the way, Max, what kind of car does your cousin drive?"

"The last time I saw him, he drove a van. Why do you ask?"

"No particular reason, just asking. Maybe we can locate him through motor vehicle records. Would you happen to know the color?"

"I'm not quite sure," Max scratches his head. "White." He blurts out. "White, that was the color."

When they get outside, Charlie turns to James. "I'm guessing we're headed for Arizona?"

"Yup, as soon as possible." James has a broad smile on his face.

"Shouldn't we try to locate him through motor vehicle records?"

"We'll do that too, Charlie, but I'm betting the van is not registered under his name. Even if it *is* registered to him, there'll be no current address. You heard his cousin—the man is a drifter. No, Charlie, Isaiah is in Yuma, and that's where we'll find him. Of course, we'll also check motor vehicles records, but I'm betting we'll find nothing."

12
JAMES FACES HIS PAST

It's late Wednesday night when James, Kathy, and Charlie get back to Colorado Springs from their fieldwork in Albuquerque. Sam is there to greet them when James and Kathy walk into their apartment with their luggage. Sam gives her fiancé a hug and a kiss.

"You guys must be hungry," Sam says. "Do you want me to throw a meal together? It won't take long."

"No, we're good," James replies. "We stopped at a roadside diner to eat on the way back."

Sam puts her arms over his shoulders and gives him another kiss. "Well, let's get you caught up with what you've been missing."

Kathy shakes her head, grabs her suitcase, and heads for her room. "Can you at least keep it a little quieter this time?" she calls back to them.

"You better put a pillow over your head," Sam yells back. "I haven't seen James in three days; there's going to be a lot of noise."

"I've got to start looking for my own place," Kathy says under her breath. She slams the door to her room.

The next morning at the office, Charlie and James are standing in front of Kathy's desk.

"Make two reservations for a flight to Arizona for tomorrow," James tells Kathy. "Charlie and I need to get to Yuma ASAP. Get us a rental car, too. Don't worry about a hotel room; we'll find something when we get there."

"What about the rest of your clients, James?" Kathy asks. "Should I tell them to go screw themselves and take their business elsewhere?"

"*What?*" Her question catches him by surprise. "No, but the Campos matter takes precedence over everything else, Kathy."

"James, I don't want to tell you how to run your business, but you made promises to other clients," Kathy continues. "There's a law firm that's doing a deposition next Tuesday. They want to speak to you about your findings in the investigation. The file is on your desk; it's been there since last week.

"And what about Juan Gomez? His trial is in two weeks; did you forget him? His lawyer wants to meet with you to discuss your discoveries. That file is also on your desk.

"Three lawyers called and have summonses that need to be served. What do I tell them? And how about Big W? You made an appointment to meet with them tomorrow afternoon in Boulder. Should I call Big W and tell them that you're not interested in their business—that they should go elsewhere? I know this kidnapping case is important, James. That poor little girl, if she's still alive, must be living in terror. You should have thought of that before you made these other commitments. Now that you have these clients, you need to pay attention to them. You can't just simply ignore all of your other existing customers."

James rubs his hand through his dark hair. "You're absolutely right, Kathy! Thank God I have you. I'm such a lousy businessman." He looks over at Charlie. "Charlie, you'll have to go to Yuma without me. You can leave in the morning. I'll catch up with you in Yuma in a few days, as soon as I'm done here. Do me a favor and take care of the three summonses that need processing today." He turns to Kathy. "Please make sure that I'm not interrupted; I'm going to be very busy over the next couple of days."

That Sunday night, Charlie calls from his motel room and gives James an update on his trip so far in Yuma. James goes back into the living room after the call. Sam is sitting on the sofa; her legs are curled under her. She has a bottle of beer in her hand. He picks up his bottle of beer from the coffee table, where it's been waiting for him, and sits down next to her.

"Where's Kathy?" he asks Sam, taking a slug of the beer.

"I'm not really sure. She may be out with Bobby. Why do you ask?"

"I need to go to Arizona in the morning. I need to speak to Kathy before I leave."

"You're going to be away again? You just came back!"

"Yes, I have to go there. Charlie's not finding anything; I'm sure he needs some help."

"Charlie is doing a good job. What makes you think you can do any better? Maybe there's just nothing to be found."

"Sam, please don't give me a hard time; I have to go. I can't just sit around on my ass while that poor girl is missing. You're probably right; there may be nothing to find. But I for sure won't find anything sitting around here doing nothing. We ran a check on the van through the department of motor vehicles. There's nothing registered under the name Isaiah Wheeler. If there is a clue, it's in Arizona, not here. I'm all caught up on my work at the office. I need to get out to the field."

"When will you be back?" she asks, taking a sip of her beer.

"A couple of days. Why do you ask? Do you need me for something?"

"We need to go back to Lorenzo," Sam tells him. "Our wedding is only a little over a month away. We need to get down there and make the final arrangements. You know, I can't do this wedding alone, James. We can go down next Saturday, right after my work. Maybe we can look in on Aggie and the kids on the way down. Remember that you promised Aggie the last time we spoke to her that we would stop by her place on our next trip?"

"Okay. Going to Lorenzo is good, but we can't stop by Aggie's place; we just won't have the time. You need to be back here by Monday night. You have work the next day."

"I'm taking that Tuesday off, so we should have plenty of time. Besides, Aggie's visit will only take an hour at most. That shouldn't interfere with our plans at all."

"I don't want to stop by Aggie's place," he says, taking a sip of his beer.

"Why not?"

"I don't want to talk about it!"

"No, I'm sorry, James, that's not a good enough answer," she fires back. "I've been very patient with you. Aggie is our friend, and we can't shun her forever. I need to know why you would generously give her more than nine thousand dollars a few months ago and now refuse to even sit in the same room with her. If you want to avoid meeting with her, you're going to have to give me a very good reason. Just saying 'I don't want to talk about it' won't cut it any longer."

He sits back in the chair, sips his beer, and looks up at the ceiling. "I had just gotten back from an operation in the DMZ during the Vietnam War," James begins. "This was the second mission in a row that I'd been on—two in two weeks. A message came in that the captain—my CO—wanted to see me and Lieutenant Zomme at company headquarters. Zomme was with me on the two previous missions.

"When Zomme and I get there, the CO told us that a guy named Sergeant Camby has come up with a plan to send out a squad of men on an ambush. The ambush site was at a place called the Rock Pile. The CO asked me what I thought of the idea, and I told him that the whole idea sucked. 'It's a suicide mission,' is how I phrased it. The CO overruled me and said the plan was on. I refused to go. The CO and I got into an argument over my refusal."

"Can you really refuse an order?" Sam asks.

James smiles. "Normally, no, but this was Vietnam, Sam. Things were a lot different. The war had become extremely unpopular. Men were always questioning the higher ranks. I read somewhere that there were more than a hundred fraggings."

"What's a fragging?" she asks.

"That's when a higher up gets killed by one of his own men. Usually when he's really unpopular or when he wants to lead the men into a dangerous situation."

"Did that really happen?"

"Yes, it did! A lot! Anyway, after refusing to go on the mission, I appealed to the captain and to his sense of fairness. I told the CO that it wasn't right that Zomme and I were going on another operation. We had just finished two major operations and it wasn't right that he was sending us right back out. Other men were available who hadn't gone out in months. My argument worked. The CO said Zomme and I didn't have to go."

James pauses for a moment and then looks at Sam. "That was the mission when Hall was killed. How do I look Aggie in the face and tell her that I refused to go, but her husband ended up going? That because I refused, I'm alive…and maybe, because I refused, her husband is dead?"

Sam shakes her head. "How was this your fault, James? I don't get it. You warned the captain that the plan was bad. You told him it was a suicide mission. James, you had every right to object to going. Zomme and you had recently come back from *two* operations. You risked your life, I'm sure, on those missions. Had you gone on the ambush, you might well be dead today, along with Hall. You have nothing to apologize for, or regret.

"Besides, James, Aggie doesn't want to talk about Hall's last mission. She wants to see you and thank you for your kindness. If Aggie does any reminiscing about Hall, it'll be about happier times—not his final moments. Please, James, come with me to look in on Aggie."

James takes another sip of his beer. "All right," he finally capitulates. "We'll go."

Sam leans over and gives him a kiss. "Thank you," she says, looking up at him. "Is that why those two boxes are thrown in the corner of your closet in the bedroom? Because of the memories?"

"There's nothing important in those boxes—just some junk," James says, trying to minimize the issue. "I just haven't gotten around to tossing those boxes out."

Sam gives him a sly glance. "If I'm not mistaken, James, those packages contain medals from the US Army. Am I wrong?"

"No, you're right." He lets out a deep breath. "I just threw them in the closet because the whole idea of medals is stupid. Hall probably got decorations, and what good did those medals do him? I'm sure Aggie couldn't care less about the medals. She probably threw them in the corner of her closet, just like I did.

"What a stupid concept. One guy does his job and nearly gets himself killed, and the army gives him a medal. Another guy *does* get killed, and the army gives his family a memento to show its appreciation. What does the act even mean? Give Aggie some money to help her out; maybe that would be an actual help. Instead they send her some stupid, fifty-cent medal." James waves his hands dismissively. "What the hell is Aggie going to do with a damn medal? She can't even hock it to feed her family."

It is midafternoon the following day when James gets to Yuma. It was a long, tedious trip to get there from Colorado Springs—two flights and four stops. He looks out of the window of the small prop plane, with seven passengers aboard, as it makes its final approach to the airport in Yuma. Near the runway, he notices tall cacti. He read somewhere that these huge plants may be a hundred or even two hundred years old. One has to wonder—how does any living thing get to be so old? Unlike humans, who seem to decay as they get older, these plants appear to grow more majestic as they age. Aging seems to agree with them.

It is sweltering hot when James comes out of the terminal. Charlie is waiting outside, sitting in the rental car. They drive to a nearby diner to have a late lunch. Because of the hour, the place is empty. They are the only customers.

"I've been to the police stations. Stopped in every single restaurant and gas station in town," Charlie says to James while they take seats in a booth. "Nobody has seen the van, the bearded man, or the girl. I've got no elsewhere to look; I think we've reached the proverbial end of the road."

"Charlie, if you were hiding out and wanted to stay out of sight, would you stay in town, or on the outskirts?" James muses.

"The outskirts," he replies.

"That's right—on the outskirts." James continues to consider. "You know, I think you've been looking in all the wrong places. Let's take a ride outside of town this afternoon and see what we can find out in the boonies. I'll bet you a cup of coffee that someone out in the sticks has seen something. I've got a good feeling about this."

Charlie grabs hold of James's arm. "It'll be like looking for a needle in a haystack—feeling or no feeling. How will you know what house he's in? It's a really big county."

"No, Charlie," James says. "I think we can narrow it down a little bit. What two things does our man need to survive?"

"Food and water."

"All right, I was wrong," James concedes with a smile. "There are three things a man needs to survive out in the boonies. He needs food, water—and gasoline for his van. We'll just concentrate on where food and gasoline are sold. Someone must have seen a bearded man in a white van. It's a pretty conspicuous combination. How many bearded men driving a white van can there be in this county?"

They spend most of the remainder of the afternoon asking at gas stations and grocery stores, on the outskirts of Yuma but they have no luck. When it gets dark, they decide to get something to eat and then turn in. They have dinner at the same diner they ate in earlier in the day, which is right down the street from their motel.

"I told you that it wouldn't be easy," Charlie reminds James, taking a bite of his taco. "You ready to give up yet?"

"You're right, Charlie—it isn't going to be easy. But I feel good." James bites into his cheeseburger, chews, and swallows. "I'm going to win that cup of coffee. The grocery stores and gas stations that we visited today weren't very crowded. They didn't have a lot of customers. When we hit upon the right one, somebody there should remember seeing our man.

"I'm pretty confident we'll find him *and* the place where they're living. I feel more sure tonight than I did when I first arrived. We'll be right back out there first thing tomorrow. We just need to hit upon the right place. If this fellow Isaiah came to Yuma, like he told his cousin he would, we'll find him. It's only a matter of time."

"Did you bring your gun?" Charlie asks him.

"What gun?" The question catches him by surprise. He stops in the middle of taking another bite of the cheeseburger. "I don't own a gun."

Charlie laughs and shakes his head. "You're a private detective and you don't have a gun? What are you going to do when you meet up with this guy—talk to him nicely and hope he turns himself in?"

"Damn it, Charlie!" James throws down his food. "I never thought about a gun. Do you have a gun?"

"Yeah, of course I do." Charlie laughs. "Lucky for you, I brought it along. You better go and get your own gun real soon. Meanwhile, you can just stand behind me if we get into a situation."

That night in his motel room, James can't sleep. He's feeling restless and nervous. Doubts are creeping in on the case. How will he ever find the kidnappers? Charlie, a cop with years of experience, can't locate these people. *What makes me think that I can do better. What if I fuck it all up. What if I get this poor girl killed because of my stupidity. Fuck, I wish I had some pills right about now.*

He decides to go for a walk. About five blocks from the motel he happens by a bar. *I'll go in and have a beer*, he decides. Inside the place is crowded and smoke filled.

"What'll be?" The bartender asks him when he takes a seat at the bar.

"A beer. Anything you have on tap is good."

"That'll be twenty cents," the barkeep says to him as he places the glass down on the bar.

James pays the man and sips on his beer. He looks across the bar at some of the people on the other side. He stops in the midst of his drink when he recognizes a face. There's a man he knows with a shot of booze in front of him. James places down his glass on the bar and walks to the other side.

"I hope that's apple juice in that glass," he says to the man when he gets there.

"Oh, shit!" The man blurts out when he recognizes James.

"What the fuck, man?" James says angrily. "You're back off the fucking wagon. Or did you lie to me you no good motherfucker? You never gave up drinking!"

"No, James, that's not true. Only tonight, I swear! I just couldn't take being in my room all alone. It just got to me. Please, give me another chance."

"Another chance? How many more fucking chances do you want me to give you? What about that story of your wife? How you were never going to disappoint that wonderful woman anymore? All fucking lies, Charlie!"

Charlie doesn't answer, he's looking down at the glass.

"How many drinks have you had?"

"Just one," he points to the glass in front of him. "This would've been my second."

"Get the fuck out of here." James says. "We'll talk about this in the morning. Be up by seven, I got a big day ahead of me tomorrow."

"So, what did you decide?" Charlie asks him the next morning.

"Charlie, the only thing that's saving your sorry ass is that I know what you're going through. I have my own problems with addiction. But you need to think long and hard. What's the road you want to be on? If you need help recovering, I'll do anything to give you that help. But, if you sneak around and don't want to help yourself, then I'm going to let you go. So, I'm warning you, this is your last chance. It's all up to you."

Midmorning, Charlie and James pull into the Sinclair station. The sign says Ralph's grocery and gas. They are some ten miles outside of Yuma. It is a dusty stop—the parking area is unpaved. The place is completely empty. Charlie parks the car in front of the store's entrance and shuts off the engine.

"Are you ready to give up?" Charlie asks. "We've been to dozens of stations. Nobody has heard of your man or seen the white van."

"What's the matter, Charlie, are you getting edgy? Suffering from DT's from lack of booze?"

Charlie looks straight ahead. He turns to James. "You know James, saying stuff like that isn't going to help. You want to fire me, then do it! Don't keep beating me up. That doesn't help."

James swallows. He knows he's gone too far. "I'm sorry. You're right. Seeing you at that bar last night was shocking. But you're a hundred percent right, remarks like my last one is out of bounds. I really want to help you Charlie. I really do. If you ever get the urge to drink, reach out to me. Please."

Charlie opens the door. "Come on. Let's get this over with."

A middle-aged woman is sitting behind the counter. She doesn't bother to get up when she sees the men.

"Pardon me, ma'am," James says to her. "We're private detectives from New York City." He's decided to start with the opening line that he's used more than a dozen times already today. "We were hired by a law firm to find a man who may be in these parts. You see, ma'am, this man inherited a whole lot of money. Unfortunately, the poor stiff doesn't know anything about the inheritance. Time is running out. If we don't find him by the end of May, the money goes to the state of New York. He's a bearded fellow who drives a white van. He has a teenage daughter. Maybe you've seen them around here."

"I've seen the man," she says, "but not the girl. Hold on a minute. I'll get my husband, Ralph. I think he may know where the guy lives." She gets up and walks to the back of the store. James looks over at Charlie and winks.

An older man wearing blue coveralls and a baseball cap with a gasoline company logo on it comes walking out. "Maggie says you're looking for the bearded guy who drives a white van?" Ralph asks when he gets to them.

"Yes, sir," James answers. "Would you know where we can find him?"

"Sure do. He came in here a few times to buy groceries and get some gas. He was living at Smitty's place, not too far from here."

"You said he *was* living at Smitty's place?" James asks. "He's not there any longer?"

"The bearded fellow moved out just before Easter, a few days before Smitty came home. He filled his van with gas and drove off. Didn't say where he was headed. Smitty says the people were squatters. They broke into his place and lived there while he was away. You should have heard old Smitty hollerin' and complaining. Apparently, they left his place in a real mess. I hope that they're long gone. I'd hate to see what would happen if Smitty caught up with them."

"How long were they here?"

Ralph scratches his head. "I'm not really sure. I'm figuring two, maybe three months."

"Did you ever see him with a teenage girl? I think she's a blonde."

"I saw him with a young girl once," the man replies, "but she had dark hair, not blonde." *Dark hair?* James thinks. *Is this the same girl?* Then it hits him. *Of course! They died her hair. That would make perfect sense. They wanted to disguise her.*

"Can you tell me how to get to Smitty's place?"

Armed with directions, Charlie and James drive to the small house made of adobe bricks. A rusted, old, blue, Ford pickup truck is parked out front. They knock at the door. A stocky- full bearded man wearing blue jeans and a flannel shirt and sporting long gray hair tied back in a ponytail answers the door.

"I really don't know the guy who was in my place," the man named Smitty responds when questioned by James. "The house was supposed to be empty while I was visiting someone in New Mexico. When I came home, right around Easter, I found this place in a mess. It took me nearly a week to clean it up."

"How long were you in New Mexico?"

"About six months."

"When you were in New Mexico, did you come into contact with a man who had a goatee and drove a white van?"

Smitty deliberates for a moment. Then his face lights up. "Yeah, I did... Isaiah—that was his name. I ran into him a couple of times. He was a real weird fellow. It always made me nervous to be around him. Is he the one that broke into my house? Boy, I'd sure like to run into him again; he left this place in a real mess."

"Maybe he's your guy," James replies. "I can't really say for sure. Do you remember if he had a daughter? A teenage girl?"

"No, I'm sorry, I don't recall him having a daughter. If he did, I never saw her."

"Do you mind if we have a look around? I promise not to make a mess."

"Well, as long as you're not planning to make a mess, you can have a look. I sure don't feel like cleaning up another one."

The place is small. There's a kitchen with a fireplace in it, an eating area, and a bedroom. No bathroom. James wonders what kind of a mess Isaiah could have made that took a week to clean up. Charlie and James walk into the bedroom and have a look around. There is nothing much to see. James is about to leave when something behind the bed catches his eye.

"Charlie, help me pull the bed out a little."

When they pull the bed out, James kneels down to take a closer look.

"What is it?" Charlie asks.

He looks up and tells Charlie, "Something is etched into the wall."

"What does it say?"

"It's hard to make out," James responds. He gets to his feet. "Here, get down and take a look for yourself. Maybe you can make it out."

Charlie kneels down and takes a look. "All I can make out is the letter *C* and the letter *T*." Charlie gets back up and dusts himself off. "The rest is scratched out. I can't really tell what it says."

"Do me a favor, Charlie—go to the car and get another piece of paper."

When Charlie comes back with the paper, James kneels back down. He copies the images that are on the wall.

James gets back up and shows Charlie what's on the paper. "What does it look like to you?"

"It's hard to say." Charlie squints. "It looks like the first scratch is either a letter or a number. The second is the letter *C*; that's clear. The third symbol could be part of another letter or possibly a number, and the fourth is the letter *T*."

James takes the note back and looks at it again. "The first symbol looks like a little circle. You see? It's smaller than the letters. The little circle could be part of a letter, or it could be part of a number. Possibly a piece of the plaster fell off. If that's true and the little circle represents a number, it would be the number six, eight, or nine. Those are the only numbers with a little circle. If the little circle is part of a letter, the letter has to be *B*, *P*, or *R*. Those are the only letters with a little circle.

"So, I'm guessing it's not a number but a letter, maybe a *P* for Penelope. That means the first two letters are *P* and *C*, the initials of Penelope Campos." He looks into Charlie's face. "Charlie, I believe Penelope carved her initials into the wall to let someone know that she was here. What do you think?"

"It makes sense, if you assume she was here. She may have carved those letters on the wall behind the bed, where they wouldn't be noticed."

"That's my thinking, too. She was trying to tell us something." James dusts himself off with one hand while continuing to look at the paper.

"What if you're wrong?" Charlie asks him. "What if these markings were scratched there a long time ago? These walls don't look like they've been painted in a while. These marks could have been made at any time."

"No, Charlie, I don't agree. The markings look fresh." James looks around the room. "Besides, if Isaiah *was* in this house, who is the teenage girl described by the gas station owner? According to his cousin, Isaiah doesn't have a daughter. The most likely explanation is that the girl at the gas station was Penelope Campos.

"The letter *C* is clearly visible." James continues examining the paper. "There's no doubt about that letter. It's not too much of a leap to assume the first letter is *P*. Putting all this together, Charlie, the first two marks are her initials, and Penelope is the one who carved the letters. Who else would have carved out these letters? No, Charlie, she did it. She tried to send a message." James is getting excited and continues to ramble on. "Now, all we have to do is try to figure out what the message is that she tried to communicate."

Smitty comes walking in. "You guys almost done?"

"Yes, Mr. Smith, we're done," James replies. "Mr. Smith, when you cleaned up the house, did you find some wall plaster on the corner of this bed?"

"Maybe so, but I can't really say; the place was so dirty."

"Well, that's all. We're done, Mr. Smith. Thanks for your help," James tells him. He and Charlie walk out to the car.

In the car, Charlie asks, "What else have you got?"

"Not much more." James is still fixated on the note in his hand. "Assuming there are no numbers in the message, we have *P*, *C*, and *T* for sure. Then the three possibilities for the third letter are *B*, *P*, and *R*. Are we looking at the initials of the kidnappers? Well, we're supposing that the kidnapper is named Isaiah, so his initials aren't part of this clue. Maybe they're the initials of Isaiah's partner? You know, both the gardener Martinez and the accused Fontana said they saw two people in the van. Maybe these are the initials of that other person?

"Or are the letters the initials of something else? Not a name, maybe a place? It's a message all right, but what the hell does it mean? That's anybody's guess."

"Charlie, I'm going to stop and visit Greenwald and his daughter in Albuquerque on the way back. We've discovered enough to get the FBI involved." He sits back in his seat. "I'm satisfied that you and I did a good job. We've uncovered a lot, but what we've found goes beyond our ability to continue our investigation. This fellow Isaiah could have gone anywhere after he left here.

"We need help. Lots of help. We need the FBI. This case is over for us, but we found enough that it shouldn't take the FBI long to catch this guy. We have the kidnapper's name, a description of what he looks like, and the color of the van he's driving. I'll give Greenwald the report and hand this case over to the feds. With their manpower, they should have this guy in custody before the month is out. This young girl should be home soon."

James starts the engine. "By the way, Charlie, you owe me a cup of coffee."

13
DEAD END

James decides not to fly but rents a car and drives all the way to Albuquerque after finishing up in Yuma. He has sent Charlie home, telling him to take a few days off and spend time with his wife and children. Charlie won't be needed on the Campos case anymore, and nothing is happening at the office. He also reminded Charlie to get back to AA. Warned him one more time that this was his last chance. He hopes Charlie gets his act together. He's grown fond of the big Palooka.

The meeting will be held at the Campos's house; Greenwald will be there, and James hopes the FBI will be there, too. Greenwald was supposed to arrange for them to attend.

The area of the search has gotten too big for James and his agency to handle. With all the information that he's uncovered, he thinks it shouldn't take the FBI long to round up this character. If the FBI gets a move on, this young girl could be home with her family before the week is out. He did not tell Greenwald of his findings yet; he will give him a full update at the meeting.

At the Campos house, Elizabeth Campos lets him in. "No one is here yet; you're the first," she tells him. She leads him into the living room. "Please have a seat." She gestures to the sofa.

James takes a seat. Elizabeth sits on a chair across from him. Elizabeth Campos is a real beauty—tall and sexy, with a beautiful figure, dark hair down to her shoulders, green eyes, and a chiseled, classical face. *She could have been a model*, James thinks. *Never mind "could have been"—she could still be a model*. He's getting aroused just sitting across from her.

"Is Mr. Campos at home?" James asks her.

"No, Mr. Campos doesn't live here any longer; we've recently separated. He will not be attending the meeting."

"I'm sorry to hear about the separation. Sometimes these tragedies put a lot of strain on marriages."

"Yes," Elizabeth says with the hint of a smirk, "and sometimes these tragedies reveal a lot of hidden secrets about a partner," she adds. "Secrets like how a partner was keeping a mistress on the side for years."

James stares intently at Elizabeth. "I'm sorry. I didn't mean to bring up anything so unpleasant."

The doorbell rings, and Elizabeth gets up and lets the visitor in. It's Henry Greenwald. James gets up to greet him.

"So, I hear you have news," Greenwald remarks, extending his hand.

"I do, sir." James shakes his hand.

"Let me take your coat, Daddy," Elizabeth offers.

"Okay, James, let's have the news," Greenwald barks after handing his jacket to his daughter. "Let's get right to it. I'm eager to learn what you have found."

The doorbell rings again before James can begin. Greenwald opens the door. FBI agents Spencer and Levin come in, along with District Attorney Simon Gold.

"Now that everyone is here, why don't we all take seats in the dining room?" Elizabeth Campos suggests.

On the dining room table are two trays of sandwiches and two trays of cookies. He has not eaten a thing since lunch the day before. He would love to reach out and grab something, but nobody else is moving for the food.

The maid comes into the room from the kitchen. "Will there be anything else, Mrs. Campos?" she asks.

"No, Magdalena, that will be all. We won't be needing anything else."

Once the maid has left, Greenwald, who is sitting at the head of the table next to James, takes charge of the meeting. "All right, James, you called us all here. What have you got?"

James looks over across the table at Elizabeth Campos. "First of all, Mrs. Campos, I have a piece of great news. It is my belief that your daughter, Penelope, is still alive. At least she was the last time anyone saw her—a month ago, around Easter."

"What?" Elizabeth exclaims, her hands covering her mouth. Tears start streaming down her face. "Oh my God, that's wonderful! Is it true? Are you sure?"

"How can you make a statement like that, Coppi?" Gold yells from the other head of the table. "I hope this isn't another one of your cockamamie theories."

"No, Gold, this is not a theory," James says in his own defense. "Let me start from the beginning." James takes a look around the table before he begins.

"There was another vehicle at the school on the afternoon when Penelope was abducted," James says, beginning his account. "A white van. The van was only there for a short time—no more than a few minutes before Penelope came out of school. There were two people inside the van. This fact was confirmed by both the gardener, Martinez, and by Fontana, the man who is locked up.

"Both Martinez, and Fontana remembered seeing the van that day, and both remembered that there were two people in the van. Unfortunately, there wasn't much of a description of those people. Neither of the two witnesses got a good look at the van occupants. The only description given was that the passenger had a beard. Charlie and I went through the thousands of tips received on this case by the police. We were looking for a caller who saw either a white van or a man with a beard.

"We got very lucky. We found a message from a caller who reported something suspicious. Two people in a white van and a teenage girl were seen across from his house. When we got there, the caller pointed us to an address where he'd last seen the girl. We interviewed the couple who lived at the house. They told us that they'd been away in Florida for six months and while they were away they let a distant relative, a cousin named Isaiah, use the home. This cousin Isaiah happens to have a beard and also owns a white van."

James pauses for a moment and looks at the trays of sandwiches again. He is starving—he would love to grab a bite, but still no one else is reaching over for a sandwich.

"Is that *it*?" Gold scoffs. "Is *that* all you've got?"

"No, I've got more," James fires back, beginning to get annoyed at Gold. "The owner of the house told me that he thought his cousin Isaiah Wheeler had gone to Yuma, Arizona. I felt this was a promising lead. It was too much of a coincidence that a man with a beard in a white van was at the school and was seen hours later with a teenage girl. We took a trip to Arizona this past week to do some searching. We finally located a gas station attendant who remembered seeing a man with a goatee and a white van.

"Of more interest, the gas station owner stated that on one occasion, he saw a teenage girl with the bearded man. Except the girl wasn't blonde. The owner described the teenager as having dark hair. It's my belief that the kidnappers have dyed Penelope's hair to disguise her appearance.

"I'm figuring that the attendant has to be talking about this fellow Isaiah. His cousin said that Isaiah was heading for Yuma—and here he was seen driving into a gas station in Yuma. More importantly, there was a teenage girl with him. When I interviewed Isaiah's cousin in Albuquerque, he told me that Isaiah had no children. The teenager had to be Penelope. Who else could it be? Where would Isaiah come up with another teenager? In any event, the owner of the gas station gave me an address of where they were living. When I got there, they were gone. The owner of the house—a fellow named Smith—said to me that squatters had broken into the place and made themselves at home there while he was away."

James stares around the room to gauge everyone's reaction. Both Greenwald and Elizabeth appear to be listening attentively. Gold seems to be annoyed. Or is James just imagining that he's irritated. The FBI agents sitting next to him aren't giving him a clue one way or another whether they're interested in what he's saying. He goes back to his account.

"Remarkably, Mr. Smith had been in Albuquerque during the previous six months and met Isaiah, the bearded man who owned the van. It's my opinion that Isaiah knew that Smith would be in Albuquerque for the next three months and that Smith's house in Yuma was going to be completely empty. We searched Smith's house for any clues that the kidnappers might have left behind. Behind the bed, I located something etched on the wall. This is a copy of what I found scratched on the wall." James hands out the paper with the copy of the etching. The paper is passed around the table.

James looks over at Elizabeth. "Mrs. Campos, it is my belief that it was your daughter who scratched these markings on the wall. From what I can determine, the second letter, *C*, stands for Campos. The first object shown on my note looks like a little circle. The plaster of the wall had fallen off and possibly erased the remainder of the symbol. I believe that the little circle is part of a letter or number.

"If I'm correct and that circle is part of a letter or number, there are only six possibilities for the first mark I noted: the number six, eight, or nine, or the letter *P*, *B*, or *R*. In my opinion, the most likely possibility is the letter *P*—which, along with the *C*, could be the initials of Penelope Campos. Penelope etched her initials into that wall to let us know she was there. If we stay with letters, instead of numbers, the third etching, that of another little circle, can only be the letter *B*, *P*, or *R*. That letter would go with the last letter, *T*, which is clearly visible. So, we would have the initials B. T., P. T., or R. T.

"Those last two letters are the initials of either a person or a place. The bearded man's name is known to be Isaiah Wheeler, so those are not his initials. There is a second suspect—the other person who was seen in the van—still unidentified. Those could be his initials. However, I don't believe that those initials refer to a person at all. I believe they refer to a place. Penelope was trying to communicate to us where the kidnappers were taking her next."

James stops and sits quietly. He turns to Greenwald. "That's it, sir. That's what I have. I don't have the manpower to do the search that's needed to locate these suspects. From now on, you need an agency like the FBI; that's why I asked that they to be here today." He looks over at the two agents sitting next to him. "We have a name of the suspect, Isaiah Wheeler, a description of him, and a description of his vehicle. You guys have resources to do the necessary search. It shouldn't take long to locate these characters." He turns back to Greenwald. "I have the utmost confidence that when the FBI catches up with this man Isaiah, we will also find your granddaughter."

Gold is the first one to speak up. "Frankly, Henry, this young man has nothing at all. He's got a bunch of things carved on a wall that anyone could have done. There's no evidence that Penelope herself made the markings. We have only his wild guess about what they might mean. The guy at the gas station—the man he calls an eyewitness—didn't describe your granddaughter. He described a dark-haired girl. Once again, James has a lot of conjecture, suppositions, and opinions—but no hard facts. He's just tugging at your heartstrings, Henry. If you follow his advice, you'll be chasing windmills."

"What's your opinion, Spence?" Greenwald asks one of the FBI agents.

"Henry, I agree with James. What he describes is worth looking into," Agent Spencer replies. "This looks very promising. There're just too many coincidences to rule out James's theory. The bearded man is in Albuquerque at the same time your granddaughter was abducted. A van similar to the one he drives was at the school. Two eyewitnesses saw this man with a young girl—one in Albuquerque, and another in Yuma."

James cannot resist the temptation of the sandwiches any longer. He reaches over, grabs one, and takes a bite.

"I'm going to recommend that we begin an investigation into this Isaiah Wheeler," Spencer continues. "We'll put out an all-points bulletin on the man and his van."

"I'll do one better than that, Spence," Greenwald lets out. "I'll go to the news media and offer a reward. A hundred grand should get us some action. We'll have everybody in the region looking for him. With that much of a reward, it shouldn't take long before someone spots him."

"I wouldn't do that, Mr. Greenwald," Agent Spencer advises him. "When you announce the reward, we'll receive thousands of calls from crackpots. My men will be tied up on wild-goose chases for months. We'll have no time for investigating. Please give us a chance to do some serious investigating instead."

Greenwald turns to James, who has a mouthful of food and is about to reach for another sandwich.

"What do you have to say, James? Should I post the reward?"

James chews his food and swallows. "I'm with Agent Spencer on this one, sir," he replies, reaching over for another sandwich and putting it on his plate. "I believe that a lot of publicity will put your granddaughter in danger. Right now, these people believe that they've outsmarted us. There's no reason for the kidnappers to panic. They believe that they've gotten away with the crime because they know there's another man in jail accused of it. They may not even be in hiding.

"If we go public, they may realize that we're on to them, and they may panic. Who knows what they'll do if they think that authorities are closing in? They may want to eliminate the only witness who ties them directly to the crime—your granddaughter, Penelope. Let them continue to believe they've gotten away with the crime. They're more likely to come out into the open, where the FBI can nab them. It's just a matter of time before they make another mistake. Wait on posting the reward, sir. Let the FBI do their job. That's my recommendation." James pauses and starts eating the second sandwich.

"All right, gentlemen. I trust James's advice. We'll hold off posting the reward for now." Greenwald begins to get up. "Mr. Spencer, I trust you will keep me and Mr. Coppi in the loop with regular updates?"

"Yes, of course, Mr. Greenwald, I will," Spencer replies. The men get up, too. Greenwald escorts them to the door. James puts down his sandwich when Greenwald gets back.

"I'm sorry, Mr. Greenwald—was it your intention to keep me in the investigation?" James shrugs. "I really don't know how much more I can offer. The FBI is your best bet now."

"No, I'm sorry, James. I don't agree," Greenwald responds. "I still believe you're my best option. You've uncovered more in two weeks than the entire police force has uncovered in four months."

Greenwald turns to his daughter. "What say you, Elizabeth? Do you agree with me? Should James stay involved?"

Elizabeth looks over at James and says, "I agree with you, Daddy. I have the utmost confidence in James. You were correct all along: he is the right man for the job."

"Good," Greenwald concludes. "Well, that's settled, then. James, you'll stay on the investigation. Don't forget that there's a large reward for you if my granddaughter is returned alive. Please continue to keep me informed as to your progress."

Greenwald stands up from the table. "Thank you, James, for all your efforts. Keep up the good work. You brought me a good piece of news today, and I know you will bring me more. Now I must leave; I have some business to attend to.

"Elizabeth, why don't you get James something to drink? Make sure he gets plenty to eat, too; he has a long journey home this evening."

Elizabeth gets up and escorts her father to the door. She gives him a kiss after she opens the door. "Don't worry, Daddy, I'll make sure James is fully satiated before he leaves."

"What would you like to drink?" Elizabeth asks James when she gets back to the dining room.

"I'll have a Coke, please."

She comes back with the Coke and sits across from him. They spend a little time making small talk. He's having a hard time making eye contact with her, because her beauty makes him uneasy. He finishes his sandwich and takes a last swig of his Coke.

"I'd better get going. Mrs. Campos, would you mind if I use your bathroom before I leave?"

"Not at all. It's right down the hall, second door on your left."

When he comes back out, she walks arm in arm with him to the door. She turns James to her and reaches up to give him a kiss.

"Thanks for all that you're doing to find my daughter."

James bends down to kiss her, assuming the kiss is going on the cheek. Instead Elizabeth wraps her arms around his neck and pulls him to her. The kiss is passionate and right on the lips. James instinctively wraps his arms around her and pulls her to him. His mouth opens and her tongue slides in. Her hand reaches down to his groin and begins caressing his already hardened member. His hands slide down her back, and he begins stroking her ass. He pulls her more tightly against him. *My God*, he's thinking, *I'm going to make love to this beauty*. Then Sam's face comes into his mind and he stops kissing her.

"What's the matter? Don't you want to?"

James tries to push her away gently. "I'm sorry, I shouldn't...I have a wonderful woman waiting for me at home."

"She'll never know." Elizabeth draws closer and her hand reaches for his groin.

James reels back. "*I'll* know." He removes her hand. "Please understand, I can't do this to her; it wouldn't be right. She doesn't deserve this—she's too precious to me."

"Wow," Elizabeth says. Then she smiles. "That's one lucky girl. Not many men would have turned me down."

"Believe me, I know." He lets out a sigh.

As he leaves, Elizabeth says, "Well, if you ever change your mind, the door is always open."

James sits in his car and takes a deep breath when he's outside. "Whew," he says aloud. "Sam, I hope you appreciate what I just did for you, and how hard it was for me to turn that lady down. Not that you'll ever know...this episode will be my secret." James starts up the car and heads for home.

Sam is lying on the couch watching television when James walks into the apartment carrying his suitcase. She immediately jumps up and runs to him. She wraps her arms around him and gives him a passionate kiss.

"I'm so glad you're home! I really missed you. Are you hungry? I can throw something together real fast."

"Let me put away my suitcase," James says to her, loosening her grasp. He reaches down, grabs his bag, and heads for the bedroom. Sam follows behind.

He slides open his closet door and shoves his suitcase inside. "I'll unpack the bag tomorrow," he says. "I'm in no mood to do any unpacking tonight."

As he turns, she reaches for him and pulls him on top of her on the bed.

Sam and James: The Missing Teen

"How about a little treat before dinner?" Sam proposes.

After the "treat," Sam takes a steak from the refrigerator. James joins her in the kitchen.

"My God, what got into you?" she remarks.

"What do you mean?"

"I didn't think you were ever going to let me go. We spent nearly forty minutes in there! You must have been really horny. How many times did you come, anyway?"

"Twice," he replies, giving her a satisfied smile. "What are you complaining about? You seemed to enjoy yourself."

Changing the subject, Sam says, "I'm cooking you a steak, I have a salad as a side dish. Do you want a potato or some rice to go along with that?"

"No, a steak and salad is good. I'm not that hungry; I had a big lunch. Do I have time for a shower before dinner?"

"Yes, you have time."

He comes out of the shower wearing his pajamas. His hair is still damp.

"Dinner is almost ready," Sam says to him when he walks into the kitchen.

He grabs her in an embrace. "What, no more treats?"

Sam shoves him off her. "You're insatiable tonight!"

James sits down in his chair and smiles, "I guess you're just getting too old to keep up with me," he says.

She puts the steak on a plate and places it in front of him. She bends down and gives him a kiss.

"I'll tell you what. If you're up for it, you can have me for dessert," she says.

14
THE MATTER OF THE MEDALS

"You slept late," Sam says to him the next morning and laughs. "I hope I didn't wear you out."

"Very funny! Has Kathy already left for work?"

"Yes, she's gone. What's on your schedule today?"

"Why are *you* still here?" he asks, ignoring her question. "Don't you have to work?"

"I'm working the late shift today."

"You're still working late shifts? I thought that when they made you manager that you could set your own schedule. How come you're still pulling the late shift?" He goes over to grab a cup from the cupboard.

"A good manager has to check on her people from time to time. So, once a week, I work the late shift to check on how they're doing—you know, to get a firsthand look at what goes on during the later shift."

"Smart move," he says as he pours himself a cup of coffee.

"You didn't answer my question. What are you doing today?" she asks. "You don't seem to be in a hurry to get to the office."

"I've got to take back the rental car, and I was hoping that Kathy would pick me up. But maybe you can give me a lift, since you have time this morning. Later, I'm going to the office. I'll be real busy, so don't wait up for me. I need to prepare for my follow-up meeting tomorrow in Boulder."

"You do remember that we're going to Lorenzo this weekend, right?" she reminds him. "We're also going to stop by Aggie's place."

"Yes, I remember," James answers, blowing on his hot coffee. "I'm going to buy toys for the twins: a fire truck for one and a police car for the other. That means you'll have to buy the housewarming present for Aggie."

"Oh. So, I walk in with a toaster and you walk in with toys?" She gives him an arch look. "That ought to make me really popular with the kids."

James begins laughing. "Don't complain. I'll put your name on the card."

She gives him a slap on the arm. "They're only three years old. They can't read."

He begins laughing even harder. "I don't know what to tell you."

"I can see that when *we* have children, you'll be the spoiler and I'll be the disciplinarian."

"Well, of course! That's the logical division of labor," James laughs. "You're the bossy one…always slapping and hitting people."

She gives him another smack on the arm. "That's so mean. How can you say that about me?"

James looks at her and looks at his arm. "You do realize that you just slapped me, right?"

"Yes, I do realize that I slapped you—but you deserved a slap, saying those horrible things about me," Sam answers smartly.

"My point exactly. When our kids misbehave, you won't hesitate to give them a whack or two. That's why you'll be the disciplinarian."

"I'm not having this conversation any longer." Sam gets up and heads out of the kitchen.

"Wait a minute!" he hollers. "Come back! I just thought of something important."

Sam walks back into the kitchen.

"Sit down," James tells her. She takes a seat across the table.

"Can you take a day off from work tomorrow and come to the meeting with me in Boulder?"

"Why do you need me? Can't Kathy or Charlie go?"

"It's a follow-up to a presentation I made to a company called Big W last week," he tells her. "I'm sure you've heard of Big W—they're up-and-coming. It's a great opportunity for the agency. The contract is worth fifty thousand to supply them the initial report, and another five thousand a month for the ongoing service agreement. It's so big that if I get the contract, I'll need to hire at least two more detectives. I've already talked to one guy that Charlie knows, and that guy is ready to come on board. He's just waiting for me to give him the word."

"I still don't understand why you need me," Sam complains. "I don't know anything about the business. I've never even seen the report that you first presented. Aren't you better off taking Charlie?"

"No. The last time I met with them, they stuck me in a conference room with seven guys who just peppered me with questions. The whole meeting was serious and somber. I scored no points with them at all. I'm surprised they even asked me back. I thought if I brought a woman along, it might loosen things up, especially someone as nice and as pretty as you."

"Why don't you take Kathy? She's also nice and pretty."

"They might wonder why I brought Kathy. They would see right through my ploy. You, on the other hand, are one of the owners of the agency. The agency is named after you. It would make sense that you'd attend an important meeting. Please, can you help? I'm desperate—I promise that all you have to do is smile and be nice. You know—use some of your Texas charm."

Sam raises an eyebrow. "So, I'm not the mean disciplinarian any longer? I'm sweet Samantha from Texas, is that right?"

James laughs. "Well, at least for tomorrow. Then you can go back to being the mean old witch that you usually are."

"You're lucky you're not near me, or I'd punch you."

"I know; that's why I'm able to speak freely. So, will you come to Boulder?" he pleads.

"Yes, I'll come with you," she answers with a sly smile. "But you'll owe me."

Kathy and James are in the kitchen the next morning when Sam walks in wearing her most conservative business ensemble.

"How do I look?" Sam asks.

"You look great," Kathy remarks. "Very professional—like a real businesswoman."

"You look *terrible*," James disagrees vehemently. "Go back and change, and come back with something that shows plenty of cleavage. It wouldn't hurt for you to expose those beautiful legs of yours, either. And make sure that cute ass of yours is noticeable."

"Are you bringing me to a business meeting or are you pimping me out?" Sam asks with annoyance.

"Don't tempt me," James warns her. "You know how important this meeting is to me." He goes over to her and puts his arm over her shoulders. "Sam, I'm not bringing you there for your business acumen. You're there to loosen up the conversation—make the guys feel a little comfortable, and help get their minds off business. I'm not asking you to work the room, but a little smile and a quick little flirty glance wouldn't hurt."

Sam gives him a knowing look and removes his arm from her shoulders. "I know exactly what you're up to. I'm beginning to feel sorry I ever agreed to come to the meeting," she says as she heads back to the bedroom to change.

"You won't feel the same way when we have enough money to buy our huge ranch," James yells at her in the hall. He heads back into the kitchen. "Then you'll thank me."

"What's this about a ranch?" Kathy asks James.

"Oh, nothing," James answers evasively. "An inside joke between Sam and me."

Sam comes back out a few minutes later. "Well?" she asks. "Are you happy now?"

Kathy and James look at Sam. Kathy quickly turns her head away but can't control herself. She bursts out laughing.

"Yeah, I know," Sam says to Kathy. "I look like a slut, don't I?"

Kathy is still laughing uncontrollably. "Where did you even get that outfit? I don't remember ever seeing it on you. Your breasts are almost fully exposed."

"I got this outfit when I was seventeen, but I was too embarrassed to ever actually wear it," Sam admits. "I just never got around to throwing it out."

"Well, I think it's perfect!" James says. He gets up to leave. "Come on, we've got to get going. We're going to be late."

"Are you really going to make me go to the meeting dressed like this?" Sam stands with her arms open.

James looks at her and waves his hand. "Yeah, you look fine. Everybody will love you."

"I'm not going dressed like this!" Sam yells. "I was just making a point about how silly you're acting."

"You've *made* your point," James replies. "Come on, let's go!"

Sam looks at Kathy, who shakes her head and is still laughing.

"Come on, let's go. We're going to be late! We've got a long ride ahead of us." James repeats, holding the door.

Sam walks out of the house with her shoulders slumped.

A few days later, James is waiting in his Mustang outside a Baptist church a few miles from Amarillo. He and Sam are headed for Aggie's place, and then to Lorenzo for the wedding preparations. Sam is inside the church at the service; she never misses Sunday church unless it absolutely cannot be avoided. When church is out, they will head east for about an hour to Aggie's place.

James glances over at the building and sees the pastor coming out—the signal that the service is over. The congregants begin filing out and walking over to shake the preacher's hand. Sam, who is dressed in her Sunday best, is at the back of the line waiting her turn. Eventually, Sam says a few words to the preacher and comes walking over to the car.

"So, are you right with God now?" James asks in an almost snide voice when she gets in the car.

Sam frowns over at him. "It's not easy when you have to pray for *two* sinners. You could make an appearance every once in a while, you know. It wouldn't hurt you. You sat in the car doing nothing anyway. Why not come inside?"

"Sam, if I walked into that church, the walls of the building would come tumbling down."

Sam is angry. They sit in silence for the remainder of the trip. They finally get to the trailer park where Aggie lives. It's a dusty lot, with no vegetation. The trailers all look essentially the same. James drives around the lot twice before he and Sam notice the twin boys playing in front of one of the mobile homes. If not for the boys, they may never have found the right trailer.

The minute James pulls up and the twins see him getting out of the car, they yell, "Uncle James! Uncle James!" and come running over. Each twin latches on to one of James's legs.

The trailer door opens. Aggie comes out, carrying her baby, Henry, in her arms. She stills looks no older than seventeen to James. She smiles when she notices them.

Sam walks up to her and gives her a kiss. "How are you, Aggie?" she asks.

"I'm fine, Sam," Aggie says. "It's so nice to see you again."

Aggie stands in front of James, staring at him but not saying anything. A slight smile is on her face. James stands still and quiet, too. The twins are still clutching his legs. Finally, Aggie speaks.

"Kids, why don't you let go of Uncle James so that he can go up the steps?" The boys let go and run inside.

"May I hold little Henry?" Sam asks reaching over for the child.

James walks up and gives Aggie a hug. Tears are welling up in Aggie's eyes. He bends down and gives her a kiss on the cheek.

"It's so nice to see you, Agatha. I'm sorry it took so long for me to get here."

"I know why it did, James," Aggie says to him. "I know why you didn't come around and why it took so long. It hurts, doesn't it? Seeing me reminds you of him, doesn't it, James?" Tears are streaming down her face. Sam turns away, as she, too, is crying. James's eyes are also welling up. Aggie reaches up and gently strokes his face.

"The hurting just means that you loved him, James. Don't run from the sadness, and please don't apologize. Aside from Henry, you are the nicest, kindest man I have ever known."

That final statement has its effect. Sam is crying uncontrollably. One of the twins looks out of the trailer and disrupts the moment.

"Mommy, when is Uncle James coming inside?" the boy asks, looking around. "And why is everybody crying?"

"We're coming right in," Aggie tells her son. She wipes the tears from her face with the back of her hand. Inside, they find the twins sitting on a small sofa.

"You sit right here, between us, Uncle James," says one of the twins. James goes over and sits between the boys.

Sam, who is still holding the baby, looks at James, shakes her head, and takes a seat on a creaky wooden chair.

"Boys, why don't you give Uncle James a break?" Aggie says.

"*No!*" one of the boys hollers out.

"You know what I just realized, guys? Sam and I have presents for you," James says. "You do *want* your presents, don't you?"

"Yay!" the twins yell in unison, jumping up from the couch.

"Come on, give me a hand. They're in the car," James gets up and heads out of the trailer. The twins jump up and rush out after him.

"Let me take the baby," Aggie says to Sam after they leave. "I'll put him in his crib. It's time for his nap, anyway."

Aggie takes little Henry from Sam and walks to the back of the trailer. James returns with the boys. Each twin is carrying a wrapped box.

"What's in here, Uncle James?" one of them asks.

"You'll have to open the box to find out…but before you do, you each have to make me a promise."

"What's that, Uncle James?"

"You both have to promise that you'll help your mom around the house. Is that a deal?"

"It's a deal!" they yell in unison. "Can we open the presents now?"

"Yes, go ahead."

The boys tear the wrapping from the boxes.

"It's a fire truck!" the first to finish yells out.

"It's a police car!" the second hollers.

"Mommy, look what Uncle James brought us!" one of the boys yells out when Aggie comes back into the room.

"Did you boys say thank you to Uncle James?"

They jump up on the couch and give him a kiss. "Thank you, Uncle James!"

"How about thanking Auntie Sam, too?" James tells the twins. "The presents are from her as well."

They run over and give Sam a kiss.

"Okay, boys, go on outside and play with your new toys," Aggie tells them. "The grown-ups want to talk."

The twins take their toys and run outside. Sam gets off her chair and sits alongside James.

"Aggie, this is for you," Sam tells her, holding out the present. "It's the toaster that you wanted."

"Thank you so much!" Aggie says. Placing the box on the floor next to her chair, she takes a seat. "So—in only about a month, the big day will be here. Are you guys excited?"

"It's beginning to get a little crazy," Sam replies. "The wedding dress, the planning, the preparations—it's a bit daunting. You *are* coming to the wedding, aren't you?"

"Yes, of course. I wouldn't miss it for the world. I'm not bringing the twins, or the baby though; I need a day out by myself. I haven't been out by myself in what seems like forever. I need one day of fun. Is that cruel of me? I mean, it's only been about six months since Henry died. Is it too soon?"

"Oh, Aggie," James speaks up, "I'm sure Henry wouldn't have wanted you to just be locked up in the house and mourning all the time. Henry would have wanted you to get on with your life."

"I know, but I don't feel right about it." Aggie looks at James sadly and pauses for a moment. "James, I'm going to tell you something. I hope it doesn't upset you. Henry considered you his best friend. Every single letter he sent to me from Vietnam mentions you. Even in the last letter before his death, he talked about you. Would you like me to read it to you?"

James is about to say no when Sam beats him by responding quickly. "Yes, we would love to hear what Henry said."

Aggie gets up to retrieve the letter. James gives Sam a dirty look. She smiles sweetly at him.

"This is it," Aggie says, sitting down to read.

Dear Aggie,

It was nice hearing from you, and it makes me happy to read that you and the twins are doing fine. I know it can't be easy on you, Aggie, what with the baby coming and all. I'm sorry I can't be there with you.

Aggie, with the baby coming, I've been doing a lot of thinking. Actually, it was a piece of advice that James gave me a few months ago. I haven't seen James for a few weeks now. He's been out in the boonies on operations. I worry about James. They keep sending him out all the time. I feel a little guilty that I hardly ever leave camp. All the higher-ups like James and ask for him to go out in the field whenever there is an action. I guess it's kind of good to not be so smart.

The last time I saw James, he was complaining that he had a rash in his butt. The rash was driving him crazy. Kind of hard to get rid of a rash like that when you're out in the boonies. No place to take a shower. Even when you're in camp, it's hard to keep clean by washing yourself in cold water. The last time James was in camp, he parked his ass in a bucket of water for about an hour.

Anyway—back to my decision. Aggie, I know I promised you that when I got home, I'd take the civil service test and become a letter carrier. But James told me that as I am young, I should shoot for the stars. He said, "If you don't do it now, you'll never do it. How do you know you can't reach the stars if you don't even try?"

So, when I come home, Aggie, I think I'm going to start my own business in tractor repair. I was always good around cars, and I think I can make a go of it. Please don't be angry with me. I promise I'll work real hard. I'll make a go of the business.

Well, that's all I have for now. Please remember, Aggie, that no matter what, I will always love you.

Your devoted husband,

Henry

Aggie folds up the letter. She looks at James and smiles warmly. "So. *You* were the one who was corrupting my husband and filled his head with all these big ideas," she says teasingly.

"Guilty as charged." James laughs and changes the subject. "How are you doing moneywise, Aggie? Do you have enough to get by? Do you need any more?"

"No, I don't need more money, James, but I thank you most sincerely for asking. I got a job at the school. I work as an aide, and the pay isn't bad. I was able to buy the trailer outright with the money you sent me. That money saved my life—I'm convinced of it. All I had was the ten thousand from Henry's military life insurance policy, and it was gone in no time—you know, with the funeral and all. I don't know how I would have survived without your gift. I'm sure I would have had to go and live with my parents. I used some of the money left over for a down payment on a car.

"James, I have a little over three thousand left in the bank that I was going to give back to you. Then I started worrying that if I did that, it would clean me out completely. What if I had an emergency? I don't want to keep coming back and asking you for money. If it's okay with you, I'll keep it in the bank. But I'll give it back to you if you ever need it."

"Aggie, don't worry about the money. It's yours; I gave it to you. You never have to give *any* of the money back to me. In fact, if you need more, please just let me know."

"Thank you, James," Aggie replies, the tears in her eyes welling up again. "I hope I never have to ask you. It is so nice to know that I have friends like you and Sam. You are really good people; I hope you guys are always happy."

"I still can't figure out how you made all that money in the army," Sam says. "Besides the more than nine grand you gave Aggie, you furnished our apartment and bought us a car. How could you possibly do it on a paycheck of less than two hundred a month?"

"I told you, Sam. I lent money to the men and charged a fee for my services. We had this conversation last year." James's voice has become a little testy; he is clearly unhappy that Sam has brought up the subject. "I already explained to you once before how it worked."

"No, you never *really* explained it to me, James." Sam's voice gets a little louder. James can see that she is not going to let the subject go. "I still don't understand how your plan worked. How much of a fee did you charge?"

"Not much." James shrugs his shoulders and waves a hand. "Five percent, most of the time."

"See, that doesn't make any sense," Sam says, continuing to press him. "Do you have any idea how much money you'd have had to lend out at five percent to earn as much as you did? Hundreds of thousands. You didn't have that kind of money to lend out. Give me an example of one of your transactions."

"Okay." James turns to her. "Let's say it's two weeks before payday and a guy is a little short. He needs money for cigarettes or maybe beer. So he borrows a ten spot from me, and two weeks later, on payday, he pays me back my ten, plus a five-dollar fee. You see? Five dollars—five percent."

Sam almost comes out of her chair as she yells at him. "That's not five percent! That's fifty percent, and that's just for two weeks. If you annualize it, it's over one thousand percent. You were charging over one thousand percent interest on the money."

James furrows his eyes. A dumb look comes over his face. "Are you sure, Sam? That can't be right. Nobody ever complained. I'm sure someone would have said something."

"Yes, James. I believe she's right," Aggie says and smiles.

"Hmm, imagine that," James says, continuing his dumb act. "All this time, I thought it was just five percent." He turns to Sam. "Good thing you weren't there when I was conducting business, Sam. You could have screwed everything up."

"Yes, it's a good thing Sam wasn't there," Aggie agrees, still smiling.

"Stop encouraging him, Aggie," Sam says. She gives James an annoyed look. "Don't be fooled, Aggie. James is just playing dumb; he knew exactly what he was doing. James is way too good at numbers not to know what the correct interest rate was. Try playing poker with him and you'll see exactly what I'm talking about. James knew all along that he was gouging the other men."

"You know, Sam, you make me sound like I'm some sort of creep." He is finally angry with her and begins defending himself. "It wasn't easy lending and collecting money from all those men. They were constantly making excuses and looking for ways not to pay me back. Besides, look at all the good the money that I earned did for you guys. Sam, you got a nice apartment and a car. Aggie got a car and her own place to live so she could take care of her family. Those men knew the deal ahead of time and they agreed to it. Nobody twisted their arms."

James stands up. "Well, that's enough of all these high-finance discussions. Sam, I guess we better get going."

Sam stands up, but before she leaves, she says, "Aggie, I noticed that you have three medals on display on the counter. Are those Henry's?"

"Yes, they are. Would you like to see them?" Aggie asks her proudly.

"I would love to," Sam answers and gives James a sneaky look.

They walk over to the medals. Aggie begins pointing. "The one to the left is called a Commendation Medal. He got that for completing a dangerous mission. The one in the middle is a Bronze Star, and it was for his last mission, the one in which Henry was killed. And the one to the right is called a Purple Heart. They give that medal to soldiers who are wounded or have died."

"You keep them displayed so nicely," Sam remarks, and looks again at James, who will not make eye contact with her. "You may find this hard to believe, Aggie, but some people shove their medals into the corner of a closet."

"Who would do such an awful thing?" Aggie says in disgust. "I'm so proud of those medals. Those medals represent what a righteous, outstanding, and brave man my husband truly was. Throwing those medals into a closet would be an insult to his memory and to his good name. The next time you see that person, you give him a piece of my mind, Sam."

"I sure will, Aggie. I'll let him know your feelings." She gives Aggie a kiss. "I'll give you a call next week."

James walks up to Aggie. She stands in front of him, looking up into his face. She gives him a coy smile. "Are you going to give me a proper kiss this time—not that little peck you gave me when you first walked in?" James lowers his head and kisses her on the lips. Aggie places her arms around his neck and pulls him closer. Sam stares and shakes her head, wondering when the embrace is going to end.

"That's *much* better," Aggie says to James when she breaks off.

"You will stop by more often, won't you?" Aggie asks him.

"Yes, I promise," James replies. "If we have time, we'll stop by when we come down before the wedding next month. I'd like to look in on the twins again. If not, I'll see you at the wedding."

As they are walking out, Aggie turns to Sam. "If you ever get tired of this fella, you send him to me, you hear?"

Sam looks back at Aggie. "Don't hold your breath, Aggie; that's never going to happen. James may not know it yet, but he's stuck with me for life."

15
ONE MORE MEMORY

When they are back on the road, Sam turns to James. "That girl *likes* you!" she says.

"I know. She's nice," James responds pleasantly. "I like her, too."

"No, I mean—she really *likes* you."

James turns to Sam, there's a puzzled expression on his face. "What do you mean?"

Sam gives him her knowing smile. "You know exactly what I mean. If you allowed it, she'd give you a lot more than a friendly kiss."

"Oh, you're crazy." He waves his hand and brushes her off. "You're saying that because of the last comment she made, but she was just being nice."

Sam's smile gets even wider. "I'm not thinking of any comment that she made. It's the way she *looks* at you, and the way those eyes try to penetrate right through you. Believe me, I know that look. That look is a lot more than being nice. That look says, 'You can have me anytime you want me, mister. Just say the word.'"

"You're nuts. You're completely wrong on this one," James says, trying to deny what Sam is suggesting. "Aggie is a sweet girl; she has no designs on me. She's not some conniving woman. She's just a sweet, innocent young girl."

"Those sweet, innocent young girls are the most dangerous kind," Sam says. Changing the subject, she adds, "By the way, Mr. Know-It-All, you owe me an apology—you were wrong about the medals. They're not hidden in a dark corner of a closet in Aggie's home; they are on full display."

"I know. I can't believe it. I would think looking at those medals would cause her pain. Instead, Hall's decorations seem to bring her comfort."

"James, you're overlooking one really important fact. You believe the war was just about *you*, but really it was about all the guys who went overseas and fought. And you're forgetting the people all of you left behind…how we sat at home and saw those awful scenes on television. How we worried about you every single day. Okay—it wasn't as hard as what you went through, but it was still difficult for us. Those are not just Henry's medals and your distinctions; they are also Aggie's and mine. They represent the sacrifice that we made for you. And for Aggie, they represent the ultimate sacrifice.

"Had it been you who had gotten killed, James, all I would have to remember you by would be those crappy three-line letters you used to write to me. You know those letters, James. I can quote them word for word, that's how brief they were: 'Hello, Sam. Thanks for writing. I'm glad to hear you're doing well. I'm doing well, too. Signed, James.'

"Do you realize that Aggie knows more about how you were doing when you were in Vietnam than I do? You didn't even tell me about the rash. You suffered for months, but you couldn't even put two lines on a piece of paper to let me know that you had a rash?"

"What difference would it have made, Sam?" James says, raising his voice. "How would me complaining about a rash have helped? And I didn't tell Aggie; Henry did! What could you have done about my rash, anyway? What I needed most was a hot shower, and you were in no position to provide that for me."

Sam shakes her head and glares at him. "What could I have done? I could have sent you some baby powder. Babies get rashes all the time, James, in that very same spot. A couple of days after you used the baby powder, that rash would have disappeared."

"Baby powder! *Of course*," he yells. "I can't believe I was so stupid! I suffered for months." James looks over at Sam. "You know, Sam, of all the fears I had in Vietnam, getting that rash was number one. I'm terrified of getting that rash again. I have such a fear of the rash that I sometimes have nightmares about it coming back."

"Is that why you shower two or three times a day?"

"Yes, exactly," he admits, "and always with scalding hot water. Now that I know baby powder can cure me, I may cut back to normal." James shakes his head. Looking out the window, he mutters, "Baby powder! What an idiot!"

It gets quiet in the car. James says nothing more for a while. He seems to be concentrating on driving. Finally he asks, "What would you do with the medals if I gave them to you?"

"I would place them in the box where I keep the letters that you wrote to me from Vietnam."

"I wouldn't have to see the medals? They would be just for you?"

"No, you wouldn't have to see the medals—not unless you wanted to."

"All right. When we get home, I'll give you all three medals."

"Three medals? I thought it was two?"

"No, it's three. Another came in yesterday. I didn't tell you—I just threw the medal in the closet with the others." Changing the subject, James says, "We need to stop for gas."

He pulls up to the pump at a gas station near Amarillo. "Fill it up and check the tires please." James tells the attendant. "The left rear tire looks a little low."

James begins walking toward the station building with Sam. As he is about to go inside, he takes a look around the lot. "Does this gas station look familiar to you?" he asks her.

Sam looks around. "No, not particularly."

"I've got to use the men's room," James tells her and walks off.

"Do you want anything from the counter?" she calls to him.

"Just a Coke," he calls back.

When he returns, Sam hands him the soda.

"This place really looks familiar," he says, repeating his earlier comment as he takes a sip. "Are you sure we haven't been here before?"

"If we have, I can't remember when," she says, looking around.

"There's something about this place that's bothering me; I just can't put my finger on what it is," James says as he walks away. "I've got to call Charlie. I never told him about the good news of our meeting with Big W."

Sam is standing next to him at the pay phone when he reaches Charlie. "Hey, Charlie, I just called to let you know we got the contract with Big W."

"No shit!" Charlie says on the other end. "How did you pull it off? I thought you said we were in big trouble."

"It was all Sam's doing. She showed them some cleavage, and they immediately perked up."

Sam slaps him on the arm. "Don't tell Charlie that."

"It makes sense," Charlie says on the phone. "Her cleavage would get my attention, too."

Sam tries to grab the phone from James, who keeps it away.

"Then she shook that cute ass of hers and the deal was sealed," James continues, smiling at Sam.

"That's not true, Charlie," Sam yells at the phone. "I didn't shake my ass for anybody."

"There's no way those guys could have resisted that ass!" Charlie responds.

Sam tries to grab the phone away from James once more. "Give me that phone!" she yells. James pushes Sam away.

"Stop it," he yells at her. "Go wait for me in the car."

"Listen, Charlie," James says after Sam storms off in a huff, "get in touch with Al, that detective friend of yours. We're going to need him now that we got the contract. He can come to our next meeting at Big W; I have an appointment with them in Boulder on Friday."

After the call, James goes back to his car and pays the attendant.

"I am so angry with you, you can't even imagine," Sam says to him as he pulls out of the station. "You basically told Charlie that I showed off my body just to get a business deal. I can't believe that you would portray your future wife in that light."

"Oh, come on, Sam. We were just having some fun."

"You, of all people, should know my feelings on the subject of women as sex objects in the workplace." She turns and points her finger at him. "Have you forgotten how that man tried to get me fired last year because I wouldn't go to bed with him? James, you are supposed to be better than that. I am *really* angry with you. That's the last time I'm doing a business conference with you."

"All right, Sam—you've made your point. I'm sorry. I got a little carried away with Charlie. I swear I'll never do it again."

"By the way," Sam says, looking over at him, "you know that cute ass that you were talking about? Well, you just keep looking, mister, because looking is all you get to do. You're not going up there anymore."

"Oh, come on, Sam! You're not really going to do that to me?"

"Oh yes. Yes, I am. You need to be taught a lesson." She sits back in her seat.

"That's not fair, Sam! Not even on our honeymoon?"

"Well, maybe on our honeymoon I'll change my mind. I want to see how you behave between now and then."

When they get to the house in Lorenzo, Sam's parents are at the door to greet them.

"Don't tell me you skipped Sunday service because you were traveling?" is the first thing Reverend Powers says to Sam.

"No, Daddy," Sam replies. She gives him a kiss. "We made time to attend services right outside of Amarillo—Pastor Flannery's congregation. The pastor sends you his regards."

"How is the old boy?" her dad asks her.

"The pastor is doing fine, but Mrs. Flannery is ill. They don't really know what's wrong with her. She's been sick for two weeks now."

"I'll have to take a ride up and pay them a visit," Reverend Powers says. He turns to James. "How did you like the service, James? A little different from what you're accustomed to, I guess?"

"Yes, a little different," James responds, "though the basic concept is the same. You know, thank God and pray to our Lord Jesus."

Sam gives James a long look. She stares at her dad who hasn't picked up on the sarcasm.

They are unpacking his bag in his room when Sam turns to him. "I can't believe how easily you just lied to my dad."

"Well, technically," James says with a grin, "I didn't really *lie* to him. Your dad didn't ask me if I attended; he asked me how I liked the service. From where I was sitting in my car, the service was just fine."

"You know, James, this past week I'm finding out a lot of new stuff about the man I'm going to marry. Lying, money gouging, and using your fiancée as a sex object. Honestly, I don't like what I'm seeing in you, James. It's making me really wonder about you."

James walks over to her and puts his arms around her. "Well, you know, honey, if you want to cancel the wedding and give this marriage idea a little more thought, I won't object. You need to be absolutely certain about the man you're marrying. There should be no doubt whatsoever—this is a very important decision."

Sam gives him a playful punch in the stomach. "Oh no, you don't. In Texas, there's only one way a guy gets out of a promise to marry. I'm pretty sure you wouldn't like that solution. You're getting married as planned, mister. I'm absolutely certain of the man I want to marry. I'll just have to work a little harder at teaching you proper behavior. You'll come around and see the light eventually"

James hugs her again, and gives her a kiss, too. "Wouldn't it be easier and more fun if you just came over to the dark side with me?"

That night, Sam walks into James's room at her parent's home It is actually Sam's brother's room, but her brother has been relegated to the couch to make room for the groom-to-be.

"James, you've got a phone call. It's Agent Spencer of the FBI."

"Oh, good! Maybe they found this guy Wheeler."

James goes into the kitchen to take the call. "What's up Spence? Did you find the guy?"

"No, but we've got some background info on your man. He's a drifter that goes from place to place. Before that he was a high school history teacher. He fancies himself as some sort of classical history buff. He always walks around quoting the masters. The school fired him because of some problem he had with one of his students. No one has seen or heard from him since he got canned."

"Spence, I don't mean to cut you off, but how does this information help us in finding the girl?"

"It doesn't but I thought you may want to get a picture of who you're up against."

"I'm sorry, you're right, Spence. Thanks for the call. How about Wheeler's partner? You got anything on him?"

"No! nothing!"

"Okay, thanks for keeping me in the loop."

"Anything, new?" Sam asks when he's back in the room.

"Not much," he replies and gets reflective. He's trying to process what Agent Spencer just told him.

"What kind of tux are you going to pick out?" Sam asks him.

"Uh? Tux?" James asks, feigning innocence. "Why do I need a tux? Can't I just come as I am?"

The truth is this whole wedding thing has been just a little too much for him to handle. His mind is on the Campos kidnapping and he hasn't paid any attention to the wedding plans. He's trying to determine his next move. Does he let the FBI take the lead or does he get more involved? More involved? How the hell does he do that? He's so confused—he really doesn't know where to turn.

As the weekend passed, he got a firsthand look at just how complicated planning a wedding can be. Flowers, chairs, tables, china, silverware, a photographer, an arbor, entertainment, food and drinks, bridesmaids, and flower girls...

And they aren't even finished yet. Tomorrow they have to write out their wedding vows, which need to be memorized before the ceremony.

"Stop being funny." Sam says. "All you need to do is get the tux and memorize the vows. *I'm* doing everything else. So, what kind of tux do you have in mind?"

"I don't know, Sam. Probably something traditional, in black."

"Make sure you tell your brother Anthony. The best man and the groom should have the same tux. Do it when you get back home, James. Please don't wait until the last minute. Don't make me start worrying about you, too. I have enough on my mind as it is."

James puts his arm over her shoulder. "All right, Sam, stop worrying; I'll get the tux as soon as I get back. I'll call Anthony and take care of that, too. And we forgot about the rings. When we get home, we need to go and buy the rings."

"Oh, that's right! Let's do that as soon as we get back. You know, I'm nervous but excited at the same time. I think I've been planning this wedding since I was a little girl." She leans over and gives him a passionate kiss. "Thank you for making me so happy. You've been wonderful throughout this process."

James pulls her into his arms, and they embrace. He pushes her down on the bed and gets on top of her. Sam shoves him off her and jumps up from the bed.

"Not in my parents' home," she hisses.

James pulls her back down on the bed. "Oh, come on. No one is coming in. Let's have a little fun."

She pushes him away again and jumps back up. "No deal. You'll have to wait until we get home. Good night. I'm going to bed. I'll be sharing my sister Maggie's room if you need me."

"Wait, don't go!" James says. "Sit back down; I want to speak to you about something important."

She sits back down on the bed. "What's up?"

James slides over beside Sam. "You know, I haven't said anything to you about the wedding. I've let you have complete control of your big day. This is your lifelong dream, and I'm in a position to help you fulfill that dream. However, I believe you should have a conversation about the cost of this whole affair with your parents. Maybe I'm mistaken, but I believe your plans might be a little more money than what your parents can come up with."

"They haven't said anything to me about the cost. I'm sure they would have said something to me if they couldn't afford to pay for the wedding."

"Your mom and dad are proud people, Sam. I don't believe that they know how to bring up the subject with you. They have two other daughters who will likely also marry someday—and let's not forget the cost of education. One of your brothers wants to go to college.

"Sam, I'm not asking you to cut back on your wedding plans. We have the money; we can kick in anything that your parents can't afford. Just ask them what their budget is, and we'll pay for the rest. You need to have this conversation with them, Sam. I don't know what a preacher earns, but I'm pretty sure your parents are in no position to pay for everything."

"All right. I'll have a talk with my parents tomorrow," Sam replies. "I'll tell Mom and Dad that it was never my intention to have them pay for the wedding, saying that you and I were planning to pick up the entire cost. They can kick in anything that they're comfortable putting in, but it's not necessary."

"That's my girl," James says. He pulls her over to give her a kiss. "You sure you don't want to have a roll in the hay?"

She gives him a shove. "Go to bed, you horndog."

On the way home, about an hour from Colorado Springs, Sam, who is doing the driving, comments, "I'm so glad we got down to Lorenzo this weekend. We got everything accomplished. All that's left is to finish picking out my wedding dress."

"How hard can that be?"

She gives him a look. "I'm going to ignore that remark because you were so wonderful this weekend. Thanks for telling me about my parents. You were right; they *were* worried about the cost of the wedding. I never realized my parents had so little money saved."

"It can't be easy raising five children on a preacher's salary."

"Well, as it turns out, we'll be paying for most of the wedding," Sam informs him.

"It's only money," James points out. "Am I out of the doghouse? I mean, since I've been so nice and all?"

She gives him a coy smile. "You're almost there, but you're still not going up my ass!"

"*What?* Why am I wasting all my time being nice to you if there's no chance of reward?"

"Because sometimes, James, you should be good just for the sake of it."

"No. I'm sorry, Sam, but I don't particularly like that idea. In fact, it does nothing for me."

James is in the bedroom, unpacking after they get home. It's late. Kathy is already asleep. Sam has been in the bathroom washing up. When Sam comes into the bedroom, James hands her three boxes.

"These are the medals," he tells her.

"Can I open them?"

"Yes, of course. They're yours now."

Sam opens one of the boxes and takes the medal out. "Can you tell me what the medals are, and what they represent?"

"That one that you're holding is called the Army Commendation Medal. You get that for being in a battle or an operation. The V on the ribbon stands for valor during the mission. Captain Myles put me in for that one after an operation somewhere near the Rock Pile. I guess I must have done something that impressed him—I don't really remember all the details. Myles always did like me."

"How about this one? It looks the same."

"Yes, it's the same medal. I got that one for something I did while on operation in the DMZ. The army couldn't admit that we were ever in the DMZ, so basically they call it 'the province.'"

"How about this one?" Sam asks after she opens the third box. "It's very impressive; it's a cross."

James just stands there and stares at the medal. "You know what, Sam? I don't want to do this anymore. You wanted the medals, and I've given them to you. Just put the damn medals in the box like you said you were going to do." It's clear that James is done speaking. He storms out of the room.

Sam takes the box from the closet and places the medals inside. She puts the box back in its place and comes out of the bedroom. James is in the living room, sitting on the couch in the dark. Sam turns on one of the lamps and sits across from him. They sit silently, saying nothing.

James finally speaks. "Aside from Hall, probably my best friend in the service was this fellow Goyette," he says. "I first met Goyette when we were in advanced infantry training together at Fort Lewis, Washington. He wasn't in my platoon at the time, so I didn't really know him until the night we were involved in a course called Escape and Evasion. It's a course that teaches a soldier how to escape from a prison camp if he's ever captured.

"As part of that course, there's an exercise that simulates a prison break. We were grouped in squads of ten and had to go through the woods of Washington State at night and reach a certain post. There are other soldiers, from another company, hunting you down. If you're caught, they take you into prison and try to get you to spill what you know.

"Goyette was in my squad during this training. It was dreary and dark that night in Washington. And, as it always does in the Northwest, it was raining. It was that cold, misty rain where it's impossible to keep yourself dry. With the darkness and such lousy weather, it should have been easy for us to evade capture and make it to our goal.

"The group I was in, however, was terrible. They bickered constantly among themselves about what path to take. Eventually, with all the arguing going on, we became confused and got lost. Getting lost led to more quarrelling among the men. The fighting got so loud that it gave away our position. That's when we heard someone yell out, 'Halt!' That meant the prison guards had found us. Everybody scattered and tore ass.

"Goyette and I climbed up a large tree and rode out the night. The next morning, when the exercise was over, Goyette and I came down from the tree. We didn't make it to our goal, but we didn't get captured, either—unlike the rest of our squad, who all got nabbed."

James looks up at Sam. "I ran into Goyette again at Fort Knox. He was in the mortars; I was with the scouts. Throughout my army tour, I kept running into him. Of all the soldiers I served with, Goyette is probably the guy I would have most likely kept as a friend on the outside. That's how fond I was of him. You would have liked Goyette, too, Sam. Easygoing, honest, ethical…and churchgoing.

"Something happened to Goyette that I wasn't aware of when we were in Vietnam. He was accused of stealing from other soldiers." James pauses and looks at Sam. "One of the two worst things you can be in the army is a thief. The other is a coward. When I heard the news about Goyette, I was in shock. I refused to believe he was a crook, even though everybody said they had the proof.

"The day that I got that last medal that you opened in the bedroom, Goyette was my radioman. We were in Laos and the whole place lit up. Bullets were flying at us from everywhere. Bombs were exploding all around us. Goyette and I jumped into a crater created by a B-52 bomb explosion. Those bomb craters are some fifty feet wide and about ten feet deep. While we were sitting in that hole, trying to ride out the fight, I asked Goyette about his stealing. Of course, he denied the stealing, and for a moment I didn't believe him when he told me the story.

"Then, he reminded me that he'd been my bunkmate for a while at Fort Carson. His bunk was right next to mine. Goyette told me that he knew my hiding place—you know, the place where I hid all my money.

"'If I'm the thief that everybody says I am,' Goyette said to me, 'then why didn't I steal from you, Coppi? You had more money than anybody else in the entire brigade.' He then told to me that he was being framed, and he told me who the guy was that was framing him.

"After he finished the story, I knew immediately that he was telling the truth. He wasn't a crook. I told Goyette to hang in there, saying that we would come up with a plan to clear his good name."

James stops at this point and stares up at the ceiling.

"What does this story have to do with the medal?" Sam asks.

"While we were in the crater talking, we heard a soldier moaning outside. We looked out, and sure enough, there's a wounded soldier about fifty yards away. Goyette wanted to run out and get the guy. I told him, 'Are you crazy? The enemy leaves wounded soldiers out there for bait. They could have finished off this poor stiff anytime if they had wanted to. They're just waiting for two saps like us to run out there and try to help this guy.'

"Goyette wouldn't let it go. He told me, 'If you don't want to go, I'm going without you.' He pretty well knew that I wouldn't let him go alone. Anyway, against my better judgment, I went with him. We ran out there under enemy fire and pulled this guy—a second lieutenant—into the crater. I believe this lieutenant is still alive today. That last medal was because Goyette and I ran out and saved this guy's life.

"Goyette was killed soon after, in the same firefight that killed Henry Hall. I never did get a chance to clear his good name. The real thief was the man who ordered Goyette to go on that last mission that got him killed."

Sam sits silently and says nothing. There is nothing more to be said. James stands up.

"Sam, now you know the complete story behind all the medals that I gave you tonight. That's the last Vietnam story I will ever tell. Please respect my privacy and don't ever ask me about Vietnam again."

16
KATHY

Dinner is over. Sam and James have gone for their evening walk and Kathy is sitting in the living room at but not watching, the television. She is thinking back to a day two years ago, the day she decided to move to Colorado Springs. It was the morning after her high school prom—her date has dropped her off at Sam's house. She knocks, the door opens and Sam lets her in.

"So, what time did the prom queen get home?" Kathy asks as they head for Sam's room. Sam closes the door behind them and they sit side by side on the bed.

"Two o'clock…and I still got punished," Sam answers. "My dad wanted me home by one. What about you? I'm guessing that you haven't been home yet; you still have your prom dress on."

"How was your date?" Kathy asks, ignoring Sam's question. "How far did you let him go?"

"He copped a few feels," Sam reveals. "He was too afraid to go any further. I didn't even have to stop him; he was probably excited that he got that far." Sam shrugs. "I'm not going out with him again; he's just not for me. How about you? How far did you go?"

And Kathy answers, "I went all the way."

"Really?" Sam yells out, latching on to Kathy's arm. "Katherine Percival is no longer a virgin?"

"I don't really know," Kathy wails. She wrinkles her nose and stares at Sam. "I *might* still be a virgin. It was over so fast."

"What happened?"

Kathy doesn't answer right away. She collects herself before telling Sam the story. "During the prom, I decided that if I got a chance, I would go all the way. What was I saving myself for, anyway? After the prom, my date and I went driving around, and after a couple of hours, we stopped at this secluded spot. We had a fifth of bourbon. To get my courage up, I drank probably half the bottle. We started making out, and frankly, he wasn't pushing me very hard to do anything. I was the one driving the process forward. Eventually he had my dress up and my panties off. I asked him if he had protection. He reached into his back pocket and took out a packet with a rubber.

"I swear, Sam, it seemed like it took him forever to open the packet and put the rubber on. He had no clue as to how it worked. It took so long that I almost changed my mind. He finally got it on. Then the fun really began when he tried to get on top of me and put his boy into me. Eventually, he finally got it in. I closed my eyes and tried to enjoy the experience. No sooner did I shut my eyes than the episode was over. Sam, I'm exaggerating if I say it took a minute. He went outside the car to take the rubber off, and I put my panties on. What a huge disappointment."

"That's horrible," Sam remarks. "You gave up your reputation for nothing."

"Who cares about any reputation? I'm not staying in Lorenzo anyway. After graduation, I'm moving to Colorado Springs."

"Colorado Springs?" Sam yells out in surprise. "Who do you know in Colorado Springs? I've never even heard you talk about Colorado Springs."

"I know Jill Morgan. You remember Jill? She was two years ahead of us. Anyway, she was down here visiting two weeks ago and asked if I would move in with her. Her roommate just left for California—moved out. Jill was looking for another roomie. She even found me a job at her office as a typist."

Kathy looks over at Sam and frowns. "I've got to get out of Lorenzo, Sam. This is the most boring place in the world." Kathy leans over toward Sam. "Why don't you come with me?" she pleads. "Jill has an extra room. You wouldn't even have to chip in on the rent until you find a job. I'm sure that Jill wouldn't mind. You can't possibly be happy here. Your dad is a lot stricter than mine."

"I'm sorry, Kathy. I can't leave my family."

"Well, what are you going to do after you graduate? You don't even have a job."

"My dad needs help at the church," Sam tells her. "I'm going to help him out until I find something."

Kathy jumps up and hollers, "Are you kidding me? You're going to be with your dad day and night? Why don't you just slit your wrists right now and get it over with?"

It was the third week of January, six months after Kathy had moved to Colorado Springs. Kathy pulls up the shade and looks out of the window at the snow, which is still falling.

"Darn," she mutters to herself. She is upset. She and her roommate Jill are throwing a big party that night. If the snow continues to accumulate, no one will

show up. She hears a knock at the door—she pulls down the shade, and walks over to see who it is.

"Oh my God!" Kathy hollers when she sees who is at the door. "It's you!"

Sam is standing at the doorway, holding a suitcase in her hand. "Is the offer for that extra room still good?"

Kathy rushes out and gives Sam a hug. "Of course, the offer is still good! Come in."

Kathy ushers her into the living room. "Let me have your jacket…it's all snowy!"

"I hung your jacket in the bathroom so it can dry out. Come sit on the couch with me, and let's talk." Kathy pulls Sam to the sofa. "What happened? What changed your mind?"

"Oh, Kathy, you were so right," Sam laments. "Working with Daddy all day and coming home at night was impossible. We fought constantly. And my mother didn't help at all. She always took his side. Finally, I had enough. I took the $ 95 that I had left from my graduation money and bought a train ticket for Colorado Springs."

Sam looks over at Kathy. "Kathy, if I'm imposing, please let me know now. I don't want to be a burden."

"Don't be ridiculous; you're not imposing at all," Kathy tells her as she gets up and pulls Sam to her feet. "Come on, let me show you to your room. I'll help you unpack. You arrived just in time. We're having a big party tonight. That is, if this snow will ever let up."

The morning after the party, Kathy comes out of her bedroom to find Sam sitting on the couch. Sam is slumped over. "What are you doing up so early? As much as you drank last night, I didn't expect to see you out of your room until Tuesday."

Sam looks up at her and moans. "Kathy, I'm worried."

When Kathy sees the look of concern on Sam's face, she immediately sits on the couch next to her. "What's the matter, dear? What's wrong?"

"Last night, I got so drunk, I can hardly remember anything. I know I was talking to some boy, and I went into my room with him. Kathy, for the life of me, I can't even remember what he looks like. This morning I woke up in bed and I had no panties on. There was sticky stuff in my private area, and the bedsheet is stained." Sam begins to cry. "Oh, Kathy, I feel so awful. Just one day from home and I act like a harlot. I was just so drunk that I didn't know what I was doing." Sam turns to Kathy and cries out. "What if I'm pregnant?"

"First of all, stop worrying. You know what the odds are that you can get pregnant in one go?" Kathy asks her. "Very, very low. Let last night be a lesson to you to stay in control."

"Don't worry. No boy is ever touching me again unless I absolutely love him and I'm sober enough to know what I'm doing."

Sam knocks at Kathy's door two weeks later.

"I missed my period," Sam reveals after she walks into the room and plops face down on the bed.

"That doesn't mean anything; you could just be late," Kathy tries to console her.

"I'm never late. I'm always on time It's like clockwork," Sam answers, looking up from the bed.

"You were never this nervous before. Just try to calm down. I'm sure your period will come. Stop working yourself up."

Two weeks later, Kathy is sitting in the waiting room of a Colorado Springs health clinic. She is waiting for Sam, who is seeing a doctor. She looks up from the magazine she is reading and sees Sam coming out of his office. Sam flops down on the seat next to her. "Kathy, just take a gun and shoot me. Please take me out of my misery."

"What did the doctor say?"

"He said, 'Congratulations, you're going to have a baby.'" Sam turns to Kathy. "I'm having a baby; can you believe that, Kathy? I can't even take care of *myself*. How am I going to take care of a baby?" Sam stands up from the chair and stretches her arms out. "How will I ever face my father with the news?" She collapses back down on the seat. "Oh, Kathy, what am I going to do?"

"How about getting an abortion?" Kathy suggests.

Sam sits up and stares at Kathy. "A what?"

"An abortion," Kathy repeats. "Lots of women who get themselves in a bind have abortions."

"You want me to kill the baby?" Sam shakes her head and looks away. "I've already committed one mortal sin; do you want me to burn in hell completely?"

"You're not killing a *baby*," Kathy explains. "You *just* got pregnant—not even two weeks ago. It's like having your period late. It's a nothing procedure."

"How would I even go about it, Kathy?" Sam begins to get curious. "I don't even know how to broach the subject with anybody. And where would I get the money? I'm sure it's not free."

"Let me look into it for you," Kathy offers. "They just passed a law last year. Abortions are now legal here in Colorado. Jill knows this girl who had it done."

True to her word, Kathy spoke to Jill and gives Sam the results.

"There's a problem." She tells Sam. "Although abortions are legal, you have to present your case in front of a three-doctor panel. It's not as easy as I first thought. There are conditions that have to be met before you qualify."

"How did Jill's friend get her abortion?" Sam asks. "How did she qualify? What are the conditions?"

"She never went in front of the panel. She had the abortion done illegally. Even though it's not legal, ever since they passed the new law, more and more doctors are doing abortions. Apparently, it's become a booming business. Jill said this bartender at a bar that she goes to hooked her friend up with a doctor. I'm going to speak to the bartender later today. I'll let you know what he has to say."

"Three hundred dollars? Where will I get three hundred dollars?" Sam yells at Kathy when she hears the price that afternoon.

"Jill and I will chip in," Kathy volunteers.

"You guys don't have any money, either. You're living paycheck to paycheck. You've already been great to me, letting me live here without charging rent. I can't expect you to do any more."

"Sam, we don't mind, believe me. Both Jill and I know you would do the same for us if the shoe was on the other foot. Let's sit down and develop a plan. And let's find you a job, too. We'll figure a way to save up enough money and get you out of this mess."

In the middle of April, Sam sits in her room and realizes that nothing has changed since her trip to the doctor, when she'd first learned of her pregnancy, except that now she is almost three months pregnant. She hears a knock on her door. Kathy peeks in. "Can I come in?"

"Yes," Sam answers.

"I came to ask you if you wanted to go out with us tonight. The girls are getting together and heading for this country bar."

"I don't have any spare money; I'm trying to save for a you-know-what. Kathy, I don't think I'm going to have enough money in time. I just can't come up with the money."

Kathy sits on the bed next to her and places her arm over Sam's shoulder. "Oh, honey, don't despair. You just started your new job at the supermarket; you'll be able to save some money."

Sam looks at her and shakes her head. "It's just a part-time job, Kathy. After all the deductions are taken out, I'll be lucky if I come home with twenty dollars."

"You just started. Once they see that you know what you're doing, they'll give you more hours. We have $120 in the fund; once you bring in more, we should be able to reach our mark. You'll be able to have enough to pay the doctor."

"I don't think so, Kathy. I'm running out of time. I'm just going to have to resign myself to the fact that I'm going to have this baby. I'm thinking about going back to Lorenzo. I can't raise this baby alone. I'll just have to face the music and tell my parents." Sam slumps back down on the bed.

"Come out with us tonight, Sam. Get your mind off your worries, even if it's just for a few hours."

"Kathy, I don't have any money to spare. I'd *like* to get out of this room, but I just can't."

"You don't need any money," Kathy tells her. "This bar that we're going to tonight lets women in for free. A lot of GIs go to this place, and, with women around, the soldiers spend more money. Believe me, those GIs will buy a pretty blonde like you a drink in a second. Come on, get dolled up, get out of this room, and forget your troubles for one night. I've been to this bar. They have a great country music band."

Inside the bar later that night, Kathy and the girls met up with some GIs. As Kathy had predicted, the soldiers were quick to buy the girls drinks. With Kathy's prodding, Sam relented and came along, but she is not really into the conversation with the soldiers. She is withdrawn and refuses to talk to any of the men.

Indeed, Sam has not gone near any guy since that episode in January. She is standing behind the girls, using them as a barrier so that none of the men will notice her. Sam looks down at her stomach, her pregnancy is still not showing.

Kathy is not impressed with any of the men that she and her friends are speaking to. Instead, she has her eye on a soldier sitting at a table by himself some twenty feet away. *How do I pull myself from these guys and get to him?* That is what Kathy is trying to figure out. The cute hunk is not even looking her way. He seems to be bored by it all. Someone drops a glass, and the contents spill all over the floor by her feet. The waitress comes over and begins mopping up. *Maybe this is my opportunity to get away from this crew,* Kathy reasons. Kathy bends down and helps the waitress clean up the broken glass.

She turns to walk toward the object of her interest, when she is greeted by quite a surprise. Sam is already sitting at the table, talking with the man. He is smiling and laughing at something that Sam has said. *Crap,* Kathy thinks to herself, *I turn my back for a second, and that shy, insecure friend of mine just walks up to him and steals him away from me. And I'm the one who insisted that she come along tonight.*

Kathy and Jill get home around two o'clock. As far as meeting guys is concerned, the night is a complete bust. The men that they met at the bar got into a fight with some other soldiers, and they all got thrown out. Sam vanished before the fight, and Kathy has not seen her since. Kathy knocks on Sam's door, but there is no answer.

"Where's Sam?" Jill asks her. "I didn't see her all night."

"I don't know. She left the bar with some guy before we got thrown out."

"That cute guy she was dancing with?" Jill asks. "He was a hunk. If she's with him, I don't blame her for staying out."

"Not Sam. She wouldn't have stayed out all night. This is very peculiar—Sam going out alone like this. I'm really worried about her."

The next morning, Kathy knocks on Sam's door, but she is still not home. Kathy starts freaking out. She has never known Sam to stay out all night. Even more worrisome, Sam has not called. Kathy gets her laundry together and heads for the laundromat. If Sam is not home by the time she gets back, she is going to look for her.

"Jill, have you seen Sam?" Kathy asks her roommate when she gets back from the laundromat. "Has she been in at all?"

"No, I haven't seen her."

"I'm worried about her," Kathy says, setting down her laundry basket. "She hasn't been back since last night. It's not like Sam to stay out all night. I can't believe that she hasn't called to let me know where she is. I'm going to put away the laundry, and then I'm going to go look for her."

"I have to run an errand, but when I'm done, I'll join you," Jill tells her.

Kathy puts away the laundry and is about to go out on her search for Sam, when she hears a key in the lock.

"Where've you been?" she hollers at Sam when her friend comes into the apartment. "I was getting worried. Why didn't you call to let me know where you were?"

"I'm sorry. I was with James and completely forgot."

"Is James the boy I saw you dancing with last night?"

"Yes, that's him; he's waiting outside. Kathy, can you drive us to the bartender you know? You know—the bartender who knows the doctor that performs the abortions?"

"Yes, I can do that, but why do you want to talk to the bartender? You don't have enough money yet."

"Yes, I know, but James said we should get all the facts. We need to find out exactly what we're up against."

"James said that?" Kathy exclaims. "Why is *James* getting involved?" Kathy shakes her head. "And why did you tell James about your pregnancy? You hardly know the guy!"

"I don't *know* why, Kathy." Sam sits down on the sofa. "There's something about James…I can't really explain it to you. I feel that I can speak to him about anything." Sam jumps back up. "Please—I don't want to keep James waiting. Can you just take us to the bartender? We can talk more about this later."

After Sam and James meet with the bartender, the barkeep takes them to the doctor that he knew who performs abortions. James pulls the surgeon aside and speaks to him. The doctor agrees to perform Sam's abortion later in the week. Kathy drops Sam and James off at their motel. Kathy is about to leave for work Monday morning, she has not seen Sam the remainder of the weekend. Sam is at the door with key in hand. Kathy wastes no time. She grabs Sam's arm, pulls her into the apartment and sits her down on the couch.

"All right, young lady, I'm not waiting one more minute," Kathy shouts at her. "I've been worrying about you all weekend. We're having our talk right now. What's going on, Sam? I know you're desperate, but you're headed for even more trouble. Staying out all weekend with a man? That's not like you! I'm sure you didn't spend the entire weekend just talking."

"All right, Kathy, please calm down. Let's have our talk. I owe you an explanation."

"Well, go ahead, start talking. I'm listening." Kathy folds her arms across her chest.

"Kathy." Sam smiles. "I just met the most wonderful guy imaginable. You're going to find it hard to believe, but I love this guy." She reaches over to Kathy and turns Kathy so that she is facing her. "Kathy, James is going to be my husband; I just know it."

Kathy stares at Sam with an incredulous look on her face, she forces out a laugh. "You meet a guy in a bar, and within hours you jump in the sack with him? You've spent a weekend shacked up with this man in a motel room and *this* is your future husband? And as if that weren't bad enough, you're pregnant with someone else's baby! What makes you think this guy will ever marry you?" Kathy shakes her head. "Can I have some of that stuff you're smoking, girl? It must be really good."

"Sounds crazy, right? But that's how I feel." Sam smiles and has a distant look in her eyes. "He made arrangements with the doctor for the abortion. It's on for Thursday night. He's going to lend me the money."

Sam looks at her girlfriend. "I've been saved, Kathy. This man flew right into my life and saved me. I was facing total doom and darkness, and he showed me the way out. There's a reason that he's here, Kathy—and I know what his purpose is."

"You haven't been saved—you naïve little girl." Kathy grabs ahold of Sam's arm. "You're jumping out of the frying pan and into the fire. This man is not giving you the money from the goodness of his heart; he's expecting something in return. This man is expecting you to keep humping. That's why he's providing you the money. He's not looking for a wife; he's looking for a mistress."

"No, Kathy, I don't agree," Sam argues, pulling her arm away. "We had already made love on Friday, right after we left the bar. He didn't know about the pregnancy. When he learned of my problems, he could have just taken off. Most men would have fled the minute they knew about my situation. He'd already gotten what he was after. I felt his sincerity, Kathy. That's why I confided in him.

And I was right. He came through. You may call my telling him about my problem the desperate act of a woman who is sinking, but sometimes that's what it takes to be saved—an admission that you need help. James says there are no conditions to his kindness, and I believe him."

"All right, Sam. I know you're not going to listen to me, but can you please slow down? This guy is very handsome, and he's swept you off your feet. There was no one like him in Lorenzo, and you're completely smitten. Heck, I might be feeling the same way myself if I were in your shoes. But can you please do me a favor? Can you please take off those rose-colored glasses and look at this guy a little more carefully? Just be a little more cautious. I don't want to see you get hurt."

17
BLACK—AND—BLUE

Two years later, back in Colorado Springs, Sam is making coffee the day after getting back from Lorenzo and having the discussion about the medals. James comes into the kitchen. She gives him a hug.

"Are you okay?" she asks him. "You were tossing and turning all night. Was it about Vietnam?"

"Yes, I'm fine," he replies. "No it wasn't about Vietnam or the discussion we had last night. This Penelope Campos thing was on my mind. I've been letting the FBI do all the work but they don't appear to be making any progress. I've got to find some time to get back on the case. I'm getting too distracted by other things. Is Kathy up yet?"

"Yes, she is. She's in her room."

He goes over and knocks at her door. "Kathy, I'm going to be late for work today," he says to her when she comes out. "I need to go to El Paso Community College and register for the summer courses. Charlie is bringing a new detective to the office that I'm hiring. His name is Al Fonte. Get him started on his paperwork—he's going to begin working for us today.

"Also, please call our landlord and tell him that I need to speak to him later today. There's an empty office right next to ours. I want to rent the space. We'll need a lot more room. I'm planning on hiring at least two more detectives—maybe three. How's our cash situation?"

"It's good," Kathy answers. "We just received four thousand from Greenwald's company. You're going to pick up the five-thousand-dollar advance payment from Big W on Friday, and there's another eight hundred that's owed to us from attorneys that should come in this month. Can I ask you why we're doing all this expanding? We don't have that many clients. We should be able to handle them with our current staff."

"We just picked up a big insurance company, Buffalo Western. They want us to handle all suspicious claims before they make payments. The management from Big W recommended us to them." Turning to Sam, he says, "Apparently, Big W was very impressed with your boss, Sam." He gives Sam a sly grin. "I got the news when I was in Lorenzo." He walks over to Sam and whispers into her ear, "I guess my suggestion for your attire wasn't so bad after all.

"All right, I'm heading for work," Kathy tells him. "I'll see you later."

"Between all that's going on with the wedding and your business, I almost *forgot* about your college," Sam says to him as she sits down with her coffee. "What courses are you taking?"

"European History and American Literature. Those are courses that I should do well in; I like the subject matter. I need a couple of As to help get my GPA up."

Sam gets up and gives him a hug and a kiss. "I'm so proud of you! We have so much on our plates, but you're still keeping your promise to continue your studies."

"So, you see why I don't want children right now?" He gets a cup of coffee.

"I do see why," she says. "With all the hard work we're doing today, we should be able to provide our children a wonderful home when we finally do have a family."

"Sam, I'm sorry about last night and the conversation we had about the medals. I'll open up about Vietnam to you at some point, I promise. I just need more time."

She gives him another hug. "That's okay, dear. Take all the time you want. Thank you for the medals. I will always cherish them."

He squeezes her tightly. "You know, Sam, when I finally do open up about the war, I'll probably go on and on. I bet you'll get so tired of my stories, you'll start telling me to shut up."

"You're probably right," Sam says and smiles.

James and Charlie drive up to the meeting in Boulder early that Friday morning. In the car with them, sitting on the back seat, is the new guy. James looks at Al in the rearview mirror.

"Al, you're going to take the lead on this account. Charlie and I will help you get started, but eventually you'll be in charge. This will be your baby."

"What am *I* going to be working on?" Charlie asks him.

"You're going to handle the other office business that comes along and the new contract we have with the insurance company. It looks like the work we're going to get from the insurance industry is going to be big. I just got a call yesterday from another insurance company, Advance Insurance. They're out of Kansas City, and they're so anxious to get started that they're making a trip to Colorado Springs just to meet with me next Wednesday. There's another law firm out of Denver that wants to give me the exclusive to their detective work. It's gotten really crazy, Charlie. I guess the word is getting out that our agency can be counted on for quality work."

"Aren't you worried that you're taking on a little too much, too soon?" Charlie asks. "All this business is good, but you can get into a lot of trouble if you can't deliver what you promise. Our reputation can go down just as fast as it went up."

"Yes, you're right, Charlie. I'm just as worried as you are. That's why I need to rely on you and Al to shoulder part of the workload. I'm planning to bring in another new man, too. If you guys know of anybody, let me know. When I get back to the office, I'm going to work on a formal business plan for our agency—budgets, cash flow, and so forth. I have an accountant coming in to help me. It's time we became a real business—no more flying by the seat of our pants.

"The only case I'm going to be working on personally is the Penelope Campos's. I've let this case go too long; it's time we brought that beautiful young girl home. I'll need you guys to pitch in on the Campos case whenever you have some spare time. I'm calling Spencer at the FBI on Monday to find out how far along he's gotten. I can't understand why they haven't caught this guy. If they had followed through on the leads that we gave them, they should have nabbed this son of a bitch by now."

It is after ten when James and the men get back to Colorado Springs. While they were gone, they spent most of the time at the headquarters of Big W. James introduced Al to all the corporate players and picked up the five-thousand-dollar advance on the project. Later that day, they visited two of Big W's department stores, interviewed the managers and department heads of the stores, and reviewed all the operations of both stores.

James is pleased with the day's work. He's gotten a lot more done today than he anticipated when he started out in the morning. Charlie's car is parked in front of James's house. The three men are returning so Charlie can pick it up.

"You guys want to stop in for a cup of coffee before you head out?" James asks the other two when they get to his place.

"No, thanks," Charlie replies, "but do you mind if I use your bathroom? I really need to go."

"Me, too," Al chimes in.

"No, of course not. Come on in," James tells the men.

They find Sam and Kathy sitting on the couch. He immediately senses that something is wrong. "What's the matter?" he asks Sam.

Kathy turns to face the men. Her face is badly bruised and battered.

"Holy crap—what the hell happened to you?" Charlie blurts out.

James runs over and squats in front of Kathy. "What happened?"

"Bobby beat the crap out of her," Sam answers for Kathy.

Kathy's face is swollen and black-and-blue. A cherry has formed on her left cheek. Her left eye is partially closed. Her lower lip is split, and a trickle of dry blood is on the rim. Kathy's left ear is also swollen.

"Kathy? Can you see me? Can you hear?" James looks into her face, she has a distant look about her. "Maybe we should take you to the hospital," he says.

"No, I don't want to go," Kathy whispers. She is crying inconsolably. "I don't hurt badly. I'll be all right. I don't want anyone to see me like this." She shakes her head and begs, "Please, James, don't take me to the hospital."

"All right, Kathy—try to calm down," he tells her, patting her hand. "We won't take you. How do you feel? How bad is the pain?"

"My face hurts, but otherwise I'm fine," Kathy responds. In addition to crying, she is now hiccupping uncontrollably. Snot is coming out of her nose. Sam reaches over with a tissue to wipe it off.

James turns to Sam. "Do me a favor and get some Vaseline out of the medicine cabinet." When Sam is out of the room, he cups Kathy's face with his hands and looks her in the eyes. "Tell me what happened."

"Bobby and I were at this bar with a few of his friends," Kathy begins. Her crying is so bad that she must stop constantly to catch her breath. "We were shooting pool—just having a good time."

Sam comes back with the Vaseline and hands it to James. He opens the jar and dips his fingers in to pull out a glob of the jelly. He gently rubs it into Kathy's face.

"Go on, continue, finish the story," he tells her.

"Bobby tells me that he wants to talk to me outside. We go outside and walk to the back of the building. 'What's the big idea?' he says to me." Kathy looks at James. "James, I didn't even know what he was talking about, so I said to him, 'What are you talking about?' He says, 'Are you trying to make it with my friend? I saw you putting the moves on the guy.'" She begins crying even louder. "James, I swear I didn't put the moves on anybody; I was just talking to his friends, politely...just being sociable."

James strokes her face gently with his hands to comfort her. "It's not your fault, baby, not your fault. Don't blame yourself." He finishes putting the Vaseline on her face, closes the jar, and hands it back to Sam. "So, what happened next?"

"I was in no mood for him and his stupid accusations. I told him to take me home. He said that if I wanted to go home, I should walk; he wasn't driving me. So, I told him, 'Fine, I'll call a cab.' I was about to walk away when he grabbed me by the hair and slapped me across the face.

"I yelled, 'How dare you slap me?' and lunged for him." Kathy looks at James and begins bawling louder. "It was just instinct, James; I wouldn't have done it if I had known what he was going to do next."

James is caressing her face again. "It's not your fault, baby; it's all his fault. You did nothing wrong."

"He punched me and knocked me down, but that wasn't enough for him. He grabbed me by the hair and kept punching me. I managed to break free. I jumped up and ran away. After a few blocks, I hailed a cab that was driving by. When the cab driver saw my face, he wanted to take me to the hospital, but I refused to go. All I wanted to do was to get home."

"What's the name of the bar?" he asks her.

"Pat's Pub."

He turns to Charlie. "Do you know the place?"

"Oh yeah—a little too well."

James gets up and turns to Sam. "Sam, keep an eye on her. If there is any change in her condition—if she gets nauseated, if her speech rambles, if her balance seems off—take her to the hospital right away. Make sure she doesn't go to sleep." He turns to Charlie. "Do you mind coming with me to the place?"

"It'll be my pleasure," he replies.

"I'm coming, too," Al cuts in.

Sam grabs hold of James before he leaves. "Isn't it better to call the police and let them handle this?"

"No, Sam, it's not. The police won't do anything. This matter gets handled and finished tonight," he says evenly. Then he looks over at Kathy. "That creep is never going to lay another hand on her."

"Come on," he says to Charlie and Al. The three men go outside. They're heading for James's car when Charlie grabs hold of him.

"Give me the key and let me drive. You're too angry to drive."

James hands Charlie the key.

At Pat's Pub, James goes straight to the back of the place, where the pool table is located. Charley and Al hurry to keep up with him. Bobby is bent over the pool table, pool stick in hand, getting ready to take a shot. When he sees James coming, he stands up to face him and is immediately met with a fist to his nose, sending him reeling backward. James follows up with a left to Bobby's gut, followed by an uppercut to his jaw. Bobby falls back against the wall.

Charlie and Al take out their guns and their badges and face the crowd that has started to form. "This is a private matter, folks, so just stand back and don't get involved," Charlie warns them.

James hits Bobby with an overhead right, sending him tumbling to the ground. Bobby puts his hands on the floor and tries to lift himself up. A pool of blood is forming under his face. James comes over and gives him a swift kick to the ribs. Bobby falls facedown into the pool of blood. James pulls his foot back and gives him another kick in the rib cage. He yanks on Bobby's hair, lifting his head up, and hits him with another uppercut. Charlie comes over and pulls James off Bobby. He stands in front of James.

"He's had enough," Charlie says to James. "You've made your point."

James is bent over, breathing heavily, his hands over his knees, looking at Bobby. "You ever touch Kathy again, I'll be back to finish the job."

James gives Bobby another kick in the ribs, turns, and storms out of the bar. Charlie hurries after him.

Al turns to the crowd. "You see what that scumbag looks like? That's what that creep did to that pretty young thing he was in here with earlier."

When the crowd hears this, they disperse. No one goes over to help Bobby. Al puts away his pistol and dashes out.

In the car, James is sitting in the passenger seat and still breathing heavily.

"Are you okay?" Charlie asks him.

James turns to Charlie. "Charlie, if you don't mind, take me to the hospital. I'm pretty sure I've fractured my wrist."

In the emergency room, James is taken into one of the cubicles. While he's waiting for the doctor, he turns to Charlie and says, "Do me a favor. Call Sam and let her know we'll be a little late. She's probably getting worried. Don't tell her I'm in the hospital."

After a while, the doctor comes in with two X-rays. "The good news is that not a single one of your fingers is broken. Just some minor lacerations, but they'll heal. You do, however, have a compound fracture in your right wrist and a hairline fracture in the left wrist. We're going to have to put both hands in casts for at least three to four weeks. I'll be right back to clean up your hands." The doctor is about to leave when he turns to James.

"By the way, they just brought in a man who was badly beaten. I'm guessing that's how you sustained your injuries."

"Yeah, that's probably the guy," James replies.

"What happened?"

"That lowlife likes to beat up women. If you'd seen what he did to my friend Kathy, you'd probably have joined me."

"I'll make sure I keep him waiting," the doctor says before he walks out.

Back at the apartment, Charlie opens the door for James. "If you don't need me any longer, I'll head home."

"No, I'm good, Charlie. Thanks for everything. Go home to your family; it's late. I'll see you at work on Monday."

When he walks into the apartment, Sam and Kathy are still sitting on the couch. Sam jumps up and runs to him the minute she sees his casts.

"Oh my God—what happened to you?"

"I fractured my wrists pounding on Bobby's face. How's Kathy?"

"Are you in pain?" Sam asks him, looking at his bandaged hands and arms. "Are you going to be all right? What did the doctor say?"

"Sam, please stop worrying, I'm going to be fine. The fractures weren't that severe. I just have to wear the casts for three or four weeks, and I have painkillers for the pain. The pills are in my pocket. My finger tips are sticking out of the cast so I can use my hands a little bit. I'm just having a little trouble buttoning my shirt. I guess I'll be wearing pull overs for a while."

James goes over and sits next to Kathy. "How's my friend Joe Palooka doing here?"

She laughs a little and says, "You should talk; you don't look so good yourself."

"At least I made you laugh. Your buddy isn't feeling so good right now. He's got a broken nose and at least four busted ribs. He was still at the hospital when I left. I can guarantee that he'll never lay another hand on you."

Kathy places her hand gently on James's face and leans over to give him a kiss on the cheek. "Thank you! If you don't mind, I'd like to turn in." She tries to get up.

"Sit back down, sweetie," he tells her. "You're not going to sleep tonight. You have a head injury, and we have to keep an eye on you. So, put on the television and make yourself comfortable." He turns to Sam. "Sam, you and I will take turns staying up with her. You take the first shift. When you get tired, come wake me and I'll relieve you."

Sam comes into the bedroom and rouses him at around four in the morning. "James, I'm a little tired. Would you mind taking my place?"

"How is Kathy doing?" he asks her as he gets out of bed.

"She's doing well. She seems to be in a good mood and has been talking all night. Maybe I'm crazy, but I think she's glad to be rid of Bobby."

"All right, get some sleep. I'll take over from here. Do me a favor and get me one of those painkillers before you go to bed?"

James walks into the living room. Kathy is sitting on the couch. The television is turned off. Sam brings in a painkiller and a glass of water, she helps James take the pill and heads to bed.

"Okay, kiddo, it's just me and you," he says to Kathy.

"How do *you* feel?" she asks.

"I feel great. I just took another painkiller and I'm feeling pretty good. Do you want one?"

"No, I have no pain."

"Who said anything about pain?" he shoots back, smiling. "Those pills are for making you feel good. Come on, let me take a look at that pretty face."

He sits next to her. She shows him her face. "I think everything's getting better. That swelling on your face has gone down, but your face is still discolored. That will take a few days to clear up. Your left ear is still swollen, and so is your lower lip. You might want to keep that swelling on your lip; it might come in handy when you're doing something with a guy, if you know what I mean."

She slaps him on the arm.

"Hey!" he yells. "You're getting just like your friend down the hall—quick with the hands."

"Well, stop being quick with your mouth and I'll stop being quick with my hands."

"You do know you're hitting a defenseless cripple, don't you?" He puts his hands up in the air to show her his bandages.

"Defenseless or not, you need to curb that mouth."

"All right, I will. Let's get serious for a moment. Tell me about Bobby. Sam says that you're glad to be rid of him. Why is that? I thought you two were hitting it off?"

"I am *relieved* to be rid of him. Bobby isn't for me; there was always an edge to him that worried me. He actually accused me of fooling around with you."

"He did? When was this?"

"A couple of weeks ago. He stopped by the agency. I guess I was in your office talking with you. When I came out, he asked me what I was doing in there with you that took so long. He said, 'Does it take that long to go down on your boss?' I was so pissed, I told him to get out. I was ready to break it off with him right then and there."

"Why didn't you? What stopped you?"

"Bobby called me later and apologized, begging for forgiveness. Said he was under a lot of pressure at school, and that his grades were falling. He promised me he'd never do it again. I was lonely and desperate, and I believed him."

Kathy and James talk until ten in the morning.

"My God," she says to James, "I can't believe we've been talking for so long. I'm so tired! Is it all right if I get a little sleep? I feel fine; you don't have to keep an eye on me any longer." She begins to get up.

"No, it's not all right. Who's going to make me my coffee and breakfast?" He waves his arms with the casts in the air. "Sam is still asleep."

"All right—I'll get right on it. What do you want for breakfast?"

"How about some hotcakes and sausages? Is that too much to ask?"

"No, I'll whip them up in no time."

After Sam wakes up, she walks into the kitchen, where Kathy and James are eating their hotcakes.

"Yum, that smells good," she remarks. "Are there any hotcakes left for me?"

"I can make them for you in a jiff," Kathy volunteers.

"Sam, while Kathy is getting your breakfast ready, can you help me take a shower? I'm not supposed to get the casts wet. And besides, I have hard time using my hands. I can't hold onto the soap."

"No, I don't mind. Let me go get you a change of clothes."

Kathy is stirring the batter for Sam's pancakes when she hears the bathroom door open. Then she hears Sam yell, "If you think that I'm doing that every time you take a shower, you got another think coming, mister." She slams the door.

Sam comes storming into the kitchen. She reaches into the cupboard, takes out a cup, and pours coffee for herself.

"What just happened?" Kathy asks her.

"James is taking his shower and I'm washing him down, lathering him up with the soap. All of a sudden, I feel this big hand behind the back of my head. He's pushing my head down into his groin and trying to stick his thing into my mouth."

"That's so cute," Kathy says.

Sam gives her a glare.

"So, what did you do?" a smiling Kathy wants to know.

"I know what I would have liked to do." Sam gives her a look. "Instead, I felt sorry for him and I did it."

"That's my girl," Kathy comments. "You're the best girlfriend ever. Here are your pancakes."

"You know, Kathy—he came to *your* rescue but *I'm* paying the price."

Kathy gives her a wary stare. "I'm pretty sure you don't want me helping you in that regard."

James comes out of the bathroom. "Sam, you left. The shirt you picked out for me has buttons and I'm having a problem. I can't button my shirt. It was hard enough getting my pants on."

"Well, that's just too bad. I guess you'll have to go around with your shirt unbuttoned."

"I'll do it for you," Kathy says. She walks over and begins buttoning his shirt. As Kathy does his buttons, James gives Sam a dirty look and she sneers back at him.

"There you go," Kathy says to him when she's done. "If you guys don't mind, I'm going to take a shower and a nap," she adds and walks out.

James places his two bandaged hands around a cup of coffee and sits at the table with Sam. "I'm glad *someone* appreciates me around here."

Sam takes a pause from eating her pancakes and snaps at him angrily. "Maybe you should ask *Kathy* to suck your cock every morning."

"You know, Sam, that's not such a bad idea. I'm pretty sure Kathy would be willing." He smiles slyly and gets up. "Let me go ask her." He starts walking out of the kitchen.

Sam grabs him and pulls him back. "Don't you dare! Remember, the only mouth your boy is going into is mine. Don't you even dream of asking somebody else."

"Well, now that's settled," he says to her, smiling, "I'll see you again bright and early tomorrow morning, before you go to Sunday service."

She releases her hold on him and shakes her head. "I'm such a big sucker!"

James bends down and gives her a kiss. "I know you're a big sucker," he whispers. "That's why I'm so willing to provide my man for your service.

"Ouch!" he yells.

Kathy comes running into the kitchen and finds James bent over, holding onto the countertop. "What happened?" she asks.

"Sam punched me in the gut."

Kathy looks at Sam. "What's wrong with you? Can't you see the guy is hurt already?"

"Oh, he's a big faker—I hardly touched him. It was just a love tap."

"I've been on the other end of your punches, Sam," Kathy reminds her friend. She walks over to comfort James. "They're not love taps."

Sam gets up angrily and storms out of the kitchen. "I've got to get out of here. I'm totally outnumbered. I can't win with you two."

The next morning, Kathy gets up and heads for the kitchen to make some coffee. She hears Sam and James in the bathroom. The shower is running. The coffee has just finished percolating when Sam comes into the kitchen.

"Good morning! Is there any coffee?" Sam asks Kathy.

"Yep. I'll get you a cup," Kathy replies. She places the cup of coffee in front of Sam, who takes a sip.

Kathy gives Sam a big smile. "Well how did it go in there this morning?"

Sam simply gives her a knowing look. Kathy laughs and says, "That's my girl."

"You know, Kathy, he's going to be spoiled rotten by the time he gets the casts off. He's not going to want to do anything around here anymore."

"Oh, come on, Sam. James helps you out a lot around the house. He does the dusting, and I've seen him do the dishes and the laundry. He folds and puts away the clothes. You never even have to ask him—he just does the work."

"That's right, Kathy, James does help me out a lot. It's taken me a year to train him. Now, I'm right back to where I started. I'm going to have to do it all over again."

18
BACK ON THE TRAIL

That Monday morning, after the shower routine has been taken care of, Sam heads into the kitchen, where Kathy is by the sink doing the dishes.

"What do you have planned for today?" Kathy asks her.

"James and I are going to choose our wedding rings, and after that I'm driving him to get fitted for his tux. I'll drive him to work when we're done," Sam answers. She pours herself a cup of coffee and sits across from Kathy.

"How are the wedding arrangements coming? Is James going to have his casts off before the wedding?"

"Yes, if everything heals according to plan, he'll have his casts off a week before the wedding. Just in time. I have another problem. I was thrown a curveball over the weekend by James. I was under the impression that just his immediate family was coming to the wedding. It turns out that not only are they coming—but also sixty other people as well."

Kathy bursts out laughing. "Oh my gosh, sixty more people? How did that happen?"

"I know—it's crazy, right?" Sam shrugs. "I didn't even invite any of those people. All James's friends found out he was getting married and called him over the weekend. They wanted to know why they didn't get invitations. So, he issued a blanket invitation over the phone, telling anyone who wanted to come that they could come. All weekend long, people kept calling to get invited. I'm afraid the whole Bronx might show up. Don't these people have anything better to do? I'm not even sure they know where Lorenzo, Texas, is located."

Kathy is laughing hysterically. "How will they even get there?"

"They're coming by car, by train, and by plane—and if there were a harbor in Lorenzo, I'm pretty sure some would come by sea. Now I have to find rooms for them at the hotels in Lubbock."

"What does James say? What about the extra cost?"

"He's not worried about the cost. He says these people are all very generous and will give us big envelopes."

"Sam, have you seen my pain pills?" James asks as he walks into the kitchen.

Both women immediately stop talking.

"Well? Have you seen them?" James asks once more when he doesn't get a response.

"Why do you need the pain pills?" Sam asks.

He gives her a wary look. "Because I'm in pain." He lifts up his bandaged hands. "What a stupid question."

"The doctor said you should only take them as needed," Sam reminds him.

"I know," he fires back, "and now I need them. So, where are they?"

"I think you've been taking too many. In two days, you've taken fourteen pills."

"If I took fourteen pills, it was because I needed them! Who died and made you queen, anyway? Just give me the damn pills."

"No, I'm not giving you the pills, James. You're abusing the drugs."

James glares at her. The pupils in his eyes appear to get smaller. There is a vein visibly beating on the left side of his head.

Sam realizes suddenly and with clarity that a major argument is about to take place and that she needs to defuse it quickly. She gets up, walks over to him, and gives him a hug.

"James, please listen to me," she pleads. "I don't want you popping pills like you did when you were in New York. Everything is going so nicely between us. Please don't let this get in our way. Won't you do this one thing for me?"

James pushes her away. "All right, Sam, you can control the pills. You don't have to tell me where they're hidden. When I need one, I will ask you. Now, can you *please* go get me one, because I am truly in pain?"

She leaves the room and comes back with a pill. He walks to the kitchen sink and turns on the water. He pops the pill in his mouth and bends his head under the faucet to get a drink. He looks at Sam and wipes his lips with the back of his cast.

"Don't think this matter is over. We're going to discuss this more, at a later time. Sam, I'm not happy with your unilateral behavior today. You should have discussed your concern about the pills with me before hiding them. Come on, let's get going!"

On the ride to the jewelry store, Sam pulls the Mustang into a gas station to get some gas. She gets out of the car to speak to the attendant. James looks out of his window just as a white van pulls up on the other side of the pumps. There is a ladder on top of the van. The company logo stenciled on the side reads A-1 Painting. A young man wearing overalls steps out of the van. He has a goatee.

Sam is getting back into the car after the attendant is finished pumping the gas. James tells her, "Get to a phone right away! I think there's a pay phone right on the corner."

"Why? What's the matter?"

"Just do it!" he says sternly.

She drives up to the phone booth.

"Come on. I need you to place the call," he orders as he gets out of the car.

"Who am I calling?" she asks him, change and phone in hand.

"Call my office and get Charlie on the phone."

When she gets Charlie on the line, she puts the phone against James's ear.

"Charlie," James says, "she's in Texas."

"Who's in Texas?" Charlie asks him.

"Penelope Campos," James replies, breathing heavily. "Penelope Campos is in Texas."

"How do you know?"

"Because I saw her, Charlie. I saw Penelope Campos in Texas."

"When were you in Texas? I thought you were home all weekend."

"I didn't see her over the past weekend, Charlie. I saw her last month, over the Easter weekend. It was before I knew anything about her disappearance. It was at a gas station outside of Amarillo. Something has been gnawing at me this entire time; I just couldn't pinpoint exactly what it was. Just now I saw this white van pull into a gas station alongside us, and it all came flooding back to me.

"Charlie, she bumped into me at that gas station. That young girl and I were in Texas at the very same gas station at the very same time. The last of the letters etched on the wall at the house we visited in Arizona? The letter T stands for Texas. Charlie, she's in Texas in a town that starts with the letter B, P, or R."

"James, do you have any idea of how many places in Texas start with those letters?" Charlie says.

"No, I don't, Charlie, and I don't care. I want you and Al to get on the phone and call every police station in towns starting with those letters. Give them a description of the van, the man, and the girl. Document everything you do—which police station you call and the name of the person you speak with. Get started immediately.

"I'll call Spencer at the FBI when I get back to the office. We need to give this information to the FBI. They have the manpower to do a proper job. Meanwhile, don't waste any time. Get started right away. We need to get Penelope home."

Sam hangs up the phone for him and opens his door of the car. "Do you really believe you'll find the girl soon?" Sam asks him when she gets in the car.

"Oh yes, Sam. I'm more confident now than ever before. I'm just mad at myself for not figuring it out sooner. We were in that same station the last time we went to Lorenzo. Remember, I kept asking about that gas station and wondering whether if we'd been there before? Well, we had, Sam—a month earlier."

Sam starts the engine and turns to him. "I'm sorry about the pills. If you want the bottle, it's in my purse in the back seat."

James looks at her and smiles. "No, Sam, you can hold on to the bottle. You were right; I was beginning to abuse the drugs. I just don't want you to take it upon yourself to dictate my behavior. If you were worried about my abusing the medication, you should have spoken to me. You need to trust that I'll listen to your concerns and act upon them."

"All right. I'm sorry. Will you forgive me?"

"Yes, of course." He leans over to give her a kiss, but accidentally presses against his bandaged hand. "Ouch!" he yells.

She leans over and kisses him. "I'm not giving you a pain pill over that little *ouch*."

"You're lucky my hands are in bandages," he warns her.

That afternoon when James is in his office, Charlie and Al come storming into his office.

"We need to talk," Charlie tells him.

"Of course," he says to them. "Have a seat."

"Al and I can't do our jobs *and* the assignment you gave us this morning," Charlie tells him. "Calling every police station and reaching someone who can answer our questions is taking forever, James. You need to come up with a different plan."

"Yeah, you're right, guys. I just got caught up in the excitement. It's not fair to you two. I was supposed to take care of this part of the investigation."

"I don't know how you're going to find the time, James," Al responds. "You've got to run this office. You have a meeting with that insurance company on Wednesday. You have another meeting with that law firm in Denver on Friday. What about your wedding? Don't you need time to prepare?"

"I know finding Penelope is urgent, but where are you going to carve out the time? The FBI is on the case. Why don't you let them handle the investigation? They're much better equipped to handle this search than we are."

"I don't think the FBI is taking this kidnapping seriously enough," James says. "Agent Spencer told Greenwald that he'd get involved, but he may have said that just to get him off his back. Anyway, this is *our* case; Greenwald is paying us good money to work on the investigation. Can I ask you to devote just one more hour at night and also come in an hour earlier in the morning? That's all I'll need.

"I'm going to call Spencer at the FBI and give him the latest news. I'll try to get a clear sense of just how seriously he's taking what I have to tell him. The investigation is my responsibility; I know that. I'll try not to interfere with your work. If you guys can give me that extra time, I'll do the rest. What do you say?"

Charlie and Al look at each other. Al nods. "Sure, we can give you the time," he says.

"All right, thanks. I'll give you each one county in Texas to cover. Cover your counties, and when you've finished, come and see me and I'll give you a new county. We'll have a progress meeting on Thursday and assess how far we've gotten. Thanks, guys. Ask Kathy to come in here, please," he adds as they are leaving the office.

"You busy right now?" he asks Kathy.

"I'm *always* busy, but I can give *you* a little time."

"Good. You're my new sidekick—and I do mean *sidekick*. We're going to be working closely together. Pull up a chair and sit next to me. You're going to be dialing the calls and placing the phone on my shoulder. Start with placing a call to Spencer at the FBI, and then go get a map of Texas."

James has just finished telling Spencer at the FBI the story of how he ran into the fugitives in Amarillo. "It doesn't matter any longer," Spencer tells James, "Fontana pleaded guilty and took a deal. Twenty-five to life. The case is closed!"

"What?" James is utterly dumbfounded. "But he didn't do it, Spence. Weren't you paying attention to what I said? The girl is in Texas. I saw her myself!"

"James, I know you believe that, but the facts point in a different direction. This guy admits to doing the girl."

"Then where's the body? If he killed her, where did he dump the body? Why won't he tell you where the body is? Spence, there is no body—she's still alive. I tell you, I saw her! Please—I need you and the FBI to be involved. I don't have the resources to do the job myself."

"I'm sorry, James, but with Fontana pleading guilty, the case is closed. I can't justify putting any more man-hours into this case. My superiors would never approve the time."

Kathy comes in and hangs up the phone receiver that is lying on his desk. "Are you okay?"

"Fontana just pled guilty," he informs her, looking at the wall. "The FBI is no longer investigating. The Campos case is closed."

Kathy sits down. "What are you going to do?" Her voice is shaking. "That poor girl is still out there."

"I'm going to keep chasing her kidnappers," he answers determinedly. "That girl is alive, Kathy, and I'm not going to quit until I find her and bring her home. Come on, come back over on this side of the desk and help me make the calls."

The phone rings. Kathy picks up the phone and puts it to his ear. It's Henry Greenwald.

"*Damn,*" James mutters under his breath. "Hello, Mr. Greenwald."

"James, did you hear? This creep pled guilty."

"Yes, Mr. Greenwald. I just got off the phone with Agent Spencer."

"What does this mean, James?"

"It means that the case just got a whole lot tougher, Mr. Greenwald. The FBI is closing the investigation. I'm the only one left looking for her."

"You still believe that my granddaughter is still alive?"

"Oh yes, I do, Mr. Greenwald. Now more than ever. I saw her, sir. I saw Penelope. She was alive."

"You saw Penelope? When did you see her? Why haven't you told me about this before?"

"I saw her on Easter, before I had even gotten the case. I bumped into her at a gas station in Amarillo. It all came back to me today. Your granddaughter is alive, sir."

"You know, James, I'm beginning to think Gold might be right about you. Maybe you are taking me for a ride. Maybe you're just soaking me for my money."

"Oh, sir, I'm so sorry to hear you say that." James is silent for a moment. "Mr. Greenwald, your granddaughter is alive. She is in Texas. Whether you keep me on the payroll or not, I will continue to look for her. After I hang up with you, I intend to call every police station starting with the letters *B*, *P*, and *R*. I'm not going to rest until that beautiful young lady comes home. If you want me to give back what you have paid me so far, just let me know and I'll send you a check."

"James, I'm sorry for what I said. This news today got to me. You keep working. I'll try to put some pressure on some politicians that owe me some favors. I'll try to get the FBI back on the case."

"It's past seven," Kathy says to him after they have spent the entire day making calls. "Should we call it a day?"

"Yes," he tells her, stretching. "I'm getting tired. We'll start back again first thing tomorrow."

"We covered a lot of ground, but we haven't made much progress," she admits. "No one has seen the people we're looking for."

"I disagree, Kathy. We made a lot of progress today. We're getting the word out to every police station. The police don't have any current information because they haven't been looking. Now that they've gotten the message, they'll be on the lookout. Something should break soon.

"My goal is to call all the police stations until it does. I'm going to keep reminding all the local police stations to stay on the lookout. Sooner or later, the kidnappers will come out into the open. Kathy, Penelope is alive. She walked right into me at the gas station in Amarillo. This young girl is coming home; I won't rest until she does."

That night, Kathy drives him home. When they walk into the apartment, Kathy cries, "What is that awful smell?"

"*Oh.* Oh no, Kathy. That's no awful smell—that's the wonderful aroma of something really tasty," James tells her delightedly.

They walk into the kitchen and find a big pot on the stove, steam is escaping from the pot in small clouds. Sam is coming out of the bedroom.

"What did you make? It smells terrible," Kathy says to her.

"I made *mineste*," Sam replies, walking into the kitchen.

"What the hell is *mineste*?" Kathy asks.

"It's an Italian vegetable soup," Sam informs Kathy. Sam walks over, picks up a fork, and sticks it into a morsel of meat on a plate. "Here, James. I fried up some fatback for you."

James opens his mouth. Sam feeds him the meat. "This is delicious, Sam!" He gives her a hug and a kiss. "You're amazing!"

"I told you I would learn to cook Italian food." Sam turns to Kathy. "Do you want to try a piece?"

"I'm afraid to," Kathy replies, but she doesn't have time to protest. Sam has another piece on a fork and is already putting it into Kathy's mouth. After holding the meat in her mouth for a moment, Kathy breaks down and chews.

"Oh my gosh, *really*, this is good," Kathy says in amazement.

Sam tells the two of them to go and get cleaned up. "I'll set the table," she adds.

"Is that *polenta* I see in the pan?" James asks her before he heads out.

"You bet! It *is polenta*, and I used escarole as the vegetable. Now that you know the entire menu, can you stop with all the questions and go get ready for dinner?"

He walks back to her and gives her another kiss. "You're absolutely wonderful," he says.

That night at bedtime, Sam is standing in front of her bureau mirror. She's just come out of the shower. A towel is wrapped around her body and she's applying cream to her hands and face. James comes in and shuts the door. He walks up behind her and gently kisses her neck.

"That was some dinner. Thank you," he says to her.

She turns her head slightly toward him as he continues his kissing. "Am I out of the doghouse yet for this morning?"

"No, not yet," he replies, loosening her towel and letting it drop to the floor. "You're *almost* out, though." He continues his gentle kissing, working his way to the small of her back.

"Oh, that feels good," she purrs. His hands slide up her sides and come to rest on her breasts.

"Are my bandages too rough against your skin? Am I hurting you?" he whispers.

"No, they're fine. You're being very gentle."

Ever so softly he caresses the lovely mounds that are pointing straight out.

With his fingers sticking out of the casts, he massages her nipples. He peeks his head over her shoulders and looks into the mirror.

"You are absolutely beautiful," he tells her, and goes back to kissing her on the neck. He moves up and nibbles on her earlobe. She lets out a sigh.

One of his hands drops down. He pulls down his pajamas. She feels his hardened member touching her skin and spreads her legs wide. He squats slightly and reaches down to guide his member into her. She lets out another moan when she feels him inside her. His fingers are still tenderly working her nipples as he slowly starts his rhythmic thrusting. She leans forward to allow him to get deeper into her. She begins keeping time with his movements. She bends her body over the bureau and clutches onto the edge. She pushes back toward him to allow his member to get deeper inside.

"Oh God, that feels wonderful. A little harder," she orders, trying to increase the pace.

He complies and begins plunging harder into her. She pushes back further and tries to get him to go in deeper. "Please, sweetie. Do me a little harder now, please."

This time he ignores her and keeps a steady, deliberate movement. She clutches tighter to the top of the bureau and begins shoving herself back at him.

"Oh, James, please don't tease—do me harder now." His hands slide down her torso, and he grabs her hips. He begins thrusting harder and harder.

"Oh yes, that's it, James! Just like that." The bureau is banging against the wall. They take no notice of the noise. "Oh yes, you've got it now, baby. Drive it home. Just a little longer, please, just a little longer." She bites her lip. "Oh God! Oh God!" she yells over and over again, until she gives a final shout and is quiet.

They hear banging on the wall. "Can't you guys give me a break?" Kathy yells from the other side.

They burst out laughing. Sam turns to James, puts her arms around his neck, and gives him a kiss.

"So, am I forgiven? Are we all square?

He gives her a smile and a kiss. "All square. That was wonderful. Thank you."

19
WEDDING WEEK

Kathy is watching television after dinner when Sam comes walking into the living room.

"Kathy, have you seen, James?"

"No, I haven't."

"He's been out every night this week. I wonder where he's been? Anything going on at work?"

"No, he's been busy on the Campos case but he hasn't been staying late. Not anything that I'm aware of, anyway."

"Um, I wonder what he's been up to? It's very strange that he hasn't told me where's he's been going?" Sam mutters to herself as she leaves the room.

James is at the wheel of the Mustang as he, Sam, and Kathy drive down to Lorenzo for the wedding. The three of them are bringing so much stuff that they have to make the trip with two cars. Kathy is following behind in her car.

Sam is not doing much talking. Neither is James. He is preoccupied with the Penelope Campos case. May has come and gone, and they have not come up with anything. He has decided that when he returns from his honeymoon, he will get in his car and drive through the entire state of Texas.

He intends to visit every town that starts with the letter *B*, *P*, or *R*. His plan is to visit every police station in every one of those towns. Someone knows something; he's convinced of that. He just needs to find out who.

The agency has recently hired another detective, Mike Stanfill. The three detectives James now has on his staff should be able to handle all the work at the office. The security report for Big W was completed, and there is really nothing much for him to do at the office, anyway. Sam will gripe about him being away, but he's not giving in to her. James knows that young Penelope needs to come home.

"Did you really have to buy the twins such a large train set?" Sam breaks the silence. "It's taking up most of the room in the trunk."

"I always wanted a train set when I was a kid."

"You *know* they're going to fight over that toy. You would have been better off buying two smaller sets."

"No, I've got that covered. I'm going to make one of the boys an engineer and the other a conductor. I'll give each of the twins a job of his own to do."

"It's really nice of you to stop in again and look in on Aggie."

"Once the ice was broken with Aggie on the last trip, I don't mind. I miss her…and those little guys, too."

"Yeah, well, I'm not leaving you alone with her," Sam warns him, sitting up in her seat. "I'm going to keep an eye on that sweet, innocent young thing—as you call her."

"Stop talking crazy. She's not going to try anything with me."

Sam gives him a look. "How much do you want to wager? I bet that she gives you a full-frontal kiss when you walk in."

"I'll bet you a nickel."

Later that day, Sam and James are on the last leg of their trip to Lorenzo.

They have just left Aggie's place. Kathy did not go with them to visit Aggie. She headed straight to Lorenzo.

"Where's my nickel?" Sam asks him.

He reaches into his pocket and hands her a nickel.

Sam has a broad smile on her face. "It should actually be a dime. Not only did she give you a full frontal when you walked in, but she also gave you another kiss when you left."

James looks over at her. "It was worse than that. She stuck her tongue into my mouth."

"Really? That *slut*. Wait till I see her at the wedding! I'm going to put a stop to this. I guess she's gotten over Henry—or at least she has when you're around." Then Sam changes the subject. "How's your hand doing today? Yesterday you said it was hurting you."

"It feels pretty good today; the pain come and goes." He lifts his hand from the steering wheel and wiggles his fingers. "The physical therapy seems to help. I just need to remember to do my hand exercises twice a day."

It is three o'clock in the morning on Thursday of the wedding week. Sam is lying in bed in her sister's room, wide awake. She's waiting for James to come home. His New York friends have taken him into Lubbock for his bachelor party. She hears the front door opening and, moments later, the door closing to her brother's room. She puts on her robe and goes into the room next door. James is putting his keys down on the night table.

"How was your night?" she asks.

"What are you doing still up?"

She sits on the bed. "My soon-to-be husband went partying with his New York friends and you thought I could go to sleep? Come on," she says, patting the bed beside her. "Sit down and tell me all about it."

"You know, Sam—I don't think that's how it works," he says to her as he sits on the bed. "I think bachelor parties are supposed to stay secret."

"Who made that rule?" she cries out. "It's unfair!"

"Shush, you'll wake everybody!"

"There *is* no such rule," she leans over and lowers her voice. "You better spill your guts; I want to hear all the sordid details."

He laughs. "All right," he says to her, "but if I get kicked out of the fraternity of men, it's your fault." He takes a breath. "There was a lot of drinking, naturally. All were drinking but me you'll be happy to know. At one point we got a little too loud and the police were called."

"Really?" She lifts an eyebrow. "I hope no one got arrested."

"No, everything was cool. When the Lubbock cops learned it was only a bunch of loud New Yorkers, they were pretty nice about the whole thing."

"That's a surprise," she says. "The cops around here aren't usually that nice."

James gives her a crafty look. "Don't you think you should go to bed? It's late. I'd like to get some sleep."

"I'm not leaving until you tell me the rest. What about the woman?"

He gives her a fake-innocent smile. "What woman?"

"Don't play dumb with me! Isn't it customary at these bachelor parties for there to be a certain kind of woman?"

James puts his arm over her shoulder and leans over to give her a kiss.

"Why in the world would I want another woman when I already have the most beautiful woman in the world?"

"Very sweet," she says as she pushes him down on the bed and climbs on top of him. His hands go under her pajama top and cups her breasts. Sam immediately jumps up.

"No you don't! Nothing for you until our wedding night."

James sits up. "Maybe I should go back and find that other woman? I haven't had any action in a week."

Sam gives him a shove. After saying, "Go to sleep!" she turns to leave the room.

"Wait a minute—come back in here." When she turns back from the door, James continues. "Friday night I'm going to go and share a hotel room with my brother. You're going to be super busy around here, and I'll just be in the way."

"Good idea. Just make sure you're here on time the next day!"

"Sure. What time is the wedding again? Six o'clock?"

"Don't be funny! You know it's at four. You better be here by three thirty!"

"I'll be here. By the way, I booked the wedding suite at the hotel for both Saturday and Sunday nights."

"Why did you do that?" she asks him, sitting back down on the bed. "We could just sleep here at my parents' house."

"Do you really want your parents to hear how you perform during one of our sessions? Maybe they'll be impressed by how uninhibited their prudish daughter has gotten in that regard."

She slaps him on the arm.

"Okay, you're right," she admits. Then she gives him a kiss and gets up. "I'm going to bed."

The morning of the big day arrives. James has just finished his breakfast and is coming out of the hotel's restaurant. He notices his mother sitting on the sofa in the lobby.

"*Mamma!* What are you doing sitting out here by yourself?" he asks her in Italian as he approaches her.

She looks up. "Giacomo, *siedi qua*." She pats the spot on the sofa next to her, motioning for James to sit down, and he does.

"So, what do you think of your boy getting married?" he asks her.

"I'm very happy for you, Giacomo. You're marrying a very nice girl. She's very good for you. You're much happier with her in your life. I can see the change that's come over you."

"Now that Sam and I are getting married, you'll come to Colorado many times, I hope. You know, because Sam and I will no longer be living in sin, according to your rules. You'll have no more excuses not to visit us."

Mamma Coppi looks over and gives him a smile. "Yes, Giacomo, I will come…even though I will still consider you a sinner."

"Me?" He sits up. "What about Sam? She was living with me this entire time, sharing my bed. Will you still consider *her* a sinner?"

His mom lifts her hand and dismisses his question. "Don't be silly. I never considered her a sinner. This whole thing is your fault, not hers. Your future wife is the nicest person. She goes to church every Sunday and prays every night. Very respectful, especially to me. She calls me every Sunday. No, she's not a sinner. You're the sinner. It's all *your* fault."

"*My* fault?" he asks incredulously. "How did you reach that conclusion?"

She gives him an arch look. "Giacomo, be honest with me. How long would you have stayed with that sweet girl if she hadn't submitted to you in *that* way? You would have gotten rid of her in a week. She's a smart girl. She knew that to get you, she had to do what you wanted. It's because of you that she committed a mortal sin. She committed those sins out of love for you. God will forgive her. It's *you* who needs to atone for the sin."

Speechless, he frowns and shakes his head. After a few moments, he throws up his hands and says, "I give up; there's just no winning with you, *Mamma*. I'm not even going to try." He gives his mother a kiss and heads upstairs to his room.

James is standing on the left-hand side of the arbor in Sam's parents' backyard at exactly four o'clock. Across from him is Kathy, as well as Sam's two sisters, who are all bridesmaids. Reverend Powers, Bible in hand, is in front of him. James's brother Anthony is standing behind him as they wait for the back door to open and for Sam to make an entrance. Every chair is filled, and a large crowd is standing on the sides and at the back of the yard.

It is a beautiful, cloudless, sunny day in Lorenzo. The temperature, for Texas in June, is actually pleasant. James is quite sure that the whole town is in the yard.

The back door opens, and the entire assembly turns to look. A little girl carrying a basket containing flower petals comes walking out. She walks slowly forward, dropping rose petals as she goes. Sam walks out behind her, fixing her dress as she walks through the door with her mother. A gasp is heard from the crowd as Sam nears the arbor. She has a beautiful white dress, and a white tiara on her head. A birdcage veil comes down to just below her eyes. Her strawberry-blonde hair is down to her shoulders and shimmers in the sunlight. James's legs buckle as he gazes upon her beauty.

"She's beautiful," Anthony whispers in his ear.

Indeed, Anthony, she is *beautiful,* he thinks. *How in the world did I manage to nab such a beauty? I've got to be the luckiest man on the face of the earth. There is no more beautiful woman in the world at this very moment.*

Sam arrives at the arbor and gives James a sweet smile. He smiles back as he walks over and stands beside her. After the reverend completes the service, it is time for the vows.

Sam turns to face James and begins. "James, from the moment I first saw you, I was in love. There was no greater love in the world than I had for you at that moment, I told myself at the time. However, I was wrong. James, every new day I wake up and love you even more. Each day brings joy and excitement into my life the moment I realize that I will be sharing that day with you.

"James, I need to thank you for coming into my life. You took a confused, foolish, stupid little girl and turned her into the confident woman you see in front of you today.

"James, I vow to you that I will always bring honor to your good name. I will cherish you and will be devoted to you and faithful to you all the days of my life. Most of all, I will always love you."

James begins his vows.

"Samantha, I'm ashamed to admit that I did not memorize the vows that we agreed on. This was not due to laziness. I wanted to wait for this precise moment to capture the exact right words to describe my true feelings. Now, I realize my plan was a big mistake. Your beauty leaves me speechless. I'm at a loss for words that would adequately do that beauty justice.

"Samantha, you came into my life a little more than a year ago. I remember that night, sitting alone in a corner. My world was a stark, dark, and dreary place. You introduced yourself to me and reached out for my hand to take me to the dance floor. Not knowing that particular country and western dance, I resisted. You smiled warmly and coaxed me gently until I stood to take your hand. Sam, throughout our time together, you have continued your soft ways and have led me out of my life of darkness—into a bright world of colors and possibilities.

"Samantha, my vow to you today is that I will always honor, cherish, and be devoted and faithful to you, but most of all that I will love you all the days of my life."

He reaches for her. Their embrace ends in a passionate kiss. The assembled crowd cheers loudly. It's a combination Texas and Bronx cheer that can no doubt be heard throughout the county.

When the reception begins, the couple kick off the affair by dancing the waltz that they had practiced for the occasion. Sam's head is spinning with joy—this is the moment that she has longed for since she was a little girl. James has learned the steps well. He glides and soars with her over the dance floor. Sam takes no notice of the people who are applauding. Her eyes are fixed on her husband, and her focus is all on the moment. The music stops. They share one more passionate kiss. *Absolutely perfect,* she says to herself.

James sits on a lounge chair in the backyard that wedding night, waiting for Sam. She comes out of the house, having just changed out of her wedding gown.

"It feels good to wear regular clothes again," she tells him, sitting on the chair next to him.

"That was a beautiful dress…you did a great job in your selection." He puts his arms around her shoulder and pulls her close to him.

"So, what was *your* favorite part of the wedding?" She looks into his eyes and beams.

"When I first set eyes on you coming out of the house. You were so beautiful—my whole body went weak. My legs almost buckled at the sight of you." James leans over and gives her a kiss. "I'm not dreaming, am I? You did marry me, right?"

"That's *so* sweet," she says. She cups his face with her hands. "No, you're not dreaming. You're stuck with me forever."

"How about you?" he asks her. "What was your favorite part of today?"

She looks up at him, smiles, and moves over to sit on his lap. "I had two favorites. The first was your wedding vow; I thought it was glorious. The second was the waltz; it was wonderful. When did you get to be such a good dancer? At the dance studio when we practiced, you were terrible."

"Last week, I didn't tell you where I was going but I snuck out every night after work and practiced with the instructor. I told her that I wouldn't stop until I got it perfect. After stepping on her toes about a thousand times, she realized that I was serious and simplified the dance into four easy steps that I could remember."

"Have you seen Aggie?" Sam looks around the yard. "I'm worried about her. She had a little too much to drink."

"She's passed out on the couch in your house," he replies. "And good for Aggie. I'm glad she let loose. She needed a day to get it all out. Raising three children by herself. Poor girl hasn't had a break in months."

Sam looks out into the yard. "Are these people ever going to leave? It's past midnight."

"These are New Yorkers; they'll party all night. I feel sorry for your parents. I'm sure they're tired and want to go to bed."

"My whole family is *already* in bed," Sam says. "I feel bad for *us!* We had a long, busy day. I would love to turn in."

"Why didn't you say so, Sam?" He moves her gently from his lap. "Let's get out of here."

She looks around. "What about our guests?"

"I'm sure they can find their way back to the hotel. Come on, let's go! I'm dying to make love to my beautiful bride." He takes her arm and pulls her away.

Sam kisses James gently on the cheek the next morning in their honeymoon suite. He is still sleeping. It is almost noon. He opens his eyes, gazes at her, reaches up and pulls her on top of him.

"Good morning," he says to her. "What are you doing up, and why do you have clothes on?"

"It's almost noon. Many of the guests are checking out and getting ready to head home. We need to go downstairs and say our goodbyes."

James pulls Sam down on the bed and maneuvers himself on top of her. "Not yet...let's have a little more fun."

She shoves him off her and jumps up. "Not now; we'll do that later. We need to say thank you and farewell to our guests. Besides, you had a *lot* of fun last night. Didn't I please you?"

James lifts his naked body out of bed and gives her a kiss. "You were amazing! I think married life agrees with you...I've never seen you the way you were last night." He begins to put on his underwear.

"You haven't seen anything yet. Wait until you find out what I have in store for you on our honeymoon," she teases him.

"If it's going to be better than last night, then let's get going right away. How far is Galveston from here, anyhow?" He goes to the closet and pulls out a pair of slacks.

"I think it's about nine or ten hours. Maybe we should stop overnight along the way."

"No, we'll leave early tomorrow morning. We should be able to make it in one day," he calls from the bathroom.

She walks to the door as he begins to brush his teeth. "James, when we get to Galveston, I want to make love to you on the beach, under the moonlight. Ever since I saw that love scene in the movies, I've always wanted to do that."

He spits out the toothpaste. "You don't have to work hard to convince me; I'm all for it."

"Did you know your brother Anthony is going back to Colorado Springs with Kathy?"

James comes out of the bathroom smiling. "He is, huh? That dirty dog. He moves fast. How did that happen?"

"They went out for a few drinks on Thursday night, and the next thing you know he's going with her to Colorado Springs. Supposedly he is taking two weeks off work."

James opens a drawer, takes out a shirt, and begins pulling it over his head.

"You've got to talk to the two of them and stop this, James."

He freezes, the shirt still covering his head. He peeks out of the opening. "Uh, what? Why should I stop it? And what makes you think they would listen to me, anyway? Last time I checked, they were both adults." James pulls the shirt the rest of the way on.

"Don't you see what's happening? Kathy is on the rebound. She can't have you, so she's going after Anthony. She's gotten the mistaken impression that one Coppi is like the other. When she realizes her mistake, Anthony is going to get hurt. Please, James, go talk to them."

"Why me?" He looks over at her. "Why don't you go talk to them? You seem to know all about these types of entanglements, and you're the one who's bothered by it all."

"Because Anthony is *your* brother, and I'm sure he doesn't want any advice about women from his new sister-in-law."

"What about Kathy? Why don't you at least speak to Kathy? After all, she's your best friend. She's more likely to listen to you than to me."

"Not this time. She won't listen to me. Please, James, go talk to Kathy and Anthony before somebody gets hurt."

James plants a kiss on his new wife's lips. "All right—stop worrying. I'll speak to Anthony and see what I can find out. Now, can we go?" he asks and heads for the door.

"Wait for Mrs. Coppi," she yells out, running after him.

He turns to her. "You just love saying 'Mrs. Coppi,' don't you? That's probably the tenth time you've said it since we got married."

Sam gives him a big smile. "I do! I just love saying *'Mrs. Coppi.'* There, that makes eleven."

Down in the lobby, Sam and James spend time saying goodbye to everyone. After his parents have left in a taxi for the train station, James is able to get Anthony alone.

"Come on, Anthony. Let's go to the bar and have a beer—just me and you."

At the bar, after the bartender puts the beers in front of them, James turns to his brother. "Anthony, I want to thank you for everything that you've done this week."

"Don't mention it big brother. It was my pleasure. I hope you and Sam are always happy."

"I hear you're heading up to Colorado Springs for a few weeks with Kathy. Do you two have a thing going on?"

"Me and Kathy? No, not at all." He lifts his bottle and takes a swig. "I wish we did; she's gorgeous," he adds.

"Then why are you going up to Colorado Springs?"

Anthony sets down his beer and looks down at the bar. "I'm a little embarrassed to tell you."

"Come on—you can tell me. I'm your brother."

Anthony scratches his head. "I was going to check out the area, and if I liked the place, I was going to ask you for a job. Kathy actually wants to do the opposite. She wants to leave Colorado Springs and head to New York. We thought we could help each other out."

"Really? You want to move to Colorado Springs? I'm surprised that you want to leave New York."

Anthony turns to James. "I need a change, James. I'm going nowhere. That job at the grocery store back home is a dead end, and I'm bored with the Bronx."

"What did Mom and Dad say when you told them about your plans?"

Anthony stares straight ahead. "They said I should do whatever will make me happy. I think they can see how miserable I am. They seemed happy that I'll be out here with you and not all by myself."

James does not say anything. He is processing the news.

"I'll work hard, James," Anthony pleads. "And I won't ask for special treatment because I'm your brother, I swear!"

"Stop it, Anthony," James cuts him off. "The job is yours if you want it. Besides, I need another detective. Just make sure this is what you really want to do."

James runs into Sam as he is leaving the bar.

"So, what happened?" she asks him.

"He's cool with it. He's not going after Kathy, nor is Kathy going after him. You had it all wrong. Anthony asked me for a job; that's why he's going to Colorado Springs. Now, where's that friend of yours? I need to speak to her."

"Why are you looking for *her*? If they're not chasing each other, why do you want to speak with her?"

"Because I learned another, just as important, piece of news that needs to be cleared up."

"What is it? What did you learn?"

"Let me find Kathy first and I'll tell you what's going on."

"I think I saw Kathy sitting in the lobby," Sam says. She starts walking toward the lobby. "I'll come with you."

James stops her. "No, Sam, I think you better stay here. I need to speak to Kathy alone. I'll tell you all about our talk when I get back."

James finds Kathy sitting on the sofa in the lounge, paging through a magazine. He sits down beside her.

"New York, huh?" he asks.

"Anthony told you?"

"Why, were you going to keep it a secret? Were you just going to disappear into the night without even saying goodbye?"

She looks over at him. "You know me better than that. I was going to speak to you about my leaving after you got back from your honeymoon. There's no immediate rush. I plan on staying through the summer."

"May I ask why you're leaving?"

Kathy's eyes well up as she looks at him. "You know why, James. I've fallen in love with you. I'll never find a man of my own as long as you're around. I'm not going away for good—just a year or two—long enough to get you out of my system and give somebody else a chance to get into my heart."

"Is that true, Kathy, you love me?" James sits back in confusion. "How long has this been going on?"

"Probably since I first laid eyes on you," she reveals. "You know, I had my eye on you too that night last year at the bar when you were sitting alone. Then my shy little friend, for the first time in her life, got up the courage to approach a man and beat me to you. I turned my head for just a split second and there she was talking to you. You know, she didn't even want to go out that night. I had to talk her into going." Kathy pauses for a moment.

"James, may I ask you a question? If I had approached you that night instead of Sam, would you be marrying me today? Would I have made you as happy as Sam?"

James looks over at her. "Come on, Kathy. You don't really want to have this conversation, do you?"

"Yes, James, I do. The thought has been eating away at me. Please, can you answer my question?"

James pauses to think it over. "It's really hard to say, Kathy. You have all the qualities I want in a woman. I really enjoy being with you. You're beautiful, smart, funny, and easy to talk to. All those traits are important to me in a woman—especially that last one."

"All right, James. Where's the *but*?"

"Kathy, you might remember that back then, I was totally screwed up. I was lost and confused. Don't you remember the tough time I gave Sam? She came onto the base just before I shoved off for 'Nam to throw the breakup letter I wrote into my face. She refused to let me break up with her. Insisted that we continue to write to each other while I was in Vietnam. Asked me to stop by for an hour to see her in Colorado Springs on my way home when my tour was over to discuss our situation.

"When I came back from 'Nam and went home to New York instead of stopping to see her, she came all the way to New York to win me back. I don't know if you would have had the same kind of determination. I'm not sure you would've gone to the same lengths to get me that Sam did. If you had that sort of perseverance—then perhaps yes, we could have ended up here today."

Kathy takes a tissue out of her bag and dabs the moisture that has accumulated at the corners of her eyes. "Thank you for telling me." She leans forward and looks straight into his eyes. "James, if I had approached you first at that bar, and if you had taken *me* to the motel instead of Sam, I would never have let you go." After a quiet moment, she asks him, "Do you have anyone in mind to replace me at the office?"

"Yes, I do."

"Who is it? Anyone I know?"

He gives Kathy a look. "Yes, you know her. You know her very well."

Kathy looks at him, somewhat confused. Then she laughs. "No!"

"Yes!" he says to her.

"Does she know?"

"No, of course not. How could she, when I just learned myself that you're leaving?"

Kathy laughs again. "This is going to get very interesting."

When James returns after his talk with Kathy, Sam begs him to please tell her what is going on.

"Well, it's not love between Kathy and Anthony, as *you* thought. We have two unhappy and restless people who are each looking for a fresh start. My brother Anthony wants to move to Colorado, and our friend Kathy wants to move to New York."

"Really? Kathy wants to move to New York? I've got to speak to her right away," Sam says and rushes off.

"What's this I hear? You're leaving me?" Sam asks Kathy angrily when she finds her.

"You had to know the situation would end this way," Kathy answers.

"He's got that much of a hold on you?"

"Yes, he does. Sam, I had a crush on James ever since I first met him. But it was nothing as it is now. After I spent the last few months living with you guys, my love for him really grew. Especially after the night when he went out and defended me against Bobby. I should have left much earlier Sam—I was so confused.

"Working with him, living with you guys, I didn't know how to get out. I decided to wait until after the wedding. I was so proud to be your maid of honor! But I paid a heavy price, Sam. This wedding was agony for me. As happy as I was for you, I was just that miserable for me. To witness firsthand my one true love marry my best friend has taken me on an emotional roller coaster ride. I'm still trying to figure out how I held it all together."

Kathy takes a deep breath and turns to Sam. "Sam, I have to get James out of my system. If I stay here, I'm going to end up doing something that I'll later regret. That something will cost me a lifelong friend—and believe me, I don't want to lose that friend. I need to find what you found. You're *so* happy. Please wish me well."

"I'm really going to miss you, Kathy. We've known each other since we were toddlers."

"I know. I'll miss you, too. You will come to New York to visit, won't you?"

"Of course. James and I are already planning a trip to visit his family during the Christmas holidays."

"Good—then we'll spend Christmas together!"

"I wonder if James will be able to find someone to replace you at the office."

Kathy looks at her. "He already has someone in mind."

"Really? Who?"

Kathy starts laughing. "Why don't you guess? I think you can figure it out."

"I haven't the foggiest. Who is it, Kathy?"

Kathy laughs even harder. "I'll give you a clue. The woman who's going to replace me is in the hotel right now."

Sam thinks for a moment and then yells out, "No! No way! I'm not doing it! There's no way I'm working for him."

Kathy is lying back on the couch, laughing.

"You can laugh all you want, Kathy, but I'm *not* doing it. I'm putting my foot down on this one. I'm not working for him."

Kathy stops laughing for a moment. "Maybe you can wear that sexy outfit to the office. You know, the one that you wore for the Big W meeting. I'm sure that would make James very happy."

"It's not happening, Kathy," Sam continues to protest. "I am *not* working for him!"

Kathy stops laughing and gets serious. "All right. Get a grip on yourself, girl. You know he's going to win. There's no way you won't give in—you always do. You can make all the noise you want in front of *me* if it makes you feel good, but when you come back from your honeymoon, be prepared to give notice at your job and start working for James."

Sam looks at Kathy and begs her, "Please, please reconsider. Don't leave."

20
THE RESCUE

It is five o'clock the next morning. The Mustang is packed, and Sam and James are ready to leave for their honeymoon in Galveston.

"I'll take the first stint," Sam says to him.

"All right," he replies, getting into the car. "I just want to tell you one more time what a great job you did on the wedding. Everybody said so."

"It's easy, I guess, when you've been dreaming about that special day your entire life."

"Really?" James gives her a sly grin. "You've been dreaming your whole life about marrying a confused Italian boy from New York City?"

She gives him a smile right back. "Yes, that's right. Why? Do you find that hard to believe?"

"Oh, no. It sounds totally plausible that a Texas girl would have a lifelong dream of going to Colorado Springs to meet an Italian boy from the Bronx and living happily ever after."

Sam drives out of the hotel parking lot. "Did you see how much money your friends and family put in the wedding envelopes? It more than covered the entire cost of the wedding."

"I told you they would be very generous."

"They certainly were. I didn't know your friends were so wealthy."

"They're not, Sam. Those envelopes represent a lot of money to my friends. Italians are like that at weddings. They feel a new couple may need a helping hand. It's their way of giving the couple a start on their new life. We'll have to reciprocate when one of them gets married. So, basically, it's a loan."

They are almost on the outskirts of Ralls, the next town after Lorenzo, when Sam says to him, "We need gas. I'm pulling into this station that's coming up. I know the owner."

"That's good. I need to call Charlie. I haven't spoken to him for a few days. I hate to bother him so early in the morning, but I really need to get caught up on what's happening at the office."

She pulls up to the pumps and they get out of the car. A young man is coming out of the garage toward them.

"Hello, Bubba!" Sam hollers out one of her famous Texas shouts.

"Is that Samantha Powers?" the man hollers back. He comes running over. "Well, I'll be! It *is* you, Sam," he says when he gets to her.

She gives him a hug. "No, Bubba. I'm not Samantha Powers anymore. I got married two days ago. I'm now Samantha Coppi."

"That's right—I heard about that. You broke my heart, Sam." Bubba turns to James. "Is this the lucky fella?"

"Yes, Bubba. This is my husband, James."

Bubba, with a huge grin on his face, extends his hand. "You are one lucky son of a gun, James. You just nabbed the prettiest girl in the county."

James reaches for Bubba's hand to shake. "Not quite, Bubba. Actually, I landed the prettiest girl in all of Texas."

"No argument there, James." Bubba smiles.

"Sam, do you have some change?" James asks her. "There's a pay phone over there. I need to make that call to Charlie."

"Nope. Sorry, James, that phone is out of order," Bubba says. "Sam, take James inside. There's a phone in the office. Daddy's inside; he'll show you where it is. What do you need on the car?"

"Fill it up and check the front," Sam tells him. "We've got a long trip ahead of us. We're going to Galveston for our honeymoon."

"Mr. Hunt, are you in here?" Sam shouts for Bubba's dad when they are inside the gas station.

A gray-haired man in overalls comes walking out. "Is that the beautiful Samantha Powers that I see?"

Sam walks up to him. "Yes, Mr. Hunt, except that I'm now Samantha *Coppi*. I got married two days ago."

She gives him a hug and a kiss on the cheek. Sam gestures to James. "This is my husband, James, Mr. Hunt."

"You got married? No wonder Bubba is walking around here moping," Hunt says to her as he extends his hand to James. "Congratulations, young man. You got yourself a very beautiful and upright young woman as a wife."

James extends his hand. "Thank you—and yes, I know, Mr. Hunt, that I'm a very fortunate man."

"Mr. Hunt, would you mind if James uses your phone to make a long-distance call?" Sam asks him. "We'll be happy to pay you for the call."

"The phone is right behind the counter," Hunt tells James, "and don't you dare try to give me any money for the call."

"Thank you, sir. I won't stay long on the phone," James replies. He goes behind the counter.

Sam and James: The Missing Teen

Sam is talking to Mr. Hunt while James is speaking to Charlie. After a few minutes, they hear James yelling into the phone. He is yelling so loudly that Hunt and Sam stop talking.

"I don't understand it, Charlie! How hard can it be to locate a man named Isaiah—a guy with a beard driving a white van who's accompanied by a teenage girl? *Somebody* must have seen them. What have you been doing at the office since I was away? Are you back off the wagon?

"Get back on the phone with Agent Spencer at the FBI; see if he will lend a hand. All we need is for him to put out a bulletin. He doesn't even have to get involved. Tell him to put out a dispatch on this Isaiah character and we'll do the rest."

James slams the phone down and comes out from behind the counter.

Hunt is staring at him. James apologizes for all the noise. Hunt shakes his head and then asks, "Did I hear you say you're looking for a bearded man named Isaiah? A guy who drives a white van?"

"Yes. Why?"

"That man comes in here from time to time to buy gas. My son knows where he lives; he fixed a flat tire for him a little while back. Just wait here a second, and I'll get Bubba." Hunt goes to the door and yells, "Bubba, get yourself in here for a minute."

"Do you remember that bearded fella you helped with the flat tire?" Hunt asks Bubba once he is inside. "You know, the guy who was driving a white van who didn't have a spare? His name was Isaiah."

"Yeah, I do. Weird-looking guy. Why do you ask?"

Hunt points to James. "James here is looking for him."

"Do you remember if there was a teenage girl with him?" James asks Bubba.

"Yeah, a pretty young thing. A little weird, though—just like her father. Wouldn't talk and refused to make eye contact. I offered her a Coke and she just *looked* at the bottle…acted like she didn't even know what it was."

"Would you happen to know where they live?"

"Sure do," Bubba says. He goes outside, motioning for James to follow, and points at the road to the left of the gas station.

"Go down this road apiece, about five miles. There's a dirt road on the right; they're about two miles up that road. You can't miss it; their house is at the end of the road, and there are no other houses in the area. Theirs is the only one."

The excitement is building inside of him. *My, God, I can't believe it, I'm so close. What a lucky break!*

"Would you happen to know where I can find a gun store in town?" James asks Bubba.

"Just take a right out of the station and head back toward town. Three miles on your left is Pete's Pistols. It's a little early, so he'll be closed right now, but if you ring the bell, he'll come down for you. He lives right above the shop. Tell him that I sent you and he'll give you a good deal."

"I'll drive," James tells Sam when they get back to the car. He pulls out of the station, makes a right turn, and heads toward town.

"Where are you going?"

"I need to buy a gun."

"Are you thinking of going after this guy by yourself?" Sam shouts at him. "Are you crazy? Just hand it over to the police. Let them take care of it."

"Sam, the police will take too long. First, they'll send someone out there to look around. If they see anything wrong, they'll have to get back to town and ask for a search warrant. Around here, getting a warrant can take hours—possibly days. No, Sam, I have the element of surprise on my side, and I don't need any warrant. That girl is getting rescued in the next hour. I just need to buy a gun and take you back to your parents' house."

"You're not dropping me off! I'm going with you!" she states obstinately.

"Now you're just talking stupid. I can't worry about you and concentrate on what I'm doing at the same time. I'm taking you to your parents' house."

She turns to him and shouts, "You listen to me—and you listen good, Mr. Coppi. I'm not losing my husband two days after marrying him. Either you go to the police station or I come with you! Those are your only choices."

James pulls into the parking area in front of Pete's Pistols. "Wait in the car. We'll talk about this more when I come out."

James rings the bell. In a few minutes, a guy looks out the window above the store.

"Are you Pete?" James shouts up at the man.

"Yeah, what do you want?" the man yells back.

James reaches into his back pocket and takes out his wallet. "My name is James Coppi. I'm a private detective," he hollers up to Pete, holding up his detective identification card. "I need to buy some equipment. Bubba sent me over and said you could help me."

"Let me throw something on. I'll be right down."

"What do you need?" Pete asks him when he gets downstairs and lets James into the store.

"First of all, I need a gun. I'm thinking of a .45 automatic."

"A .45 automatic? That's a heavy piece. Are you sure you don't want something a little lighter?"

"I got used to the .45 when I was in the service. Besides, I want something big that will scare the crap out of a person when I point a gun at him."

Pete opens the counter case, takes out a .45, and hands it to James, saying, "Here you go."

"Let me have a box of ammo, too. And are those handcuffs I see in the glass display case at the end of the counter?"

"Yep. Do you want to see them?"

"Yes. And I'll take a pair of binoculars as well."

Pete goes to the end of the counter and gets the handcuffs and binoculars. He comes back and places them on the desk in front of James.

"What's this all about? Are you after somebody? Do you have someone in mind? Anyone I might know?"

"No, I don't think so," James replies, loading the bullets into the magazine of the .45. "Besides, it could all be for nothing. I'm not even sure it's the right guy. Can you show me how to work the cuffs?"

"It's really easy." Pete picks up the cuffs. "You can do it with one hand. Here, let me show you. Stick out your hand. Just click over the wrist. It's self-locking." He puts a cuff on James, showing him how it's done. "You can cuff a suspect in seconds."

"Good. Let me have another set." James tucks the .45 into the back of his belt, under his shirt.

Pete hands him a second set. "Don't you want to try out the gun? I have a target range out in the back."

"Yeah, sure. Let's give it a try."

Out in the back are half a dozen silhouette targets.

"How far are the targets?"

"From behind that line right in front of you, it's twenty feet."

James takes out the magazine with the bullets and slides it into the .45. He releases the safety, and with one hand holding the gun, he puts three bullets into the silhouette's head.

"I'm impressed," Pete says. "Not too many shooters could have done that well with one hand."

They go back inside and settle the bill.

"Good luck," Pete says to him after James has paid and is heading out the door.

When James gets back in the car, he looks at Sam. "All right, Sam, I don't have any time to waste. No more arguing; you're going to your parents' house."

"James, I'm going with you." Sam has her hands folded across her chest. "You're not winning this one, so save your breath and let's get going. There's a young girl waiting to be freed so she can go back to her family."

James looks over at her. Sam is staring straight ahead. He starts up the car and looks over at her again.

"Okay, Sam—you win. But when we get there, you better listen to everything I tell you. No more arguing."

James turns up the dirt road where Bubba told him that Isaiah is holed up.

"Are you sure this is the way?" Sam asks. "This doesn't even look like a road. There's nothing around."

"Yeah, I'm sure. There's fresh tire marks. See, look in front of you."

Sam sits up and takes a look. "Why are you driving so slow?"

"I don't want to kick up any dust and give them a warning that someone is coming."

"There it is." James points to a small, one story house. "There's the house." He stops and makes a U-turn.

"Where are you going?" Sam asks him. She looks back at the house. "Why are you turning around?"

James gets about a half mile away from the house, stops, and makes another U-turn.

"I want to keep the car out of sight and have a look before I approach the place." He parks the car behind some shrubs. "Wait in the car." He grabs the binoculars and gets out. "I'm going to go have a look."

James gets behind the shrubs and lies down flat on his stomach. He takes the binoculars out of their case and looks through them. Someone comes crawling up behind him, and he nearly jumps out of his skin. He turns to find Sam lying flat next to him.

"Christ, Sam, you nearly gave me a heart attack! Didn't I tell you to stay in the car?"

"I couldn't see anything from the car. What did you see?"

"Nothing yet. I'm too busy dealing with you."

James puts the binoculars back up to his eyes. "That's Isaiah, outside in the front, working on a piece of farm equipment," he tells her. "He fits the description. He's got a beard. I don't see the van. That means his partner isn't there."

"Where's the girl?"

"Good question. I hope she's not out somewhere with the partner."

"Wait a minute! I think I see someone coming out the back door of the house." Sam points. "See, over there."

James points the binoculars toward the back of the house. "That's her!" he whispers fiercely. Penelope has a bucket in her hand and is heading for a well in the backyard. A few chickens that are loose in the back go scurrying away as she walks by. The teenager draws water from the well and fills her bucket. She lugs the bucket back into the house.

"Why doesn't she just run away?" Sam asks him. "There's no one watching her. Are you sure it's her? Maybe it's someone else."

James is still looking through the binoculars. He replies, "That's her; I have no doubt. Except for the color of her hair, she looks just like the photograph." He aims the binoculars at the front of the house. Isaiah is still working on the equipment.

"Come on—let's get back in the car. I've got to get started. We need to hurry before his partner gets back," he says.

"Sam, listen to me," James continues when they are back in the car. "This is important. Please follow the plan exactly as I lay it out or someone could get hurt—maybe killed. Please—no more going off on your own. I'm going to work my way through the field in the back of the house. Then I'm going to make my way into the house from the back door and through the place to the front. As long as he's busy working on that piece of equipment, I should be able to surprise him. His partner is out somewhere, so I think Penelope must be in the house all alone."

"I'm going to give you the binoculars. Keep watching the front of the house. When I wave to give you the all clear, get in the car and come up to the house."

James turns to face Sam and says sternly, "Sam, keep a lookout for the partner. He could show up at any time. If you see the van driving up, jump back in the car and give me a warning by blowing the car horn twice. Then drive off immediately and go get the cops in town. I should be able to hold them off until you get back. You got that?"

"Yes, I got it."

He looks at her closely and warns her firmly, "No deviation, Sam. You see a van coming, honk twice and go get the police."

"All right—I've got it," she assures him. "You better get going."

James hands her the binoculars and picks up the two sets of handcuffs from the floor. He gets out of the car and hurries across the field. Sam gets out and crawls belly-down back to the shrub. She points the binoculars to the front of the house; the man is on the ground working on the underside of the equipment. She looks to the open field in the back and sees James running from shrub to shrub.

James's movements are deliberate. He runs behind a shrub, pauses to look around, and heads for the next shrub for cover. It's not long before he's hiding behind a tree that is behind the rear door of the house. She sees him hesitate and wait; he makes no move toward going in. *What is he waiting for?* she wonders. *Is there someone else in the house?*

Suddenly, she notices the man in the front start to get up. He dusts himself off and begins picking up his tools. Sam realizes that he'll soon be heading back into the house, and James will have no warning that he's in there. Instead of James surprising the target, James will be the one getting the surprise. Even more troublesome is that this man may have a weapon in the home. Sam jumps up and races to the car. She hops in, starts the car, and drives for the house. The man stops to look at the Mustang coming down the road.

James is looking into the house from his position behind the tree. *What if I'm wrong?* he begins thinking. *What if his partner is still in the house? Better play it safe and assume his partner is still in there. No need to screw this up now.* He reaches behind his belt, pulls out the .45, releases the safety, and makes his way very quietly to the back door. He has his gun pointing at the door, and he's fully ready to shoot and kill—a thing he learned in Vietnam. Killing someone is not as simple as one might think; you have to be mentally prepared. Your mind needs to know in advance; otherwise, you might hesitate and falter at the crucial moment.

He slowly opens the back door and enters an empty room that turns out to be the kitchen. The next room is dark. He peeks in, holding the .45 in front of him with both hands. Penelope is sitting on a stained and threadbare couch. He quickly moves into the room and points his gun at the opposite wall. No one is there. He walks over to the Penelope and sits next to her. She looks away from him toward the door.

"Penelope, your grandfather sent me to rescue you," he tells her. "Is it just you and the man outside?"

She nods her head. James notices the girl shivering.

"Don't be frightened!" He tucks at her arm and smiles. "You're going to be okay. It'll soon be over. Wait here and don't make a sound. I'll come back for you," he instructs her.

James gets up and walks to the front door. The door is open, but the screen door is closed. He looks outside. Isaiah has his back to him and is talking to Sam. James shakes his head. *She just will not listen,* he thinks. The two of them are about thirty feet away.

James suddenly knows that he's *done* it. Despite the sudden appearance by Sam, he's got the drop on the man—and he's extremely accurate with a .45 within thirty feet or less. If the man makes any sort of move, James is ready to take him out. There will be no need to take him prisoner.

Carefully, he opens the screen door. It creaks a little, but Isaiah doesn't hear the sound. Sam is doing a great job of keeping the man preoccupied. James walks quietly up behind the man and puts the gun to the back of his head, touching his skull, so that Isaiah can feel the metal.

"If you make any kind of move, I'll blow your fucking head off," he calmly tells Isaiah. "Now listen carefully. Slowly put your left hand behind your back."

When the man complies, James clips a handcuff to his wrist. "Now, put the other hand behind your back." Once again, the man complies. James locks the other hand into the cuff. James puts the gun to his side and releases a deep breath, relieving all the tension that had built up within him. Isaiah turns to James, about to say something. James hauls off and whacks Isaiah in the nose with the back of his .45. Isaiah falls backward to the ground.

James points to him. "You lie there. Don't move and don't make a sound." Blood begins to trickle out of Isaiah's nose.

"Damn it, Sam, didn't I tell you to wait until I called you?" he yells at her. "Don't you *ever* listen to me? You nearly screwed everything up!"

"I saw him heading inside and I had to stop him. I was worried he might have a weapon in the house!"

"I was ready for that possibility," James fires back. "What I wasn't ready for was seeing my wife out here having a pleasant talk with the kidnapper. What if he took *you* hostage?"

Isaiah turns on his side and tries to get up. James kicks him in the ribs. "I told you not to move."

Isaiah groans. James uses his foot to push Isaiah's face into the dirt. "You just stay there and eat dirt. If I see you move or hear you make a peep, I'll finish the job."

James turns back to Sam. "All right—let's not argue. We'll talk about this later. Penelope is inside, sitting on the sofa. Please go get her and bring her out." As Sam is about to walk away, James reaches for her and pulls her to him.

"Sam," he says in her ear, "be gentle with her. She has been badly traumatized."

Sam goes inside. The place is so dark that she can barely make out Penelope sitting on the couch. She walks to the couch and squats in front of the girl.

"Hi, Penelope. My name is Sam. I've come to take you home." Sam reaches for the girl's hand, but Penelope cowers back.

"Don't be afraid—no one is going to hurt you."

"He said he will kill me and my whole family if I try to escape."

Sam gives her a smile. "Well, he might have said that, but he won't, sweetie. James has him restrained with handcuffs. That evil man can't hurt you any longer. Come outside with me and you can see for yourself."

Penelope gets up. She clutches Sam's arm as they walk outside. Sam can feel the girl's body trembling against her. Isaiah is lying on the ground; James is standing by the car.

Sam turns to Penelope. "You see, honey, he can't do anything to you. James has him in shackles. That evil man can't hurt you anymore."

James walks over and reaches for Penelope. She immediately cowers away from him and clings more tightly to Sam.

"Okay, Penelope, I won't touch you. I promise," James says to her. "You hold onto Sam."

"Sam, put Penelope in the front seat of the car and come back." As the two girls walk toward the car, James walks over and gives Isaiah another kick in the gut. Then he bends down, pulls Isaiah's head up by his hair, and whispers in his ear, "I should blow your head off for what you did to that little girl. But that would be going too easy on you. A lifetime in prison is what you need—you miserable bastard."

Sam opens the car door for Penelope. "Just sit here for a moment, sweetie. I'll be right back."

Penelope sits down on the seat, but she won't let go of Sam's arm. She refuses to get fully into the car and holds on even more tightly. Sam squats down and faces Penelope.

"It's just for a minute, sweetie. I promise I'll be right back. Just let me help James for a sec, and then I'll come sit in the car with you."

With that assurance, Penelope releases her hold. Sam walks over to James. "That animal must have done some kind of number on that poor girl," she tells him.

"I can't even imagine. Listen, Sam, take this gun and keep it aimed at him." He hands her the .45 automatic. "I've got to get the car ready to haul this guy off to jail. If he makes any kind of move—pull the trigger. Don't hesitate." He gives Isaiah another kick as he walks by him.

James opens the trunk of the car, takes out the luggage, and puts it in the back seat. Penelope is sitting in the front and will not look at him. He looks back and Isaiah is trying to get up. Sam walks up to Isaiah and decks him with an uppercut. Isaiah falls back to the ground.

Sam walks up to James and hands him the gun. "That felt good!" She rubs her fist.

"I'm afraid our honeymoon is going to be a little delayed," he tells her. "Sit in the car and keep Penelope company while I finish up."

James walks up to Isaiah. "Come on, get up!" He reaches down, grabs his collar, and pulls the man to his feet. They walk to the back of the car.

"Climb in," he orders Isaiah, pointing to the trunk.

"I'm not getting in," the man yells back. "You wanna shoot me, go ahead and shoot me. Get it over with right now."

James takes the gun and whacks Isaiah in the back of the head, sending him face-first into the trunk. "Don't tempt me," he tells him, lifting up the man by his legs and flinging him into the trunk.

James lifts up the man's head by his hair once more, bends down, and whispers, "Now, you listen to me—you worthless piece of shit, and you listen carefully. You're going to lie down in this trunk nice and quiet or I will come back and shoot you. It doesn't matter to me if I bring you back dead or alive; I get paid the same. But before I shoot you, I will cut off your dick and stick it in your mouth." He gives Isaiah another whack on the head with the side of his pistol and slams the hood closed.

21
Going Home

James walks back around the car and gets behind the wheel. Once again, he takes a deep breath and heaves a sigh. Penelope is sitting in the same seat with Sam. Her body is against the center console squeezed tightly against Sam, sitting almost in her lap. She is still pointedly not looking at James.

"It's times like these I wish I didn't have bucket seats," he says to Sam.

"That's all right; I don't mind at all," Sam replies. She gently strokes Penelope's hair. "It makes me feel good to be holding her. Where are we going?"

"We're taking Penelope home to her grandfather."

"Don't you think we should go straight to the police station?"

"No. They'll want to hold Penelope for questioning, and then there's the matter of jurisdiction. They'll have to initiate extradition proceedings for the man we have in the trunk. That's a matter that could drag out for days—maybe weeks. I don't want Penelope to spend another day away from her parents and home. Tonight, Penelope is going to be sleeping safely in her own bed." He turns to Penelope and asks, "Isn't that right, sweetheart?"

Penelope burrows her head more deeply into Sam's shoulder. James looks over at Sam and shakes his head.

"Why are we taking her to her grandfather?" Sam asks. "Why not the mother?"

"Because, Sam, Greenwald is the one who hired me. He's the one paying the bills. I'll call ahead and have Mrs. Campos meet us there."

The car ride is quiet. No one says a word. Penelope remains clinging to Sam, refusing to look at James. She has not picked up her head. They are just outside Amarillo.

"Do you hear a noise, James?" Sam asks him. James looks over at her.

"No, I don't hear anything."

"I hear a noise. It's coming from the trunk." Sam turns and looks at the back seat. "Do you think he's trying to escape?"

James pulls the car to the side of the road. He gets out of the car, pulls out his gun, and opens the trunk.

"I need to use the john," Isaiah says to him, his eyes are squinting in the bright sunlight.

James takes his gun and shoves it into Isaiah's groin. "How would you like it if I just pulled the trigger right now? Without a dick, you wouldn't have to worry about needing to piss, now, would you?" He lifts up the gun and slams it on Isaiah's head. "I don't give a fuck if you go in your clothes, do you hear me? You can sleep in your own piss and shit; I really don't care. You're not getting out of that trunk until we get to the police station in Santa Fe. If I hear another sound from you, I *will* shoot your dick off."

James slams the hood down and walks back to the driver's side. He gets in the car and resumes driving.

"James, Penelope heard everything you said," Sam tells him.

"I'm sorry, Sam—I just lost it for a moment. I'll be more careful. I'm going to pull into the next station and call Greenwald. I want to tell him the good news."

A few minutes later, he sees a gas station and pulls in. He drives up to the bank of phone booths. "Sam, why don't you take Penelope inside; she may want to use the ladies' room. Maybe you can get her a soft drink and a snack, too. I bet she's hungry."

Sam tries to get out of the car, but Penelope pulls her back.

"Penelope, we need to get out. I need to use the ladies' room."

"No," Penelope answers. It's the first word she's uttered on the trip.

Sam and James look at each other.

"Penelope, sweetie," Sam begins, with a gentle, reassuring tone to her voice, "you need to let me go. I have to use the restroom. James will stay here with you—or, if you prefer, you can come with me. We'll walk arm in arm; I won't let you go."

Penelope looks at James and then turns back to Sam. She releases her hold.

"Do you want to come with me?" Sam asks her. Penelope nods. The two get out, heading for the building. Penelope clings to Sam the whole time.

James gets out and heads for the phone to call Greenwald. He's put on hold for a minute by the receptionist, but finally he's transferred to Greenwald's office.

"Mr. Greenwald's office," Helen, his secretary, answers.

"May I speak to him please, Helen? This is James Coppi."

"I'm sorry, Mr. Coppi, but Mr. Greenwald is in a meeting and cannot be disturbed. May I take a message?"

"Would you please slip him a note that his granddaughter, Penelope, is with me and that she's safe?"

"What? Hold on, Mr. Coppi. I'll get Mr. Greenwald right away!" As James will learn later, Helen puts James on hold and jumps out of her chair. She runs down the hallway and bursts into the conference room.

"Oh, Mr. Greenwald! I'm sorry, sir, but James Coppi is on the phone. He says he has your granddaughter, Penelope, with him." She speaks so excitedly and loudly that everyone in the entire office hears.

Greenwald hurries to his office. "What line, Helen?" he yells back at her.

"Line one, Mr. Greenwald."

Greenwald puts James on the speakerphone. Everyone is gathered by his office door. "James, is this true?" Greenwald says the moment he's on the phone. "Do you have Penelope?"

"Yes, it's true, Mr. Greenwald. Your granddaughter is with my wife and me right now. We're at a gas station just west of Amarillo."

The whole office lets out a cheer. James can hear the roar at his end.

"How is she? May I speak to her?" Greenwald asks. James can hear the tears in his voice.

"Not right now, sir. She's in the ladies' room. Sir, can you take me off the speaker? I'd like to talk to you in private."

Greenwald immediately picks up the phone and takes James off speaker. "Helen, would you please close my door?" After she closes the door, he says to James, "Go ahead, James. We have complete privacy now."

"Sir, I haven't called the police yet. I thought you might want some time with Penelope. Once the police get involved, they'll want to interview your granddaughter. I suggest you call Mr. and Mrs. Campos and have them meet us at your office.

"I would also suggest to you that you may want to call a child psychologist. I believe Penelope has been severely traumatized. Physically she appears to be fine, but I believe she will need some psychological care. I have the man who kidnapped her. He's handcuffed and in the trunk of my car. I'm bringing him back as well."

"Okay, James. How long do you think it will be before you get here?"

"I'm thinking it should take about four hours. I don't plan on stopping again unless it's absolutely necessary."

"All right, James. Drive safely. Bring my granddaughter home to me."

James is about to hang up when he hears his name.

"James?"

"Yes, Mr. Greenwald?"

"Thank you! You've just made an old man very happy."

After hanging up the phone, James sees Sam and Penelope coming from the gas station. Penelope's hands are free; she's not holding on to Sam. She has a Coke in one hand and a bag of chips in the other. Sam is also carrying a bag of chips, but she has two Cokes. She hands one of the Cokes to James. They get in the car and he drives off.

James turns to Sam. "Can I have some chips?"

Sam is about to hand him the bag, when she notices James shaking his head no. She is momentarily confused but then gets the picture.

"No," Sam tells him, "you should have gotten your own."

"Really, Sam, you're going to eat all the chips. You are really mean and cheap. I bet Penelope is more generous." James turns to Penelope. "Penelope, can I have some of your chips?"

Penelope looks up at Sam for direction. Sam smiles at her and shakes her head no. Penelope turns back to James. "No," she tells him, and looks back up at Sam with a huge smile on her face.

"Oh, wow! She's just like you, Sam. No wonder you guys are holding on to each other. You gals are both the same—mean and cheap."

Penelope begins laughing and buries her head into Sam's side. A few moments later, James sees a hand coming toward him with a chip in it. It's Penelope, offering him a chip.

James takes the chip. "Thank you, Penelope!" He turns to Sam and winks. "You could learn something from this girl, Sam."

Penelope has a smile on her face.

By the time they get to Greenwald's office, Penelope has opened up and is now talking freely. James looks at the girl and is truly amazed by the strength of the human spirit. This unfortunate child has endured terrible, unspeakable horrors, and yet within hours she has been able to set them aside and have a happy moment. He knows there is hope that someday she will overcome this tragedy.

James parks the car in the parking lot at the back of Greenwald's office. Before they can get out, Penelope yells, "I don't want to go!"

"Why not?" Sam asks.

"I'm scared."

Sam turns to her and lifts up her chin. "Penelope, do you know who is waiting for you upstairs? Your mom and dad. And your grandpa is there waiting for you, too. They have all been very worried about you, and they have missed you so much. They want to see you really badly."

"But I'm scared," Penelope pleads.

"I'll come with you. You can hold on to me, the way you did when we went into the ladies' room. You were frightened when we first got to the gas station—but with me by your side, it all worked out. I won't let you go. I promise."

"You will hold me the entire time?"

"Yes, of course."

With that, Penelope relents and they walk into the building.

"Elevator or stairs?" James asks.

"Elevator," Sam and Penelope reply in unison.

Upstairs, in the office, they walk up to the receptionist. The moment the receptionist realizes who they are, she calls Greenwald, who immediately rushes out with his daughter, Elizabeth. Other office workers notice the trio and gather around. Penelope is overwhelmed by the presence of all these people, she buries her head in Sam's shoulder. Her mom, Elizabeth, hurries to her side.

"Penelope, it's me—Mommy," she says, but Penelope will not look at her mother. She continues to hold onto Sam.

"Mr. Greenwald," James says, "all this attention may be a little too much for Penelope. Can we go into your office?"

"What did that animal do to my daughter?" Elizabeth says to a man who has just come out of Greenwald's office.

"You need to reconnect with Penelope very slowly, Elizabeth," the man replies. "She must be very frightened."

"Take her into my office," Greenwald orders James.

"Sam, please take Penelope into Mr. Greenwald's office," James tells Sam. He turns to Elizabeth whose eyes are full of tears. "Mrs. Campos, she'll open up, give her a little time."

As Elizabeth and the girls leave for the office, James turns to Greenwald. "Mr. Greenwald, can I speak to you in private for a moment?" James turns to the stranger. "I'm sorry, sir, but I don't know who you are."

"Dr. Sidney Greenbaum. I'm a child psychiatrist."

James extends his hand for a shake. "It's nice meeting you, Dr. Greenbaum. Maybe you can go in with the girls and help them out. Penelope is pretty shaken up, for obvious reasons."

After the man leaves, James and Greenwald go into the conference room.

"So, what happened?" Greenwald asks him. "How did you find her?"

"I got a tip early this morning by someone who told me of Penelope's location. My wife, Sam, and I immediately rushed out to the place. After a little reconnaissance work, I rushed the house and we rescued your granddaughter. I also managed to apprehend the man who kidnapped her. I've got him handcuffed in the trunk of my car. He's got a partner who wasn't at the house and is still on the loose."

"Why didn't you just shoot the bastard?"

"I'm sorry, Mr. Greenwald, but killing is a little more than you paid me to do. I brought Penelope here directly to you, so you and the family can have a little time with her right away. We'll need to call the police and the FBI. They'll want to spend time with Penelope. They will want to get all the information they can on her abduction and captivity. I'm glad you have the shrink; he should stay with her during this process. Your granddaughter is pretty shaken up."

"All right. Can I spend a little time with her before you call the police?"

"Yes, of course."

When James and Greenwald get back into his office, Penelope is sitting on the couch between Sam and her mom. She still has her head buried into Sam's shoulder. James squats down in front of Penelope.

"Penelope," James says to her in a soft voice. "Don't you want to hold your mom's hand?"

She shakes her head no and refuses to look at him.

"Would you mind if I held your mom's hand?"

Without looking up, Penelope shakes her head no.

James reaches over and takes Elizabeth's hand. "Wow, your mom has the nicest, softest hands," he says to Penelope. "It's amazing how soft your mom's hands are, considering all the dishes she must wash."

Penelope looks up at him. "Mommy doesn't do the dishes. Magdalena washes the dishes."

The room bursts out laughing. James takes Penelope's hand and places it in her mom's hand.

"See how soft her hands are?"

Penelope holds onto her mother's hand. Her head is still on Sam's shoulder but is no longer buried in it.

"Penelope, are you hungry?" James asks her. "I know I am. I only had that one chip you gave me. Sam wouldn't even give me *any*; she ate the entire bag by herself."

Penelope looks up at Sam and smiles.

"How about a grilled cheese sandwich and french fries?" James asks. "How does that sound?"

Penelope nods her head and sits up, holding Sam's hand on one side and her mother's hand on the other. James looks up at Elizabeth, whose eyes are still full of tears as she gazes at her daughter.

"James, what will you and your wife have?" Greenwald asks, telephone in hand, ready to order the food.

"We'll have the same—grilled cheese and fries, Mr. Greenwald. That's if Penelope says I can have some." Penelope gives him a smile and nods her head.

When lunch arrives, Penelope seems to be more comfortable. She isn't holding on to anyone. James turns to Greenwald. "Can I see you alone again in the conference room?"

"What's up?" Greenwald asks him when they are alone.

"We need to contact the authorities. I still have the prisoner in my trunk, and the news will eventually get out."

"Yes, I agree. I'll call Gold and Spencer."

"Mr. Greenwald, I hate to bring this up at this time, but you didn't forget that matter of the bonus, did you?"

"No, James, I haven't forgotten, but I generally don't have a hundred grand lying around. Give me a week or two and I'll get it to you. That money is well deserved; you've earned every penny."

Not long after Greenwald makes the call, various types of law enforcement personnel show up at the office: Gold, the district attorney; Spencer of the FBI, with two other FBI agents; and the two local lead detectives who had worked the case—Fallon and Rodriguez.

"James, we're going to take custody of the criminal," Spencer tells him. "He committed a kidnapping and he took her across state lines, so the crime falls under federal jurisdiction."

"Fine by me," James tells him. "Come on. Let's go downstairs, and I'll hand Isaiah over to you. He's in the trunk of my car."

As they are all riding down the elevator, Detective Rodriguez whispers in his ear, "Why didn't you just shoot the motherfucker?"

"Believe me the thought crossed my mind," James responds.

James opens the trunk of his car. Isaiah squints as the light hits his eyes. One of the agents reaches in and helps him out of the trunk.

"Look at me!" Isaiah yells out. "Look at my bloody face! He beat me while I was handcuffed!"

"My understanding is that you put up a fight resisting arrest," Spencer yells back, grinning as he looks at Isaiah's battered face. "James had to do what he did in order to restrain you." Spencer turns around and winks at James. "You should count yourself lucky, Isaiah. If it had been me, you'd be a lot worse off!"

James gives Spencer the key to the handcuffs. The agent leads Isaiah to his car. James is walking away when Rodriguez yells out, "Nice going, Coppi. We owe you a big apology."

James gives him a wave without turning around and goes back into the building. As he is walking into Greenwald's office, Gold pulls him aside.

"There's going to be a news conference today at five at my office. You should be there—it'll be a nice plug for your agency."

"All right, I'll be there," James says to him. Then he starts toward Greenwald's office. Gold pulls him back. "I'm sorry for the way I treated you. Thank God that you didn't listen to me and stuck to your convictions instead."

"Forget it, Gold," James says to him, about to head to the office. But then a thought comes to him, and he stops. "You know what, Gold? You can make it up to me by sending some business my way every once in a while. How does that sound?"

"It's a deal," Gold says, smiling.

Back inside the office, Sam is still sitting on the couch with Penelope and Elizabeth. The frightened girl is holding Sam's hand again. James squats down in front of Penelope.

"Penelope, do you think you can let go of Sam? Sam and I need to leave, but your mom will stay with you."

"No! I don't want her to leave," Penelope cries out and moves nearer to Sam.

James waits a few moments. "Penelope, can you please look at me for a second?" The girl turns to look at him.

"Do you know what a honeymoon is? You know—after two people get married, they go on a vacation to get to know each other a little better?"

"Yes," Penelope answers.

"Well, Sam and I were just married two days ago, and we were about to begin our honeymoon when we learned where you were. You were so important to us that instead of starting our honeymoon, we turned right around and came to rescue you. Now that you're safe, Sam and I would like to take our holiday now. You wouldn't want Sam to miss her honeymoon, would you?"

Penelope turns to look at Sam. "Can I come, too?"

Sam lets out a laugh. "No, darling. A honeymoon is just for a husband and wife."

"I'll tell you what," James continues, "on our way back from our trip, we'll stop by and look in on you. We'll have lunch together—just like we did today. Maybe your mom will make us grilled cheese and fries. Then Sam will tell you all about the honeymoon. What do you say? Can Sam go?"

Penelope releases her hold on Sam's hand and looks at her. "You *will* stop by on your way back?"

Sam gives her a hug. "Of course, dear. I wouldn't miss it for the world. So, what do you say—can I go with James?"

"Yes, you can go."

"Penelope, can you do me another favor? Please tell Sam to share her potato chips with me on the way. Sam will listen if *you* ask her."

Penelope begins laughing and looks up at Sam, who shakes her head. Penelope turns back to James. "No, she doesn't have to share. You have to buy your own."

Sam and James leave the office. As they are about to press the call button for the elevator, Elizabeth Campos comes running out.

"I never got a chance to thank you both personally for bringing my daughter home!" Elizabeth says. Then she turns to Sam and smiles warmly. "Congratulations on your marriage; you have a wonderful and utterly faithful guy here. I'm sure he'll make a great husband."

At eleven that night, Sam and James are on the road again. James has given his statement to the police. A press conference has been held—not for just the local media, but also for the national press. James has given four press interviews—all in all, it's been a good publicity day for the agency. He's doing the driving.

"I don't know why we didn't just rent a room and stay in town overnight," Sam says to him.

"I'm all fired up; I couldn't sleep just yet. We'll find a roadside motel and pull over when I get tired."

"Do you think that poor, sweet thing will ever recover?"

"Yeah, I think so. It's not going to be easy. She must have a thousand thoughts running through her head—not the least of which is probably the shame she feels for having been violated. She seems like a tough young girl, so I feel hopeful that she will be able to put this behind her. I'm happy that she's sleeping in her own bed tonight."

"I can't even imagine the condition I'd be in if she were my child. I'm pretty sure I would have killed that man."

"In that case, I'm glad, Sam, that she isn't your child. We might be bailing you out of jail."

"What about Isaiah's partner?" Sam asks. "Do you think they'll ever catch up with him? If I were Penelope's family, I'd be very worried knowing he was still on the loose."

"They picked her up about an hour ago in El Paso."

"Her?" Sam looks at him in disbelief. "The partner is a woman?"

"Yes, a woman. She's his wife."

"The whole thing is making me sick. How can a woman be married to a sick animal who would do those horrible things to such a beautiful young girl? What kind of woman is she?"

With that last question lingering in their thoughts, they drive quietly for a while. Suddenly Sam blurts out, "That was an odd statement Elizabeth Campos made to me back at Greenwald's office this afternoon, don't you think?"

"I don't remember what she said. What was so odd about her statement?"

"She said that I have a wonderful and *utterly faithful* husband. Don't you find that a little strange?"

"No, I don't see anything wrong with her comment. She was just trying to be complimentary."

Sam sits up in her seat and looks over at him. "You don't think it's peculiar that she used the word *faithful*? Who uses that when giving out a compliment—unless for a dog, maybe? The lady barely knows you, but she says that you are faithful. Why would she use that particular word?"

"Well, maybe she misspoke." James is beginning to worry about where Sam might be heading. "Maybe she was looking for another word, and that's what came out." He tries to lead Sam off that train of thought. "You know, everything was all busy and confusing back at the office. She *just* got her daughter back and she was not in the best frame of mind, I'm sure."

"Yeah, maybe you're right. Maybe she just misspoke." Sam turns, takes a long look at him, and then hollers, "All right, mister, spit it out! You're holding something back. That lady didn't misspeak. She knows something, and I want to know what it is!"

James pauses and swallows. "A few weeks ago, when I was at her house, Mrs. Campos made a play for me, but I turned her down. That's what she was referring to when she used the words *utterly faithful*."

Sam grins smugly. "I knew there was something. Why didn't you tell me? Why did you hold it back? Why be so sneaky?"

"Sam, you're missing the important point of the story," James protests. "*I turned her down!* I wasn't being sneaky; I just didn't see any reason to *tell* you. What's the point of us having this conversation when I didn't do anything wrong? You don't tell *me* every time a man makes a pass at you when you turn him down."

Sam settles back in her seat and smiles. "I've got to admit—it's quite impressive that you turned her down. She's a stunning woman. A lot of guys wouldn't have been able to resist such temptation."

"A lot of guys don't have a woman like you at home."

She gives him a wily smile. "Really slick, Mr. Coppi. You got yourself out of this one very quickly."

Sam and James arrive late the next night at their motel in Galveston. Their room is right on the beach. James is listening to the waves roaring as Sam is changing into her bathing suit in the bathroom.

"How do I look?" she asks when she comes out in a bikini.

"You look great," he remarks and goes over to give her a hug. He looks over at the bed. "Are you sure you don't want to wait a bit before the beach?"

She gives him a shove. "On the beach, darling. I've always dreamed of making love on the beach—and there's a full moon tonight. It's almost midnight, and the beach will be empty. It'll be perfect! Come on."

She picks up the blanket from the bed and grabs a few towels from the bathroom. They find a secluded area on the beach and open up their blanket.

James looks out at the moonlight reflecting brightly off the dark waters of the Gulf of Mexico. "This is nice," he comments. He lies down on the blanket and gazes up at the Texas night, hundreds of stars are sparkling above. Sam reaches back and unfastens her bikini top.

"Come on," she says, letting her top fall off and freeing her beautiful breasts. "Get your bathing suit off and let's go for a swim."

She removes her bathing suit bottom and runs off toward the water. James jumps up and quickly tries to remove his suit. In a hurry to run after Sam the suit gets tangled around his ankles, he trips and falls. He kicks the suit off him, leaping to his feet and running after Sam, catching up to her as she is about to dive into the water. They both dive in together. Sam wants to play, but James has something else on his mind. He wrestles her down in the shallow water and gets on top of her.

"Not here!" she yells, spitting out water that she's inhaled. "I'll drown while you're making love to me." She flips him over, gives him a shove, pushing his head under water, and runs back to lie down on the blanket.

She's laughing as he jumps on her and pins her down. She tries to push him off, but he holds her under his weight. Her look turns serious as she gazes into his face. She grabs a hold of the back of his head and pulls him to her. His lips are moist and salty as she makes contact. Both of her hands are caressing his head as his tongue enters her mouth. She lies flat on the blanket as he moves his body on top of hers. He nibbles her earlobe. She tilts her head back, inviting him to kiss her neck. He complies with her request and gently nips at her neck. He shifts himself on top of her, and his hardened member slips inside her jewel without any urging.

She pulls him tightly on top of her and whispers, "Don't move, baby. Stay just like that!" She's staring up at the starry night. The full moon is visible just over his right shoulder. Gently, she strokes the small of his back with her fingernails. He works his tongue into her ear. Sam lets out a moan, grabs James by the hips, and pulls him tighter to her. His manhood is now fully inside. She tenderly picks up the sexual rhythm. James has still not responded to her invitation. She closes her eyes and increases her pace to urge him on.

He can resist no longer and responds in kind, thrusting himself into her. Digging her nails into his backside, she increases her hold. Her thrusts from below reach a furious pace. Her legs wrap around his body as she moans with delight. Her eyes open and she stares out at the night to take in the full view. With a final groan, her body begins to quiver. She closes her eyes as she senses his fluid entering her body. The hardened member is pulsating within her. She holds him tight, refusing to allow him to get off her and trying to hold on to the moment. *Absolutely perfect,* she thinks to herself; *more wonderful than in my wildest dreams.*

Sam finally releases her hold on him. James falls onto his back. She turns over to her side and gently strokes her fingers over his chest.

He gives her a smile. "So, was it as good as you imagined?"

"Even better." She smiles and gives him a kiss. "Be prepared: you're not going to the room tonight."

He smiles and gives her a kiss. "I'm at your mercy."

The next morning finds them sitting on the blanket watching the sunrise over the blue water. James has his arm around Sam's back as the sun begins to slowly make its appearance in the horizon. Sam has two towels wrapped around her, she is resting her head on his shoulder. They made love three times during the night.

"Shouldn't we turn in?" James asks watching a lone walker strolling on the beach a distance away from him.

She lifts her head up and smiles. "Do we have to?"

"No, we don't. This is really nice. So tranquil and peaceful." He turns to her. "Sam, will you call your job later today and tell them you need another week off for your honeymoon? It took us two full days to get to Galveston. It's going to take at least another two days' travel to get home. We'll have no time at all to enjoy our honeymoon. We'll have to leave tomorrow."

"You do know that they'll probably fire me." She sits up. "I've already been off more than a week, but I guess me getting fired is exactly what you want, right? Then I'll have no choice but to come to work for you when Kathy leaves. Isn't that your master plan? That's what you told Kathy, isn't it? You want me to come to work for you?"

James looks over at her and smiles. "Your friend Kathy has a big mouth." Then, seriously, he adds, "Sam, you're not coming to work *for* me. I want you to come work *with* me. You'd be great at the job. You're my partner—I named the agency after you *and* me, because the agency is half yours. This is such a great opportunity for us. Together, we can build a great company and a bright future for ourselves."

Sam turns him to face her. She puts on her stern face. "Tell me the truth, James! Are you going to consider me your partner? Are you going to treat me as a coowner and not your wife? Are you going to listen to my ideas?"

"Yes, of course. You are my *equal*. That's what *partner* means."

She takes a long look at him. "Why don't I believe you?"

"So, will you do it?"

She nods. "Kathy said I'd give in. Yes, I'll do it." Sam falls back onto the blanket. "I've got to be the world's biggest sucker."

James looks down at Sam. "That sounds familiar. Haven't we had this conversation before?"

22
Sam's Master Plan

Sam and James have just left the home of the Campos family after their honeymoon and are driving back to Colorado Springs.

James is at the wheel. He turns to Sam. "Can you believe the change in Penelope? It's hasn't even been two weeks and she's already smiling, talking, and laughing. It's so nice to see her happy."

"It is truly amazing," Sam replies. "You can't tell from her behavior what happened to that poor girl. No one would guess from speaking to her now that just two weeks ago she was experiencing unspeakable horrors from that monster."

"It's going to take a little time, but I think she's going to pull through just fine," James remarks. "I'm glad they got her a tutor to allow her to catch up with her schoolwork. I think it's important that Penelope keep up with her classmates…get back to her life as it was before this sordid episode."

"Yes, I agree. The sooner Penelope gets back to some of her normal routines, the better."

"That was nice of you to invite her up to come and visit us for a few weeks this summer," James states.

"I've taken to that young lady, James," Sam remarks, sitting up in her seat. "I've become very fond of her. I intend to stay in contact with her as long as she will allow me in her life."

"She's taken to you, too, Sam. She really likes you."

Sam adjusts herself in her seat. "You, too, James. She really likes you, too."

"Me?" He shrugs. "Not so much. She hardly spoke to me."

"She doesn't have to say anything. It's that cute smile she gets on her face whenever she looks at you. You need to spend some time with her when she comes up to visit, James. It's important for that girl to know that not all men are monsters—especially now that her parents are separated and getting a divorce. She needs some older men in her life. Penelope needs to know that not all men are creeps."

"I'll do my part. I promise."

"That was nice of Mr. Greenwald to come all the way down from Santa Fe to thank us again. What was in that envelope that he gave you?"

James turns to her. "You mean you haven't looked? I was wondering why there was no reaction from you."

"No, I didn't look inside—I just stuffed the envelope in my purse. I assumed it was some sort of personal thank-you letter addressed to you."

"It's a check for money he owed me on the case." When she doesn't do anything, he gives her a long stare. He asks, "Aren't you going to look?"

"I'll look when we get home," she responds indifferently.

"You have no interest in our business? The money coming in doesn't interest you at all?"

"All right, I'll look. Stop making such a big deal about the envelop. I was just waiting until we got back."

Sam reaches down, opens her purse, and pulls out the white envelope that's folded inside. She opens the envelope and takes out the check. There is a stunned silence. She turns to him.

"Is this a mistake?"

He lets out a laugh. "What does it say? How much is the check?"

"A hundred thousand dollars," she reveals, her pitch getting higher and her lips quivering.

"No, that's right—there's no mistake. That's the correct amount."

"Oh my God!" she yells out, bouncing up and down in her seat. "I'm going to pass out. This is unbelievable. Why didn't you tell me? What's this money for?"

"That's the bonus I got for bringing Penelope home. That was the deal I made with Greenwald. If I brought Penelope home alive, I'd get a hundred thousand dollar bonus."

"What does this mean? Has your contract with Greenwald ended? What about the agreement that you have for a thousand a week?" She is so excited that the words come tumbling out of her mouth.

"No, that's still good. In fact, Greenwald just gave me another assignment today. He wants me to review the security procedures at his railroad warehouses."

Sam has a broad smile on her face. "What are we going to do with all this money? I can't believe we have so much money."

"Really?" James looks at her dubiously. "You can't come up with one single thing that we can put this money toward?"

She gives him a brilliant smile. "I guess we could start looking for the ranch…"

"Now you're talking!"

Sam leans over and gives him a kiss. "You are simply amazing."

It has been nearly three years. Now Sam is sitting in the dining room of the home they have built, sipping her morning coffee. The house is a huge ranch-style home presiding over a thousand acres of land. James would have built her a castle, just as he promised, if she hadn't stopped him. Still, at five thousand square feet of living space, the house is much more than they need. The bunkhouse where the ranch hands will sleep has just been completed.

There are two barns on the property. James came up with the idea to rent a stall or two in one of the barns to people who want to board their horses, as a way to offset some of the costs of upkeep of the property.

The other barn will be used to house his racehorses. They only have two yearlings so far. The horses are too young to race yet, but their first races will come later this year, when they are two-year-olds. Sam took up riding when the ranch opened and is getting quite good at the activity, particularly at equestrian jumping. James also took up riding, but he's not very good and does not really have time to devote to getting better. The detective agency and his other activities keep him quite busy.

"Would you like me to make you something for breakfast?" the elderly maid asks, interrupting Sam's thoughts.

"No. Coffee is fine, Gilda."

"Will you be home today, or will you be going to work?"

"I'll be going to work," Sam answers, taking a sip of her coffee. "But I'm going in a little late today."

Gilda begins to head out.

"Oh, Gilda, we won't need you tomorrow, so you can have the day off," Sam calls out. "I want to spend some time alone with James after the graduation ceremony."

"Yes, Mrs. Coppi," Gilda responds. Then she turns back to Sam. "You must be very proud of him graduating from college. I don't know how he found the time to study—he's so busy with work and this ranch."

"Yes, I am very proud of him. And he graduated in three years—exactly as he promised he was going to. And you're right—he did that with all the other duties that he has. Quite an achievement."

Sam *is* very proud. She goes back to her thoughts after Gilda leaves. Not only did James graduate in three years, but also he raised his GPA from the D plus he had when he started college to a B plus—and he did all this while building the ranch and growing a thriving business. The agency now has sixteen detectives, and James is looking to open another office in New York City.

The new bureau in New York is a matter of controversy and has been a topic of conversation between them for months now. Everyone wants the expansion—except for her. She's concerned that James is taking on too much and will be traveling constantly to New York. This expansion could screw up the plans *she's* getting ready to set in motion. She's been plotting for months on how to approach James with her new proposal. After the call she got from Kathy in New York last week, her scheme has finally come together. Kathy was the final piece of the puzzle. Without Kathy, Sam's plot would most certainly fail.

Tomorrow, after the graduation, she plans to spring her proposition on James. It will not be easy. James can be quite determined, and he is very shrewd. He knows all her weak spots and is not afraid to play on them. She's ready for him this time, though. This matter is so important to her that she's not about to let him win. She takes a final sip of her coffee and heads to work.

"Mr. Coppi has called twice for you," her assistant, Helen, tells Sam when she gets to her office. "His door is closed, but he said you should go right in."

"Thank you, Helen. Can you get me a cup of coffee, please, and bring it to his office for me?"

James's door is closed. Sam knocks and she lets herself in. There is a middle-aged man sitting across the desk from James. Both James and the stranger jump to their feet when she enters.

"Oh, good," James says. "You got here just in time." He comes over and gives her a kiss. "I want you to meet Rodney Davis. We're going to be bringing him on board next month. He's going to head that government program we discussed at our last staff meeting."

Sam looks at the clean cut, silver-haired man in the navy-blue suit.

"It's nice to meet you, Mr. Davis." Sam offers her hand to shake.

"The pleasure is all mine, Mrs. Coppi," Davis responds, smiling and shaking her hand. "Please call me Rodney."

"Well, in that case, you can call me Sam." She releases his hand and takes a seat.

They hear a knock at the door. Helen walks in with Sam's coffee. She places the cup on the desk.

"Does anyone else want a cup?" Helen asks.

"No, I'm fine," James answers.

"I'm good too," Rodney lets her know.

"Sam, I wanted you to meet Rodney before he leaves for Washington this afternoon," James says, after Helen leaves. "Rodney is a director at the CIA. He'll be retiring next month, and then he'll come to work for us to launch the government business. If what Rodney tells me is correct, the government sector could be a huge part of our company going forward—larger than any of our other segments."

"That's great news, Rodney...and welcome aboard." she says.

"Thank you, Sam," Rodney says. He rises from his chair. "Now, if you'll both excuse me, I need to go home and finish packing my things for the flight this afternoon. James, I'll call you in a few days." He turns to Sam. "It was a pleasure meeting you, Sam."

"I'll walk you out," James says to him.

"Is that all?" Sam asks James when he gets back into his office.

"No, that's not all." His tone has changed and gotten sterner. "We need to discuss the New York office again. We need to decide, once and for all. No more delays, Sam—we've procrastinated long enough. This matter needs to be brought to a conclusion."

"I don't know why you're asking *me*," she says, speaking harshly back at him. "You never listen to me, anyway. You don't value my opinion; you never have. You do whatever it is you want. When we have a staff meeting, you never ask for my feedback. This is the first time you've included me in a decision."

"What the hell are you talking about?" he shouts at her, sitting back in his seat. "Of course I value your opinion. You're at all the staff talks. Why do you think I include you at the meetings? I always ask for everybody's input. When you don't speak up, I just assume you're on board with the proposal.

"This is the first time you've spoken up and objected, Sam." He stretches his arms out wide. "And as you can tell, we haven't gone forward with the idea. Without your approval, we won't open that branch. That's how much I value your opinion. You're an equal partner—so if you don't want to go forward with the New York office, we won't. I just need to know your objections, so that I can explain them to the staff."

She fidgets on her chair. As usual, he's too quick for her and she's lost the upper hand. She pauses for a moment to regain her composure.

"First of all, I just don't see any purpose in taking on the additional work and responsibility," she says. "We're doing well financially without the New York office. Our business has grown nicely; we now occupy half of the floor space in this building. Why take on the additional headaches?"

"Okay, Sam. If that's how you feel, that's how it will be. However, you've got to realize that the rest of the staff doesn't agree with you. They want the agency to grow. Growth means raises in their paychecks and bigger bonuses at the end of the year. If we don't open the office in New York, we'll have to give up some of our East Coast clients. It's not fair to the employees to require them to travel back and forth constantly and be away from their families."

"What about you being away from *your* family, James? If you open an office in New York, *you'll* be traveling back and forth."

"No, I won't, Sam. Anthony is going to run the new office. That's why I'm opening up the place—so that I don't have to do the traveling. I want to spend more time on the ranch. I've finished college now and I have time to devote to the ranch. I don't want to fly back and forth to New York. If we don't open the office, I'm going to give up the East Coast clients. Nothing is going to come between me and my family."

"Well, if you put it that way—I will go along with the plan."

"Really?" he asks as a hopeful smile crosses his face.

"Yes," Sam responds. "The only thing that was bothering me was the possibility of increased demands the New York office would make on *you*. I didn't want you to be away from home so much. Now that I know that you won't be traveling, I'm fine with the idea."

"Why didn't you tell me about your concerns in the first place?" His smile gets even bigger. "We could have put this matter to rest long ago."

Sam walks out of James's office feeling pretty good about the meeting. She's lost the battle on the New York office, but she is now confident that she will win the war. She is much closer to achieving her goals. James may not realize it yet, but he nearly conceded to her plans at this meeting. Tomorrow, after the graduation ceremony at Colorado College, her plans will come to fruition. Everything is set, and all systems are go.

Sam is sitting in the hot Colorado sun, fanning herself with the program at the commencement exercises for James's graduation. The graduation ceremonies are being held on the field of the football stadium. Seated around her are thousands of family members who are proud to see their loved ones graduate. She, also, is very proud to see her husband get his degree. James is sitting closer to the front among the other students wearing their caps and gowns.

The speeches and honors are over, and they have just begun calling the students up to the stage alphabetically to accept their diplomas. Every time a student's name is called, the entire family jumps up and cheers. When Sam hears the name Coppi, she immediately jumps to her feet and begins whooping and hollering so loudly that James stops to look back at her, startled. He smiles, shakes his head, and hurries up to the stage to get his diploma.

After the assembly, he comes over to her. "You were so *quiet*. I didn't even know you were here. Couldn't you have shouted a little louder?"

"I'm sorry; I got excited," she says, giving him a kiss. "You have no idea how proud I am of you today. Put your cap back on your head; I want to take a picture."

He puts his cap back on and she snaps the picture.

On the car ride home, he asks her, "So, what do you have planned for me today?"

"Nothing fancy." She looks over at him. "I know you don't like a big fuss.

I gave Gilda the day off, and I'm making you a nice, romantic Italian dinner. Afterward, I'm going to put on a sexy outfit I bought just for this occasion."

James gives her a look. "Is it what *I* would consider a sexy outfit, or is it what *you* would consider a sexy outfit?"

She glances at him deviously. "I look like a slut in it. Are you happy now?"

"Yes," he says, smiling broadly. "Very happy. Let's forget about the dinner."

"No way, Graduate. You'll just have to wait. We're going to have a romantic dinner. We're going to talk and reflect on these past three years. I want to take it all in and really enjoy the moment. We have a lot to celebrate. I bought a magnum of Dom Pérignon just for the occasion."

After the dinner, James sits back and rubs his belly. "Was it your master plan to fill me up? To fill me up with so much good food that I won't be able to perform in bed?"

"You better be up for the performance," she tells him. "I've got big plans for you."

"Well, all right." He shrugs. "If you insist. Shouldn't you be going to the bedroom and putting on your special outfit?"

Sam glances over at the clock. It reads twenty to three. *Perfect*, she says to herself. The timing could not be better.

"In a second," she tells him. "I want to talk to you about something."

"What is it?"

"I'm not taking my birth control pills any longer," she admits, watching him carefully to gauge his reaction.

He looks over and offers her a smile. "All right."

"You don't have a problem with that?"

James reaches over and grabs her hands. "No, Sam, I don't have a problem with that. You made it quite clear when we first got engaged that you wanted a family—and so do I. Frankly, you've been more than patient. You're absolutely right—it's time to get started." He beams. "I'm so looking forward to this next chapter of our lives. I can't wait!"

This part of her plan has gone more rapidly than expected; she's not quite ready yet. The second part of the plan has to be sprung, but she needs to buy a little more time.

"Can you get me another glass of champagne to celebrate the moment?"

"Sure," he says, getting up from the table. "Where did you put the bottle?"

"I put it in the fridge so that it would stay cold."

James walks over to the fridge and brings back the bottle to pour them each another glass. "Here's to the beginning of the Coppi family of Colorado," he says, raising the glass in the air. Sam clinks his glass with hers, takes a sip of the champagne, and then puts it down.

"Sit down for another sec. I want to talk to you about something else."

"Can't it wait until after?"

"Just one more thing," she pleads, "then we'll have the rest of the day for fun—no more interruptions. You'll love what I have planned for you—I promise."

"All right. What's up?" He sits back down.

She pauses for a moment and then drops the bombshell. "When the baby is born, I want to leave the agency to take care of the child, James. I want to be a stay-at-home mom. I want to stay here and take care of the ranch and raise our family."

"What? Why?" The news catches him totally off guard. "Why can't you do both?" he begins to argue. "You have Gilda to help you. If you need more help, we can hire more. Sam, I need you at the office. You run the entire operation. Without you, I'd be lost. You're far too important. There's no one in that office who can take your place."

She knew that this would be his reaction. Now her strategy has to be put into effect. "We'll find someone, James. I'm not indispensable. There are plenty of competent people out there. And I'm not leaving right away—we'll have time to search. And when we find someone, I'll train her."

"Sam, it's just not a matter of competence," James says, continuing his resistance. "It's also a matter of comfort. You know my every mood—when to approach me, when to stay away, or how to proceed with a personal problem one of the workers is experiencing. No, I'm sorry." He shakes his head defiantly. "You're too important to let go, Sam. I can't let you leave."

She has anticipated this reaction, and now she is ready to drop the bombshell. The timing is perfect. She looks at the clock once more, just to be sure.

"Don't be stubborn," she tells him. "Try to keep an open mind. I'll tell you what I'll do. Let me look around. If I don't find someone suitable—someone who is truly to your liking—I'll give in. *You* have the final say."

"All right. As long as *I* have the final say, you can look." James looks straight into her face. "But I'm warning you, Sam—you're wasting your time. There's no one who can replace you, so don't get your hopes up. I'm telling you right now that this won't work. You can do all the looking around you want, but it will be impossible to find someone who can replace you."

Just then, the doorbell rings. "Now, who the hell is that?" he hollers, throwing down his napkin.

"Well, go and see."

James goes to the front door and opens it.

"Hello, stranger," the lady says to him.

"Kathy!" he yells. "Oh my God, it's you!" He gives her a hug, lifting her off her feet. He puts her down and has a good look at her. "You look terrific. What are you doing here?"

"You didn't think I'd miss your graduation, did you?"

"You came all the way from New York just for my graduation?"

Sam and James: The Missing Teen

"May I come in?"

"Of course," James says. He places his arm around her shoulders and escorts her into the house. "We were just finishing dinner." He brings her into the dining room. When Sam sees Kathy, she jumps up from her chair and runs over to her.

Sam squeezes Kathy tightly. "Oh my God, Kathy, it's so great to see you!" Sam releases her hold. "What's it been—over a year?"

"Yes, over a year," Kathy replies, looking around. "Did I come at a bad time? Am I interrupting anything?"

"No, don't be silly," Sam tells her. "Have a seat. Are you hungry? Would you like something to eat?"

"No, I'm not hungry," Kathy answers as she sits down. "I will have a glass of that champagne, though, if it's all right with you?"

"Of course," James responds. He runs to get her a glass. He rushes back in and pours her some champagne.

"Here's to your graduation, James." Kathy holds up her glass of champagne and then takes a swallow. She puts the glass on the table. "James, with all that you've been doing the past three years, I don't know how you found the time—but you got it done." Kathy lifts up her glass once again. "Here's to you!"

"Thank you," he says as Kathy drains her glass. He takes a seat across from her.

Kathy puts down her empty glass. "James, I have to be honest with you: I have an ulterior motive for coming here today." She looks at him for a reaction but gets none, so she continues. "As I told you six months ago, I got engaged to an aspiring lawyer. Well, three weeks ago we found out that he has passed the bar exam. We want to move back to Colorado Springs, where he's going to start his own practice."

"You're moving back!" Sam cries. "That's great news! Oh, Kathy, it's going to be so nice to have you back. You have no idea how much I've missed you. We've got so much catching up to do!"

"How about you, James? Did you miss me?" Kathy gives James a wry grin.

"What? Are you trying to be funny? Of course I missed you. You were about to tell us your ulterior motive for coming here today..."

"James, I need a job. With my fiancé just starting out and opening his practice, we won't have any money coming in for a while. We have enough saved up to get the practice going, but we need money to live on. Since I worked for you before, I was hoping you'd give me a job."

"You want a job at my..." James stops in his tracks and turns to look at Sam, who has a devious look on her face. He turns back to Kathy, who is also smiling slyly. James frowns and turns back to Sam. "You are so damn sneaky!"

"So, what do you say, James? Do you have a job for me?" Kathy asks him.

James shrugs his shoulders and shakes his head at Sam as resignation sets in. "I am such a sucker!"

CPSIA information can be obtained
at www.ICGtesting.com
Printed in the USA
BVHW081823100221
599809BV00005B/543